SMOKEBIRDS

SMOKEBIRDS

by

DANIEL BREYER

RARE BIRD
LOS ANGELES, CALIF.

RARE BIRD

THIS IS A GENUINE RARE BIRD BOOK

Rare Bird Books
6044 North Figueroa Street
Los Angeles, California 90042
rarebirdbooks.com

FIRST HARDCOVER EDITION

For more information, address:
Rare Bird Books Subsidiary Rights Department
6044 North Figueroa Street
Los Angeles, California 90042

Set in Adobe Garamond
Printed in the United States

10 9 8 7 6 5 4 3 2 1

Library of Congress Cataloging-in-Publication Data

Names: Breyer, Daniel, author.
Title: Smokebirds / by Daniel Breyer.
Description: First hardcover edition. | Los Angeles, Calif. : Rare Bird, 2025.
Identifiers: LCCN 2024056773 | ISBN 9781644284452 (hardback)
Subjects: LCGFT: Ecofiction. | Novels.
Classification: LCC PS3602.R4826 S66 2025 | DDC 813/.6—dc23/eng/20241204
LC record available at https://lccn.loc.gov/2024056773

PART 1
August

1

The Petersons, without Cole, go to Kauai

Those first years only seemed bad, Richard thought, staring at the gray sky and smelling it too. It was early, and the sun sat behind the gray like some pale eye stretching to see, a scornful reminder of spring in San Francisco. Of course, there had been plenty of problems. But better than this. Richard inhaled a bouquet of smoke.

He had new masks in his suitcase and dozens of old ones in the basement. The oldest were from 2017 when the fires first rendered them necessary. Over a decade ago. There weren't many options to choose from back then. People wore surgical masks, pink and blue. They wore whatever they could find. The masks didn't work, not really, but people went about their business, thought they were better than nothing. Said the smoke would pass in a few days, and it did. Until October 2018, when it came back. In 2019 and 2020 too. When the pandemic hit, at least the masks got better. COVID was good for something.

"We should move," Lily had suggested after several bad fire seasons in the Bay Area.

"We can't," Richard said. His dad's business, the Peterson Lumber Company, was headquartered a few hours north in Redding and Richard's job was to invest Peterson Lumber Company money.

They compromised eventually, agreeing to escape the city every fire season and go to Kauai.

Richard stepped inside, closed the balcony door, and wondered aloud if there was something he was forgetting.

"There's always something," said Lily, who somehow heard him from the depths of their walk-in closet. He approached to find her buried among shoes, too many to count.

"Well," Richard said, "what do you think I'm forgetting?"

She turned around and snapped, "How would I know?" Then she went back to her shoes. Head bowed and focused, she looked young. She usually did. Facelifts, Botox, and fillers worked miracles. She also took all kinds of supplements and had tried, it seemed, every wearable on the market. Most of these she discarded after a few weeks, but she still wore a Slendra™ around her ankle (supposedly it boosted her metabolism) and a Sunni around her wrist (supposedly it boosted her mood).

He turned to see himself in the mirror. Graying hair, a slight stomach bulge. A few wrinkles on his forehead. But all in all, pretty good for forty-five. He could pass for ten years younger, maybe. Lily was lucky to have him, wasn't she? Then again, there was always room for improvement. Maybe he should try wearing a Slendra™.

"Richard," Lily started. She looked up and softened. "It's the air. We'll feel better in Hawaii. We always do."

"I feel great."

She stood. Delicate thing in a bathrobe. He wanted to fuck her. She wrapped her arms around his waist. It could happen…

She whispered, "Can you check if the boys are ready?"

—

NOT EVERY SCHOOL IN San Francisco ran on the alternate schedule, December to August, but the good ones did. And Emmett Peterson attended the best private high school in the city, where tuition was eighty grand a year and, according to his mom, well worth it—a good education is priceless. Emmett was one of the most popular kids in his class and liked school, but he loved going to Hawaii for break. In Hawaii, his parents seemed genuinely happy. Not that they didn't pretend to be happy in San Francisco; he saw they tried their best. It was just different in Hawaii. In Hawaii, the Petersons fit in perfectly. The other families were like theirs: successful, friendly. It wasn't like that in San Francisco. Sure, they had friends, but it was a small circle and the city was filled with all kinds of people Emmett had nothing in common with.

Their neighborhood in Hawaii was filled with striking and impressive homes. Soaring ceilings, koa wood interiors, infinity pools, gardens with outdoor showers nestled between fruit trees. The homes shared a golf course, tennis courts, and a private beach. There were even private firefighters stationed on the land—even Hawaii had fires now, although still nothing like the ones in California. Most importantly, there was also plenty of booze, and this year Emmet was bringing a blue duffel of treats: ketamine, cocaine, weed.

"Don't bring that," a friend had warned him days prior. "You could get caught."

He'd laughed. "There's no security. I won't get caught." He had to explain these things to his friends who didn't fly private. Some families, despite their wealth, refused to pay the increasingly expensive carbon offsets that private jets required. The financial aid kids didn't leave the city at all during fire season.

Emmett brought the blue duffel and his other bags downstairs. He was athletic and tall and carried all four bags with ease. He had wavy hair, a toothy, confident smile. He wasn't the best surfer, but he could at least look (and dress) like one.

Cole was already in the living room, his backpack by the front door. He was shorter than Emmett and always stooped over. Lately he had been combing his hair back. It made him look older and younger at the same time, like he was stuck between adolescence and a coveted political career. Cole was twenty-two, five years older than Emmett, but they almost looked the same age. Sometimes people even thought Emmett was older, a mistake that seemed to drive Cole crazy.

"That's all you're bringing?" Emmett asked.

"Yes," Cole said, and that was that. The brothers weren't close, not anymore. There was a time when Emmett used to worship Cole. He would copy everything his older brother did, from what he ate to what he wore. But Cole had become nasty and bitter and seemed habitually on edge. He was a loser. He had no girlfriend. He didn't drink or smoke or do drugs. All he talked about was climate change and wealth inequality and other depressing shit. He always wanted to pick a fight, but never with his fists. In a fistfight, especially against Emmett, Cole stood no chance.

Emmett went to his parents' room to see if they needed help. "Which of these are you bringing?" he asked, noticing the pile of suitcases.

"These for sure," his mom pointed, and he picked up all three. "Are you okay?" she asked.

He should be asking her the same thing, but it would be pointless. She would say she was good. She was never honest when things were bad.

"Yes, I'm good!" he said. Then he smiled.

"You look tired."

"No, I'm fine. Dad, do you need help?"

His dad was in the bedroom, staring through a window at the gray light outside. He didn't seem to hear Emmett. So Emmett asked again, yelling over the air-purifier. This time his dad looked back.

"Oh, um, no, I got it." Then he lifted a bag in each hand. "Of course I got it."

—

As THE BLACK SUV left the gate, Lily ran through a final mental checklist. The alarm was on. The lights were off. The trash was empty. The air filters were off. She swiveled her head around to make sure her family was all accounted for. Emmett and Richard in the middle row, and Cole alone in the very back. The car—electric, of course—was quiet. It smelled nice inside. It had one of those new purification systems that smelled like lavender.

"Is this your car?" she asked the driver.

He nodded. His name was Michael and even inside the car, he wore a mask. He was a new driver, and she wondered why Richard's assistant hadn't booked one of their regulars. Tracy was always fucking up, and it's not like the job was that hard. Lily nagged Richard incessantly, "*Please* have Tracy call the hotel to make sure our room has yoga mats…*Please* get her to confirm that we'll be in the dining room and not at the bar again…" and so on. But then they'd get to their hotel room in Paris or wherever and there wouldn't be yoga mats. Or they'd get to the restaurant and be escorted to the bar. It was such an easy job; if Lily were an assistant, she would crush it.

"It's a very nice car," she said to be polite. After all, it wasn't this guy's fault that Tracy had called him.

"Thank you."

There was no traffic, and they barreled through the smoky streets.

"Are you from the city?"

"Yes," said Michael, who, considering the way he was driving, had to be. "I grew up here." He had white hair and was well-mannered, and Lily felt bad for him. She wished she could take everyone with them to Hawaii. She really did.

She turned up the vibrations on her Sunni and clicked the euphoria track. According to the app, in a matter of minutes, her mood would elevate and she would have more energy. She had been wearing the Sunni for a few years but still didn't know if it did anything.

"We're lucky," she explained to Michael, "that we get to go on a trip right now."

"Where are you off to?"

"Kauai."

From the middle came Richard's voice. "Can you play the *New York Times* daily briefing, please?"

"Of course, sir."

She didn't have to look back to know that Richard appreciated being called sir. He liked that kind of respect from people he considered beneath him. The fact that his dad was the billionaire and responsible for Richard's status, and to be fair *her* status, too, didn't seem to bother him when speaking to the help. When he was with anyone self-made though, he ended up trying too hard to show he was one of them. Of course, him trying so hard was enough to convince others that he wasn't their peer—not really. This wasn't his fault. Yes, he had been given a lot, but he worked hard and was a good investor. She wanted to be proud of him. *No*, she reasserted to herself, *she was proud of him.* Still, why couldn't he *actually* listen to news briefings, instead of just pretending to? He was almost certainly playing stupid games on his phone.

Michael found the *New York Times* app on his dashboard display, selected August 2, 2028.

"Hi, I'm Andrew Rosario from the *New York Times* and this is your daily briefing."

As Andrew droned on about civil war in Nigeria, protests in Europe, and the latest round of impeachment proceedings, Lily consulted her phone, which had far less doom and gloom than the *New York Times*. Her social media feeds were rife with smiling friends, all headed out of state. Like the Bradleys in Florence, grinning in the Boboli Gardens. It was probably 100 degrees, but they looked happy enough. Blond and blue-eyed, people probably thought they were a perfect family, Mormons or something.

Lily knew better though. Their fifteen-year-old daughter got expelled for selling drugs at school. Emmett had told her. She liked that Emmett told her those kinds of things. When she asked if he was selling drugs at school, he had just laughed at her. "Why would I need money?"

It was a good point. He used his family credit card liberally. But wasn't that true for the Bradley kid too?

She would post her own photo once in Kauai. Perhaps this year in front of a palm tree. A photo with the family, something worthy of a Christmas card.

"I've always wanted to go to Kauai," the driver said.

Lily shot a look back at Richard. She wanted him to chime in and bail her out of the ensuing conversation—she had never intended for it to go the whole drive. But of course, Richard wouldn't look up from his game to speak to a chauffeur.

She turned to face the driver, whose name she had already forgotten.

"It's a special place."

"I bet."

"We go every year, all four of us. It's very special to get everyone together, you know, all in one place, even though the kids are older now." She smiled at the thought. Richard loved that too about their annual trip, a Peterson family tradition. The four of them all in one place, eating together, hiking together, actually having conversations. She liked when friends stopped by at breakfast or dinner—how they'd say, *You have such a lovely family.* She'd smile sheepishly, *We're very lucky.* She looked at the driver—was he judging her for being spoiled? "I haven't seen a mask like that before. Is it new?"

The driver's mask had some kind of water filtration. It bubbled when he breathed. "Yes. It was given to me by a longtime client. Maybe Mr. Peterson knows him?" But Richard still didn't look up.

"We might know him," said Lily.

"Anyway, it's a good mask. I have asthma, and it seems to help."

Lily was on the board of InhaleAfrica, a fact she liked to insert in conversations whenever possible. "We give Africans over 100,000 masks every year," she explained. "You know there are a lot of bad masks on the market there, knockoffs and even ones with harmful chemicals. And the asthma rates have skyrocketed in recent years, so good masks have never been more important. I'll have to tell the board about yours. Can I ask who makes it?"

"It's an Aqualung."

"Aqualung," she made a note in her phone out of politeness. "I'll let the rest of the board know."

"It's an expensive mask, though. I don't know if you should buy them for Africa."

Lily's eyes narrowed. "We try to get the very best masks." Silence from the driver. Lily continued, "We have sent only top-quality masks. I think people assume that poor people should be fine with any mask. But that, you know, is a very privileged position."

"Hmmm," said the driver.

"We put on a big gala every year," Lily said.

Lily wanted the driver to ask about the gala, but he didn't. He was quiet until they arrived at the terminal and even then only said, "Okay. We're here." As if they didn't know. As if they hadn't been going to the same private terminal for the last five years.

—

THE TERMINAL WAS SPACIOUS AND COMFORTABLE. Couches and armchairs surrounded glass tables speckled with magazines. There was a coffee bar and a salad bar, and a real bar. There were TVs everywhere. Cole remembered that the TVs used to play the news. Now they only played sports. Because these rich fucks couldn't bear to watch the news. Too many protests, floods, record heat waves, corrupt politicians, corrupt businesspeople; it was all very unsettling. They dismissed it as woke propaganda. Unless they were under a fire evacuation order—then they watched.

Normally Cole would have had the thought and squashed it, reminding himself, *you are one of them*.

Not today, though. Today he would have his chance to show his family that he wasn't one of them, and so he let the thoughts flow. *These rich fucks*.

"Richard! Lily! How are you?" A man cornered them. He had slick blond hair and a blue sport coat.

"Frank! Good to see you!" When his dad spoke, Cole grimaced. So corny. So fake sounding. "Have you met my boys? Emmett and Cole." Emmett shook the man's hand. After a moment, Cole did too.

Frank laughed. "Is that what you call a handshake?" He left his hand out, tempting Cole to try again. "Come on! Lay it in there. Let me feel the meat of that hand!" Cole acquiesced. He squeezed as hard as he could.

"There it is!" Frank said.

"Frank runs things at GreenOaks," Richard explained.

"Not for much longer."

"An early retirement?"

"I hope so. Unless these carbon offset prices keep going up. My God, Richard, can you believe this shit? Why not just shut down all planes. Stop all travel!" Frank turned, "Lucy! Lana!" His wife and his daughter came over. Lucy was beautiful and Lana, perhaps Emmett's age, was a carbon copy.

"So, are the Petersons heading to Hawaii?" Frank had a greasy smile.

"You know it!" Richard said. "And the Martins?"

"Big Sky!"

"You have a place there?" Emmett asked.

Cole was taken aback by his brother's confidence, butting into the conversation like he belonged, like he was all grown up.

"Oh yes," said Frank. "We have a ranch. You should come by, all of you. Doesn't Hawaii burn now too?"

"Well, in 2023 Maui did, but we're at The Preserve in Kauai," Richard said proudly, as if that settled things. "And there are firefighters stationed on the property." He put a hand on Frank's shoulder. "Do you have a moment?"

The two stepped aside, and then Lucy took Lily aside, and Emmett stepped closer to Lana. "Are you in college?" he asked.

"No. I have another year of high school."

Emmett smiled. "Me too. What school?"

"I'm gonna go to the bathroom," Cole said, slipping away.

The men's room was marbled and clean. Cole was glad to find it empty. He looked at himself in the mirror. He was dressed nicely. Polo shirt, blue jeans. He had fair skin and green eyes and still looked childish. He wished he could grow a beard. He went inside a stall, not to shit but to sit down and wait.

He heard two men enter the bathroom, one he recognized as Frank. They spoke by the urinals. They were talking football. "I never believe any reports from training camp," Frank said.

"Yeah, yeah…"

Then Frank got quieter. "By the way, you know who's here?"

"Who," said the other man.

"Richard Peterson. You know him?"

"No."

"The guy invests his dad's money, has done one good deal in like twenty years. Thinks he's hot shit though. I'm always polite, of course."

"Of course." They laughed.

Cole had read that his dad was known as a one-hit-wonder investor. But he hadn't known that he was a laughingstock, that they thought of him as a nepo baby. It made sense though. He didn't want to be around his dad any more than Frank did. It would be nice to tell him so in a few minutes. In front of Frank and everyone else. He went over the words in his head. *I'm not coming with you. I'm not coming with you.* His family looked forward to their Hawaii trip every year; even while in Hawaii, all they talked about was future trips. The trips never lived up to expectations, but that didn't stop his mom and dad from pretending they did. Hawaii, to them, was always a utopia, and any disappointments while there were disregarded and ignored when it came to imagining the next trip, or even the next family excursion on the trip. This year would be different. He would disappoint them. They would be shocked. His pulse quickened.

When he heard the men leave the bathroom, he waited a moment and then left too. He took a seat on one of the couches and flipped through the magazines. These were no plebeian magazines. They featured ads for mansions and cars. Aston Martins, Lambos, Ferraris—all electric. The houses all advertised clean inside air, reduced emissions, little to no energy costs. All for the price of ten, twenty, or thirty million.

Emmett approached. "Our plane's ready."

"Okay."

Slowly, the Petersons congregated. "Frank's a good guy and a good VC," Richard said to no one in particular. "I'm going to give him a call, see what kinds of deals he's looking at."

"You can follow me to your aircraft," said a flight attendant.

"One second," Cole said. But he must have said it too quietly because his family and the flight attendant started to walk. Cole's heart was beating fast.

His mom turned back, "Cole? Come on."

"I'm not going." They all stopped, the flight attendant included.

"What?" said his dad. "Come on, the stewardess says it's time to go."

"I'm not going."

"Cole, this isn't funny. Come on. You're already at the goddamn airport, let's go." His dad whispered the words. His face was red-hot and knotted.

Emmett rolled his eyes. "Oh, let him stay."

"Honey…" Lily was the first to move toward him. "What's this about? You love Hawaii!"

"I'm not coming with you." He watched the words hurt her.

"Why?" She asked.

"Cole, you're coming on this plane," his dad whisper-hissed.

"No, I am not." Cole's heart thumped, but he was in it now. He felt better when he noticed his dad survey the room, taking note of all the gawking faces. There were few things his dad hated more than a scene. Cole stood up taller. "This year, I'm staying in San Francisco."

"Not in our house." His dad said it like he had him now, like this was the shattering blow.

And for a moment, it was. Cole's plan had been perfect. Make the point at the airport, when it would be especially inconvenient. But then go home, lie down in his king bed, run the AC, blast some music, read a book, relax and recuperate before making his next move. He had to roll with the punches though. He wouldn't give them a win. "No," he said, feigning confidence, "not in your house."

"Where then?" His mom asked, budging ever so slightly.

"With a friend." He expected them to probe. Which friend? You have friends?

But Emmett cut in. "This is, what? Some protest? Because you don't want to ride in planes anymore? Because they're bad for the earth? Because you hate this family?"

At least this was a way out. Cole nodded. "I won't fly."

Lily cried, "We pay the offsets!"

"Honey, quiet." Richard put a hand on his wife's shoulder.

Cole saw her squirm. He turned around and started to walk toward the door, not knowing if they would follow. They didn't. He was outside, Uber app open, and walking just far enough away to get a ride where he wouldn't be seen.

2

Duke tests his daughter

Duke Peterson's Redding, California, home was an architectural treasure. Nestled along the Sacramento River, it was a sprawling, baronial dwelling, much too big for its lone occupant. It had been his wife's project, mostly, until she died eleven years ago, leaving him alone in this big house. Fires had come close many times, but the house still stood.

There were other homes on the property. Sometimes friends stayed in these. Sometimes, Richard and Lily would come and stay with their kids, and his daughter, Eliza, lived close by and would come visit often. It was always a relief when they left though. Five guest cottages, a pool, a home theater…empty but for the staff that rarely approached Duke. He liked it that way.

Sometimes at night, when he drank whiskey, he missed his wife and his kids and resented his loneliness. He would look at family photos and wallow in nostalgia. But usually, he would catch himself before too long. He didn't have time to be sentimental. There was always work to do and he liked the work. The more phone calls, the better. The more meetings, the better. Duke was seventy-four years old but worked like he was twenty-four.

"Slow down, Dad," Richard would say. "You don't have to work so hard anymore."

But without his work, Duke was nothing.

They called him the last lumber baron of California. He was worth three billion dollars, and his company owned the most private land in the state.

"You need to come with us to Hawaii this year," Richard had told him. "Your lungs can't take another fire season."

"I've been breathing in smoke for fifty-five years."

"Let's not make it fifty-six."

He agreed to go. Not because he was scared of the smoke but because it was time to pass the torch, at least for the sake of appearances. Two years ago, *New York Magazine* had released a hit piece on Peterson Lumber— admonishing their post-fire logging business. He had hired a PR team to respond and they did an admirable job. It wasn't a hard position to argue. Fires were inevitable. The fact that Peterson Lumber profited off of them was shrewd business, and not unscrupulous like the article suggested. Still, this was a different era. Fake news could ruin organizations, even strong ones. So despite the fact that the company was stronger than ever, taking in record profits and expanding its footprint, he had to find new leadership. The board initially gave him a year to implement a succession plan. He convinced them to make it two. Now his time was up. He would go to Hawaii and let his daughter Eliza and his COO Chris take the reins. For the next few months, a trial period of sorts, they would be co-CEOs. Then he would choose the best candidate as his successor, the person who was most amenable to being his puppet, the person most willing to let him run the company as he always had, just this time with the title "chairman." Whoever he chose, he wouldn't tell them that the title was symbolic. He would let them think they were running the company; he would even let other people think so, but while he was still breathing, he wouldn't let Peterson Lumber fail.

Eliza could be the right choice. She was earnest, eager to please, but soft. Did softness matter? Maybe in this case it would be an advantage. Still, he couldn't help but look down on her. His kids were soft because they never had to be tough.

He had always wanted Richard, his firstborn, to work in lumber. Richard had refused, which was disappointing but bearable, especially since Duke had offered him a meager fifty thousand dollar starting salary. "There will be no nepotism in this business," he had explained. But then Richard had continued to disappoint him. He had invested in one good company— some virtual reality nonsense—with capital from his trust fund and then, on the other side of that success, convinced Duke that he was ready to make venture investments for the family office. The family office had been established to diversify the family's holdings, mostly through investments in stocks and bonds— conservative investments that Duke could wrap his head around. But Richard's investments with the family office capital hadn't done well. He was, it seemed, a one-hit wonder, and Duke had long since lost patience. Richard's latest proposal was to back some bitcoin mining company in Russia. For the last month, he had been pestering his dad to approve the investment, but to Duke it sounded like bullshit, and he didn't trust his son's intuition more than his own.

Even if Richard had turned out to be a good investor, Duke wouldn't have been impressed with his son. Investing, as he saw it, involved a lot of luck and country club gossip. Not that his daughter's work was so hard. Eliza was technically Chief Business Officer at the company, but the title was for her ego.

The night before leaving for Hawaii, Duke called Chris. Chris always answered right away, even after-hours.

They talked about new regulations, various loopholes, cash on hand for fire season contracts.

"Oh, Chris. One more thing." Duke took another swig of whiskey.

"Yes—"

"You and Eliza will be running things when I'm gone."

"Me and Eliza?"

"Yes. Together."

He imagined Chris on the other line. Perhaps in another room, so his wife could sleep, and far enough away from his two kids to wake them. Chris, in his fifteen years with the company, had never once expressed disappointment, at least not to Duke. That's why he could call Chris but would have to meet Eliza tomorrow in person. She would bitch and moan about sharing the role, he was sure. Chris, though, was professional as always, his response routine and emotionless. "I look forward to working with her more closely."

Thank God for Chris. To his biological children's dismay, Duke considered Chris, privately and publicly, a son. Sometimes, he even called Chris "son." The man was smart, dedicated, but more than that, uniquely ambitious. Whereas his family had been handed everything, Chris had been handed nothing. One of Duke's crowning achievements was seeing the potential in Chris and deciding to give him a shot. With each passing year, Chris proved himself. First in the forest and then in HQ and finally as Duke's righthand man. Chris would be a great CEO, but whether he would continue to let Duke call the shots was still unclear.

"Thank you again, Chris, for your commitment to this company, to this family." Duke believed in the American dream, that his own success was proof that the dream was healthy and well. With hard work and courage, anyone can make it, he would say to family, friends, and auditoriums of strangers. He liked to give others opportunities that they wouldn't have had otherwise. Chris, a midwesterner from a poor farming community, was given such an opportunity. "You're just like me," he would tell Chris, "an American success story."

No one ever mentioned that Duke had inherited $25 million dollars from his dad. It was an open secret, perhaps, but one that even Duke tended to forget.

DUKE AWOKE THE NEXT MORNING AT 5:30 a.m., per usual. The mornings used to be easier, but now they reeked of lethargy. Showering, dressing, making coffee—each activity was a separate battle, and it took him until 7:00 a.m. to win the war. Then came video calls and even an in-person meeting with a logging contractor. This man said he was honored to be inside Duke's home. It was the right thing to say. But Duke didn't agree to a partnership. He didn't agree to anything unless he was certain he was getting the better end of the deal, and this guy was proposing a revenue share. Sharing was another word for stealing.

Around 1:00 p.m., Eliza arrived. Instead of living on the Peterson compound, she lived a few miles down the road. Redding was cheap compared to San Francisco, and though she had trust fund money to build a mansion of her own, she lived in a modest house next to modest neighbors.

She was his daughter, and he loved her, but unlike some fathers who cannot see their children's flaws, in Eliza, Duke saw more flaws than he could count. He saw, for example, that Eliza was overweight and habitually weary. On this afternoon, she was caked in makeup. Duke wondered if she was respected at the company. She was unmarried, probably devoid of prospects, childless, and, Duke assumed, maintained a poor social life. All negatives aside, he liked that she didn't use her trust fund. That had been his late wife's idea and because the trusts were irrevocable, he hadn't been able to reclaim the assets. He knew Eliza didn't use them out of respect for him, unlike Richard, who had no problem indulging and seemed to ignore Duke's sermons about spoiled children.

They sat down in the dining room and Duke's chef, Santiago, approached. "My daughter will be joining me today. Any special requests, Eliza?"

"No." She smiled at Santiago and then dipped her head. "Whatever you want, Dad."

Duke wanted a cheeseburger. Eliza got one too.

"You're leaving tomorrow?" she asked.

"Yes. Which is why I wanted you to come by. Were you at the office this morning?"

She nodded. The office was a few miles south of the house. Duke usually stopped by, but today he had lots of packing to do.

"Are people in good spirits?"

"Yes." It looked like she had something else to say. He waited, but nothing particularly significant came. "You know, we're monitoring the fires. I think we'll win some big contracts this year." The business took in hundreds of millions of dollars each year from post-fire logging. The burnt wood was cheap and, ninety percent of the time, salvageable.

He asked, "What do you think about the Nesbit plot we looked at last week?"

She seemed to search him for clues, but he gave nothing away. "What do I think?"

"Should we buy it?" He didn't know what she would say, but he knew the correct answer. It was a large plot adjacent to Peterson land, but it had been poorly maintained. The answer wasn't so cut and dry.

To his surprise, she said as much. "Not for what they're asking."

"Do you think we can get it for less?"

She sat on his question. He could see her brain working, like she had been asked a trick question. It wasn't a trick question, though. Chris would have seen that, would have answered directly. She couldn't bear to be tricked. Her gears turned, but then, once again, she surprised him.

"We can get it for less, but we shouldn't. No one else will buy it. It sits too close to us, so any new buyer's expansion potential will be capped. They'll have to put it up for auction. Then we can get it for much less."

Duke wiped his mouth. "Maybe an out-of-stater will bid us up?"

"Then we let them. And in two years, they'll be selling it right back at an even steeper discount."

"I think that's right." He prepared his announcement, forming the words in his head. "When I'm in Hawaii—"

She cut him off. "Was that a test?"

"A test?" He was taken aback, more by the fact that she interrupted him.

"Did I pass?" This display of confidence didn't faze him. Beneath the show, she looked as she always did: nervous, obsequious.

Santiago brought the burgers, and Duke took a bite. She lifted hers but then put it back down. She looked right at him when she spoke. "After all these years, you still need to test me?"

Duke chewed. "It wasn't a test."

"You knew the answer, but you asked me anyway."

"Eliza—"

"Why can't you trust that I know what I'm doing?"

To his surprise, Duke found himself on the defensive, needing to control the situation, regain the conversation. "I do trust you. You should have let me finish."

It looked like she was going to interrupt him again, but she didn't. She waited with her hands clasped in her lap.

"When I'm in Hawaii, I want you to run the business—" He saw the slightest smile, "alongside Chris," he finished. The smile retracted.

"What?"

"Chris knows. He'll brief you on everything."

"I just… I'm confused, I guess." Her mask of confidence, which wasn't convincing to begin with, disappeared. "So it's like another test?" she tried again.

"No. I just think it's the right move for the business."

"What will my title be?"

"You and Chris can figure that out together."

"And when you come back from Hawaii?"

"I'll pick the best person for the job, and I'll move to chairman."

—

ELIZA WALKED OUT INTO the hot and smokey driveway. She put her mask on and, from her car, waved goodbye to her dad, who had followed her out to see her off. The man wore no mask, despite the smoke. Each visit, he looked older. The only hair left was white and on the sides of his head. Wrinkles branched from his eyes, running like tracks to his sad pursed lips. But his eyes still glowed green as ever. Like a reptile. The lumber baron of California.

She drove off and let the air purifier run for a moment before removing her mask. She hadn't expected this, and she didn't know how to feel. If her dad had named her CEO, she would have accepted graciously. If he had passed her over, she would have left the company in a show of defiance. Or at least she would have considered it. Being named co-lead felt like purgatory, and now she would have to prove herself yet again.

She caught a glimpse of herself in the rearview mirror and didn't recoil. She even let her face linger there for a moment. She didn't feel pretty, she never had before, but she felt okay. Like being a co-lead—not great, not bad, but okay. Maybe she should be happy about it. Despite the half-measure, it was the nicest thing her dad had ever done for her. He respected her now more than he used to. Certainly more than he had when she was in eighth grade and she overheard him talking about her one night after her parent-teacher conference. Her parents assumed she was in her room. She had wanted a snack. She had to sneak snacks because her mom had put her on a diet. So, she waited by the stairs for them to leave the kitchen.

"So she needs extra help," her mom said. "We'll get her the help."

"It's not just that—" Her dad sounded tired.

"It's mostly that. You can't stand that your daughter needs extra help."

"What about her not fitting in?"

"Eighth grade is hard on everyone."

"Not the ones who do fit in!"

"Duke—"

"Something's off about her. You look at her, and it's like her gears are spinning, always spinning, endlessly."

Eliza waited for her mom to defend her. No defense came. She went to her room and cried.

The words still stung. She had spent her whole life trying to convince him that she was worthy. It seemed that she had half-convinced him. She called Richard while at a stoplight.

"Hey. I just had lunch with Dad. He said I'll be running things with Chris."

"Congrats." There was noise in the background.

"Where are you?"

"Oh, sorry. We just landed. We're stepping off the plane."

She passed the street that would lead to her house. She decided, on a whim, to keep driving to the office. "How is everyone?"

"Good. Great. So what did he say?"

"He said I'll be running things with Chris while he's in Hawaii. And *then* he'll decide who will take over the company."

"What does that mean?"

"It means he's playing some fucking game."

The noise died down, and she could imagine her brother getting into a car. No part of her was jealous of the annual Hawaii getaway, fire season or not. She would have nothing to do in Hawaii. At least in Redding, she had a job. She was like her dad that way, only content when busy, only okay when she wasn't thinking about feeling okay. "Well, I just wanted to thank you, for the support." She had begged him to take Duke to Hawaii and he had agreed. It hadn't been an easy conversation, but the guilt-tripping had gotten through to him. "*Come on, I have to work with him every day. It's been like that for years. You talk to him, what, like once a week? I talk to him every day! Just give me this, it could make him retire, finally retire.*"

But she hadn't called her brother out of gratitude. She had called to complain, but it was obvious that he didn't want to hear it.

"I'm glad, Eliza. I'm proud of you." She doubted it was true. He was obsessed with distancing himself from Duke, proving that he was his own man. Of course, Richard still worked for Duke, just not directly for the lumber company. It was a distinction without a difference, a sad compromise for her brother.

"Thanks. Send everyone my best." Then to be polite, "Are you all excited?"

There was a pause on the other side. She assumed her brother had lost service, but then his voice emerged. "Well, Cole didn't come with us. But it's fine!"

"Oh."

"He says he didn't want to go on a plane, that's all."

"But you pay your offsets."

"I know. It's fine. We're fine."

"Yikes."

"Just, well, he might come by Dad's place. I mean, I have no idea. Just keep an eye out, okay?"

"Okay."

She had no time to think about Cole or his juvenile activism. She pulled into the Peterson Lumber lot, wielded her mask, and headed inside the office. It was a big building, smartly furnished and well-ventilated. Still, this was the time of year most corporate employees started working from home or relocating, and the office was quiet.

But Chris was there, of course. She found him in his corner office on the phone, and she took a seat. He didn't stop speaking. She tapped her foot. "That sounds great, Ethan," he said, and, "You got it, Ethan." Finally, he hung up.

Chris smiled at her. She was skeptical of Chris and, at times, critical. This wasn't unique to Chris. She guarded herself against most people because she moved through life with the assumption that most people didn't like her.

"I'm coming from my dad's. He told me that we'll be holding down the fort together."

"Yup. It'll be great to work more closely together." He said it matter-of-factly, but she still picked up a layer of disappointment, even condescension.

"I'll be across the hall." As she was stepping out, he called her back.

"I guess I would have normally run this by Duke, but—well, it's our call now."

"What's up?" She reminded herself to stand up straight, to look into Chris's eyes.

"It seems that the controlled burn we initiated on our eastern plot has spread."

She knew the spot. They owned a strip of land that wasn't close to any of their more western centralized holdings. "How bad has it spread?"

"About five-thousand acres so far, depending on wind speeds, it could get worse."

"Do we still have a crew up there?"

"Everyone seems safe and accounted for, and our private firefighters are on-site."

She whispered, "And you're sure we started it?"

"It seems that way."

"Fuck." And then an idea flashed in her head. The eastern plots that were burning were surrounded by mostly Nesbit Lumber plots, and Nesbit Lumber was in trouble, starting to sell off some of their more minor holdings. If the fire were to spread through Nesbit territory, she could buy a massive chunk of the ravaged land for much less. It was the type of deal her dad would love. But there were risks, of course, and if things went wrong her dad would despise her.

Maybe it was time to finally take that risk. For years she had played it safe. And what had that gotten her? Another test. Another step in a long-winding, never-ending ascension. If she didn't gamble, then Chris could become CEO. He probably would become CEO. And then what? She'd have nothing left to aim for. She would wallow as his number two, or perhaps he'd demote her further.

"Do you think it'll get out that we started it?" she asked.

"What?"

"Will it get out?"

"Eliza, we should cooperate. I was about to call—"

"Don't call anyone. Let's talk this out."

There were no guarantees that the fire wouldn't cross into more of their territory or any of the towns around Lake Almanor. But there were precautions they could take, at least to protect themselves. She was gambling, but it was a smart bet. "What if we cut our eastern border? Or burn it?"

"We'd be putting the men in a tough spot. Nothing's predictable about—"

"Fire," she finished. "I know. But we have some time?"

He shrugged. She liked that he didn't agree with her. If it worked, it would mean more glory for her. The result would be unambiguous. Eliza did this. Just Eliza.

"Dad hasn't left yet," she said, "let's let him decide." She knew Chris wouldn't like that. They'd both look incompetent.

"No. It's okay. Let's cut the eastern border. I'll keep you posted."

"Great. Thank you." She walked out without looking back and shut his door. She went to her office. It was smaller than his, for now.

3

The Petersons do rich-people things in Hawaii

The Maluhia Nature Preserve, a private residential community located on the southern tip of Kauai, was developed in partnership with the Hawaiian state government. For an outrageously expensive fee, members like the Petersons gained access to a private beach, three pools, two spas, two golf courses, two bars, four restaurants, and an abundance of other amenities. Members of Maluhia were required to buy land and encouraged to build homes. The members liked to say that the best part of being a Maluhian was that half of one percent of their fee went toward maintaining the natural beauty and sustentation of the land, or *aina*.

Richard and Lily had built a sizable house near the mangrove forest. Their home had an ocean view and was a fifteen-minute walk to The Preserve's best restaurant. They would have preferred one of the beachside lots but had bought in too late to claim one. Richard complained about this often. Whenever he encountered one of the beachside families like the Wilsons or the Bells, he would whisper something contemptuous to Lily. She wouldn't encourage him. The Wilsons, the Bells, and their beachside peers were good people, like them.

In San Francisco, Lily told herself that the months in Kauai were her favorite of the year. But upon arriving, she didn't feel excited. Perhaps it was Cole's fault. She wished he was with them and kept expecting to find him reading, typing, or brooding around the house. She had expected him to outgrow his chronic scowling, but even last year, even in this beautiful place, he had persisted. He wasn't affectionate like Emmett, or even polite, but she sensed his vulnerability. While he never said so out loud, she saw when he was nervous or insecure, and in those moments, all she wanted to do was comfort him, even if he rejected her. Now, she was unable to comfort him and it made her feel uneasy.

Maybe Cole wasn't causing her unease at all; maybe she was in a funk. She didn't like to think about that. She ignored the discontent until it was impossible to do so. When it became impossible, she took pills, or strapped on a wearable, or drank wine, or went to sleep.

Richard seemed unaffected by Cole's absence—at least he pretended to be. At the garden restaurant for breakfast, he said, "He's old enough to do his own thing. I was like that, you know, at his age."

Lily had been engaged to Richard when he was Cole's age, and he had been nothing like that. Perhaps Richard had attempted to resist his father's pull at first, but he was never able to break away. For Richard, doing his own thing was a fantasy. He talked about independence the same way she talked about moving to Europe. Fun, but infeasible.

Cole, meanwhile, barely spoke to them. He wouldn't even tell them if he had a job or where he was planning to live. After graduation he'd mentioned something about consulting but didn't elaborate. There was no reason to probe. He would just scowl.

"It was pretty rude if you ask me," Emmett said. "After everything you guys do for us." Then, like the thought suddenly occurred to him, he asked Lily, "Are you okay? About him not being here?"

She nodded. "I think so." He was a sensitive kid that way, always trying to make her feel better. She constantly reassured him that she was fine, but he never seemed to believe it. "I'm going to peruse the buffet." She rose and went first to the fruit bar. She took some papaya and mango. Then she went to the omelet bar. The omelet chef, Peter, had been there for years.

"Good to have you back," Peter said with a smile. Maluhia was a nice place, with or without Cole. Lily had to remember that. She had to tell herself that again and again. She took a deep breath and conjured one of her affirmations: *The perfect moment is this one.*

While Peter prepared her order, she found bacon, fresh bread, a chocolate croissant, lobster ravioli, sushi, and sashimi. She wouldn't come close to finishing her plate but wanted to taste everything. She was a meticulous calorie counter and, after years of food circumspection, knew what she had to eat to maintain her figure. "Thank you, Peter," she said and sat back down with her truffle omelet and abundance of sides.

Richard and Emmett returned with their plates just as Cathy Haden walked over. She was a popular woman on The Preserve, always planning events and getting people together. She and her husband, Bret, lived in one of the nicer houses with a beach view. Lily got the sense that Bret thought he was better than Richard, but if Cathy also felt that way about Lily, she hid it well.

"So good to see you, Cathy!"

"And you, Lily! And you, Richard. And…Emmett?"

"Yup." Lily found herself matching Cathy's tone. They sounded like contestants in an exuberance pageant.

"Did your other son come?"

"Cole," she explained, "is working in San Francisco at a consulting firm."

"Oh, well, that's wonderful," Cathy said. "You must be proud of him. Even though I'm sure you miss having everyone together. It's always nice to see happy families like yours here."

"Well, yes, we miss him but we're very proud. Are you here with Bret and your boys?"

"Yes! And you know what?" Somehow Cathy's smile found more room to grow. "We brought along an exchange student," she raised eyebrows in a show of suspense and then finished, "from Nigeria!"

Richard put down his fork. "You don't say."

"Yes. He's wonderful. And, honestly, he's taught us so much."

"What's his name?" Richard asked.

"Michael!" Cathy, too, seemed to find this amusing. "You'd think it would be Chaka or something, but it's Michael."

"You don't say." Richard laughed. "I hope we'll get the chance to meet him."

"I'm sure you will!" Then, speaking right to Lily, "Let's catch up later today. Are you coming to the meditation hall at two for the Hakalau sit?"

"Hakalau?"

"It's this ancient Hawaiian kind of meditation. A real native will be teaching. You have to come!"

"Well, oh, okay. I'll come!"

"God, I just love this place. Don't you?"

"Of course."

After Cathy left, Lily stopped smiling. The truffle omelet wasn't very good. They were probably using Chinese truffles. Cathy wouldn't have cared. To Cathy, everything at Maluhia was perfect.

—

EMMETT HAD AGREED TO intern for his dad this fire season. It had been his mom's idea originally. She was nervous that his extracurriculars weren't unique enough to get him into Stanford. Emmett could work for his dad and then write in his Stanford application about gaining lots of responsibility and experience at a young age. His college counselor had already sent him an outline. In his essay, he would acknowledge how fortunate he was to be getting this kind of experience while also demonstrating that he had taken full advantage of the opportunity he had been given. Cole, the hypocrite, had done the very same.

At the breakfast table, long after Cathy had left and they were all full, Emmett asked his dad what he should do.

"I have a call this afternoon that you can join for."

Emmett was excited. "With who?"

"It's with the bitcoin mining company."

"The one you're trying to invest in. Didn't Grandpa say he didn't like it?"

"I'm just running down the deal. Your grandpa doesn't have the context." It seemed like he had more to say, but instead, he changed the subject. "You want to golf?"

"When's the call?"

"At three. We have more than enough time to golf."

They changed and drove their golf cart to the Gold course. The weather was overcast and warm at the driving range, perfect golf weather. But when they approached the first tee, it started to drizzle, and by the time Emmett hit his drive, it was raining. "Shit," he said. He had hit the ball far out into the trees. "Can I take a mulligan?"

Neither father nor son acknowledged the rain. Emmett hoped it would go away if they ignored it. But by the end of the first hole, it was still raining, and by the end of the second, it was raining harder. Finally, he asked, "Are you sure you want to keep playing?"

"Come on! It's just some rain!"

Emmett kept asking his dad about work, but Richard was evasive. He would provide short answers or no answers at all. He knew his dad was successful, but Cole and Duke always seemed to imply otherwise. He liked when his dad confirmed what he knew, but it wasn't always easy to get there.

30

It was time for a different strategy. "Cole says that all VCs are doomed, that no one will care about tech when the world's on fire."

"They'll care about VR."

"You think so?"

"Will you watch my shot?"

"Okay."

Richard hit his nine iron into a sandtrap. "Fuck!"

"Do you think we should invest in more VR?"

"Yes, I think so."

Richard's best, and perhaps only great investment, was in the VR company Trance. He had invested in the first round at a sub $30 million valuation. Eight years later, the company had gone public at a $12 billion valuation. Some of the best VR games were Trance exclusives, and while there were plenty of competitors, only Trance had nailed the Metaverse. Players could win skins, weapons, power-ups in one game and seamlessly bring them to another. Once a player started on Trance, they rarely left since everything they earned would be useful for years to come, even as older games became outdated.

Cole believed that Richard had just gotten lucky with his investment in Trance. "The founder was Dad's freshman roommate," he said to Emmett once. "I bet he didn't even know what he was investing in. Plus, I heard it was a tiny check. Dad was only asked to join the board because he would be a yes-man."

Emmett took a different position. His dad was always playing video games—on VR, on console, on the computer, and on his phone. The man was obsessed and must have known that Trance would be big after hearing the pitch. Emmett knew it had been a while since the Trance investment, though, and had overheard his parents worrying that Grandpa was going to stop funding new investments.

As they rounded the back nine, it started to pour. "We can wait it out in the clubhouse?" Emmett suggested, wondering if he sounded as desperate as he felt.

Richard, who looked to be melting in the rain, finally relented. "I guess I could use some lunch."

The restaurant was crowded with other soaked patrons. They took a seat at a corner table and ordered cheeseburgers.

"Beef or impossible meat?" asked the waiter.

"Beef," Richard said.

"Beef," Emmett said. Then, when the waiter was gone, "Do you think you can get Grandpa to eat an impossible burger?"

Richard laughed. "I'd be shocked."

"Do you think he's worried about leaving his business behind and coming here?"

"I don't think your grandpa will be leaving anything behind. He says he's a video call wizard."

Emmett had tremendous respect for Duke. On every family trip to the Redding compound, he made sure to ingratiate himself as the favorite grandson. As far as Emmett was concerned, Duke had few flaws. The man exuded grit and hard-won triumph. "He doesn't seem that worried about climate change. He says his business will be fine. Cole says—"

"Cole's right." Emmett didn't expect this response from his dad. "At least people will be up his ass about it. There was an article two years ago, in some big magazine, that basically said Peterson Lumber was evil. It's really a shame. Everyone is so angry these days. They're looking for scapegoats."

"Scapegoats?"

"They're pointing fingers at people like your grandpa, like me, who make a lot of money."

"Because they're jealous?"

"I think that's part of it. I think they're also scared."

"Of climate change?"

"I'm doing my very best to position us, just so you know, as being on the right side of history. In fact, this is a good lesson for your first day of work—remember this." He pointed a finger. Emmett nodded in anticipation. "Good branding is everything. Everything. We don't have to back every green company, every sustainable solution—most of them are absolute trash. But we have to talk about them like we love them, like we're always looking for the next Tesla. Then when the mob comes, they won't come for us because we'll be the good ones on their side. It'll be those other rich people," he gestured around the room and lowered his voice, "that'll get the brunt of it. No one follows money; they follow words. When people are angry, you have to distract them. If we want to hold on to this life, all of this, we'll have to distract them. Even if they go down, we don't have to go down too. I'm working on that."

"You're so smart, Dad," Emmett said, and on cue, his dad beamed.

—

WHEN LILY ARRIVED AT the meditation hall, Cathy, Jenny, and Becca were already seated, talking loudly. Lily waved at a few of the other people clustered about, then joined her friends. The hall was a wood-paneled window-lined oasis of a room, the gem of Maluhia. She liked the room but, despite years of trying, didn't like meditation. It was too hard and never made her feel better. Yet here she was.

"I hear he studied in Nepal for twenty years," Becca said.

"But he's Hawaiian, right?" Cathy asked, scanning the room, then smiling at Lily as she sat down. "We're talking about the teacher."

"Oh."

Cathy scrolled on her phone. "His name is Koa! He has to be a real Hawaiian."

"He might be Asian," Becca said. "Asians have all kinds of names."

"Shhh…" Jenny said. "He's here."

But it wasn't Koa, just a staff member. "I'm sorry," he said, "there has been some confusion. Koa isn't able to make it today."

Lily heard sighs across the room. She pretended to be sad too, but now could get a massage before dinner. Much better.

"What do you mean he isn't able to make it?" Cathy asked.

The man looked nervous. He was new here. Lily squinted at his name tag. Jeff.

"There was a mix-up with his scheduling," Jeff said. "We're very sorry for the inconvenience."

The other people started to get up and return their pillows and mats. Cathy and her friends didn't budge. "So what are we supposed to do?"

"Um." Jeff read from a piece of paper. "There is a lei-making workshop at four in the rec center and sunset snorkeling at five."

Then a voice in the back announced, "For anyone who wants to stay for the Hakalau, I can guide us." It was an irritating interjection, declared boldly, and before turning around to face the speaker, Lily hoped the woman would be ugly or old. Sometimes people couldn't pick up on social cues.

Lily had been raised right and never embarrassed herself publicly. Lily locked eyes with the woman and saw she was pretty with blown-out hair and a sundress. She emanated some nameless but breathtakingly significant essence that permeated outwards and left Lily speechless and acutely self-conscious, staring back at this woman like a schoolgirl.

The woman noticed Lily's stare. "Hello," she said right to her, only to her. And then to everyone in the same loud voice, "It's not that hard. I looked up the instructions. You all came here to learn the Hakalau." She read from her phone, standing in the center of the emptying room. "Hakalau Meditation is an ancient Hawaiian practice that uses peripheral vision to bring you into a meditative state."

Cathy, Jenny, and Becca were already near the door. Lily stood and started to follow them but the woman stepped in front of her. She was smiling and didn't seem to mind the all-encompassing disinterest in her offer. It was the type of rejection that would cripple Lily, the kind that she did everything to avoid. Who did this woman think she was, saying she could lead them all in meditation, as if they didn't want to sit with a real master?

"Do you want to meditate?" the woman asked. She looked about Lily's age.

"Um. Well—" She wanted to follow her friends out the door.

"It's fine. We can just talk."

"Oh, well—"

The woman sat down on the floor, legs crossed, totally at ease. "It's not like you have anything else to do?"

Lily wished she had the confidence to say she did or, even better, tell the truth that even if she had nothing to do, nothing was preferable to this. But Lily couldn't do anything but nod.

On her most recent InhaleAfrica video call, she had been silent for two hours. Only confident enough to occasionally nod and say goodbye at the end. What had happened to her? She was supposed to have been a high-powered lawyer or politician or business executive. But she had gotten married so early and then had kids and that wouldn't have been good for the kids. She agreed with Richard on that at least. And to his credit, he had asked her: "You want to be a good mom, right?"

But maybe she wanted to be more than a good mom. It took this presumptuous pariah of a woman to surface these doubts, but they multiplied once they were there.

"I'm Patricia." Patricia extended a hand.

Lily noted that Patricia did not reference a last name or husband. So Lily, uncharacteristically, followed suit. "I'm Lily." She shook her hand but didn't join her on the floor. Then, in a veiled show of superiority, asked, "Is this your first year at Maluhia?"

"Yes. I bought the Bell place."

Lily noticed the *I*. The Bell place was one of the beachside mansions. Any feelings of superiority vanished. "Congratulations. I didn't know the Bells were selling."

"They weren't, not officially. But I had a friend broker the deal, and one thing led to another. You know how these things go." Patricia trailed off. "It's good to meet you, Lily!"

"Oh, and you too. Are you here with your family?"

"Yes, my daughter."

"Oh, that sounds nice—"

Patricia doubled down. "My ex would have fucking loved this place." She laughed. "Too bad..."

"Oh," said Lily. She didn't know what to say next.

"You're here with your family?"

"Yes, well, my husband and my son Emmett. We have another son who had to stay back. He's a consultant."

"It would be great to do dinner together, but maybe next week? You know we just got here, and I'm settling in." Lily nodded but vowed never to join this woman for dinner. It wasn't just the meditation comment, or the fact that she had singled Lily out, or the way she spoke as if everything she said was important. It was mostly the fact that she made Lily feel small. "What do you do, by the way?"

Lily felt even smaller. "I'm very lucky to not have to work full time, my husband—"

"Is that your usual spiel?"

"Um. I'm sorry?"

"Don't apologize. I just asked a question."

Lily couldn't look at Patricia anymore. The freak of a woman. No social skills. No class. No wonder her husband left her. "I don't know what you mean."

"I'm just fucking with you." She laughed.

Lily tried to laugh too. She sounded like a whimpering cat. "What do you do?"

"I run my own company. I'm CEO."

"Oh."

"I'll tell you about it later."

"Okay."

"You can go. I can tell you want to go."

Lily looked up, shook her head. "No, no, not at all. It's just I should see what my friends are doing. That's all."

"I'm gonna meditate. I'll see you later, Lily."

Outside Lily tried to shake off the encounter but couldn't. Who was this woman to judge her for not working? So what if she ran her own company? Lily didn't need to run a company. She had a husband and a family to think about. And she had friends, unlike Patricia—that condescending, uppity bitch.

4

Cole accidentally goes to a food bank

Cole blamed his family for the world he was inheriting, and for the world his kids would inherit (should a woman ever decide to bear his children). He reserved an extra dose of vitriol for his grandfather, the lumber baron. But the whole family was to blame. His dad invested blood money, his mom spent it, and his brother cherished it and longed for it and saw himself as deserving of it.

After his freshman year at Stanford, Cole had returned home eager to convince them of their moral failings. He would point to smoke pollution and the far too hot San Francisco days. These were things his family supposedly cared about. Things that made even their flagrantly comfortable lives a little bit worse. His mom and dad would say all the right things. They even said they were proud of him for fighting for what he believed in.

But when it came to making changes to actually help the earth or the skyrocketing wealth divide or even the homeless men and women on their city sidewalks, they did nothing. Well, not nothing. They bought a new security system for their house and stuck a Black Lives Matter sticker on the window. "That way, we won't be a target," his dad explained.

Cole had always been rebellious, but until college had kept that part of himself hidden away.

He was an outcast growing up. He had few friends in elementary school and even fewer in middle school. In high school, he had one real friend, a fellow outsider named Thomas, but even that relationship was short-lived.

Thomas taught Cole how to mine bitcoin and access the dark web. They would spend their weekends side by side in Cole's room, installing bitcoin miners (eventually they had six, all purchased on Richard's credit card) and looking up the most disgusting things they could think of on the internet: porn, gore, anything with a nsfw hashtag was fair game. Sometimes Thomas would show Cole 4chan posts from an anonymous user. They were threatening and violent and mentioned specific classmates and teachers at their school. Cole suspected that Thomas was responsible but bit his tongue. Then one day, someone at school found the posts, and when they called Thomas in for questioning, he confessed. His defense—that he was expressing himself and wasn't going to harm anyone, not for real anyway— fell on deaf ears. Thomas was expelled and moved away shortly after.

So Cole turned to self-help gurus on the internet. From YouTube videos and expensive online classes, he learned how to be a "real man," or in one specific class, "How to get inside her!" That class was the most expensive.

The videos told him to focus on "lesser targets," but he wasn't willing to wait. There was only one girl he wanted to be with. Her name was Carrie. She was beautiful and intelligent and popular. One time in French class, she turned around and asked him how long their presentations were supposed to be. He said, "Five minutes and then five minutes of Q&A."

"Thanks," she said.

That night all he thought about was the way she said thanks. It was a very sexy *thanks*.

The next day, feeling confident, after watching a video about how to "make her NEED you," Cole asked for her number. "What?" She was confused.

He tried again. He told her he had some questions about the presentations. She relented. That night he texted her five times.

Hey, it's Cole.

Five minutes later. *I actually don't have questions about the presentations. I just wanted to see if you'd like to hang out sometime.*

He felt good after that one. The videos said, "Be direct. Be vulnerable."

An hour later. *I just think you're really cool.*

Ten minutes after that, he lost his confidence. *If not, that's cool too.*

Two hours later, at 1:00 a.m. *Is this your real number?*

The next morning he got a Facebook notification. It said, *Carrie Deckard tagged you in a post.* The post said, *Like this status if you think Cole Peterson is a creepy simp.*

Her post had 150 likes. There were only 140 people in his class. He didn't go to school that day and cried for hours under the covers. He got up twice to go to the bathroom but didn't look in the mirror. He knew he would hate what he would see.

In college, he made his first real friends since Thomas. He saw that the social activist clubs on campus were among the most popular, so he flocked to meetings and met fellow warriors dead set on building a better world. These friends gave him the confidence to let his anger show, to even take it home with him. They pushed him to help his family see the light. He wasn't invited to their parties or anything like that, but during club meetings (he was a member of Sustainable Stanford and Stanford Socialists), they listened to him. He was sure that his club members, unlike his parents, believed in him.

"We're proud of you for fighting for what you believe in," said his mom. "Absolutely," said his dad.

But then they flew their private jets and escaped to Hawaii every fire season. He hated them for it. In them, and especially in his brother Emmett, he saw Carrie Deckard and the insufferable people just like her. They were perfect and rich and popular, but cruel—to him and to the planet.

He was grateful to be leaving them behind and extra grateful when his Uber Black pulled up outside the private airport. The UberX drivers were striking again, which he, of course, supported, but that left Uber Black as the only option.

He couldn't find the exact address of his destination, but some internet blogs pointed him toward the Dogpatch neighborhood of the city. Once inside the car, he took off his mask. In another universe that seemed far more plausible than this one, Cole Peterson was on a jet with his family, Hawaii-bound. He would grit his teeth through family dinners and golf outings and hold his tongue when Grandpa Duke started lecturing. He would telecommute on weekdays to a lucrative consulting job and he would spend his evenings reading. It was a life that others would kill for. And yet, as he moved away from that life, the car immersed in smoke, he didn't feel a sense of loss.

His driver stopped on Twenty-Second Street and Illinois. Supposedly, the real love of his life (not Carrie) was working one block away, between a rock climbing gym and a food bank.

COLE MET BELLA in a moral philosophy class his senior year. They had some overlapping friends, although her activist group was cooler than his. He fell in love with her when he first saw her and then fell in love with her again when he heard her speak, and he seemed to fall in love with her, again and again, each day, whether he saw her or not. She was the most intelligent person he had ever met, much brighter than Carrie. He didn't let himself think otherwise because, in that moment of falling in love, he rendered Bella flawless. He disarmed himself of all cynicism and genuflected before her perfection.

He thought about her and spent nights scrolling up and down her Instagram, masturbating. He knew every photo, but he had his favorites. Once, while attempting to zoom in, he double-tapped and liked one of her high school bikini pics. He was mortified. She would get a notification *Cole Peterson liked your photo*. Extra bad because it was so far down her feed. And extra extra bad because she barely knew who he was. That awkward guy from the philosophy seminar. Maybe the notification disappeared after he unliked the photo, immediately after. But what if she had push notifications on and saw it before? Perhaps she was sitting with friends. *Who the hell is this guy? Oh my God, Bella, he liked your high school bikini photo. What a creepy simp.*

He waited two weeks after liking the photo and then approached her after class. He knew she was involved in Aid for Earth on campus, which was smaller than his other clubs, but had some of the same members. "Can I come to your next meeting?" he asked.

"I don't know," she said smiling, "can you?"

"I'm Cole, by the way."

"I'm Bella. Why do you want to join Aid for Earth?"

"Well, I guess, um, well…I grew up in a crazy rich family. You know, I should have been one of those rich Stanford kids you hate."

She teased him. "What makes you think I don't hate you?"

"Well, I wouldn't blame you if you did. I know firsthand how unfair the world is."

It seemed like the message resonated with her. "Sometimes," she said, "I feel like most kids at this school don't know anything about how Americans actually live."

"I'm sorry," he said. It was the wrong thing to say, but she just smiled.

"Why are you sorry?"

"I just mean—"

"You mean you feel bad for me because I'm a black girl from New Orleans at a school with people like you?"

"No!" He was mortified. "I mean, yes?"

"See, here at Stanford, I'm the special one, but everywhere else, I'm normal." She walked away, but then turned back, "See you at the meeting."

There was nothing normal about Bella. Brilliant, courageous, beautiful. She saw the world as he saw it: broken and unjust. It didn't get her down, though. She was ferociously optimistic. "Things are changing," she announced at the first campus Aid for Earth meeting he attended. "I can feel it."

Aid for Earth was a climate justice organization that had gained national attention for its unconventional protest tactics. Leadership would organize rallies in front of climate offenders like big banks and fossil fuel companies. Sometimes the protests turned violent.

But Aid for Earth rose to real prominence in 2025 when the organization targeted senators who had taken money from fossil fuel lobby groups. The attack tactics ranged from in-person protests in front of private residences to leaked emails, phone calls, and photos. Photos of Texas Senator Earl Grady screwing his mistress led to his prompt resignation. Other cases were less clear-cut.

Martha Clancy, the Democratic congresswoman from Michigan, had a phone call leaked where she told an aide that if a natural gas company became a donor, she would vote for a pro-natural gas bill. The Aid for Earth warriors didn't care that she was a Democrat and a staunch green policy defender. Everyone knew that senators voted to appease donors, but something about the blatancy of the leaked call set protestors off. They surrounded her family's lake house and camped out for days. The affair ended nastily for all involved when a subset of the protesters vandalized the extravagant home, breaking windows and coating the walls with graffiti. A few offenders were arrested, and the protest subsided. Martha lost her re-election campaign in a landslide. Her Republican challenger called her Corrupt Clancy, and the rest was history.

One night, after an Aid for Earth meeting, Bella invited Cole back to her place for drinks. He knew that it was a friendly invitation, not a romantic one, but was still excited.

They opened a bottle of wine, and Bella told him about why she volunteered for Aid for Earth.

"It's white people and rich people who are adapting to climate change, who are even thriving. But most of the world is being left behind." In the previous meeting, they had discussed floods in Nigeria, locust swarms in Kenya, and the sea-level rise in Indonesia. It had been a depressing meeting. Well, not for Cole. He enjoyed any chance to see Bella.

"I care too," he told her, feeling a little buzzed. "I want you to know that I care too."

"I know you do." They were on opposite sides of a table. She leaned in close. "You want to know something else?" Her brown eyes beckoned him toward her until they were almost touching. "I broke Martha Clancy's windows." She smiled. "What do you think about that?"

"I think she deserved it."

Bella clapped and sat back, grinning. "I knew you'd get it, Cole Peterson. I fucking knew it."

After that evening, Cole longed for a second invitation, but it never came. He considered asking her out, but he couldn't summon the courage. Cole had slept with only one woman in his life one time, and the sorry event had involved considerable amounts of alcohol from both parties. Consenting parties, he reminded himself when he was feeling insecure, often in front of a mirror where a creepy simp looked back.

STANFORD, LIKE OTHER CALIFORNIA SCHOOLS, had switched to the fire season alternate schedule. Graduation was on July 1, and it wasn't until after the ceremony that Cole had a chance to speak one-on-one with Bella again.

She told him she wished him the best. He hated hearing that. It sounded like a final goodbye. But then she added, "Unless you come join us…"

"Join you? At Aid for Earth?"

Bella was joining Aid for Earth's corporate chapter full-time.

Cole had accepted a consulting job that would pay him far more money than Aid for Earth would, but Aid for Earth had Bella.

"We could use someone like you," she winked at him. "You know, with an insider's perspective."

He was about to respond when she hugged him. The hug was so unexpected and so overwhelmingly appreciated that he forgot what they were talking about. By the time he remembered what she had said, she was already gone, lost in the zoo of graduates. He trudged off to find his parents.

"We're very proud of you," they told him.

He nodded while he looked for Bella, without success.

In the subsequent weeks, he plotted how he would get out of his family's annual retreat to Maluhia so he could work with Bella. It would have to be last minute, or else they would try and stop him and possibly succeed. He wished he could message Bella in between, but he didn't have her number, and he wasn't about to pop up on her Instagram and resurface any conveniently forgotten trauma.

THE SMOKE WAS BAD TODAY, and Cole took short breaths through his mask as he studied his surroundings. He had spent little time in Dogpatch, despite growing up in the city. There were a smattering of trendy shops and eateries and then the occasional homeless camp or abandoned warehouse.

He walked on the opposite side of the street to bypass a cluster of tents and then crossed back to find his destination. The climbing gym was shuttered, but the food bank had a long line of people. Some wore masks. Cole didn't make eye contact with anyone. As he stood in front of the building that he thought was Aid for Earth, he felt afraid and unsafe.

To make matters worse, the warehouse appeared run down from the outside. There were no signs and seemingly no people inside. The walls were graffitied and, in some cases, punctured. The windows were boarded up with wooden planks, and it looked like exactly the kind of building someone of Cole's background would avoid at all costs.

He approached what he assumed was the front door. There was no handle, no doorbell. On the side was a rusty keypad. He looked for a call button but couldn't find one. He knocked on the door, first quietly and then loudly.

Then he glanced to his right and saw that he was attracting attention. This hooded boy banging on what seemed like a forsaken warehouse. He didn't let his stare linger. He knocked again and made himself wait. It was painful. No one came to the door, not that he had thought anyone would come to the door, and he was beginning to regret not getting on the family jet.

He could feel his pulse thick in his neck and his body tight and agitated. He could go home, wait it out, and try again tomorrow. It was an alluring idea. The food bank line and those hungry faces made him sick. At the front door, he pressed a few buttons on the keypad. They didn't seem to register. He knocked again, this time much more loudly.

He told himself to wait five minutes. A minute passed, and a voice from the food bank line called out to him. "Your girlfriend live here?" Laughter followed.

Cole turned and faced his audience. These were not Stanford people or tech people. These were the city's forgotten. He saw broken teeth and wrinkled skin, ragged clothing. "I'm looking for Aid for Earth," he managed. The words sounded meek and pitiful and were met with more laughter. He was worried for his safety; he knew it was wrong to think that way, but he was. What if they went through his backpack? What if they took his wallet, his laptop, his phone—he would buy new ones of course, but it would still be terrifying.

A woman spoke this time. She was wrinkled. She wore a pink surgical mask and souvenir-shop sunglasses. "Well, it seems like nobody's home."

Cole had no reply. He banged again. He tried to buy some dignity from the sneering mob. "They're supposed to be here."

Now his skin was flushed and his body electric, and he was certain he was going to leave. Already the steps formed in his mind. Call an Uber, call Mom, apologize profusely. In less than a day, he could be in his Maluhia bedroom reading a book and free from this hellscape.

Then he heard a beep from the keypad and then a husky voice. "Hello?"

"Hi!" He shouted. "I'm a friend of Bella Jones." His mouth was pressed against the key box.

"What's your name?" said the box.

"Cole Peterson."

There was a long pause, and then the box said, "One sec."

He turned to face the food line, redeemed. "See," he said. Pink-mask lady was looking the other way. Another man called out, "What?"

"Oh, I found it," he said, now aware that he shouldn't be saying anything at all but unable to stop. "They're coming."

"What?"

"They're coming!" Cole shouted back. Through his hot mask, he could hear his breath roll in and out, and it smelled musty, and he prayed that if he were allowed inside, Bella wouldn't smell it.

Then the door opened. It was Bella. Cole threw his hood down and removed his mask so she would recognize him. She stared blankly, and he was seized with panic. Then she smiled in her usual way, like he'd hoped she would, like he was a welcome surprise.

5

Duke misses the fresh smell of burning forest

When Duke arrived at his son's Maluhia house, it was 3:00 p.m. and hot. He was no stranger to the heat. His slice of California was prone to scorching summers, even more so during the last decade. But this heat was different, somehow more exhausting. He chalked it up to the humidity, and not his age or the flight.

The family seemed thrilled to see him. Lily gave him some kind of tropical juice, and Emmett took his bags for him. Richard asked about his trip and the drive over and his health, and so on.

"Where's Cole?" Duke asked.

"He had to stay in the city for work," Lily said. "He's working for a consulting company."

"Ah. So he bailed on you?" A week ago, Richard had told him the whole family was coming.

"You know how these things work," she said.

He didn't.

"Want a house tour?" Emmett asked.

The rooms were spacious and adorned with plants and flowers. His bedroom looked out on a tropical forest. The house had rooms for yoga and VR, two offices, and outside there was a big yard and a grill and a telescope. Emmett showed him a fire pit. "At night, I like to sit out here and look at the stars."

Duke was tired but agreed to see more of The Preserve. They piled into a golf cart. Richard drove to the beach and then to a golf course. The roads were lined with tiki torches protruding from flower beds and volcanic rock. They ran into another family that Richard introduced as the Fujis. "They're from China or Japan or somewhere over there." And then a woman that

Lily seemed friendly with, "She's friends with a bunch of celebrities." After a while, the different restaurants, pools, and hiking trails that Richard was pointing out blended together until Duke had no idea where he was or what he had seen.

"You'll get used to it," Emmett said. "It's a big place."

Back at the house, after they changed for dinner, Duke was asked what he thought about Maluhia. The family, all three of them, awaited his answer.

"It's nice." Richard looked proud, even smug. Duke continued, "It's not my kind of place, that's all." There was nothing wild about Maluhia, nothing natural. He hated cities for the same reason, except this was even worse. At least a city knew what it was. Maluhia was pretending to be untamed, even spiritual. The pretending made things so much worse.

They went to the restaurant close to the house, the best one on The Preserve, they assured him. It was a Californian-Hawaiian fusion restaurant called Heiau. They sat on a terrace under a blanket of string lights. In the corner, a heavyset man played ukulele and sang into a microphone.

"Dad," Richard said with a sad shy smile, "I was hoping we could talk about the mining company."

"And I was hoping we could enjoy dinner without talking about bullshit."

His son's smile faded. "We can talk about it later."

Duke grunted. "How often do you eat here?"

"It's our favorite spot," Richard said, deflecting Duke's gruffness.

Lily cut in, "So Duke, how has Eliza been faring?"

She looked down when he met her gaze. He seemed to have that effect on people. He liked that he did. "Faring at what?"

"At, um, running the company?"

"She's not running the company."

"Oh. Richard told me she was."

Duke took a sip of water and then took a closer look at the woman his son had married. She was pretty enough but bland, habitually bored, and worst of all, always throwing her husband under the bus. He and Margie had had something special, undefinable chemistry, an unbreakable commitment. Margie was always on his side. If she ever wasn't, she held her tongue, as a good partner should. They had been real that way, always on the same team. She had brought out the best in him, always setting him up in conversation to talk about what he wanted to talk about. It was because she understood him and believed in him, and after his success, she stayed the same way, in love with him and not his money. It wasn't like that with Richard and Lily. It was their generation's way, he couldn't blame them entirely. He mostly blamed Lily's parents, people he had met only once at the wedding, but must have been responsible for raising a quarrelsome daughter.

Richard ordered a bottle of wine, and Duke ordered a bourbon for himself. When it arrived, Duke took a small sip and then a series of larger ones. He lost focus on the conversation and listened to the fat man play ukulele. All of it was nauseating. Heiau reeked of decadence and pageantry. The lights, the music, the Hawaiian-shirt-wearing waiters. *It was like Disneyland*, he thought, and then said so. "It's like Disneyland here."

"Why do you have to hate everything?" It seemed that Richard had no intention of being polite. Duke didn't mind. Tonight, he was in a nasty mood and hoped that he would get nastiness in return.

"You eat here every night?"

"No, Dad. Not every night."

"How much is it?"

"Excuse me?"

Duke looked down at his menu. It had today's date on it, indicating the menu changed every night. There was a tasting menu and an à la carte option. Both routes were expensive.

"Royal Ossetra Caviar, Summer Truffle Mac and Cheese, Snake River Beef," Duke read aloud. He looked around at three grim faces. "Tell me, what's so special about Snake River Beef that it should cost ninety-seven dollars."

"We don't usually get the beef," Emmett said.

Richard shook his head. "Oh, don't humor him. So what, Dad? You don't want to eat here?" He kept his voice low. He sounded more sad than angry. "We try to take you somewhere nice, you know? We wanted to show you—"

"Show me how you live here, I know." Duke finished his whiskey. It had only been five minutes. "Do you know why this country is fucked?"

"Because you keep burning it?" Richard smiled.

Duke ignored the jab. "It's because no one works anymore. The rich don't work, and the poor don't work, but the rich are especially bad because they don't work and eat a hundred-dollar steak."

"Oh, come on, you picked the most expensive one." Richard pointed. "This one's sixty, for fuck's sake."

"Richard, stop it." Lily gestured toward Emmett, who was seventeen but apparently was too young to hear the word fuck. She doted over him like he was still a toddler. She didn't seem to care about talking back, though. No, *that* was fine for Emmett to hear.

"Sorry," Richard said. But then again to his dad, "Sixty!"

"I worked to get here," Duke continued.

"You don't think the people here work?"

"You don't. You just spend my money."

"Hello, Petersons!" Duke looked up from his drink to see a tall, smiling man. He, like the waitstaff, wore a Hawaiian shirt. He, unlike the waitstaff, sported a Rolex.

"Con Man!" Richard stood up, his weariness suddenly wiped clean from his face. He shook Con Man's hand and then patted him on the back. Some country club gesture. Duke wanted more bourbon. "How are you?" Richard asked.

"Oh, so good. So good. Lily, hello! Emmett, hello! And you are?" His teeth were shiny and white. He looked like everyone Duke hated. The guy probably spent hours in front of the mirror. Probably had all kinds of ointments and creams and other crap. Duke only used sunscreen and only because his doctor told him to. So what if he looked like a slob in his old jeans and an old blue T-shirt? That's how men should look, how they used to look.

"This is my dad, Duke. Dad, this is Connor."

"Duke, it's such a pleasure." Connor extended his hand, and Duke shook it. "We're golfing tomorrow!" Connor pointed at Richard. "Don't weasel out of it, Richie."

They made their plans and laughed. Lily asked about his wife, Emmett said something about colleges, and Duke looked down into his empty glass.

"Tomorrow, Richie! See you on the first tee. Bring your A-game."

Connor swaggered off. "He's a real estate developer," Richard explained. "We call him Con Man because—"

"Richie," Duke raised a finger. "I think you have me confused with someone who gives a shit."

The ukulele player decided to take a break and silence engulfed the table. Duke called over the waiter.

"I would like another bourbon, and I think we're ready to order."

"Tasting menu again, Mr. Peterson?" The waiter asked Richard.

"I think we'll do à la carte tonight. Thank you, Jackson."

Duke ordered a salad. It was the cheapest entree on the menu. He did it on purpose. He knew they would notice. But they ignored him, so he said, "It's only thirty dollars for the salad."

"Dad, please, *please* try to enjoy this."

"Honey, let it go." Lily put a hand over her husband's.

"No. It's not okay." Richard spoke quietly though. Were people listening to them? Duke looked around, saw mostly consumed, self-involved faces. Half of them were on their phones, unaware of anything in their surroundings, let alone Richard. But leave it to his son to be paranoid, always afraid of what others would think of him. "We invite you into our home for three months. We give you a full tour. Lily makes you juice—"

"It was good juice," Duke said with a sardonic smile.

"Thank you," Lily said.

Richard groaned. "He's fucking with you."

"I am not. I liked it."

"Thank you," she said again.

Richard stopped him before he could prod further. "How could you possibly hate this place?"

Duke's second whiskey arrived, and he took a sip. He hated the place but even more than that, he hated the people here. They made their money behind computers, manipulating financial markets and closely tracking graphs. Duke supplied them with wood for their first homes, and second homes, and third homes. They didn't work with their hands; they didn't seem to work at all. And the worst part was that his son was part of their sorry flock. He had always known this but seeing it firsthand made it so much worse. Especially since his son was galivanting on Duke's dime, enjoying things he hadn't worked for and didn't deserve. "We just like different things, that's all. You're the type of people who like this. That's fine."

It wasn't fine, but they left it there. For now.

Lily and Richard's wine arrived, and Duke ordered two more glasses of bourbon. Jackson, the waiter, was confused, "You mean a double?"

"No, Jackson. I mean two glasses."

Jackson brought back the glasses. Duke handed one to Emmett. He waited for Jackson to say something. The man looked miserable but stayed silent.

"Dad," Richard whispered, "He's seventeen."

"When I was seventeen—"

"We know all about how hard you worked at seventeen."

"I was managing a whole site!"

Emmett leaned in, his eyes wide and earnest. "They let you manage the whole site?"

Duke smiled as Richard rolled his eyes, and Lily feigned interest. He knew he had told the story a dozen times—Emmett had even heard it a few times—but it was a better story than whatever stories they had to share. Drama for his family revolved around golf wagers and tax disputes. They didn't know the meaning of real drama.

"When I was seventeen, I took up with a lumber crew in the Canadian Rockies. It was a tough job. It was raining all the time. We were always wet. And everyone was always tired. It was like we were in a labor camp. And with the amount they were paying us, we might as well have been. People kept getting injured. One guy even lost a hand and had to be helicoptered out of there. And then, to make things worse, the bears started coming." He was happy to see that Emmett was clinging to every word. "It didn't take long for the men to stop working hard. It wasn't out of laziness, as much as fear, but the result was the same. Lots of feet dragging, you know? Lots of complaining. The supervisor asked me to get morale up, to set a good example. And I did my best, but, and this is a good lesson," he pointed at Richard, middle-aged and still in need of lessons. "But I knew it would take more than words. My chance came a few days later, a mother grizzly walked right into camp. I got out my rifle and—"

Richard cut in. "And you shot the bear."

"Can I tell my own story?" A tacit nod. "Well, yes, I shot the bear. And after that, there was no more complaining, no more backtalk. They called me 'Bear Killer.'"

"Bear Killer," Emmett said. "I think I'll call you that too."

"Feel free."

"You shot it in the face?"

"No. Right in the lungs. The lungs are the best target for a bear because—"

He was interrupted by the ukulele player's return. The crowd quieted, and Duke quieted too as the man spoke into the mic. Something about being grateful to play for such a good audience, to Duke it was all nonsense, so he didn't listen.

The servers arrived and placed a covered plate in front of each diner and then removed the covers with flawless coordination. To most diners, this was welcome entertainment; to Duke, it was gratuitous. He scoffed when his cover was removed and glared at his salad. The plate was all aesthetics, no substance. Three red beets, a bed of cheese, and some flowers on top. Maybe they were edible, but they didn't look appetizing.

"Bon appétit," said Jackson.

He was going to say something aloud about his delicate portion. Perhaps, something like thirty bucks for a decoration, but he was suddenly tired. He drank his whiskey and watched the others eat. When Lily asked him what he thought, though, he was reinvigorated.

"I think it's thirty bucks down the drain."

She looked sad. He didn't feel bad for her though. She was eating a steak.

Emmett drank a sip of his whiskey and coughed.

"Too strong?" Richard pried.

"No." He took another sip and winced but did not cough. He looked to Duke for approval.

"Do you like it?"

"It's good," Emmett said. "I just don't usually drink whiskey."

"Good. I'll get you another."

As the dinner continued, everyone got drunk. By Duke's sixth bourbon, he was light-headed and slurring his speech.

"I'm not surprised you like it here, Richie. I'm not surprised at all."

"Why, Dad?" He looked and sounded defeated.

Duke squeezed his glass and narrowed his glare. "Because God forbid, you go somewhere and actually be productive. Your whole life is just one never-ending vacation. Here in Hawaii. Back in SF—"

"If you don't like it here, you can leave," Richard muttered. For a second, Duke felt bad for his son. Especially when he took Lily's hand and said, "We like it here," and it was obvious that she didn't like it at all and definitely didn't like him touching her hand.

But then Duke drank another sip and didn't feel so bad. "If you want me to leave, I'll leave."

"We want you to stay," Emmett said. "Lots of people work from here."

"You can't work here. It's a playground. 'The most successful people on the planet.'" Duke laughed. "Maybe they're rich because they took daddy's money."

Richard didn't take the bait. He pressed on, voice still low, eyes still pointed at his plate. "You can go home, but you have to let Eliza do her job. It'll be her company soon."

Duke squeezed his glass and imagined it shattering in his hand. "It's my company, and it'll always be my company. I built the damn thing. And it's not even Eliza's job! It's Chris *and* Eliza's job. Look at me." Richard continued to look down until Duke snapped his fingers in his son's face. Then, and only then, did Richard's eyes rise, like ornaments on a string, to meet Duke's. "You and Eliza don't know what it means to suffer. You can't work without suffering. Work and suffering go hand in hand. Together, they make you a man." Then he turned to Emmett. "Or else, you'll be like your father, weak and womanly."

That was it for Richard, the piece of dynamite that made the whole thing blow. He squeezed his fists. The Richard that hated making a scene, hated being picked on, hated being anything but good guy Richard became someone unrecognizable. His face flushed red, and his eyebrows turned in. He shouted. "Shut up! Damn it! Please!"

Duke hadn't seen his son lose it since he was a child. Richard would push back, but never really burst. He was weak that way. But for the first time, Richard had burst. Lily looked equally surprised, although also vaguely impressed.

The ukulele player had stopped playing. Heads swiveled. Every pair of eyes on the patio closed in. Richard looked around, saw that he had lost himself, and shriveled up. "I'm sorry," he whispered. "I'm sorry for yelling."

Duke knew he would also feel sorry, but later. He knew he might even apologize. Now though, his mind searched for a witty response, a winning blow. He spoke so only his table would hear. "See, womanly. You're proving my point."

Richard sat, crumbling in place until the music started again.

6

Emmett lies to a girl and Richard lies to himself

Emmett left the Peterson home around 9:00 p.m. He was drunk and wasn't allowed to take the golf cart. "But, Dad," he protested. "I'm barely buzzed."

Richard crossed his arms. "No. You walk, or you stay here."

His mom was less accommodating. "I think you should stay."

"Mom, please…" She gave him a familiar look, part maternal anxiety, part hopelessness. "I'm fine, really. I'll walk."

"Please be safe." It looked like she was sending him to war.

"I'm going to Logan's house! He lives like five minutes away!"

"I know," she said, with that same look. "Okay."

His friend Logan lived twenty minutes away down a steep hill. Emmett hoped he would be fucked up enough on the walk back to make the ascent bearable. He had a couple of grams of weed, a bubbler, and some pre-rolled spliffs in his backpack. He hoped to put the awkwardness of dinner behind him, walking under a bright Hawaiian moon on the well-paved, torch-lit Maluhia streets. He hummed to himself as he strolled along.

He was trying to feel good. Seeing his family fight like that was an awful experience, and he felt simultaneously like everyone was blameless and culpable. He was worried that his grandpa wouldn't stay. All he wanted was a nice normal family that didn't fight with each other, that actually loved each other. Instead, he was a Peterson.

At the bottom of the hill, he lit up one of his spliffs and inhaled. The smoke hung in his mouth, and he breathed again, letting it waft through him. When he listened, he could hear all kinds of insects, rustling noises, and even some voices out in the distance. It was dark but for the cherry red spliff and the torchlight, and when he exhaled, a ring of mist floated outwards, disappearing into the warm night. It was all very serene until his phone rang. It was his girlfriend, Kacey. He didn't think about her all that much. He didn't like her all that much. They were a popular couple at school though. Everyone said they were great together. He was just as happy, though, when they weren't together. But here she was, calling him.

He picked up after a few rings. "Hey."

"Hey." Kacey seemed annoyed, and he wished he had let it go to voicemail.

"What's up?"

"Does there have to be something up for me to call you?"

"No—"

"I haven't heard from you for days."

"I've been busy."

And then she started to complain about her sister, and then her dad, and finally about her family's fire-season sabbatical in Mexico, where it was way too hot. It was all so depressing that Emmett tuned her out.

"Are you even listening?"

"Huh?"

"Damn it, Emmett. What did I just say?"

He took a deep inhale of his spliff and coughed into the phone. Sober Emmett would have been all over an apology. He didn't feel like apologizing now.

"Emmett?" Kacey asked. "Are you there?"

"Yes." But then, "I think you have me confused with someone who gives a shit."

The big red button beckoned. "What the hell, Emmett—" He pressed down. Back came the insect noises and the rustling and the moon. When she called back, he turned his phone off. He drew from the warm spliff. He smoked it until it was small, and then he stomped it out.

He felt wretched and knew that Kacey had paid a price for it. Still, he wouldn't call her back tonight. He needed to escape.

Logan lived in a mansion next to the surf club. It wasn't on the beach but just a few minutes away, and the second and third floors had ocean views. Logan's dad was a hedge fund manager, and his mom was a corporate attorney. Logan was proud of his parents and talked about them a lot. In response, Emmett usually talked about Duke. Not that his parents weren't successful; he knew his dad was a good investor (no matter what Cole said). But Logan's parents were *really* successful, in magazines and shit. So Duke was the better counter. Not that he was competitive with Logan. Emmett had first met him five years ago at Maluhia. Since then, they had grown close.

"Emmett, buddy!" Logan shouted when Emmett approached the back door. They embraced.

Logan and Emmett were the same height. They dressed the same: board shorts, tank tops, flip-flops. Emmett had wavy hair though, which made him look more like a surfer and made him feel like he belonged in Hawaii. Logan with his parted hair seemed stuck in the Bay Area. But they were both good-looking, and girls seemed to like them equally. Not that they ever competed. They were real friends that way, always helping each other stand out and look good. Emmet, of course, didn't do anything but flirt, not while he was still in Kacey's clutches.

Inside the house, others beckoned. There were maybe twenty people there, congregating in small circles. The drinks were flowing. The music was bumping, loud enough to make conversation possible only mouth to ear. Emmett liked it that way, intimacy when he was close to someone and anonymity when he was far. He moved from conversation to conversation, but couldn't take his eyes off a girl in the corner. She swayed to the music, coyly smiled, drank from a red solo cup and made it look sophisticated. Everything she did looked sophisticated and adult, and he wasn't just obsessed with her blue eyes and pinned-up blonde hair and perfect figure, but her presence. Once he saw her it was impossible not to see her. It wasn't a unique insight, she was surrounded by people, all wanting to talk to her or be near her. He whispered to Logan, "Who is that?"

"That's Chloe."

Logan led him over. "Emmett, meet Chloe."

"Do you want to smoke a spliff?" Emmett asked, squashing his butterflies and looking at her dead on. With his family, he had to play catch-up, always a step behind their vacillating moods and anxieties. They made him submissive, desperate to placate, eager to fix. Talking to girls was an arena where he could shine. He just needed to get his family out of his head: his dad's humiliated face, his mom's faux-placidity. He couldn't think about Kacey either. If he showed even an ounce of insecurity, of indecisiveness, he would lose his chance.

"I don't like tobacco," she said.

"I feel that. How about a joint then?" He raised his eyebrows, smiled when she smiled.

"Okay."

He left to roll a joint on a corner table. He worked quickly, but she had moved on and was among a group of others when he was done. He joined the circle and laughed and joked but was just waiting for the right moment to pull her aside.

She shared small details about herself, and he built her into something he could conceptualize. She was rich and smart and cool. Cool in a European sense, like a go-out-at-3:00-a.m.-high-on-who-knows-what sense. She said she had lived in Spain for a summer and was studying abroad there next year. She was older than him—a rising sophomore at Brown, taking a semester off to work with her mom.

"What's your name again?"

He double-checked that she was looking at him. "Emmett," he said.

"How about that joint?"

The confidence came back. He didn't show his excitement. He just said, "All right."

They went outside. He asked her more questions. This was, he had already grasped, her first year at Maluhia.

"Lucky me," he said.

"Why?"

"I'll get to show you around." He lit the joint.

"Hang on," she said. She pulled out a phone and took a selfie. Then another one and then another. He saw they were for CrissCross—an influencer app he had downloaded but never used.

"You like it?"

"I get paid a lot," she said. Then clarified, "not that I do it for the money."

"Why do you do it?"

"I don't know."

She looked bored. "Where are you from?" he asked.

"Seattle."

"What do your parents do?"

She pulled on the joint, it lit up her face, and he couldn't help but stare. She was much prettier than Kacey, and smarter.

"Many things," she said. "But they spend most of their time being assholes. We can't stand each other."

"Oh. I'm sorry." She probably wanted to hear about his parents, but he didn't know what to say. They weren't assholes. They weren't hedge-fund gods either. "What are you studying?"

"Art," she said.

He wanted her to ask him a question, but she didn't. The silence killed him. He searched for something interesting to say. He wasn't used to being tongue-tied. All he could think of was the unfortunate dinner. "This is the first year my grandpa is here with us."

"Uh-huh." He couldn't tell if she was listening.

"I don't think he likes it here. He thinks it's a playground for rich people." She smiled. She *was* listening. When he took the joint from her, he grazed her hand and stepped closer. "He thinks that the people here are lazy, that they don't deserve to be here."

"Is he poor?" There was contempt in the question.

"No. He's loaded."

Chloe passed back the joint, and now she stepped closer. They weren't touching, but if she were to lean his way, they would be. "As loaded as Logan's parents?"

"Definitely."

"I mean Logan's pretty rich."

"Well, my grandpa is the lumber baron of California." She seemed confused. "That's what they call him."

"You're funny."

"You're cute." He watched the words land and then wished them back.

She raised her eyebrows. "You're young."

"I'm twenty," he lied, and regretted the lie immediately. She would find out very quickly from Logan or someone else that he was seventeen. But he didn't correct himself. "What do you think," he managed, "about Maluhia?"

"Oh, I like it. I mean, I'm here with my mom, that sucks. But like your grandpa said, it's a playground for rich people! Pretty sweet."

She finished the joint and said thank you, and then returned to the house. He wasn't feeling so great anymore, but he followed her in. He felt like a child.

RICHARD LAY ON THE BED, an arm's distance away from his wife, transfixed on his phone. He was playing a new game called Beetle Wars and wasn't very good yet, which he couldn't stand. "Fuck. Shit. Fuck." His fingers danced on the screen, and he blinked only when he had to. His beetle was going to die any second. He was going to be the first player in the twenty-person match to die.

When it happened, he let out a more dramatic, "FUCK!" and dropped the phone.

"Do you want to talk about tonight?" Lily asked.

"No." He picked the phone back up and clicked on a different game. He was much better at this one, a zombie shooter, and only said "fuck" twice. Shooters were better games anyway. He had fast reflexes and there wasn't as much strategy. Beetle Wars had too much strategy.

"Can you put your phone down?"

"One second."

He was respawning after a kill streak when she brought it up again. "I think we should talk about it."

"Why? It's fine."

"Do you really want to deal with him for the next three months?"

After a conversation with Eliza, in which she begged Richard to bring Duke along, Richard had agreed, despite Lily's not-so-veiled aversion to the idea. He loved his sister but, more strongly, he pitied her. The Peterson Lumber job was everything she had. And he was the only one in the world who knew what she knew: that their dad was a tyrant to work with, never satisfied, perpetually unimpressed, marked by a boundless capacity for meanness.

"We just have to deal with him," Richard said. Then he said, "Fuck yeah!" and exhaled.

"What?"

"Oh, nothing, I just won a battle."

"Maybe he misses your mom?"

"No." Richard sat up and, for the first time since coming home, set his phone down. "That's not it. It's not about Mom. He's always been like this."

Richard, for his whole life, had never been good enough for Duke. Occasionally Duke would say, "Good work, Richard." Like after Trance went public and again, shortly after, when he was interviewed on CNBC. But the approval didn't last long. A night or two later, Richard's phone would ring, and Duke would ask, "Do you even work?" He would usually say it in a comical way so that Richard would seem sensitive if he reacted badly, but Richard had heard it enough to know what his dad meant.

Richard was never going to be good enough because, compared to his dad, he was nothing. From Duke's perspective, he had given his kids the world, and no matter what they did with it, it would never be enough. "If I had your start, I'd—" he would say.

"You'd what?" Richard would counter as calmly as he could, "Have ten billion dollars instead of three?"

There was no way to reason with Duke. Everything he did was always the right way to do things. He worked the right job, a man's job, and drank the right liquor, a man's liquor, and so on. But Richard knew deep down that his dad wasn't proud of himself. The reason he wanted to keep working despite being seventy, the reason Hawaii was his first vacation in almost twenty-five years, was because he believed that he wasn't good enough, not yet. If he did, he would have stopped working years ago.

"He called you a woman. In front of Emmett!" Lily said.

"I know."

"He treats you like you're nothing."

"I know." As if an investor in Trance could be nothing. Who cares that it was a small first check or that he had long ago spent his gains and was back to living off his trust fund? Richard knew one thing for sure: investing wasn't any easier than lumber. "The worst part is," he told Lilly, "this next investment in the bitcoin mining company could be just as good. But he won't fucking approve it. You heard him, right? He won't even talk about it! We're leaving billions on the table. You'd think he would trust me by now. Trance changed the world." She looked tired and he wondered if she was understanding the importance of what he was saying. "The *fucking world!*"

He wished she would say more about his greatness, but she didn't seem to be catching on. Or maybe she did understand and just didn't feel like it. He felt weak as he asked the question but asked it all the same. "You're proud of me, right?"

"Of course."

It didn't sound like it. She must have noticed his grimace.

"You've given me such a good life." He nodded, expecting more. Instead, she said, "I wish you were proud of me."

He didn't like where the conversation was going. Lily had a tendency to make things about her. But he wasn't in the mood for a second fight in one evening. "I am proud of you. You are a great mother—"

"See." She got out of bed. "That's the problem. I don't like that you think of me as a mother."

"Where's this coming from?"

"Well, I met someone today." He felt a whirl of jealousy. "Patricia something." He relaxed. "I didn't like her or anything. I'm not saying I want to be like her—"

"Well, why are you talking about her."

"She's a CEO, that's all. I just know I could have done that too."

"You don't need to work—"

"When I was in college—"

"Lily, why isn't anything ever enough for you? Do you know how many women would love to come here and get to sit by the pool and relax and…" He trailed off and closed his eyes. He was so tired. So sick of conversations like this one. He expected her to walk out. When he heard her feet move toward the door, he opened his eyes and reached for his phone. But she stood still in the doorway, unwilling to grant him a full retreat.

"I just wish you respected me. I don't know when you stopped."

He rubbed his eyes. "Of course I respect you."

She continued, undeterred. "And yet you expect me to respect you."

The knowledge of what was coming next, what always came next when she wanted to pick a fight, roused him to his feet. He walked toward her, big-chested, stretched tall. Towering over her, he said. "You're so ungrateful."

"Oh yeah?"

"I work my ass off for *you*. I get you everything every woman would DREAM of. But it's never good enough." He stepped away and massaged his neck like he was about to enter a boxing ring.

"You're feeling really good about yourself, huh?"

He paced back to the bed. Sat and ran his hands through his hair. "Just get out of here. Please."

"Fine. Go work your ass off for more of your dad's money." She walked closer.

"Get the fuck out of here."

She picked up his phone and mashed the screen like she was playing a game. "Oh first place, second place, OH NO, fifth place."

"What are you even doing?"

"I'm working my ass off, like you!"

"Give me that." He reached for the phone, instead he caught her wrist. It was delicate, so thin that his fingers were touching his thumb. It would take one squeeze to teach her a lesson. He looked at her. Did he see fear behind the disgust? He let go.

She laughed. It was the worst thing she could do. Until she did something worse. With a terrific heave, she threw the phone against the opposite wall.

"What the hell!" He sprang back up, grabbed his phone to find the screen cracked. "What the fuck is wrong with you?"

She was gone though. He heard the front door slam. He saw his reflection on the phone screen. Handsome man, red-faced and wronged. But there were cracks everywhere in his reflection and one big one between his eyes, right down the middle.

7

Eliza gives a speech

The Lasco Fire ravaged 100,000 acres of Nesbit land. It stopped short of the Peterson holdings to the West and instead turned South, burning through Lassen National Forest before decimating the town of Chester. When the fire was extinguished on August 14, eighteen civilians had lost their lives, as well as five prison inmate firefighters. Chester, a popular hunting, fishing, and boating town, would never be the same.

For the two weeks that the fire burned, Eliza had impressed herself by staying calm. Site supervisors would call every hour with updates, "Twenty thousand acres now," and then a few hours later, "We're at twenty-five." They didn't know anything that the news didn't, though, and she was keeping close tabs on it every day. No one at work seemed particularly interested in the fire. There were bound to be a few big ones every year, and everyone knew Peterson would get the salvage contract. Chester burning was sad, but then again, it was only a matter of time before it went up in flames. People said as much around the office. Only Chris knew about Eliza's decision to cut the eastern border. Before starting their all-hands meeting, he told her that the Chester casualties weren't the company's fault.

"Of course, they weren't."

Chris should be congratulating her, not consoling her. And anyway, she had nothing to do with a controlled burn gone wrong, whether or not she was co-CEO at the time. Her job was to protect the company and foster its success. Letting the fire burn was a tough decision but the right one. Not only was the vast majority of their land safe, but she could now potentially acquire Nesbit land for a much lower price and win a government contract to salvage the burned Lassen lumber. If things continued to break her way, the company would have a record-breaking quarter. In less than a month she had established herself as a capable CEO. She wanted to share her win with her employees, show them who was really running the show. But Chris (of course) had reservations. A minute before starting the event, when they were already seated side by side on the platform, he whispered, "Let's leave the fire stuff out of it."

"I think they should know what's happening."

"Does your dad know?"

He had her there. She wanted to ensure she had good news before reporting to her dad, and too many balls were still in the air.

Monday was the only day of the week when local corporate employees had to report to the office. Since Covid, Peterson Lumber had embraced a more flexible work-from-home policy, mainly to stay competitive and retain talent. Duke had pushed back, convinced that people were naturally lazy and would slack off when beyond the scope of his supervision. Eventually, though, making people come into work every day proved impossible, especially during fire season when no one wanted to drive or spend even a short stint in the parking lot, breathing toxic air. Of course, working from home was only a possibility for the corporate employees—a small fraction of the Peterson Lumber headcount—most were in the forests every day, chopping trees and breathing fire and smoke.

For the corporate employees, Mondays were for in-person meetings and, once a month, the company-wide all-hands. Duke called them his "famous all-hands," but there was no reason why the meetings should be famous, since her dad had ripped the concept off from far more innovative companies and the meetings themselves were routinely uneventful. But Duke cared so much about these meetings and put so much into them that most employees walked away, if not feeling inspired or recommitted to their jobs, at least less likely to quit. He had that kind of power and charisma. He made everyone feel special, like they were working for something bigger. When he said things like, "We are the custodians of the forests," no one laughed or questioned him. When Duke spoke, no matter what he said, everyone listened.

So as Eliza prepared for her first all-hands, she was torn between thinking that the meeting wasn't a big deal and that it was the biggest test she would face in her career. She followed a similar preparation process to her dad, writing opening remarks and then an agenda. She had no one to practice with, so she read her speech out loud six times before deciding that she was good to go.

She could have chosen a less important topic than the future of Peterson Lumber but, in the end, forged ahead. This was her chance to show everyone, especially Chris, that she was in charge. While a few employees had spoken to her directly about the leadership transition, she could tell that they were all thinking about it, talking among themselves about what would happen to the company under her and Chris's tenure, with some considering other options. Eliza couldn't tell if anyone at the company respected her, but she knew that no one liked her. Maybe after her all-hands speech, they would like her more.

She couldn't help but resort to an old habit, thinking, *but why would they?* In middle school, high school, and college, no one liked Eliza. They had tolerated her, in some cases, talked to her, but no one had ever dared get close to her.

She had been in one long-term relationship, eighteen months, with a college sweetheart. He had picked her out of the senior econ seminar as a fellow bottom-feeder. Like her, Marvin was terrified of rejection and equally insecure and self-critical. But he had managed to make two courageous moves in his life. The first of which was approaching her after class. He was short with a thin face and beads of sweat on his forehead. He could barely say the words, "I was wondering if—"

He would find courage a second time in his life when he told her, in the same shaky voice and with the same thin face and beads of sweat, that he wanted to break up. He did not know her, he said, and could never know her. He said she was always wearing a mask, that she was never her real self. "This is my real self," she told him. "This is me." He didn't budge though, and she knew then that it wasn't a question of not knowing, it was a question of not liking—it had to be. Even Marvin, who she didn't like but had told herself she loved, could not like Eliza Peterson. She didn't push back. Instead, she said, "I'm not surprised."

"I was never with you for your money!" He stammered. She wished she had asked him, *Then why were you with me?* But she didn't. She let it go like she let so much else go because she was afraid of the question, even though it meant losing her only friend with little closure. And she didn't make new friends after that. She called Richard sometimes, and he helped her and talked to her because he pitied her (she assumed), but he was not her friend, and if they were not siblings, he, too, would not like her.

"It's my fault," she had explained when she first started seeing her therapist, a year ago. At forty-three, she had turned to therapy after reading about its business merits in a Sheryl Sandberg book. If she wanted to be an effective operator and take Peterson Lumber to new heights, then therapy seemed necessary.

Eventually, her therapist dropped a truth bomb. It was one someone less credentialed and less expensive could have deduced, but she buried the lede until session eight. "It's because you don't like yourself. Would you be your friend? If you were someone else?"

"Um."

What followed was session after session focused on self-love and self-forgiveness. The therapy was working. She had affirmations to repeat when she was feeling down, tone-setting exercises to do in front of the mirror in the morning. Her toolbox was growing, and with it, her influence. The fact that she had confronted her dad and won the job, or half the job, was proof enough. But those displays of confidence seemed performative. She agreed in principle with "fake it till you make it" but couldn't shake the belief that she would always be faking it.

She told herself she was a hard worker because she loved her work and was good at it. At night, she had two choices: work or waste away. To her credit, she didn't live a life of perpetual doom and gloom. For months at a time, she "played around" on dating apps. Tinder, Bumble, Hinge, and worst of all, Trance Date. The latter option's parent company had, of course, been partly funded by her brother, a fact she couldn't shake when on the other side of a VR date.

It should go without saying that VR dates were the worst kind. The photorealistic avatars were a sham, Eliza herself had paid to make hers look better. But, desperate and fueled by her therapist's encouragement, she wasn't in a position to be picky. So she put on her headset and pretended like the date was normal, like she really was a runway model and her co-conspirator some cyberpunk hunk.

Luckily, today she could spend the next hour focused on something else. Forty or so employees gathered around, with perhaps eighty more remote workers and medical exemptions video-calling in. Even Duke couldn't put a stop to the medical exemptions.

She was determined not to look weak now. As she approached the mic, she smiled and waved at the gathered crowd. She wasn't used to the attention, to the barrage of faces sizing her up. But she wouldn't show them that it was new to her. She walked and composed herself as though she had given hundreds of speeches, as though this was a routine event.

"Thanks for joining us on this gorgeous day." No one laughed. "In all seriousness, thank you for coming. I know Duke is sad to miss his favorite day of the month, and, frankly, I miss him too. But he's doing his best to enjoy Hawaii, even though I know being away from this kills him. He calls me three times a day asking about all of you."

This time she heard chuckles, even some laughter. She saw Chris grimace. Reassured, she slowed down and looked outwards, seeing her audience for the first time. She knew enough about them to make small talk when appropriate. Matt from legal liked to play fantasy football. Kara liked to hike. But she didn't know any of them, not really, and they, in turn, didn't know her. They thought of her as their boss's daughter, not as their boss. But faking it to make it, she continued. Head up, shoulders back, and now making eye contact with the few faces that seemed mildly entertained or, at minimum, in the top percentile of wakefulness.

"As you know, I'm lucky to be your CEO, with Chris, of course. Most of you know what I'm about to say." They certainly didn't, but maybe each would assume others knew her better... "But at the risk of repeating myself, I thought I'd share a bit about what this company means to me and the direction I think we can go. Then you can ask me questions, and I hope we'll all have a little more clarity about the leadership transition and how things might or might not change going forward."

She told them that Peterson Lumber was never a company to her, but instead an ideal, a future worth fighting for, a family. More than the sum of its parts, Peterson Lumber was both its history, time-tested and grand, and its future, pioneering and prescient. "My dad founded this company because he felt a duty to the earth and to the forests—to heal them, protect them, and harness them. That duty is in my roots, if you may, and if anything, has become something more than a duty—perhaps a purpose, or a destiny, or even the very reason I am on this planet."

She hoped to see engaged, even impressed, faces. But she saw a room of listless stares. What had seemed so inspiring the night before appeared now an alternate history, hyperbolic and corny, too much for the all-too-common setting. Whereas Duke had jokes to temper his grandiosity, she had only grandiosity.

The last paragraph of the opening remarks was her favorite, but she did not enunciate and sped through it, blurring one word into the next. "Like the trees we shepherd, we are stronger than ever, but at the same time, as flexible as ever…proud to be of service, growing upwards in search of a dream greater than us all. And it's my honor to, like my dad before me, lead us through the great thicket ahead, cutting through the bramble of adversity, treading carefully but boldly, embracing each sapling of opportunity that falls our way."

First, there was silence and then a smattering of claps. She could imagine Duke in her position taking a thespian bow, reveling in the importance of his speech. She settled for a half bow, but it seemed the employees were more confused than amused by the gesture, which must have looked like a spasm or stumble.

When she asked for questions, no one raised their hand. They looked disturbed and on the verge of laughter. When Chris said, "Thanks for the sermon, Eliza," they laughed, all of them, even the telecommuters on the monitor.

It wasn't just sexism, as much as she wished she could pin it all on that. It was the anti-Eliza sentiment that had always followed her, even here where she supposedly ruled, or co-ruled, supreme. "I know that was a lot to take in," she managed. "Future remarks won't be so…intense, I promise. And we'll answer questions about anything, big or small."

"That's right," said Chris, "We took too much time already. This is your time."

Then rose one tepid hand. Bruce, from accounting, one of the younger employees. She conjured his résumé, Chico State, rugby. "So, um, Duke isn't coming back?"

Chris answered. "Duke will remain on the board, and I'm sure we'll be seeing plenty of him."

"And you're taking over," Bruce continued, "Together?"

They all looked interested, even though she had answered the same question in an email blast three weeks prior and then again in a second email blast just the other day.

"Eliza and I have both been named acting CEOs," Chris said.

"As I wrote in a number of emails, Chris and I are co-CEOs, and Duke is stepping into the role of chairman."

Chris nodded, "For now. One of us may become the solo CEO."

"Yes," Eliza said, "one of us may."

"This co-CEO thing is temporary," Chris said.

Eliza gulped, and several hands rose into the air. "I don't think that's the right messaging," she tried to sound very professional. Could they hear her faster heartbeat, sense her growing unease?

"What's important to know is that we are all aligned—Duke, myself, Eliza. Our day-to-day roles have not changed."

"Except for my role," Eliza said.

"Well, you were chief business officer, and I was COO, and we're doing the same things, but are acting as co-CEOs."

"I *am* co-CEO! Not acting as co-CEO." The awkwardness could no longer be contained. Chris sat still with his fingertips pressed together in a gesture of deep contemplation.

"Chris and I will send an email tonight to everyone, clarifying all these changes, so they're in writing, and we will all have a reference point going forward."

She stood up, but Chris stayed seated. This should have put her in the position of authority, but it had the opposite effect. He, in his chair, seemed composed and thoughtful, while she seemed rattled and on alert.

"Eliza," he announced, "I think people can sense that we're still figuring this stuff out. And that's okay. It's like you said in your wonderful speech, we're a team, we'll weather the storm—"

"Bramble…"

"Weather the bramble!"

The phrase was *cut through the bramble*, but she didn't say so out loud. Instead, she listened to Chris's rousing defense, which was sounding more convincing by the second. "I started here when I was nineteen, in the field. Duke saw something in me and gave me a chance to grow, alongside all of you, alongside Eliza, who I've known since she was fourteen. She was literally still growing—"

Chris had a family, friends, a life. Eliza only had the job, and she had given it everything. She wouldn't let that work slip away. Not now, in front of these people, the people who were supposed to listen to her, respect her, worship her. And so her shyness parted; her insecurities dissolved. And this time, she was not faking anything. The feelings were real and born from a primitive instinct to survive.

"Still growing," he said again with a smile.

"Stop it." What came from her mouth was not her ordinary voice, but instead something sterner and deeper with the dynamic current of anger that they had seen from Duke, but never from her. It was the same anger. It was for the Peterson's alone, heritable and exclusive, her irrevocable claim.

"Excuse me?"

"Chris, with all due respect, I invite you up here to share this stage— something that my father has never done for you, would never do for you. I include you here beside me in a gesture of good faith…of generosity. And you want to cause a scene in front of everyone. I am Duke's daughter. I love this company in ways that you will never understand. Peterson is my last name. This isn't the Chris Hill Lumber company. It's the Peterson Lumber Company. And I will honor that and always honor that, and Duke knew it and knows it, and that's why I am leading beside you. Okay?"

Everyone was frozen. Then they exchanged smiles, nervous glances, signs of giddiness. And why shouldn't they—didn't Duke always put on a show?

"You didn't invite me up here," Chris said. "I have a right to this seat as much as you do."

"We'll see."

He laughed. "Yes, we will."

"Everyone, in a few days I'll have some news about a recent development," she said. "This company has never been stronger, despite how it might seem today, I assure you."

"I think we should end the meeting."

She shrugged like she could stay up there for hours, but he was too weak to join her. Now, the people knew who was in charge. Even as they scattered or logged off of video, she knew they knew.

Chris leaned over, whispered in her ear, "That was embarrassing. You embarrassed this company." She walked toward her office, trying not to pay attention to the stares. He chased her down. "You have nothing to say?"

She didn't respond until they were in her office. "Oh, cut the shit. If you have a problem bring it up during the board meeting."

"I have tons to bring up."

"Well, save it then. I have work to do."

He stormed out and slammed the door. He was very mature that way, real CEO material.

8

Bella wanted to change the world and really could have but now is a paper pusher at a tier two nonprofit

Those who knew Bella before college were surprised when she decided to work for Aid for Earth. Bella, a high-achieving, New Orleans-born prodigy could have gone somewhere much more prestigious. While other kids played video games, watched Netflix, and did drugs, Bella won science fairs, junior hackathons, and piano competitions. She did all of this while remaining the idol of every video game-playing, Netflix-watching, and substance-consuming peer. She never rubbed her success in anyone's face. She treated everyone with respect and compassion. So unlike other high-achievers on her middle-class block, Bella was admired by all.

No one was surprised when she received a paid-in-full scholarship to Stanford. Her parents, friends, and mentors had expected nothing less. Nor were they surprised when she interned at Goldman Sachs her freshman year and then for a high-flying AI startup her sophomore year. Some were skeptical when she started to take time off from school her junior year for a medley of activist crusades but were even more impressed when she continued to get perfect grades.

When Bella committed to joining Aid for Earth full time, almost everyone was shocked. Her parents tried to talk her out of it.

Bella's mom was a force of a woman. Every day during Bella's childhood, she would prod her daughter to work harder, even if that meant late nights and tired mornings. Usually, Bella handled the stress well, but even she had a breaking point.

Eighth-grade Bella wanted to go to a school dance with her friends. Except, the state middle school mock trial championship was less than a week away, and Bella was ill-prepared. "It'll be a disaster," her mom had explained. "You have five days to get up to speed, or you'll embarrass yourself."

"I know the case—"

"You don't!"

"I *fucking* do!"

"*Excuse me?*"

"Everyone else…"

"You're not like anyone else." The compliment was laced with bile. "Now, learn the case and watch your mouth."

Bella didn't relent easily. For the next hour, she lashed back. There were tears. There was screaming. But sure enough, she ended up back at her desk with an open case book. That night was a reminder to her that as exceptional as she was on her own, she was nothing without her draconian mother.

In time, Bella required less prodding. Her mom relaxed when her daughter accepted a scholarship to a prestigious East Coast boarding school. "We're very proud of you," she would say to a smiling Bella, who agreed that it was all for the best, even though leaving her friends and family for a different state at fourteen was a harrowing proposition. If she wanted to be someone special though, she couldn't be like anyone else. She would work harder. She would be better. She had big dreams.

Bella didn't feel as accepted in high school as she had in grade school. Her boarding school classmates were from some of the wealthiest families in the country, and she had to straddle two worlds: one where kids and families were so rich that they didn't have to think about money and one where thinking about money was routine.

Her high school cafeteria had a twenty-five-station salad bar, but still, many kids ate off-campus, often at some of the swankiest spots in the posh New Hampshire town. Everyone but her, it seemed, had a parent-paid credit card. The smart ones caveated each expense with *we know how lucky we are* as if this slim degree of self-awareness could excuse each indulgence.

Bella had spending money, too, but nothing compared to what her classmates had. Growing up in New Orleans she had never felt poor. Her dad was a dentist and her mom was a teacher. They had two cars, ate out on the weekends, and went on family vacations over the summer. In New Hampshire though, she went to a country club for the first time, stayed at a five-star hotel in Boston during a weekend trip, and watched in awe as friends spent hundreds of dollars on meals, drinks, and drugs. In those instances, she felt out of place. Peers covered her share without hesitation, and even though she always thanked them profusely, she wondered if her professed gratitude was enough to mask her discomfort.

The discomfort she felt wasn't just about herself—she was a terrific and well-liked student. If people wanted to treat her that was fine—but she couldn't help wondering what her friends back home would think about so much extravagance. She had grown up around all kinds of people. She had friends whose families struggled to pay rent and aunts and uncles who relied on her dad and mom to help pay the bills. This was a life they could only dream about, and they weren't any less deserving.

By her senior year of high school, she heard about friends from childhood working three jobs, trying to stay afloat. Meanwhile, her "day friends" talked about riding horses and going to the Bahamas for spring break.

SHE WAS BORN IN 2005, the same year that Hurricane Katrina decimated her city. She obviously didn't remember anything about the hurricane itself, but some of her first memories were of its continued aftermath. Her family had rebuilt their home, and while her dad said it was tough, he seemed to take it in stride. "We're lucky we had the ability to bounce back," he told her. So many people she knew never bounced back, not completely anyway. Her aunt had to live with them for four years. Her uncle was always asking for money. Uncle Henry's face in those moments was impossible to forget. He was a proud man, strong and capable, and having to ask for help seemed to suck the life out of him. He would show up to dinner like everything was fine. But after dinner, he would ask her dad to talk. Bella was told to go to her room, and they would go to the living room, but she would sneak down to listen in the corridor and watch. "I'm almost back on my feet," Henry would say, always looking down, sometimes running his hand through his hair. Her dad was generous and always greeted the request with a smile. "We're family. Of course, I'll help you."

Years later, the script was flipped, and she was on the other side of the conversation. "Come on, Bella," her friends would say, "just come with us. We'll spot you."

"You don't have to."

"No come on, we *want* to. We want you to come."

It wasn't the same but maybe it felt similar. It felt unfair. It was unfair that her friends could spend whatever they wanted on her, without a second thought, without even a call or text to their parents. And it was unfair that a hurricane had crippled her uncle, so many of her friends, and her city. The ones who bounced back, as her parents had, didn't seem any more deserving than the ones who didn't. But that was the way it was. The wealthiest people moved away, the middle-class people found their footing, and the lower classes lived in the hurricane's shadow for decades.

It was the summer between her sophomore and junior year of high school when she first decided to do something about it. Her parents were planning on taking her to Europe for the first time. Her mom had spent months planning the itinerary. Her dad had spent two years saving up for the trip. But in April, just a few months before their flight, she called her house and told her parents that she didn't want to go. "There's a nonprofit called Aid for Earth in San Francisco. They're offering summer internships to high school students. I want to go."

There was some pushback and some sadness, but in the end they agreed. Hurricane Katrina had happened sixteen years earlier, but there were more natural disasters every year. The earth was warming, the world was changing, and just like in her hometown, only some people were bouncing back. Every day, around the world, people were trying to bounce back but weren't able to. She wasn't going to stay on the sidelines.

She went back to Aid for Earth the next summer. At Stanford, she started the first university chapter and helped spread the organization to other schools. While she also enjoyed her summer stints at startups and investment banks, the work paled in comparison. So, in her senior year of college, she committed to joining Aid for Earth full time.

"It's not good enough," her mom said. "You won't get hired anywhere after."

Few people could make Bella tick, but her mom was one of them. Too many years of pressure. Too many years of fighting for approval. But she didn't let her emotions show. This was too important a moment and too important a decision. "I'm doing this," she said. "My whole life has been leading to this."

Aid for Earth SF had six full-time employees. Bella would be number seven. The organization had thousands of volunteers and many vocal supporters, but the boots-on-the-ground management was small and close-knit. They followed their fearless leader, the organization's cofounder and current CEO, Brandon Towns.

Brandon was tall with an athletic build and short curly hair. He was in his mid-thirties but looked younger. When he spoke in his deep and slow voice, he came across as wise and confident.

When Bella told others about why she picked Aid for Earth, she talked about New Orleans, the hurricane, her first-hand experience watching a community come together after a terrible tragedy. Deep inside, she knew that Brandon was a part of her decision. She didn't know him well, but she had become enthralled with him as an intern. He said once that she had a terrific mind. And he didn't throw compliments out to everyone. A compliment from someone with his credentials and his dynamism went a long way.

Though she had developed a crush on him, she had never expected anything to come of it. When he started to flirt with her a week into the job, she began to question if he had hired her for her work or her body.

It happened one night during her second week as a full-time employee. It was a late Friday night. They were working away. There were drinks. He took her hand on the couch, put his laptop on the floor, and then kissed her. She felt doubt, she felt some discomfort, but she started to kiss him back. One thing led to another...

Their liaisons, of course, were secret. Not even her best friends knew, certainly not her parents. It was better that way. Hotter too, he assured her, equally invested in maintaining secrecy.

Other than that first time, they were strictly professional while in the office. Bella worked harder than everyone else and—she was sad to see—was more capable than everyone else. She quickly became indispensable. She took on bigger projects and managed people ten years her senior. As everyone got to know her, no one was surprised. Boss, they called her, only half-facetiously. Except for Brandon, who was strictly professional. Except when he fucked her in his SOMA studio, usually about twice a week.

Bella wasn't in love. She didn't think about love. She thought very analytically about relationships and sex and so on. She was young and didn't have time to fall in love. She did like Brandon. He was smart and confident. Notably, he was never sycophantic. Nothing made her lose interest faster than a toady "nice guy." Quick with the compliments and then, once rejected, quick with wrath.

She had few complaints about Brandon as a lover, but many about Brandon as a boss.

To complicate matters further, she only aired these grievances before sex when Brandon had no choice but to indulge her. Like at 2:00 a.m. on a Tuesday morning, after eighteen hours of work.

"Take your shirt off—"

"I'm just saying, we're playing too safe. It's not what I signed up for."

"I'm all for danger," he smirked.

"I'm not talking about sex! I'm talking about work! I spend all week writing the policy briefs that NO ONE reads."

"Bella, come on—" His eyes darted between her bra and her face.

"What happened to the old Aid for Earth? We used to—"

He turned away. He would look back, she knew it. She crept closer.

"It wasn't sustainable. We have to build something legitimate."

"I used to see you guys on the news screaming into the cameras, wearing fucking masks, scaring the shit out of everyone! Now you want to play by the rules; we'll get nothing done."

His eyes flashed back to her body. She unpinned and dropped her bra. He looked ravenous. "Why do we need to talk about this now?"

"It's the only time you listen."

"You're so fucking sneaky." She came closer, and he wrapped his arms around her bare back.

She said her last piece. "If we don't do something bigger, I'm out of here." The rest could wait.

The next day at the office, Brandon made an effort to do something big. Professional as ever, as if last night had never happened, he said, "We're going to work with the ACLU on a lawsuit. I want you to run point."

"What lawsuit?"

It was important stuff: a natural gas company was preparing to build a pipeline on indigenous land. But as she listened to the pitch and perused the summary, it still seemed small. The Navajo would settle, or the gas company would find another route. There had been a thousand of these. It wasn't changing the world. She heard her mom in her head. She bristled.

"Okay?" Brandon asked.

"Okay." She smiled. She would tell him later that it wasn't good enough. Brandon had been arrested multiple times at protests. She suspected he had even been behind some of the arson in 2021, which Aid for Earth had, of course, denied responsibility for. When she used to volunteer with him he had been passionate, visibly angry. She had liked that about him, how his emotions and his activism were one and the same. But now, he was straitlaced and, by Bella's standards, too diplomatic. He spent all day talking to donors in a monotone lifeless voice. He was committed to building a larger Aid for Earth. One that had more reach and was well-respected. Noble goals, but he was a sellout. Aid for Earth would become like every other impotent nonprofit. Soon they would put a sign out front…soon, they would throw a banquet.

She wished she had been full-time five years earlier, when Aid for Earth and the charge of "eco-terrorism" went hand in hand. Those pundits were wrong, but it still said something about the work. Talking about change wasn't good enough, she wanted to fight for it.

Bella looked around the Dogpatch warehouse. It looked the same as it did five years ago. There were activist posters, and a mutilated Trump piñata, and graffiti on the walls. It *looked* very revolutionary.

She put on her headphones and read about the pipeline until Marcus tapped her on the shoulder. "Someone's outside for you. Cole Peterson? He says he's a friend."

9

The Petersons attend a luau

There was a Maluhia luau every week. Emmett loved the luaus. In addition to the band and a dozen or so hula dancers, there were buffet stations, waiters coming by with hors d'oeuvres, and carnival games. The luaus were right on the beach, and this evening was especially beautiful.

Even Duke said as much.

"You're right," said Lily as they were escorted to a table. "It doesn't get nicer than this."

"Only the best for Richie." Four days after the Heiau dinner and Duke was still calling his son Richie.

Emmett found it hilarious. "Richie," he chimed in, but only because his dad didn't seem to mind.

They had their own table close to the water. For a moment, Emmett looked at it and found it pretty, but these musings passed through him, and then were replaced by more urgent matters. Like Chloe. He hadn't seen her since Logan's party. He scanned the other tables.

"I'm going to say hi to Logan."

"Okay, but come back to eat with us."

He passed people he knew, waving and smiling, but didn't get sidetracked. Logan was eating with his parents and some others at a large communal table.

"Emmett! Give me a hug!" Logan's mom was hot. Fake tits and a dolled-up face. He savored his hug. He talked to Logan's parents for a moment before he was able to nudge Logan. "Have you seen Chloe?"

Logan pointed. Emmett moved on.

Chloe was in line at the soufflé station. He tapped her on the opposite shoulder; she looked the wrong way. "Gotcha."

"Oh," she smiled.

"Emmett," he reminded her.

"Hi, Emmett."

"Already on dessert?"

"I guess so."

"How was dinner?"

She looked around. His lust at Logan's house had not been misplaced, despite the alcohol and weed. She wore a blue romper and flip-flops, and he saw that she had a swimsuit underneath.

"It was just…okay."

"You didn't like it?"

"No. But maybe this soufflé—"

"Do you want to sit with my family? You can meet my grandpa, the lumber baron." He wondered if she remembered. He couldn't tell.

"I can't. I'm sitting with a friend."

"Oh, not your mom?"

"That bitch?"

"Um."

"You can come sit with us? My friend's cute. You'll like her."

"I like you."

Chloe rolled her eyes, but playfully, perhaps flirtatiously. She was handed her soufflé, and they walked to her table.

Chloe's friend was tall with a long, equine face. She wasn't as pretty as Chloe but she was glamorous and radiated rich-girl energy. Her name was Stephanie. She introduced him to her parents, Mr. and Mrs. Dean. "Call me Harold," said Mr. Dean.

Harold was fifty, maybe. He had speckled gray hair and a double chin. He sat regally.

Mrs. Dean, who had not given her first name, who, in fact, had said nothing to Emmett at all, looked more polished than beautiful, like some antique figurine.

Emmett felt unwelcome as he pulled up a chair. When no one said a word, he looked over his shoulder. "I should actually—" But he made the mistake of speaking too softly, and Harold addressed him. "We were talking politics."

"Oh, okay."

"Do you know anything about politics?"

"Um, a little, I guess." He knew his parents said they were independents, but Cole said they were center-right.

Harold chewed on a lobster tail while he spoke and seemed torn between eating and speaking, so he made the bold choice to do both simultaneously. "Nobody knows anything about politics but they vote anyway. They vote for radicals and anarchists and then wonder why everything is going to shit. Maybe you're too young to notice that everything's been going to shit, huh? All you've known is this crap."

"I'm not too young—"

But now Harold was speaking to himself more than Emmett. "Why would any businessman worth his salt build in America? Every incentive is broken. Every single one."

"It's appalling." Mrs. Dean shivered when she spoke. Her voice was birdlike.

"And the Left wants to get rid of cap gains? The engine of innovation. The only incentive we have left. It's so stupid." Mrs. Dean shivered again.

Harold swallowed his lobster tail and then coughed. "It's socialism, everywhere. We work hard and create thousands of jobs, and what do we get in return? Higher taxes. The nation's spite. That's the worst part. The spite! I pay the taxes, but does it help the spite? No. They're an insatiable mob. They're insufferable."

"Insufferable!" chirped Mrs. Dean.

"Why would I work? What's possibly in it for me, for us? I tell you." He slurped another forkful of lobster. "The world is going to utter shit!"

Emmett tuned him out. Harold sounded like a dumber Duke, and anyway, the world didn't seem so bad. He watched as the last smatterings of the sun fell beneath the ocean, and a hot wind swept sand across his feet. He was drawn to the music from the band and the dancing women. He wanted to get up (and take Chloe with him). He wanted to be there, not here.

But then came Harold with a question for him. "What does your family do, Eric?"

"Um, well, my dad's an investor."

"Mm-hmm. What does he invest in."

"Companies."

Harold laughed. "Yeah, like what kind?" Emmett reddened.

"Well, he's best known for being an early investor in Trance. The VR—"

"Trance! Your dad invested in Trance?"

"Yes."

Harold laughed. "What a deal that must have been!"

Emmett felt better. It was nice to be noticed. It was nice to hear his dad being noticed.

"Do you guys come here every year?" Harold asked.

"Yes."

"We're just renting for a few weeks. We're moving after! Out of this godforsaken country. I'm sick of it! Aren't you sick of it?"

Now that it was getting darker, the Maluhia staff started to light candles and torches.

"Where are you moving to?"

"Belize!"

"It's very nice there," said Chloe. "You will love it."

"I know it's nice!" Harold said. "Nice to have taxes that are twenty-five percent! No matter how much you make, twenty-five! Now that's a lot, don't get me wrong! That's a fourth of a man's livelihood. It's outrageous that I'm in love with twenty-five. I should hate twenty-five. But goddamnit, in this shithole of a world, I love it. I can't wait to pay twenty-five!"

Emmett felt something graze his leg. He looked down. It was Chloe's foot. In the firelight, she looked magnificent. More so when she said, "Your dad invested in Trance?"

"Yes."

"I love Trance."

"You play games?"

"No, not the games. I love the VR concerts, though."

"Yeah, me too."

He sat for a few minutes longer. He made plans to hike with Chloe and Stephanie, and he got Chloe's number. "I'll see you two tomorrow?"

"Great," said Stephanie, but he wished she would get sick or cancel.

"Thank you for letting me sit with you."

"Of course," said Harold. "Where is your family sitting?"

Emmett pointed. "Close to the water near the sushi station."

"Maybe I'll say hi, a little bit later. I'd love to hear more about that Trance deal."

Back at Emmett's table, Duke was nursing a drink and picking at a lamb chop. His dad and mom were sharing a sushi platter and a bottle of wine, and no one seemed mad that he had been gone.

"How's Logan?" asked his mom.

"He wasn't with Logan," said Duke. "He was seducing that blonde girl."

Richard perked up and looked around.

Emmett left to get food. When he returned, no one was speaking.

"You guys okay?" he asked.

Duke grumbled.

"You feeling okay, Grandpa?"

"I think so. Your dad's talking my head off about this goddamn bitcoin company. I might go for a walk. Do you want to come?"

Emmett popped a piece of sushi in his mouth. "Yes!"

As they moved away from the luau, the noise faded, as did the firelight. The moon rose, and stars cut through the sky. Neither Peterson said anything. In his right hand, Duke swirled his bourbon glass. He would take small sips and long audible breaths.

Duke walked away from the water, up to denser sand, and finally to the trees. Emmett pulled out his phone for a light, but Duke muttered something about not needing it, not wanting it. The man ambled through the thick sand but didn't look weak. He looked methodical. Meanwhile, Emmett managed to step on every variety of stone, shell, and branch. He didn't vocalize his discomfort. Was Duke doing the same, he wondered, pricking his bare feet but masking the pain?

Duke reached out to touch a tree. "It's a eucalyptus," he said.

"You know that, even in the dark?"

He laughed. "Of course. Your grandma knew even more than I did. She wouldn't even have to see the tree. She could have smelled it, touched it; that was enough."

His grandma had died when Emmett was six. He didn't remember much about her besides some dinner table rants. She hated Democrats. Even at age six, he had grasped that much.

He remembered how his dad would laugh at her grumbling prognostications, and she would, in faux defiance, lash back. "Are you

Democrats now!" she would demand to know. "We're Independents," Richard or Lily would say, which seemed good enough for her. It was always friendly. Emmett had been comfortable at those dinners.

She would buy him and Cole dozens of Christmas presents each year. She picked them meticulously. Cole got fancy pens, cuff links, one year, a desk carved from Peterson lumber. "It's because you're mature for your age," she told him, "and an intellectual." Emmett, her athlete of a grandson, got signed baseball cards, a set of golf clubs, a punching bag. The trunk, when they left Redding after the new year, was always full.

Emmett didn't know she died until a month after it happened. They told him it was heart disease, which he didn't understand but imagined was a sad way to die, like her heart hadn't been given enough love and he was somehow responsible.

He remembered the first Christmas without her. Duke gave them each one present. Eleven-year-old Cole got a leather-bound *Death in the Afternoon*. Emmett got an illustrated *Tom Sawyer*. From that point forward, every Christmas, they each got a book. Anything more would have spoiled them. Cole seemed to like the books. Emmett didn't care for them. When Cole was nineteen, Duke splurged and gifted him five Steinbeck first editions. "He's a communist, like you," Duke said to Cole. Emmett got Shelby Foote's Civil War histories—three thousand pages that remained unread.

Cole devoured Steinbeck, despite the communist cheap shot. Their relationship had been like that, ideologically opposed but grounded in mutual respect. Duke thought Cole was smart and told him so. From Duke, there was never a mention of Cole's weirdness or awkwardness or creepiness. Even when Cole's political positions moved to what Duke called "Marxist revolutionary," he treated Cole with respect.

Perhaps now Emmett could change his mind and show Duke that he was the better grandson.

"Cole says that you cut down more trees than any other lumber company." Duke didn't respond. He was still staring at the tree, perhaps thinking about his wife.

Finally, he said, "We plant more trees than we cut."

"You do?"

"Yes, we do. But people like your brother get mad all the same. People get mad about everything."

"Cole is always mad."

Duke drifted back toward the water. In the distance, they could see the light of the luau—a golden beacon in the black and blue.

"Cole says a lot of things about you."

"Hmmm."

Should he drop the subject? He waited for a hint, but none came. He couldn't help himself. "He says that you don't care about the earth because when you die, it won't be your problem."

"Why does he think I don't care about the earth?"

Excited now. "He says you profit off of fires."

"It's a lousy argument." Finally, some heat. "Someone has to salvage that land after a fire. It's either us or someone else. You can't just leave it, you have to clear it so new forest can grow."

"I wish you could tell him that."

"He knows it. He's smart." When the beach became rockier, Duke turned around. "How's working for your dad?"

"It's okay."

"Just okay?"

"I don't really do anything. I just listen to some of the calls."

"Do you like listening?"

"I guess."

"You're a good kid, Emmett. I think you should work for me next time you have a break. Your dad won't teach you anything."

Emmett was glad it was dark. He could hide his face. He had hoped his grandpa would ask and never would have predicted it would come so soon and so easily. But he hated hearing the gripe at his dad.

"I would love that," he said, masking his embarrassment.

"It's good work. You won't just listen to calls. I miss it."

"You miss it?"

"Oh yes. I mean, I miss being there, in the thick of it."

"Why did you come here?"

"The fucking board is making me pick a new CEO." He took another sip of bourbon. "And your dad begged me to come."

Emmett hoped Duke would say something about being with him. "I'm glad you came."

Duke faced Emmett. They locked eyes. Emmett became self-conscious, desperate to look away, but something rooted him in place. It was like Duke was looking into a mirror, studying himself more than his grandson. Only when Duke looked down was Emmett free to do the same.

"You're seventeen?"

"Yes."

"I would do anything to be seventeen. I would give up everything. Every single thing."

What did that mean? Things like his money? But also perhaps things like his dad and Aunt Eliza, and by extension, him and Cole? "We can get your youth back here!" He tried to laugh away the seriousness. "Just leave it to me!"

Duke didn't seem to hear him. When he spoke again, he didn't seem to be speaking to Emmett. "I guess when I'm here, I want to go home, but when I was home, I was ready to come here. I don't know if I feel good anywhere anymore. I feel like the world is moving faster than me. I feel like it's leaving me before I can leave it." He sat down slowly. His body was stiff and mechanical, a twitching silhouette in the dark. He let out a deep sigh. "I got mad the other night, I think, because I don't understand things anymore. I feel like things used to be simpler, but I don't even know if I used to feel that way or if I just imagine I felt that way. Maybe things were always confusing and moving fast, and only in retrospect did they seem so simple. I guess that's comforting." He turned to Emmett sitting beside him. "I don't know if you should work for me."

"No?"

"I don't know. I worked one way my whole life, and then, all of a sudden, everyone says it's the wrong kind of work. It's bad for the earth. It's bad for the forests. That one hurts most of all. My whole life has been about forests. It's all I know. I feel like everyone has lost their minds. But it's just me that thinks that way, so it must be me that's losing mine."

"You're not losing your mind." Emmett saw another route to his grandpa's affection. "It's my generation that's confused. We grew up with phones in our faces. We make friends on the internet. I feel like it's bad for us, but we can't do anything to stop it." He sounded like Cole.

Duke was up again and walking toward the water. Emmett followed. Duke put his feet in. So did Emmett. It was cold until the sand, warm and sticky, seeped between his toes.

Had Duke even heard him? Perhaps the point was so bland, so expected, that it was dismissed. He saw Duke reach down and pick up a piece of plastic. He put it in his empty whiskey glass. "Damn trash," he said.

"I can hold it."

Duke ignored him. "It's all gonna catch up to me. I guess that's what I feel most of all. Like I've been running from it my whole life. But something is coming."

"Something?"

"I don't know, but I've felt it ever since your grandma died. And it feels so close now."

Emmett needed to try another joke or change the subject. What he really needed was a bong rip or a line. It was always his family that made him feel that way. Duke was supposed to be the exception, strong enough not to need his help, proud enough not to seek it. But here he was putting Emmett in an all too familiar position. Emmett would fix him if he knew how. He wanted nothing more than to fix him and Mom and Dad and yes, Cole too. But there wasn't anything he could do but stand there and absorb it. "Let's walk back?" he asked, praying that his grandpa would agree. When he did, Emmett felt better. His duffel of drugs was waiting for him, perhaps thirty minutes away. He could make it another thirty minutes.

10

Eliza wants billions, but Chris has a conscience

A few days after the all-hands, Eliza received a board deck presentation from Chris with the section CEO commentary filled in. She skimmed it and didn't like it. There was too much minutia, too many details to get lost in. This was the first update where Duke wasn't CEO. They needed to send a strong message about the state of the business and their plans to take Peterson Lumber to the next level.

Her dad had always been in charge of the CEO commentary. He put the bad news first, and no matter how well the company was doing, there was more bad news than good news. She knew Duke would be calling in for the board meeting, so she did her best to follow his lead. With a glass of red wine by her side, she typed, *Bad News.*

She highlighted some operational challenges up North. She even referenced an HR dispute. But she found that she had little else to say. It seemed that business was humming along.

So she moved to *Good News*.

We are particularly proud of the Peterson Lumber Company team this month. Despite the societal and economic turbulence we have encountered as a country, the team pulled together, optimized for sustainable growth, and delivered excellent work...

That night, after sending the presentation and her commentary to the board, she slept well.

The next day at the office, others seemed to notice her. They smiled back more fully when she smiled at them. Miranda, their head of people, said, "Eliza, you're glowing today!"

She wasn't used to being complimented, but she didn't show her surprise until she was alone in Duke's office. Then she grinned and pulled out her phone to look at herself. She was glowing! She almost looked attractive. But then came the usual swarm of unflattering thoughts: *You're too fat. You're too stocky. You have a man's face…*

Chris knocked and entered. "You ready?"

She tried to recapture some confidence. "Yes."

They had avoided each other since the all-hands, only communicating over email and only when absolutely necessary. But she had agreed with his latest message that they should put on a good face for the board meeting. "We're both adults," she had responded. "I don't think that'll be a problem."

They met on the top floor around a long wooden table. Peterson wood, her father had told her when she was young. She sat in a wood chair, also Peterson wood, at the head of the table. Her dad's spot.

Only Mark would be joining them in person. Duke, Ronnie, Heather, and Seth would be calling in. The room was equipped with a big screen for remote participants. It was Duke's first time calling into a board meeting and Eliza's and Chris's first time presiding over one.

Mark arrived and took a seat next to Chris. He was a gray-looking man. It wasn't just his hair but his pale skin and eyes too. He was even older than her dad. He had been a board member for over twenty-five years. At one point in time, he had run a large lumber operation in Washington state. Duke had acquired his company, and even though most of the Washington land had been sold since, Mark remained a proud board member of Peterson Lumber.

"Good to see you." Eliza shook his hand.

Mark was wrinkled and small and spoke softly. "Glad to be here." Eliza didn't know if he had missed a single meeting in his two-plus decades with the company.

Seth, Heather, and Ronnie showed up side-by-side on the display. Seth was the company lawyer. Legally, he was required to attend meetings, but he would always quickly go off camera and keep his mouth shut unless absolutely necessary. If Seth had a problem with how Duke did business, he never said so. As the company's lawyer, he was supposed to protect the company, but to Eliza, it seemed like he cared more about staying in Duke's good graces.

Heather was an outside board member, the former CEO of a home renovation conglomerate, and Ronnie's dad had been an early investor in Duke. Since Ronald Senior's death, Ronnie presided over the board seat.

Eliza suspected that Ronnie had asked Duke to step back and install a new CEO, perhaps after the unflattering *New York Magazine* story two years ago. If Ronnie had really asked Duke to step aside, that would have been a painful conversation for both parties. If true though, she hadn't heard it from either of them directly.

Small talk ensued until Duke showed up on screen, and then all attention shifted to him. He didn't say anything interesting. It was too hot in Hawaii, there wasn't a lot to do, nobody was working, and so on. But it was the way he spoke, with force and a dry smile, that made even his insignificant words significant.

"Shall we start the meeting?" she interrupted. She watched the faces settle into what seemed like embittered anticipation.

"Yes," Duke said. "Is that bot in the meeting?"

"Yup, it'll send us the transcript after." Every meeting they had was transcribed by a bot and then sent via email to the participants. She imagined that Duke would read the one from this meeting more closely, wanting to review her performance, and Chris's too. It was all part of his plan to make them compete. But she wasn't in a position to disagree, and she planned on doing a good job anyway.

She began, "We moved this board meeting up because there are a couple of critical decisions ahead of us. The Lasco fire has put us in an opportunistic position, and I want the board's advice on how to proceed. You see..." She filled them in on the fire, without mentioning its origins. She watched her dad's face and waited for a smile or an approving nod. He was still.

When she was done speaking, it was Mark who said, "Thank you for the context."

And then Heather, "Do we have an open dialogue with Nesbit?"

"Yes," Eliza said. "I have a meeting planned—"

"Chris," Duke interrupted his daughter. His headshot filled the display, and even from Hawaii, he loomed over the room. "What is your view on all of this?"

Chris rubbed his temple. When he spoke, eventually, he spoke only to Duke. "I think we have steered the company into a great financial position, sir."

Chris had always called Duke sir, and Duke had never told him to stop. "Say more," said Duke.

"I think we'll end this year with more land and deeper pockets. I think that's positive." It was as if he spoke with a gun to his head. Everyone could see it. He wanted them to see it. He wanted them to think Eliza was holding the gun.

"Chris feels that—"

"Eliza." Duke's voice blared from the speakers. "I asked Chris, not you."

Sapped of all authority, she hunched over, while Chris continued with his hostage video charade. "I think we'll get the Nesbit land for a discount. I think we can win the salvage contract from the state." He took a long pause.

Eliza noticed her right leg was shaking. Once conscious of it, it slowed. But not before Mark saw. He was looking at her. Pitifully?

"I've been proud to be a part of this company, sir. Until this month."

No one spoke. Eliza didn't look up.

"Why?"

Her board meeting, in fifteen minutes, had been hijacked. She felt sick and small, and she wished she were anywhere else.

It was like she was in eighth grade all over again. *You look at her, and it's like her gears are spinning, always spinning, endlessly.*

"Sir," Chris said, "Eliza should have mentioned that the Lasco fire started on our land. It was a routine controlled burn, but it got out of control."

Seth, for maybe the first time ever mid-meeting, spoke, "Perhaps we should take this offline."

Duke swatted his hand. "No, Chris, continue." And just like that, Seth muted himself. Most company lawyers were sycophants, but Seth took obsequiousness to another level, something that Duke demanded from everyone in his orbit.

Chris's charge, even though she was expecting it, was rousing. Back came her strong voice, her confident posture. "Chris, you said the opposite, two days ago! You said—"

"I know what I said." He glanced at her before turning back to Duke's face on the big screen.

"You said—"

"I said the causalities weren't our fault. I meant it. They weren't. It was an accident. But then I think about Chester and those people and those families…"

"Me too, Chris," Eliza said. "But this is a board meeting, not a therapy session." He didn't flinch. She felt like a bomb primed to explode. So fast was her pulse, so hot were her hands.

"What would you do, Chris?" Duke asked.

Eliza sensed anger in her dad's voice. She wondered if it was meant for her. Chris seemed undeterred. He looked around the room. "I think, perhaps, we should cooperate with investigators and then rebuild Chester. We owe it to those families. They have nothing left." He added, when the words had been digested, "Sir."

Eliza didn't know what would happen next. Either she would be humiliated, or Chris would. She glanced at her dad's face to find a clue.

Duke was still. He gave nothing away. "If we didn't provide testimony, what is the likelihood that investigators would discover the truth?"

"Low," said Eliza. "They're already calling it the Lasco fire, which is south of the Harvey Valley plot that burned. The men who were on-site will cooperate with the right incentives. And we can make the fire trail hard to follow…"

"Do you agree, Chris?"

Chris shrugged. "I guess that's right."

"And if you had your way now, Chris, you would call the investigators anyway and tell them we started the fire?"

"We have the liquidity right now to make a difference, and it's the right thing to do."

"And then what?" There was the clue. There was the turn. Eliza's anticipation, now stripped of its foreboding, was marked by a gleeful expectancy. No more shaking leg, no more downcast eyes. Duke repeated himself, with more venom now. "And then what, Chris?"

"We would still have a strong quarter, sir. The town of Chester—"

"A strong quarter? HOW?" Duke hissed. "How much money are we set to make if we proceed with your plan, Eliza?"

"Wait," Chris interjected, "we can still cooperate with an investigation and purchase the land."

"How much money, Eliza?"

"The short-term salvage contract will lead to a couple million. Overtime gains on the Nesbit land could amount to tens of millions. If it's good land and we hold for generations, hundreds of millions."

Duke liked that answer. "Hundreds of millions. Chris, how much money are we set to lose if we proceed with your plan?"

"It's unclear."

"Let me get this straight. You would defer hundreds of millions of dollars to get us wrapped up in a scandal, that could cost this company billions?"

There was no more looking at Duke, not for Chris. He looked around for an ally, finding none. "We could still get the Nesbit land and the contracts." Chris lost his performative tone. Defensive, he sounded angry and shrill. "We would be doing right by the people of Chester. We—"

Eliza spoke again, this time proudly. "If we get caught up in a scandal like this, Chris, you know as well as anyone that we might not win another government contract. Who knows if even the Nesbits will want anything to do with us." Duke nodded. That elusive nod of approval, at last, filling the big screen. It gave Eliza more confidence. "No one wants fire to hurt people. We're not monsters, but we are a company. We owe it to this board and our stakeholders to do what is best for this company."

"That's right," said Duke. "We have to win the Lassen National Forest salvage contract, and we have to buy from Nesbit before someone else does. If you feel differently, Chris, you can follow up with an email. But you better be more persuasive than you were today."

"Yes, sir," Chris muttered without looking up. Eliza let his shame linger for a moment before continuing.

"And that brings us to the next slide…" She was back on track. In a few minutes, the room settled. Chris didn't participate for the rest of the meeting.

11

Patricia is a psycho but Lily (kind of) likes that about her

One evening by the pool, Lily felt especially uncomfortable. She had her own cabana and a good book, and in the distance, she heard birds, and rustling, and all kinds of other beautiful sounds. She lay back and closed her eyes. Instead of peace, came rolling unease. She opened her eyes to make it go away. It didn't.

She read three pages of her book and internalized nothing. If she were asked what had happened on those pages, she would have had no answer. She put her book down and fell into her phone. More distracting, more exciting. She had four social networking sites that she checked every day and three or four others that she checked every once in a while. By the pool, in her cabana, she was distracted as she checked them all.

Until she spotted a shadow. She looked up to find Patricia.

"Hi," Patricia said.

"Hi."

Patricia eyed the cabana. "Can I join you?"

"Sure." Lily moved her things off of the adjacent seat, and Patricia lay back on the reclining chair. It was an unwelcome intrusion, but Lily would be polite. "How are you?"

"I'm good." Patricia described her day: phone calls, a board meeting, some pricing debacle.

"My husband, Richard, invests in companies."

"Yeah?"

"Yeah. He invested in Trance. He was an early investor."

Patricia's lips curled downwards. "He sounds like an important person."

"Oh, um, I didn't mean it like that."

"How did you mean it?"

She looked stern now.

"I just meant—"

Then Patricia relaxed, and the smile returned. "I didn't mean to be rude."

"No, um, I know."

"I just mean I don't want to hear about Richard. I want to know about you."

Lily gulped. "I told you, I—"

"Tell me something about you."

"Um…I'm on the board of a nonprofit."

"Okay."

"It's called InhaleAfrica."

But as she explained, even this fact sounded unimpressive. Lily, watching Patricia's reaction closely, lost confidence. She started stumbling over words and explaining things poorly. "I'm sorry."

"Don't apologize… Lily, can I ask you something? And you don't have to answer. I know we just met."

"Sure…"

"I couldn't stop thinking about you after you came up to say hi the other day."

She wanted to say that's not what happened—Patricia had approached her. But instead she said, "Oh."

"Not in a romantic way. You just had this magnificent mask, this… On the surface you looked so happy. But beneath it all, you looked, and well, you felt, so sad. I couldn't shake it. I felt this need to help you, like I wanted to tell you that you have no reason to be sad, that everything's okay. Since then, I haven't stopped thinking about it. Now you're sitting here, and I feel it. It's like a deeply hidden sadness."

Lily's heart started to beat faster. First came embarrassment and then a swarm of defensiveness.

"I don't mean it in a bad way. And I know this is odd. I know it's odd hearing this. But I just, well, I couldn't get over it, and I couldn't get over it now. There is a tremendous sadness in you. It's beautiful. Even if it hurts, it's really beautiful."

Lily couldn't look Patricia in the eye. She wanted to run to Emmett, or Cathy and describe this vile woman, this lunatic. She would tell everyone at Maluhia. Here she was relaxing in her cabana, just enjoying herself, reading a book, and then bam, out of nowhere comes Patricia. A first-year. A narcissist. Saying that she senses unhappiness in *Lily*, a woman who has everything.

"Was that too much? I feel like I shouldn't have said anything." Patricia seemed earnest.

"I don't know what you mean. I think I want some time to read; if that's okay."

"I'm sorry if I offended you."

She didn't look sorry but all the same, in came Lily's social instincts. Ready to tide things over for the time being. Ready to avoid further awkwardness at all costs. And then later, from afar, she would bite back. "It's okay. I was just actually enjoying my book."

"What are you reading?"

Lily had to flip back to the title page. "*Apocalypse Never: Why Environmental Alarmism Hurts Us All.*"

"Oh, it's excellent."

"Yes."

"I'll leave you to it. But Lily?"

"Mhm-hm."

And the woman inched closer. After saying she would go away, here she was, closer. Lily felt shaky, acutely unsafe. "You can tell me anything."

But they had just fucking met!

"Because I was sad once too. I think that's why I wanted to say something. I think I used to be just like you."

"Patricia, we just met, how do you know—"

She took off her sunglasses and then put her hand on Lily's. "It's what you said about your husband, and your life, and…I was the same. I was the bored housewife on antidepressants."

"I'm not on antidepressants!"

"Oh."

Except she was. No one knew. Not even Richard knew. And she took more than antidepressants. She took fifteen supplements in addition to the antidepressants every day. But they didn't seem to get the job done. So she did breath work and she wrote affirmations and she did yoga and she took Ambien to fall asleep.

"Why do you think I'm on antidepressants?"

"There's nothing wrong with antidepressants."

"I know!"

"Lily, it's beside the point. I'm just saying, you remind me of myself. I had to say something. I had to. Because after I saw you, it stuck with me. I've met a hundred people here, and no one stuck with me except for you."

Now in Lily's mind churned flattery and embarrassment and sickness. "You stuck with me too."

"Why?" Back came a knowing smile. It teased Lily.

"I found you impressive."

"Ah! That's kind of you." She removed her hand from Lily's. "And you wanted to feel…impressive?"

"I don't know."

Patricia stood and laughed. She walked to the shadier side of the cabana and reached for Lily's water. "May I have a sip?"

"Sure."

She took a sip. "You are impressive. But you don't know it. Tell me this, then I'll leave."

"I just wanted to read my book. I didn't mean that you should leave. I didn't mean—"

"It's okay, Lily. We're past that now. You don't have to be so polite." They had spent, it again occurred to Lily, ten minutes together, max. "Just answer this for me, okay?"

"Okay."

"When you were little, what did you want to be when you grew up?"

"What?"

"I'm serious."

"I don't know."

"Yes, you do!" Patricia sat down again, and back came the hand on top of Lily's hand. This time she squeezed harder, an aggressive *tell-me* squeeze.

"I don't know." But she could have said that she wanted to be a lawyer or a doctor or, you know, all the usual stuff. Instead, she repeated herself, "I don't know."

"You don't know?"

"I guess not."

Patricia shrugged. "I bet you wanted to be somebody!"

"I am somebody…"

"You wanted to be important."

"I don't know."

"Don't you see it, Lily! I was like you. I was married. I had a kid, or well, have a kid, but I wasn't working as hard back then. We flew around on a private jet. We ate in all the best places. It was very relaxing. But I'm happier now. I can't even describe it to you: so much happier. It's like I got my life back. I'm finally who I really am, you know, who I was supposed to be!"

That was enough lecturing, enough unwarranted unhelpful advice. "You know what?"

Patricia seemed unfazed, fashioned a cocky smile. "What?"

"I don't have to justify myself to you."

"Well, of course not!"

"But that's what you're saying, right? You're saying I need to be more like you. I don't. I'm very happy. I'm still married."

"Ouch." But still smiling.

"I didn't mean it like that."

"You did, though."

"What do you want to hear?"

"It's not about what I want to hear."

"It clearly is!"

"I want you to tell the truth."

"I am telling the truth." But she wasn't. In the spirit of truth, she could have said, *I go to a hack psychiatrist who prescribes me anything and everything and I have no idea what I'm doing with my life…*

"How do you feel right now?" Asked Patricia.

"What do you mean?"

"Right now, how do you feel?"

"I'm fine."

"I don't think so."

"You wouldn't know."

"Come back here tomorrow, same time."

"I don't think so."

"I'll be here. I want to hear from you."

"You're crazy!" Lily scooted away, head bowed, fists clenched like she would have to fight the woman.

"No. I think I'm the only sane one at," Patricia's hands became quotation marks, "The Preserve."

12

Cole is unwanted and then, seemingly, wanted

When Bella smiled, Cole relaxed. The relaxation quickly abated when she asked, "What are you doing here?" Bella's face turned from bemused to inquisitive. Before he could speak, she asked, "Are you okay?"

He sought a casual response. "Yes. Of course." But it wasn't the right response because she didn't usher him in. The secrets of Aid for Earth, it seemed, required more than a friendly face.

Not that his face was friendly, especially not now. At least he didn't think it was. He tried to look very friendly as he said, "I didn't go with my family to Hawaii this year."

"Oh."

"I guess I chose this instead." He gestured behind him to the pale, bleak, and smoky morning.

She didn't budge. He scratched his scalp and looked away. "I wanted to see if I can help."

He wondered if she remembered their graduation discussion. Perhaps his Aid for Earth job offer had been a polite suggestion made only because she was so sure he would refuse. Any sane man would have understood that. Here he was, though, in the sooty streets, pointedly insane. He itched his chin.

"You want to help?" She asked.

Still looking down, now kicking the ragged doormat, "I thought I could."

From the corner of his eye, he saw the food bank patrons shuffling. He heard their voices and imagined they were talking about him. *Look at the loser. Look at him hover.*

"It's just, um—" He had heard Bella speak hundreds of times, mostly in class, and rarely to him, but speak all the same. And never, in all those cases, had she struggled. Leave it to him to leave her tongue-tied.

"I'm sorry. I guess I shouldn't have come."

"No. That's not what I—"

"I don't really know what I was thinking. I just thought—"

"Come in."

He looked at her now. She seemed at ease, and as he let his eyes linger, he saw her again for all her beauty and confidence.

"Come in!" She said again and this time stepped aside. He walked through the door to find a warehouse entirely different than what the exterior foreshadowed. Tables and couches littered an open space, garishly decorated, walls speckled with art, posters, graffiti. He looked around to find other faces and only found a few. Despite the size of the room, it was sparsely populated. "This is a big space," he said, as he followed Bella from one end of the room to the other.

"Yeah, you know, it's just seven of us now, but we hold events in here. The building was donated to us."

"I see."

"Do you want anything to drink?" She opened up a fridge and grabbed a kombucha. He refused but then wished he had taken the kombucha. His mouth was dry, and he didn't know what to do with his hands. When she sat on a couch, he sat on a chair opposite and fidgeted.

"I'll introduce you to Brandon, but he's on a call right now."

"Got it. Okay. No worries."

She sipped her kombucha. He wondered if the time they'd spent together had meant anything to her, or if it was barely a blip on her radar. He knew a lot about her, of course. What she hadn't told him, he had discovered through internet searches. Her name had surfaced in several newspaper articles. Most articles were from her high school days. Local papers covered her victories in a variety of competitions. More recent blogs contained interviews and, in one case, a Substack hit piece. "What's wrong with Gen-Z" was the headline. It was replete with mostly conservative drivel about the rebelliousness of the young-left and the misplaced anger of one of their "firebrands," a certain Bella Jones.

The evening they had shared that had been the pinnacle of his college experience seemed, to her, just another night. "So," she said at last, "you decided not to go on your fire season vacation?"

He nodded.

"What? Too hot in Hawaii?"

He was happy to be teased but didn't know how to tease back. "I couldn't go this year. I couldn't do it."

"Is it so bad?"

"For those of us with morals."

"Ah," she laughed, and it was that full-body laugh he remembered. He imagined them together, in a serious relationship. Would his parents be surprised that he was dating a Black girl? They were practically bigots, so he couldn't put it past them—and if they were shocked, it would be incredibly satisfying.

"We leave our state behind as it burns, and then we come back every year when it's over. Rinse and repeat. I couldn't do it this year. It just felt wrong. After everything we worked for in college, you know?"

Bella turned and drew Cole's attention to an approaching man coming from one of the few rooms in the warehouse. He walked over, nodded at Bella, and then regarded Cole. The man was tall and handsome.

Bella stood. "Brandon, this is Cole. He's a friend from school."

Brandon managed a smile. Cole stood and shook his hand.

"Bella, can I speak to you for a minute?"

They went a few paces away and out of earshot. Cole looked away from the conversation. He had a good idea of what they were saying.

You let this guy in?

He just showed up.

What does he want?

A job.

What?

Brandon and Bella came back. "Thanks for coming by," Brandon said. And then he was walking back to what must have been his office.

Bella started to explain, "So now just really isn't the best time."

"Oh, um, no problem. I understand."

"It's just we have some big projects. We're working on a lawsuit and—"

"I'll go."

She walked with him to the door. He plotted the next steps for his day, week, and life, but all that arose was a longing to curl up in bed with a book and hide from the world. Not just because he was distraught but also because he had the cruel intuition that the world deserved better than what he had to offer. Only a loser would have come here. And then, when he managed to look at Bella again, this time by the door as she waited for him to exit her life forever, he knew that he never had a chance with her. He never would.

"Do you have my number?" She asked.

"No." This was the perfect opportunity to explain away his insanity. "That's why I just showed up here. I would have texted first."

"Here," she handed him her phone. "Add yourself."

When he was done, she took her phone back and texted him. *Bella Jones* read the message.

"I'll text you tonight," she said. "I'm going to see what's possible."

"Um."

"We need smart people here. Like I told you at graduation."

———

WHEN COLE WAS GONE, Bella walked back toward Brandon's office. She was interrupted on the way by Toby, their head of marketing. Toby was lanky with glasses and a mustache. She suspected he liked her, but he was too timid to ever say so.

"Who was that?"

"A friend. He wants to work here."

"And do what?"

"I don't know."

"I don't know if we have the budget right now to be hiring."

She stopped, and like a heeling dog, he followed. She was already in a bad mood after Brandon had dismissively told her to handle "that boy." Now she had Toby giving her advice.

"I don't think we have the budget for your podcast," She snapped back. Bella had never spoken to him that way before, but she didn't regret it. It was about time he realized that his nine-to-five lazy commitment to the organization wasn't good enough. "Toby," she continued, "we need to think bigger."

"What does that have to do with the pod?"

"Nothing."

"Do you even listen to it? We just had a great episode about photosynthesis rates slowing due to climate change. People loved it."

By people, he probably meant his mom. Practically no one listened to *Climate Cadets*. "I need to talk to Brandon." She kept walking without looking back and imagined Toby sleuthing away to his half-assed work. She knocked once on Brandon's door. No answer. She knocked again harder and, this time, let herself in.

He didn't look up. His eyes were glued to his laptop screen. They seemed to pierce through it as he typed.

"Hey," she said.

He stopped typing but didn't look up. He sighed. "What now, Bella?"

She closed the door and approached the desk. She stood with her hands on her hips and her head raised. She waited until he looked up, and when he did, she shot him a mean look. "Don't dismiss me like that."

"Dismiss you?" No one else in the building would speak to him like that. He may have thought that she did it because she fucked him, but that wasn't it. She did it because he had no power over her, despite what his seniority suggested. If he let her go, she would find another job in a heartbeat, and they both knew that Aid for Earth would be worse off. For now, though, she was here, determined to restore the organization to its former glory, back to how it was when she was just a volunteer—when corporate bullshit was mocked, not embraced.

"Don't talk to me like that. When I have something to say, you need to listen."

"You're lecturing me on how to talk to you?"

"Brandon, I've told you a hundred times that I won't stay here unless we start actually doing big things."

"Do you really want to have this conversation now?"

She sat down opposite his desk in a wooden chair and scooted herself forward, so they were face to face. He was taller than her, and her chair was lower to the ground. She didn't like the dynamic, so she stood again. He watched the display with eye-rolling scorn.

"Look, I didn't invite him here. He showed up."

"You said that."

"But you didn't let me finish out there, so I'm sure as hell going to finish in here. I think we're making a mistake by not even hearing him out."

"What's his name?"

"Cole Peterson."

Brandon typed it in on his computer and snarled. "Stanford and the family business, so what?"

"Do you know the family business?"

"It looks like some…venture shop."

"Look up Duke Peterson."

"That's his dad?"

"His grandfather."

Brandon did and scanned what must have been a Wikipedia page. Bella walked around to confirm and leaned over to read the profile. She had read it a couple of times after hearing Cole's story in college.

"Okay, he's the trust fund baby of a billionaire. So what?"

"A logging billionaire."

"So?"

"Logging is the single biggest source of carbon emissions in Oregon and top three in California. And you should hear about all the other shit his family does. When the forests burn, they profit."

"What?"

"They profit off of fire."

"So he's a trust fund baby from an evil family. Am I supposed to be impressed?"

"I think he could help us do something big. Something like Aid for Earth used to do, like you used to do. When I first volunteered, it was like war out there. We were fighting. It wasn't like this." She put her arms on his shoulders and shook him. She saw him smile, and she smiled too. He was budging. "I want to do that stuff again, and Cole can help. Fuck it! Barely pay him for all I care. Let's just make him an intern."

"And tell him what? That we want dirt on his family?"

"Not so directly."

"You're crazy."

"Maybe, but it's worth a shot. They profit off of forest fires! These people are evil."

"And he's going to help us take them down? You watch too much TV."

"I don't watch TV."

Brandon leaned back. "Why would he help us?"

"He hates his family."

"It's rich guilt; we've seen it before. It goes nowhere."

He had a point. Most of the activists at Stanford were legacy kids, eager to play renegade for a few years. It was a low-stakes game. They had cushy jobs waiting for them on the other side, parents who would forgive them for their college politics. The difference here was Cole was obsessed with her. "He'll do what I say, though."

"Because you're so great?"

"Just give him a shot. Give me a shot. If it doesn't work, it's on me. I'll make it up to you."

"Okay, we'll hire him as an intern. But you owe me one." Brandon reached for her hand, but she stepped away.

"Sure." It was supposed to be a flirty *sure* but it didn't sound that way, and she didn't feel that way. She left the office with a sinking feeling in her gut.

13

Emmett feels good for ten seconds and then feels really bad

Chloe showed up to the trailhead alone.

"Is Stephanie coming?" Emmett asked.

"No. She couldn't make it."

He stepped closer, suppressing his delight. "Have you hiked this trail before?"

She hadn't.

"Did you bring water?"

She nodded. She had a backpack that hung over her bare left shoulder. With her tank top, shorts, and flip-flops, she looked better prepared for the beach than for a hike. That was good for him because it was a steep trail. He hoped that Chloe would reach out for his hand to climb over a big rock or ledge. Or even better, she would slip, and he would catch her.

"You ready?" He asked.

"Let's do it."

Emmett had only been away from Kacey for a few weeks, but he was already sick of her. She texted him multiple times a day, wanted to FaceTime every evening, and when he didn't respond or couldn't make a time work, she punished him with a swarm of allegations. He had apologized for hanging up on her—what more did she want?

He vacillated between being angry and dismissive, which only made things worse. When she was sad, he would calm her down and say he was sorry and loved her. When she was curt, or rude, or angry, he had no problem telling her he couldn't speak.

He still had one more year of high school, and their circles were so tightly intertwined that breaking up with her now would throw a wrench into his social life. And the truth was, when he was around her, he liked her.

When alone with Kacey, he could be comfortable and vulnerable. He never felt judged.

She was the only person he told about his parents and how they weren't the perfect people they pretended to be, and how they needed him to support them and make them feel good about themselves.

When they were apart, though, those intimate moments of trust became irrelevant, even silly; their authenticity stood no chance against time and distance. Kacey was the second girl he had slept with and the first girl he had dated. He was Kacey's first everything. When away from her, he rationalized their impending breakup. Sometimes it seemed like they were only together because all their friends said they were great together. It all seemed so surface level, so high school.

Chloe represented possibilities beyond Kacey. She was prettier, more mature, more worldly. He would have to wait, though. Because Kacey, despite her comparative failures, deserved better than a cheater. She felt safe with him. She told him that often. She would curl up in his arms and say that with him, she could be herself. Breaking that trust would gut her.

But when he looked at Chloe, Kacey disappeared from his mind.

The beginning of the trail was well-paved and flat. When the steps came, Emmett slowed his pace. He knew the trail well and knew that there were many more steps to come. He heard Chloe breathing. "It'll be worth it at the top," he said.

The top was an hour away. This was the steepest hike on the Maluhia Preserve but also his favorite. When she wanted to rest, he told her to go for two more minutes. "There's a bench up there."

She trudged along behind him. When he asked her questions, she answered with one-word responses between exhalations. At the bench, she melted. Sweat on her face, she reached for her water.

"Does it get easier?" she asked.

"We can take our time. Trust me, the top is worth it."

"Are you even tired?"

"I've been training for this my whole life." He laughed, proud of himself. He did not tell her that his whole life was seventeen years.

When she had caught her breath, he asked her about her night. She and Stephanie had had a few too many drinks. That's why, she explained, Stephanie didn't make it. And that's why, she said, "I look awful."

"You don't look awful."

"I feel awful."

"We can go back…"

"No! We're gonna do this!" Her smile made every statement captivating.

They began again, this time more slowly. He let her go in front to set the pace and had a view of her butt and bare legs. They got to a muddy part of the trail, and she started to slip. He outstretched his arms to steady her, extending one around her waist and the other against her back.

At the top of the trail, she collapsed on the ground, hands spread out like a snow angel. "Finally!"

"Yes, but get up."

She shook her head. So he reached out and grabbed her hands, pulling her up toward him and onto her feet. Her face was close to his. "Look," he said again, this time pointing.

In the distance was the ocean. Much closer, they saw hills of green and then, on an adjacent peak, a waterfall. "Come with me," he said, taking her hand.

"I thought this was the end," she whined, but didn't resist.

Emmett led her off the trail and down into the shade. There wasn't a marked path, but he knew his way. They only had to duck under a few branches. He led her, and she gripped his hand, and when he released it to clear a route, she grabbed it again before he could offer.

They arrived at the base of the waterfall. When the water hit the lagoon, the surface bubbled and foamed. It looked perfect. The surrounding pool was clear and shimmering in the heat, and from their vantage point, the scene looked magical and unspoiled as it did every year and every time he came.

He saw awe on her face. "It's my special spot," he said.

"No one else knows about it?"

He led her to a log, a few feet away from the water. He sat and untied his hiking shoes. "Logan knows. I'm sure others too, but I've never seen anyone else here."

"You're going swimming?" she asked.

He was wearing board shorts. He took off his shirt, socks, shoes, and backpack and set them on the log. He walked to the edge and felt the water. It was cool and comfortable. "Have you ever swam under a waterfall?"

"I don't have a suit."

He grinned. "Sucks for you!" He jumped in and swam to the waterfall. He let it fall on his shoulders first and then his head. He went inside, and as he stepped back, he found a familiar ledge to rest his feet against. "Come on!" He called. But the noise of the waterfall was deafening, so he swam back. She was standing by the log, watching him. Her face flushed. "I don't have a suit," she said again. "Can we just talk here? Is that all right?"

"Yes." He felt guilty and wished he hadn't gone in the water. But it was too late. He was half-naked, dripping and wet. He sat on the log, and she joined him. "It's a pretty spot though, right?"

"Stunning."

She pulled out her phone and took a picture for CrissCross. Then asked him to take one with her in it. He saw she had almost one-hundred-thousand followers. "Do you want a filter?"

"I'll edit it, just take a few on my camera."

"Okay!"

She knew exactly how to pose, how to smile. "You look amazing."

"Do they look good?" She came back and peered over his shoulder. "Can I hire you as my photographer?"

"I'll do it for free!"

She smiled and for the first time ever looked shy. "I'm not one of those social media–obsessed girls. I don't want you to get the wrong idea. It's just I make a lot of money."

"I thought you didn't do it for the money?"

She didn't look shy anymore, but instead conflicted, a little embarrassed. "I don't want to live off my mom and dad, you know. How about you?"

"Me?"

She sat back down so their knees were touching. "Do you want to live off your parents or the lumber baron?" She said it sarcastically, like he had said it to her when they first met.

"I don't know."

"I mean, there's nothing wrong with working for your parents, if you do good work, that is."

"Yeah. I work for my dad now, actually."

"You do?"

"Yeah. I'm kinda his right-hand man, helping with investments, helping the companies. We invested in Trance."

"You told me."

"Oh."

"Would your dad let you do an investment yourself?"

"Well, we're kind of a team. We do everything together."

"Yeah, I also need to help my mom with some work stuff."

"I thought you hated her?"

"I do, it's complicated. We're always fighting. But I said I'd help her." She looked down and then suddenly right at him, now with a grin on her face. "Let's go swimming!"

"What?"

"Turn around."

"Um, okay. Yeah!"

He turned around, but not all the way. From the corner of his eye, he watched her peel her tank top off, then her shorts. She had a white bra, and a matching thong; her body was everything he imagined it would be. "So this was your plan?" She waded into the water. He splashed after her. They swam to the waterfall. She put her head under and screamed out, "Whoa!"

"It feels good, right?"

She put her head in again. "It's like a massage."

He could barely hear her. He swam through the falls to the other side, where it was still loud but so were their echoing voices. It was a tight space, and they were pressed up against each other. "This is crazy," she yelled. She swam back out and then back in again, and he put his feet on the ledge. When she came back to join him, she was grinning, and she was at once angelic and immodest, and when she pressed against him, it took every ounce of willpower he had not to kiss her.

How would Kacey feel? He moved away and sat back against the ledge.

"It's okay," she said. She took his hand to steady herself and pulled herself up on the ledge too. Her wet bra was translucent.

He closed his eyes and saw what was going to happen. Then images of Kacey surfaced. Her soft voice whispering that she needed him, that she would be so lonely without him, that no one understood her, not her family, not her friends…only him, the love of her life. Weren't they so lucky to have each other?

But when he opened his eyes and saw Chloe staring back and then looked down again to see her bra and what it failed to conceal, he knew he stood no chance against his inner virtue.

"You know what I like about you?" she asked.

"What?"

"You're more mature than you look."

He beamed.

"No, really," she said. "You're already making all these investments, running things with your dad. It's so cool."

"Yeah, um, thanks."

She put her hands on his shoulders first, and he went for her chest, and she laughed and kissed him. He kissed back and grabbed and squeezed every part of her like he was playing some debauched game of whack-a-mole.

She led him out of the water, and he pulled a towel out of his bag and spread it on the ground. He lay down, and she sat on him and removed her bra. "My God…" he said. She shushed him and pulled his shorts off and took him in her mouth. Within seconds, he was close. He pushed her head away, stood, flipped her on her back, took off her thong. "Can I?"

She nodded.

He thrust five times and then finished on her stomach.

"I'm sorry—"

She was laughing.

"It's just because you're so pretty!"

She kept laughing.

"It's okay," she said. She stood up and went back to the water. He followed, again apologizing.

He looked at her naked body in the water and resented its perfection. When he met her eyes, he saw cruelty and didn't know if he was putting it there himself or if it was cruelty he hadn't seen prior, and he lowered his gaze because he didn't want to find out. He suddenly remembered all of Kacey's good qualities. She never laughed at him for finishing quickly. She didn't make him feel like this.

He put his suit back on, sat down on the log, and waited for Chloe to come back. But she didn't.

He relented. He returned to the water and found her behind the falls. Her face didn't change when he approached. She looked peaceful, maybe a little bored, and she ran her hands through her hair. He wasn't going to ask her to put clothes on, but he wished she would.

"Are you okay?" he asked because she wasn't speaking, and he had to say something.

"Yes."

He put his butt against the ledge and ran his hands through the water.

"I should be asking you, though," she said.

"What?" He didn't look up.

"Are you okay?"

He felt like a child, and he hated himself for it. "I'm fine." He hoped his tone conveyed that he was, in fact, not fine. He wanted to blame her for it. She didn't take the bait, though. After another minute of silence, he said, "We can go back now if you want?"

"Do you want to go back?"

"I don't care. But if you want to go back, we can."

"Maybe in a little."

"Okay."

He wanted to go back and call Kacey and have a normal conversation. He would ask her all the routine things he used to ask her and hope that in their predictability, Chloe would fade from his mind. Now though, he was here with her and couldn't do anything but run his hands through the water.

"Did you bring a joint?" she asked.

"I can roll one!" He was thrilled to have a job to do, one he could do well, and he swam to the shore. When she emerged, she dried herself with the towel and then put her underwear back on and then her shirt. But she didn't put on her shorts, and when she lay down on the towel, he looked away because he knew that he would want her again, and the guilt, without the lust, was enough of a burden to bear.

He lit the joint and took a tepid puff. He sat up and passed it. It took a few rotations for her to speak. She didn't look at him, and he didn't give her a chance to. "You have a girlfriend?"

He nodded.

"And so you feel bad?"

"I guess." He tried not to think about Kacey, but couldn't help himself.

"We won't tell her, okay?" She blew a cloud of smoke in his face. He swatted it away, and she laughed. "How old are you?"

He planted his hands on the ground. "I told you—"

"No, really."

He groaned. "Seventeen."

She laughed. "Fuck, they could arrest me."

"Fuck you."

"You tried." He stood and walked away, back toward the log. And in a hurry put his shirt on and struggled to stretch his socks over his wet feet. "It was a joke!"

"It's fine."

"You can fuck me again."

He didn't know if she was serious. He was determined, this time, not to find out. She approached the log and dressed.

"You ready?" he asked.

"Let's finish this."

He handed her the lighter, and she relit the joint. When she spoke, she looked at the waterfall. "You know, I have a boyfriend too. I think you're making too big a deal of it. I can see that you're making a big deal."

"I'm not. I'm just—"

"Why are you so angry?"

"I'm not angry!"

She swatted her hand through the air. "Generally, people are angry. Everybody all the time spends so much time being angry. I thought you were different. I thought you didn't care and just wanted to be happy. I liked that about you."

"I'm just tired."

"You feel bad for your girlfriend?"

"I don't know."

"If it wasn't me, it would have been someone else."

"Hmm?" He looked at her again.

"Life is too short to be angry. We have the best lives."

If Cole were here, what would he say? He imagined his brother's scowl, his conniving eyes. Cole would say that the world was falling apart and it was their family's fault. The rich spend extravagantly as people all around the world sink into deeper wells of destitution. Clean air has become a luxury good, and with it, health and safety. But don't feel bad, Cole would say mockingly, because life is short, and we have to live our best lives.

"I don't want to spend my whole life feeling bad about things," she explained. "It's not healthy. I just want to live, you know?"

"Yeah, me too." But he couldn't help feeling bad and didn't want her to notice. His best move was to change the subject. "So, what are your plans for the rest of the day?"

"I don't know. I'll probably have to spend some time with my mom."

"You have to?"

"Yeah, I think so. She's working all the time but is taking the afternoon off. I promised her."

"What does she do?"

Chloe sat on the question. "She has a company. She wants me to help her with some things."

"That's cool."

"You know what would be really cool? Me and you working together."

"Me and you?"

Chloe nodded. "There's something that I'm working with my mom on. We're looking for partners."

"Investors?"

"Yeah. I mean, we don't *need* investors but it would be fun, you know. That way we can stay in touch even when I have to go back to school."

"That would be cool."

"I'll send you a presentation. But first, you should talk to your dad. You know, to make sure he'll let you make investments."

He wasn't sure his dad would let him do anything or, for that matter, that his dad could do anything without his grandpa's approval. "It won't be a problem. I make investments all the time."

"It's cool how your dad respects you so much. I wish it was like that for me. I need to show my mom that I can do stuff first, you know? That I can make a difference. I'm going to try."

"It's cool that she tells you all about her business."

"She tells me everything. Too much."

They sat watching the waterfall. "It's not like that with my parents," Emmett said. "They're pretty closed off." Then he caught himself. "Not with work stuff, though. My dad tells me everything about the work stuff."

"Hmmm. But closed off in other ways?"

"Yeah. Like always pretending to be things they're not."

He stood and started putting things in his bag. He didn't want to talk about his parents.

14

Eliza makes a deal

The diner was on a side street. It was 10:00 a.m., and its garish sign looked especially worn out in the morning haze. Eliza didn't have to walk far in the smoke, but inside the air seemed only negligibly better. Two air purifiers whirred. They were old models. They stood no chance.

Still, Eliza took her mask off because it was the polite thing to do. She breathed in the smoke and surveyed the room.

Gary was seated in a booth. He watched her, and when their eyes met, she smiled. He didn't. He looked old and withered and destined for the smoky air and grungy innards of the low-trafficked, antiquated diner. She had always thought of Gary as a wealthy man, a rival of her remarkable father. But the man sitting here didn't look anything like the Gary she had prepared to see.

Eliza had met Gary Nesbit twice before. Once when she was young, at a charity banquet. Gary's hand went out for Duke's and hung there for too long. At last, Duke shook it. When Gary left, Duke whispered something to Eliza's mom, and that was that.

At ten years old, Eliza was perceptive but not particularly interested in her dad's business. That passion, that drive to impress him through work, would come later. But she remembered that exchange because it was the first time she saw how others perceived her dad. Gary didn't say anything or do anything to show his fear and reverence, but even as a ten-year-old, she could feel it. She could tell that her dad felt it too and liked it.

She didn't see Gary again until she was a twenty-year-old Peterson Lumber summer intern. He came by the Redding office and spoke to her briefly before following Duke to a conference room. When he walked out, he betrayed nothing on his face. He nodded goodbye to her and a few others. But as the elevator doors were closing, she saw his expression shift from stern to satisfied. The man that she remembered being so afraid looked anything but.

"What was that about?" she asked Duke.

"I bought some land," he said.

"Oh."

Then in a rare moment of transparency, her dad said, "He thinks he's cheating us. I let him think he's cheating us."

"Cheating us?"

"He sold us bad land. But I don't want the land for lumber. I want it for the access to his good land."

She didn't understand, and he didn't explain. As she continued to work for Duke, though, she saw the brilliance of the purchase. When Gary decided to sell off some of his holdings, there were few buyers. His land was hard to access without cutting through the Peterson plots first. And when prospective purchasers called Duke about using his roads and paying for the privilege, he refused them.

Gary grew desperate and started to sell to Duke at a discount.

Nesbit Lumber had once been the largest private lumber company on the West Coast. In the 1980s, Peterson Lumber had ten percent as much land. By 2015 the companies were nearly the same size. Now, Peterson Lumber was the behemoth and Nesbit was a dinosaur.

Duke never missed a moment to enlighten Eliza and Chris. "It's really a shame," he would say. "I used to look up to the Nesbits. Gary's father was a force." From there, Duke explained why second-generation wealth faltered, and third-generation wealth failed. "The second-gen lacks the drive but has the smarts. The third-gen has neither."

After these talks, Eliza would do her best to show her dad that she had drive. She would put in extra long hours. She would run projects by him, too many to count, hoping for words of encouragement, or even approval. Sometimes she got the feedback she looked for, but even then, it seemed insincere. She couldn't make Duke proud no matter how hard she tried. He must have seen her as another Gary. Well-intentioned but lazy. Or worse, like she had skipped a generation and was well-intentioned but dense.

Now she was in her forties, a co-CEO, and on the verge of earning her dad's long-awaited, long-fought-for approval. If she could close this deal, she would get it, at last, she was sure.

Gary didn't stick his hand out this time. So she did him the honor. And it was almost like he, too, remembered that banquet from many years ago because he didn't take her hand, not right away. He let her hold it out and feel all the nervousness that comes with a social faux pas, with a convention ignored or gone awry. Then, like Duke, he relented.

"Thanks for meeting me," Eliza said.

"Sure."

Gary's face was folded up and wrinkled, his lips chapped. He wore a red golf hat because, she assumed, he had little hair.

"You live in the area?" he asked.

"Yes. By the river. And you?"

They volleyed back and forth until they had coffee and a food order placed. It was Gary who brought up the subject first. He did so without looking at her. For the first time since she sat down, he looked at his hands. "It all depends on the offer, you know. I'm not going to do anything stupid. There's lots of time."

"Oh, I know. We would never give a lousy offer. Like I said on the phone—"

"I said that you could give your offer, and I will think about it. I'll think about it, and then I want to speak to your dad."

"You can speak to him, but it won't make any difference. He's just chairman now. He trusts me to do these kinds of deals."

She shouldn't have to explain herself. But Gary, even then, wasn't satisfied. "Eliza, with all due respect, I don't know you. I don't know how you do business. Your dad and I have known each other for a long time."

"I know that, and believe me, he's in the loop. But he's in Hawaii now, and I'm running the company."

"When we are done, I will call him."

"It'll be a waste of time."

"It won't be. He understands something about this business, about respect and relationships."

What was he remembering? Handshake deals with her dad that made them both better off? Win-wins? That history was fiction. Perhaps concocted by Gary's old mind, drawn to some glory days fable. The evidence was clear enough. After Gary took over, the Nesbits started to lose. And yet, the man sought Duke, all the same, imagined that they were peers.

She wouldn't degrade herself. She wouldn't report to her dad that she couldn't get the deal done, not without his help. "You can call him, but it won't do you any good. He'll be insulted. We might walk away." He might tell Gary that she wasn't really running the company, and any credibility she had would dissipate.

Gary scoffed. "You won't walk away."

"If you call him on his vacation and say you don't trust his daughter? You don't want to work with her? That's a reflection on his judgment. He won't like that."

He would have to sell to them. He knew it, and she knew it. The Nesbits hadn't invested any money into their salvage business. Peterson Lumber was the only player with salvage expertise in the Nesbit's geographical vicinity. "The longer you drag this out," she explained, "the more risk you take that more fires will burn your land. Then what? You'll be more desperate. We'll give you a fair offer now."

Their food arrived. Gary skirted around the details. He complained about the fires. He blamed her for mismanaging their forests.

"There are hundreds of fires burning right now all over the state. It's not on us, Gary."

"I guess it's on all of us." He looked sad. She didn't comfort him or contradict him. She just nodded. It was a hard world for the lumber companies, especially those that weren't built to profit off fire. They would die a slow death as the earth got hotter. In the short term, they could cut more trees, but fires were a long-term problem. The national forests would burn, and because it was so hot, they would burn faster and for longer. No one was safe.

At least Duke had found a way to make a profit.

"I got it." She passed their waitress her credit card.

"How generous," he said.

"Our counsel will send our offer later today. We look forward to a response."

"We'll see," said Gary. But it was clear she had already won. Maybe he would push back on some of the terms, but he wouldn't get far. She held all the cards.

—

Duke was getting ready to sleep when his phone rang. It was 10:30 p.m., which meant it was well past midnight for Eliza.

"Is it too late for a call?" she asked.

"It's never too late for work."

As she filled him in, he heard himself in her. The strain of work, the assault of a fire season. "Around five million acres have burned so far this year. That's just in California." She didn't sound surprised. She had no reason to be.

"Better than last year," Duke said.

Last year, by the end of August, nearly eight million acres had burned in the state.

The fires were good for business but bad for morale. Peterson Lumber Company did better than every competitor in the salvage business and won all of the contracts they could handle. But the fires marked an end to the old way of lumber work, when good business equated to the number of trees cut and sold. The industry had changed and was changing still. Would they have holdings in the future? Or would they be salvagers exclusively, the clean-up crew for an ever-burning earth?

Less than a decade ago, some people were still optimistic that the government would manage the fires. Duke had even served on committees, advocating for controlled burns and clear-cutting. But the committees accomplished little. Politicians and voters resisted controlled burns and clear-cutting due to its carbon footprint. The issue, in Duke's mind, was more complicated than people realized. Climate change was playing a role, but so was poor forest management.

Now, it seemed like it was too late to fight either battle, and he had few personal incentives to do so. When the fires came, Peterson Lumber was one of the only beneficiaries.

Despite the fact that he was making more money, there were reasons to be concerned about the business's long-term health. It was, for example, harder than ever to hire talent. People didn't want to work in the forests and breathe poisonous air. Even in Redding, the air was too toxic for most. He was lucky that Eliza and Chris wanted to stick around. His other top people were either leaving or were already gone, and their replacements often left after one or two fire seasons. There were better masks and air filters now, but at best, they made life tolerable. People wanted more than that. As Duke stepped out on the porch and smelled sweetness in the air, he couldn't blame them. Not that long ago, he would have stepped outside in Redding and felt a similar pleasantness.

He didn't know what would come to Hawaii, but something would. He would be dead then.

Then again, he used to say the same about climate change in his forests. It seemed so far away, and then all of a sudden, it wasn't. He remembered reading about fires in Maui in 2023. Maybe everything was already happening, and he was just numb to it.

"How's the smoke?" he asked.

"Three hundred and sixty AQI outside. In other words, very toxic."

"How's Chris?"

She mumbled something about him being fine. "I met with Gary."

"Oh?"

"He'll accept our offer. What do you think?"

What did he think… Of course, it was a good deal. If he were in her shoes, he would have done the same thing, maybe even gotten better terms. But she didn't actually want to know what he thought; she wanted praise. She wanted a pat on the back, for him to say *good job, I'm proud of you.* He wasn't going to say any of that, so all he said was, "Keep me posted."

PART 2
September

15

Lily dumps her drugs

Lily had never met anyone like Patricia. What made her unique wasn't her bluntness or her confidence. Lily knew blunt and confident women. Instead, what seemed to set Patricia apart was her unapologetic genuineness, her I-don't-give-a-fuck-ness. It occurred to Lily she was a bona fide psycho, albeit compellingly so. Whatever was wrong with Patricia that made her fearless was something that Lily wanted for herself.

After her first few encounters with Patricia, Lily had tried to avoid further interactions. She would dodge Patricia's invitations to meet for breakfast, and when they ran into each other, Lily would make excuses to get away. She didn't have the mental bandwidth to consider what she was afraid of. Those early conversations had been awkward but also thrilling. Still, Lily shirked from the prospect of anything further.

Patricia eventually lost patience. After two weeks of Lily playing the rodent in an exhausting game of cat and mouse, Patrica cornered her by the pool.

"You're avoiding me." Patricia didn't look nervous nor particularly happy. This seemed, to her, a banal point, so obvious that stating it aloud was merely a convention.

"I am not."

"Don't lie. It's unappealing."

Lily looked down. "You can't take a hint, huh?" Lily seemed more surprised by her own words than Patricia's. "I mean—"

"It's okay."

"I just mean, I've been busy, okay?"

"That's not what you mean. You have to say that because it's the polite thing to say. All you ever say is the polite thing because you're so afraid of saying anything else. Say what you want to say, what you really want to say."

Lily couldn't think of anything to say. She felt the urge to run.

"You think I'm crazy, obsessive, weird…"

"I don't—"

"You do."

"Well—"

"You think I want to fuck you."

"I do not!"

"I don't, sorry."

"Well—"

"We're going to have lunch. And after lunch, if you don't want to see me again, that's fine. I will disappear. I'll lose your number. We can smile at each other politely from across the pool. Okay?"

"Okay."

At lunch, they drank too many cocktails. At first, as Patricia probed, Lily was able to deflect. But then she started to get drunk, and Patricia started to ask the right questions. With a morning bickering match fresh in her mind (Richard kept complaining about his dad and that stupid Russian bitcoin investment, but refused to actually do anything about it), she opened up. "He thinks he's some fucking outlaw or something because he doesn't work for the lumber business. But he's investing for his dad. He has to confirm every investment with him, like a child!" They laughed. Lily drank melted ice from the bottom of her drink.

"Let's get another."

"I don't know. I don't usually drink so much at lunch."

They got another. "Is he even good at investing?" Patricia asked.

"No! That's the thing. He had one good deal, and it was a small check. All the others have been shit."

"You should be doing it."

"What?"

"You should be doing it. You're smarter than him."

"Oh, I don't know." She was glowing, from the drinks and the compliments. After Patricia paid, they walked along the beach. Lily confessed that Patricia had been right about the antidepressants. "I take a lot of things. I want something to work so badly."

Patricia took her hand and squeezed it like she had done so hundreds of times. "Don't you dare be hard on yourself!"

"What?"

"Everything you take is because you care about yourself, because you want to feel better. There is goodness in that. You have to see that too. You must."

"I guess."

They sat in the sand and watched some kids snorkeling. They sat for maybe an hour, Lily didn't know for sure, but even though it was quiet, it was all comfortable.

"So?" Patricia asked, breaking Lily out of a trance. "Do you want to see me again?"

"Yes. Yes! I'm sorry for before. I am. Really."

"What did I say about being sorry?" She was smiling warmly.

From then on, it was Lily who sought out Patricia. Patricia became her first real friend since college. She had other friends, of course. Women she would meet for coffee or wine—women like Cathy. They would gossip and laugh and leave exhausted and relieved to be done with each other. It always felt like they were acting, like everything said had been scripted in advance. With Patricia, she was given permission to be herself. She said things out loud that weeks ago she wouldn't even think. Like, "I don't even know if I love my husband." And at one point, "I think he cheats on me."

They were walking by the tennis courts. It was a cooler evening, and the path was wet from an afternoon storm.

"How do you know?" Patricia was, all of a sudden, alert.

Truthfully, this was the first time Lily had entertained the scenario. She explained her rationale. The business trips away—what work did he have to do in Thailand or Greece? The lack of calls or texts—couldn't he at least respond to her? She didn't believe for a second that he wasn't using his phone to play games. Then the overcompensation after his trips. Showering her with gifts and boyish excitement. His behavior, which never lasted more than a few days, hiding some inner guilt that she was too blind to notice, until now. "Why wouldn't he cheat?"

"Is it such a big deal?"

"What? Of course."

Patricia stopped walking and went from casual to stern. "I mean, you don't really know if he's cheating, do you?"

She was used to Patricia pushing back on her, but it always seemed performative, even playful. This felt formal, even punitive, like Lily was on the wrong side of an interrogation table.

"How does it make you feel when you think about him cheating on you?" Patricia asked, still with an unsettling intensity.

Lily tried to answer the question honestly. "I don't know. I guess I feel nothing other than a feeling that I'm supposed to feel something, and the fact that I don't is disturbing."

"Maybe it's all your meds."

"Maybe." And it occurred to Lily that Patricia would, in fact, be a very bad therapist. "So, what should I do?"

"Whatever you want."

"I don't know what I want."

"Let's sit." Past the tennis courts, on an offshoot from the main trail, they sat on a bench. In the distance, they could see a golf hole and, farther out, the ocean. They often walked together and then found a bench to talk. It became one of those unspoken routines that Lily clung to and refused to say out of fear that in naming the thing, she would diminish it. On this bench, on this evening, now willing to imagine her husband's infidelity, she felt like she was outside her crowded mind, free from its dictatorial whip. Patricia guided her as she mused about what she really wanted in life. The trivial answers were pushed aside, cleared for the solution that Patricia demanded. As Lily circled it, Patricia grew impatient and at last blurted out, "You want what everyone wants: to be seen."

"To be seen?"

"To be appreciated, respected, listened to."

"That's what you want too?"

"That's what everyone wants, even if they don't know it."

They returned to Lily's house. No one was home. They poured glasses of wine and sat outside. The stars were already poking through the darkening sky as they drank and lay back on reclining chairs. "I talk about InhaleAfrica so much," Lily explained, "because it's the only thing I'm proud of. But you know, if you saw me in those meetings, you'd be disappointed. I don't sound like you. Every time I speak, my heart beats like crazy. I just speak to say something, you know?"

Before every board call, Lily studied the materials. She would even write down questions and comments in hopes that she would have the courage to share them. She never did. Facing her computer in a Zoom room with twelve others, she failed to say anything of interest. When she spoke, it would be to compliment someone else's suggestion or provide sterling feedback on the group's work. Mostly she just nodded. "I hear you on your calls, and you sound so confident."

Patricia ignored the compliment. "So you want to speak up more in your meetings?"

"Yes."

"That's too small."

"Excuse me?"

"It's too small. Think bigger."

"Well, I don't know."

"You should invest with Richard."

"He wouldn't let me."

"Make him."

"It's not that easy."

Patricia shrugged. "Everyone told me that I couldn't start my own company, that the idea was stupid." She parroted a patronizing voice, "'*It's not that easy, Patricia.*' Well, fuck them. I'm glad I did it anyway! I'm on a rocket ship." She threw her head back and laughed. "I mean, there's still room to grow but starting this thing was the best thing I've ever done. That," she nudged Lily, "and getting divorced."

"But that's you. I don't even know where to start. I'm not an investor."

"Stop thinking about what you aren't and start thinking about what you want to be."

"I don't know anything about business. I don't even know anything about your business."

"You know enough to know that Richard sucks at business! That's more than he knows. You're freaking out over nothing."

"I'm not freaking out."

"Look! I'll tell you what…and I'm only doing this because I love you; I'll let you invest in my company. We don't need the money, and I've turned away everyone else, but for you, I'll make an exception. And you can join my board. Not Richard, you."

It was an insane offer. What had she said to convince Patrica that she was worthy? And how quickly after watching Lily butcher a board meeting would Patricia change her mind? "That's really sweet of you, it's just—"

"It's just *what?*"

"I don't even know what your company does!"

"Oh, well, that's simple. We're revolutionizing the health and wellness field through personalized, patient-centric, and evidence-backed interventions." Before Lily could interject, Patrica raised a hand. "Whatever excuse you're about to say, save it! It's like I'm handing you a golden ticket. Everyone would kill for a chance like this." She softened. "Just consider it, okay? I want to help you. After a deal like this, everyone will want Lily Peterson to be their investor. Richard won't know what to do with himself."

WHEN RICHARD CAME HOME, he said something about how awful his dad was and something else about hearing nothing from Cole. Lily must have responded because he didn't press her further, but she had no idea what she'd said. She had been distracted, thinking about Patricia's offer. When Richard wanted to fuck her, she agreed, and for those five minutes, was again gone. He finished, and she showered. She came back to earth just before bed.

"What do you think I'm good at?" she asked.

"This again?"

She nodded.

"A lot," he said.

"But what specifically?"

"You're kind. You're caring. You're sweet. You take care of your family." She didn't say anything. "Feel better?" he asked.

She turned away to the opposite wall. "Yes."

"Good!" he said, and she heard him tapping on his phone, playing some game.

She didn't know if Richard had ever complimented her intelligence or ambition. She had been valedictorian of her high school class and graduated magna cum laude from Stanford. But he didn't care. When she was younger, he had called her cute. Now that she was older, she was caring. Pre-Richard she had been smart, post-Richard she was caring.

She married him for her mom. Everything she had ever done had been for her mom, and then her mom handed her off to Richard like she was a rag doll. And everything she did in her life was for Richard. It wasn't like her mom had arranged the marriage, but she might as well have. For as long as Lily could remember, her sweet-in-society, harsh-in-the-house mother told Lily what a good life for her would mean.

Lily wanted to enjoy her childhood, but instead, she was placed before a piano. Every day she played, and then her mom said she should also play the violin. Then she had piano, violin, and pageants.

The pageants were the worst. She had to dress up and smile and be horribly polite.

After the pageants, there was homework to do, sometimes volunteer work, and always church on Sundays. Even her friends were arranged for her. At first, very directly. Her mom would schedule playdates with kids from families she approved of. Then it was less direct, but still never Lily's choice. Every interaction with a prospective friend was an interview. The question was never said out loud but was necessary all the same: what would Mom think of you? Even when the question faded and became, what do I think of you, the "I" was not really Lily. She had internalized the opinions of her mother and had become her mini-me.

When Lily did as she was told and ideally won the pageants and the piano competitions, her mom said she was perfect. "You'll see," her mom explained, "you'll thank me when you're older." It was all part of a grand plan for Lily to be perfect and find a perfect man. He would be rich and take care of her and help her climb to the top of society. This man, Lily realized, would be the polar opposite of her absent father, who had left when Lily was five and died a few years later.

"No way," Lily's mom had said. "You won't marry someone like that." And like everything else her mom said or suggested, she agreed.

When she announced she was going to Stanford at age seventeen, it was what her mom wanted to hear. It was what Lily wanted too! Or so she thought.

And it had been that way with Richard too. There were other men, but her mom especially liked Richard.

Lily never considered what she wanted. After her mom met Richard, "the son of a BILLIONAIRE"—Lily could still hear the way her mom said it—the rest was history. "Listen to him, or he'll leave you," her mom said. Richard wanted to get married right away. He wanted kids right away. She complied. She didn't want him to leave her.

Lily turned to look at the "son of a BILLIONAIRE" she had married. He didn't look up from his game. His face was askew in mouth-breathing, lip-nibbling concentration.

Had she ever loved him? In college, what had he been like? Mostly the same. Funnier, perhaps, but even then, dull and conventional and so obsessed with not being dull or conventional that he collected experiences like a boy collects baseball cards. At parties, he talked about the same things: skydiving, his backpacking trip in Europe. When Lily would grill her friends for input, they would tell her that he was very nice and, in some cases, very interesting. She believed them until the fifth or sixth party when he was still bragging about the same things.

He thought he was such a rebel for not joining his dad, but he had no problem investing his dad's money. Did she too bask in his rebellion as if it was interesting? She looked at his saggy face. Only his fingers moved.

She got out of bed and looked in the mirror. She had been given all the best treatments, and her face, for forty-five, was flawless. She wanted those treatments back now. She wanted to see what she would have looked like without them.

It was too late. Everything all of a sudden felt too late. What could she do now to change? What choices did she have? Patricia's offer seemed miles away, construed in some fantasy land. Richard would laugh at her. She'd have no response but to laugh at him. The night would go from bad to worse.

She opened her medicine cabinet. There were all kinds of mood enhancement supplements: 5-HTP, L-Theanine, Lithium, and ashwagandha. Then there was the good stuff: psychiatrist prescribed. Most recently, she was on one called Lamictal. She was sure that when this one stopped working, Dr. Schumer would have another on the docket.

She heard Richard approach behind her. "What are you doing?" he asked.

"Nothing." She closed the cabinet and started to wash her hands. And then he did the unthinkable, something she had never seen him do before.

He opened up the medicine cabinet and tilted his head, closely reading the names.

"What?" she asked.

"I don't think you should take these." He wasn't trying to offend her, she knew that. From his perspective, he was stating a fact. But she found it offensive. So much so that with a terrific swipe of her hand, she knocked the vials, all of them, to the ground.

He looked at her bug-eyed.

Some of the lids fell open and the dislodged pills, multicolored and of various shapes, looked like some Halloween bonanza.

"What the hell, Lily?"

"You happy?" She asked.

"What?"

"Are you fucking happy?"

16

Bella says, "Where there's smoke, there's fire"

A few weeks after Cole joined, the team gathered in the conference room for their monthly strategy meeting. Bella took her usual seat and noticed that Cole stood outside the circle, twitching his foot. "Sit here," she said, gesturing for him to share her couch. He sat with a firm back and clenched fists. Then he deflated, perhaps in some futile attempt to be more casual.

"Are you okay?" she asked as others shuffled in.

She got the sense that Cole was always nervous, that he lived life in a perpetual state of fear. Some of his nerves, at least at the office, seemed justified. Aid for Earth was a small close-knit team, and no one had made any effort to make Cole feel welcome. Behind his back and, for that matter, hers, the team called him a weirdo. Brandon told her so.

In Cole, they saw nothing but rich guilt and fecklessness. His assignments didn't present the opportunity for him to prove otherwise. Brandon had him crunching numbers for their email marketing campaigns and even getting coffee.

Bella was sure they were all wondering: why was she friends with this loser?

It was the right question.

After his first day, she'd asked him, "What do you think?"

"It's," he rarely looked at her when he spoke, he usually looked at his feet, "it's exciting. Thank you again." He had thanked her dozens of times already.

After his third day, he no longer thanked her. When she asked him how he was doing, he said, "Fine." And then he skirted off.

Now, with the meeting about to start, she tried to help him relax. If he couldn't pull it together and get at least someone else on the team to like him, he'd be gone. "These are just opportunities for people to share their work," she said. "You know, ask questions, gather feedback."

He nodded.

"How's everyone doing?" Brandon asked. He stood while they sat, sipping a Cole-bought coffee. The group discussed. She commented on the lawsuit. She purposefully brought Cole into the conversation. "Cole, maybe you can share more about the type of engagement we're getting on the emails. When we do go public with the lawsuit, we'll want to drum up as much support as possible."

"Um." He looked like a ghost. In a show of support, she nudged him with her elbow, but he contorted his body away. "Sorry," he said, aware that the shirk was obvious.

"Go ahead," she said. "Tell us about what you're seeing."

He, with impeccable precision, rattled off every important metric. The problem was, when he spoke, he sounded insecure. When he was done, no one asked any follow-up questions.

"Great," Brandon said flatly. Then there was silence. "Okay. Jennifer?"

"Wait," Bella interrupted. "If Cole's right about the conversion rates, then we should invest more."

"The emails don't work, Bella," said Toby, who had been combative since she had dissed his podcast.

"Was anyone listening?" She raised her hands. "They're working! For the first time, they're working. Cole, you said email-campaign donations are up twenty percent this month."

"Versus last month, which was low."

"Because we stopped putting any effort into the emails," said Toby.

"If we can do twenty percent month over month, then the emails will actually be worth it. Cole, if we grow at this rate, what will we be at next year?"

He seemed to run some numbers in his head and then pulled out his phone. No one looked as riveted as Bella. "Almost ten-K a month."

Everyone laughed. "See!" Toby said. "That's after a whole year, and that's assuming we can maintain a twenty percent increase. I don't see it. We've done it for one month."

Cole didn't speak again for the rest of the meeting. He looked miserable, and he seemed determined to hide his misery behind some sad excuse for a smile. She couldn't tell if he was on the verge of tears or a temper tantrum.

They blamed her, she knew, for bringing Cole on, and worse, they blamed Brandon for playing favorites and letting her.

THE NEXT DAY, Cole arrived at the office hunched over, red in the face, tired.

"Good morning," she said.

"Good morning."

"You don't look so hot."

"Oh, um, I'm tired. I had to move to another place yesterday and, long story short, the city's expensive."

"You don't have a place—"

"I'm not going to stay at my parents' house. It wouldn't be right."

"So you've been crashing…where?"

"The hostel near mid-market. But my booking got mixed up, and I found another, but it was late."

Bella went to find Brandon. He was in his office. She knocked, because he had told her a few days prior that it bugged him when she didn't. "Come in."

She shut the door and approached his desk. At last, she was ready to have the conversation. "Cole can help us, but we're not giving him a chance."

"Bella, for God's sake, we're giving him a chance. Everyone is up in arms about it. You should hear what people are saying. If you're going to get him to do something for us, go do it!"

"You have him on email marketing!"

"Which seemed to impress you in yesterday's meeting."

She rolled her eyes. "Listen to me."

"All I do is listen to you."

"What?"

"I just think that I listen to you too much. I'm running this thing. Not you. We shouldn't have brought Cole on. It's fucked up the whole culture."

"He's not that bad."

He put his hands in air quotes, "'Not that bad.' Listen to yourself. You promised, what?" He tried to remember her exact words, "'Something big.'"

"You're right."

"That's nice to hear you say."

"But it's your fault. We need to figure out how to use him."

"You want dirt on his family, yeah? Well, what are you going to do? We can't just ask."

Then they heard a knock on the door. "It's, uh, Cole."

Brandon rolled his eyes. "One second!"

"Do you think he heard us?" Bella whispered.

"Who cares." Then louder, addressing the door, "Come on in." Cole entered and looked around like he was being confined to a cell.

"It's all right," Bella said. She gestured at a seat. "Sit down."

"What?"

"Come on, sit down."

He did. There were two chairs facing Brandon's desk, but she stayed standing.

"I had a question about our mail client. Hubspot is kinda outdated now. I think we should switch to something different."

Bella walked around the desk so she was on the same side as Brandon. She leaned over and met Cole's eyes. "Do you really want to work on emails?"

"Um. I didn't know I had a choice."

"You do. We're all good at different things. And you're good at a lot. Email marketing is a shit job, but you still managed to make it work. That was my point yesterday. It was impressive."

"Thanks." The eye contact was gone, and he watched his feet.

"Look at me." He did. "Brandon," she asked, still staring down Cole, "Can you give us a minute?"

He sighed. "Bella, it's my office."

"Please," she said. She didn't stop looking at Cole and listened to the sound of Brandon's fading footsteps and then a closing door. "A lot of people were born with everything, but I haven't met anyone else who knows it, really really knows it. Lots of rich people will say they know it. We've both heard it. They say how lucky they are, and maybe they do some bullshit like attend a BLM protest or vote social democrat. But then they drive home in the nice car daddy bought to the nice home daddy bought…but not you."

Cole smiled. It was the first time she had seen him smile in a long time, at least genuinely. She kept going. "I have no doubt that you can work here and, like everyone else, make a marginal impact. I know you can do more than email marketing. The truth is, though, that after that, the grass is only a little greener, the tasks a little more important, you know? Maybe you get stuck on the SEO team or the fundraising team, or maybe you even work with me on policy and advocacy. I know you would do a great job, but the bigger question is, could someone else do just as good a job? I don't know. What do you think?"

"I guess so." No more smile, but he was following her words, hooked on them or her face or both, and she didn't care because she had him now, bait and switch.

"But you have something that nobody else here has. Honestly, probably something that few people in the world have. You said it the first time we met. *I should have been one of those Stanford kids you hate.*"

"You remember that?"

"Yes. But you're not one of those kids I hate. You want to be different. You really do."

For a moment, she almost felt bad for him. He would say yes to anything she asked, and that kind of power felt immoral. But she wiped those doubts away and reminded herself of the cause. It was bigger than them both.

"So, what do you think I should do?"

"Help us show the world that families like yours aren't playing by the rules." He didn't flinch. She went further. "They're not playing by the rules, right? You've told me." She took his hand and squeezed it.

"There are tax loopholes," he said. "And I guess some legal loopholes."

She put a hand on top of his and shook it. "No! Come on, more than that. How about the forest fires? You said your family profits off of fires."

"But everyone knows that. I don't think it's illegal."

"Where there's smoke, there's fire." She smiled. He didn't.

"What do you want me to do?"

"Maybe go see what you can find?"

"From my family?"

"Come on, I know you can do it. You'll be my hero."

"I just don't know what I'll find."

"It doesn't have to be anything that'll get them in trouble, just something to help us think about wildfire advocacy. Everyone knows there's a problem. It's so fucking hot, these fires burn forever and spread so fast. It's awful. It's gonna get worse. We all know that! But we don't know what the lumber companies are doing about it. Maybe it's good? I don't know." She doubted it. "But it would be good to find out. Just some information, okay? That's it."

He still looked unsure.

"You'd be my hero."

"Okay."

"Okay?"

"Okay."

17

Richard is confused

Richard knew that something was wrong with Lily but wouldn't ask her about it. He was scared that by asking, he would make things worse, that whatever anger lay dormant in his wife would expose itself, viciously, ruining the Hawaii trip for everyone.

It had started with the pills. If he could go back in time and never say anything about them, he would. But the damage was done. She was a delicate thing. It was his job to protect her from the worst parts of the world. If she wanted to live in ignorance about the drugs, so be it. Maybe they did make her happy. She was certainly happier before she spilled them.

Later that night, around one or two he caught her staring out the window. Her phone was by the bed charging, and she didn't have a book or magazine. She was staring like some psycho, like some woman possessed. The light of the moon on her white face between the dark blinds did not help. "Lily, honey, are you all right?" he asked.

"Yes," she said, without looking back. She kept staring. It wasn't clear she was breathing. Like a doll, she was so still.

"Lily?" He managed again.

Then she turned, slowly, way too slowly, "What?"

"What are you doing?"

"I can't sleep."

"You can't sleep?"

"No."

"Lily?"

"Go back to sleep."

A few days later Richard awoke alone in the bed, as he had every day that week. In his boxers, he did a quick walkthrough of the home, expecting to find Lily somewhere. It was early and a Sunday. She was nowhere to be found. Back in the bedroom, he sat and looked out the window like she had been doing every night and wondered what was so fascinating about the view. It was pretty. He saw palm trees and the ocean. But at night she would see nothing but darkness, maybe some obscured stars.

Then he heard steps in the kitchen, and he knew Emmett was awake. He walked in and tried to seem okay, even upbeat.

"You want to go out for breakfast?"

"Nah. I'm gonna surf with Logan. But, Dad…"

"Yeah?"

"Are you and Mom all right?"

Richard was reminded that Emmett, despite his height, confidence, and independence, was still a child. He was in need of assurance that the life he knew was safe. When Richard and Lily fought, especially when Emmett and Cole were younger, it was always Emmett who came running in, screaming out to be heard above the fray, "Are you going to get divorced?"

One time Richard said, "Maybe." He'd meant it. She had crushed his VR headset with his putter. Neither gadget was salvageable. All because he didn't want to talk about fucking InhaleAfrica for the thousandth fucking time.

Luckily Lily had recovered her sanity and could de-escalate. "No, honey. We're just having a disagreement."

Now, seventeen but still the same boy, Emmett was asking again.

"We're fine," Richard said. "We're really good. Don't you love it here?"

"Yes, of course, I do." He nodded for extra emphasis, and it looked to Richard like overcompensation.

What could he tell Emmett anyway? *Your mom is a demon woman.* There was no one he could talk to. He felt very alone and wished Lily would come back and be herself.

Lily returned that afternoon. She smiled and said hi, and it was all the same except for the distance between what she showed and what she felt, the obvious contrast between surface Lily and her grudge. Again, he was too scared to say anything, but he followed her into the bedroom. He watched her change and shower and brush her hair and so on. It was like he was a movie patron voyeuristically viewing a celluloid scene.

Then he started to cry. He was surprised; he didn't know the last time he had cried but knew it was a long time ago, and he did his best to stop.

The tears came with a weight in his chest. Lily saw, and her calm face shattered into authenticity.

"What's going on with you? What's wrong?" Only now did he have the courage to ask. He wiped his tears away.

She sat at the foot of the bed, naked, bare back to his gaping face. "You wouldn't understand."

"Try me." When he touched her, she shivered and slunk to her window. He couldn't tell if she was crying because her head was turned and there was no noise. He hoped she was crying. He didn't want to be the only one. "Come on, talk to me."

"Richard," she said at last, still not looking. "I'm miserable."

"Without your pills? We can get more! I'll order more!"

"No, it's not the pills. I picked up the pills." Then she turned, and he saw tears on her face and red eyes. "I've always been miserable."

"Here? In Hawaii?" They were ten feet apart, and he didn't dare move closer. To move closer, he knew, would scare her. His Lily now like some deer in a scope.

"I don't know," she said. "I don't know."

"Did something happen?" His voice sounded warbled. He had stopped crying but didn't trust that the composure would stay.

"No! Yes. I don't know."

"I want you to know you can talk to me. I'm always here—"

She sobbed. "No, you're not. You're here, but you're not here."

He didn't realize he had his palm up—some subconscious soothing gesture.

She noticed. "Stop patronizing me."

"Patronizing?"

"Patronizing!"

"I'm sorry, okay?"

"What are you sorry for?" She hung by the window. She was beautiful even in her anger, especially in her anger, and he felt an agonizing desire. More agonizing because he suspected it would lead nowhere. "What are you sorry for?" she asked again.

"Patronizing you?" She didn't look impressed. "I mean, I don't know."

"Yeah. I didn't think you did." Then she relaxed, "You think I'm crazy."

"I don't."

"I feel pretty crazy."

"Yeah?"

"Crazy but also not crazy. Like for the first time in my life, not crazy. And that's what's crazy."

"Okay."

"I want to invest with you."

"What?"

"I want to invest in companies with you."

"Um. Okay."

"What? Really?"

"Sure, go find some companies." Inside he was laughing. She wouldn't know where to start. Probably type "top startups" into ChatGPT or something...

"I already have one."

"What's the company?"

"It's a once-in-a-lifetime deal. No other investors can get in. I'm getting a stake because the founder wants me to join her board."

"Okay, but what do they do?" He saw a flash of insecurity in her face.

"Don't make me pitch you."

"What? That's the job..."

"Don't you dare make me pitch you. You'll just shoot it down. Find a bunch of holes to make yourself feel smart. All because it's my deal. If this were your deal, you'd be all over it. But because it's mine, it's a big fucking interrogation—"

"Lily..."

"Don't Lily me! Say yes."

"I don't even know who we are investing in or how much we're investing! Or what the terms are!"

"Just say yes."

"Fine! Yes. Fine. Whatever. Will it make you happy? Will you stop fucking moping around?"

"Maybe." She whipped around and left Richard standing alone, still confused. Even if it was a good deal (and he doubted it), his dad would probably block it.

18

Cole (almost) uncovers a conspiracy

When Cole used to go to Redding to visit Duke and Eliza he traveled by car. Usually, his dad drove the family in one of the Teslas, or he would drive one of his dad's Teslas. This time he traveled by bus. He wasn't spoiled like other rich kids, and he was going to prove it to himself and the world and Bella.

It was the first time he had ever been on a bus, at least a *real* bus. The party buses after Peterson Lumber events were a different species of transportation, replete with drinks, snacks, and neon lighting. The bus he found himself on now was filled with vagrants. The man next to him smelled and fidgeted. He had a dandruff-blown beard and a rashy face. It was better to look out the window for the whole five-hour ride. When they arrived at the Redding stop, Rash-Man followed Cole off the bus.

Eliza texted that she was running a few minutes late.

He wrote back, *I'll just Uber to you.*

Don't be silly. I'm coming.

He wasn't being silly. He was being practical. Redding in the summer was like being inside a cigarette. Still, he wouldn't take it out on Eliza. Of everyone in the family, he was most like Eliza, for better or worse. They lacked the confidence of their siblings, were both introverts, and were more self-aware.

"Have a good ride?" asked Rash-Man.

"Um yeah. Would have preferred an electric bus though."

Rash-Man stepped away, shook his head, spat on the ground, and lumbered off. It was a small win, but Cole was still stranded (albeit temporarily) and feeling sick to his stomach. The last few weeks had been lonely. When he left his family on the airstrip, the future had seemed bright with Bella in his mind. Instead of excitement and romance, what had followed was awkwardness and solitude. He knew that hostels were cheap, but he hadn't expected them to be so grimy. Even when he paid up for his own room, he found himself in springy bunks with cracked walls and stained floors. The noises were unbearable. He had expected, to some degree, the cars and the honking and the sirens. He hadn't prepared himself for the screaming. Every night, someone, no matter the hostel, was screaming.

At one point, he almost broke down. It was a Thursday. He had been at Aid for Earth for three weeks, comfortable enough in a single hostel room, when he had been informed that they had an existing reservation and his single was no longer available. Committed to maintaining his everyman identity and paying for things himself, he moved into a quadruple. Then at 1:00 a.m., someone outside screamed. Then dogs started to bark. Then Doritos started to fall down on him from the top bunk. He lay there with his eyes open as the chips rained down and the street sounds blared, and he was about to give in. Pac-Heights was twenty minutes away. He could be back in his bed. He would have the whole house to himself.

But then he remembered what his dad had said, the words crueler three weeks later: *not in our house*. And his words, *I'm staying with a friend*. He couldn't tell them the truth. *Mom, Dad, I'm staying with Dorito man*.

One night at a time.

He made it through, but things only got marginally better. The office was an unwelcoming place. Behind his back, people sneered. Even Bella seemed to regret bringing him in. Not that she said so, but he could tell.

Most of all, and he could never have imagined this being the case a month ago, he missed his family. He missed his dad's stupid jokes and how he made everything seem comfortable and predictable. He missed his mom's warmth, her love, her trust in him. And he even missed Emmett, his bullheaded confidence, his fuckboy charm. He wanted to be with them but was too proud to do it.

Instead, here he was, running some covert operation and feeling lonely, scared, and guilty.

Eliza came ten minutes later. They hugged. She ushered him into her Tesla. "I thought we could get dinner later and then maybe go see a movie or watch one at my place." She spoke quickly. "Only if you want that, of course!"

"That sounds good, it's just—"

"I just need to run by the office, if that's okay."

That was more than okay. "I'm actually behind on work. Can I just work with you from the office?"

"I'm sure you can work from the house. I want you to be comfortable. I just need a minute."

"No, I like the office! I think that would be great."

They worked from the office for a few hours. The walls were white and bare, the rooms cool, and everything from the black swivel chairs to the wooden desks seemed optimized for minimalistic efficiency. The place felt ripped from the nineties, and while he had little to base that assumption on other than the Aid to Earth warehouse, it felt accurate. This was a corporate machine and furnished like one, and he resented the fact that he had to be here, trapped inside a place that he wanted no part of. But it was comfortable and the air was clean inside and since he was mostly alone, no one looked at him or judged him. Within a few minutes, he felt better than he ever did at Aid for Earth, where he wanted to belong but seemed not to. He was a Peterson and intrinsically belonged here, at the place with his last name etched onto the building.

He didn't have anything to do so he just browsed Reddit. He had an Excel spreadsheet open in another tab populated with nonsense. When Eliza checked on him he switched over and typed numbers. Finally, around 8:00 p.m., Eliza asked if he was ready to go home.

"I'm actually in a flow, you know? Can I stay here?"

"Um, well." She seemed a little letdown, but he knew she would say yes. They weren't close enough for her to say no. "I guess you can stay here. I'll leave the back door at the house open for you in case I'm asleep."

After Eliza left and the floor seemed empty, he went to Duke's office. Duke's computer was password protected. He texted Eliza, *My computer just died, and I forgot my charger. Do you know Duke's password?*

Try Margie, Eliza wrote back.

He was in. He had no idea what he was looking for.

Most of the files he opened were impossible to decipher. Legal jargon or company forms. He found a strategic update presentation, but the content was benign, even philanthropic. It looked like the family was starting some forest education foundation. On another deck, he learned that Peterson forests sequestered 150 million metric tons of CO_2. He didn't think that was a big deal; after all, planting new trees actually made fires worse. The new fuel burned faster. But that wouldn't be what Bella wanted. He needed more.

He remembered something she had said before their campus Aid for Earth chapter. "You don't become a billionaire by playing by the rules." It had seemed so convincing then, but now he doubted the statement. What the fuck was he looking for?

By eleven, he was as lost as before. He called Bella. No answer. He felt entitled to an answer. Here he was combing through his grandpa's computer at 11:00 p.m.—the least she could do was answer. He called back, and this time she picked up.

"One second." He heard someone else in the background. A familiar man's voice. He couldn't place it. Then the voice was gone, and it was just Bella, intoxicating even from 200 miles away. "Did you find something?"

Her voice thawed his anger. "Not yet."

"Is everything okay?"

"Yes!" He put her on speakerphone so he could type and, to no avail, searched ill-defined pejorative terms like scandal and criminal. "It's just…I don't know what I'm looking for."

Neither did she, he discovered, by the silence on the other line. Then he heard that male voice again, and this time it was unmistakable. "You're at the office?" he asked.

"Uhhh, yes."

"Just you and Brandon?"

"Just, well, yeah. Cole, I need to call you back."

But in a wave of urgency and jealousy, he snapped back, "Wait! You need to give me some direction here. It's almost midnight. I'm snooping on my grandpa's computer. I don't know—"

"Put everything in my Dropbox."

"What?"

"Copy the files and put them in my Dropbox."

When she hung up, he inhaled and then nearly choked on his breath. The door, which he had closed (he had made sure to close), was now open, and in the vacant space stood a man.

"Cole?" The man said with a smile.

"I'm helping Eliza, um, with some—"

The man sat down. He didn't look suspicious or angry but instead, effortlessly casual. One knee on top of the other and hands folded over his stomach. "It's been a long time."

Cole was frozen.

Then the man extended a hand. "Chris. Chris Hill."

Images of Chris Hill filled his mind. Duke's right-hand man. A friendly presence at company Christmas parties. "You have a beautiful family," he remembered his mom saying to him. And he remembered thinking that it was true, and that he liked Chris. Even more so after Chris had said with a big grin, "Stanford, congratulations, you're a genius like your granddad, I can tell." That was the last time they had met, and the last holiday party Cole had attended.

"Um, of course." And he offered a limp and soggy hand.

"What are you looking for?" Chris looked relaxed, amused. He sprung up from the chair and walked around the desk. Cole did not move, could not move. He shuddered.

"I just—"

The search bar was populated with a sole and lonely word: *conspiracy*. Cole, noticing much too late, spazzed over the backspace button.

"Hmmm," Chris said, "conspiracy."

Cole didn't look up at Chris, but he felt his condescension. "It's for a project. I..." He trailed off because he knew Chris had heard his conversation with Bella. Anyone on the floor would have heard.

"I didn't mean to surprise you."

"It's fine." The future, very much not fine, flashed in his mind. An angry Eliza, Bella, Dad, and Duke. How angry? He imagined going to jail. Was this criminal? It had to be criminal. It was Chris's word against his own. "I don't know what you think you heard."

"What?"

Cole realized he had muttered the words, perhaps inaudibly.

"I said," this time louder but still with a tremble, "I don't know what you think you heard."

"I saw conspiracy."

Cole made the mistake of looking up and finding Chris with an enormous grin. "Eliza told me—"

"To look through her dad's files for a conspiracy, of course!"

Cole couldn't stand it. He backed away from the desk. By the door, he was called back. "How about your backpack?"

He went to get his backpack and, in front of Chris, put his things in one by one. It was probably a few seconds, but it felt like a lifetime, and his hands were shaking the whole time. He willed them to stop, but they kept going.

"Hey, it's all right." There was a change in Chris's voice. "Sit down."

"I need to—"

"I'm sorry for messing with you. It's fine. Sit down." Confronted with this new, seemingly compassionate Chris, Cole sat. This time on the opposite side of his interrogator, who took a seat himself in Duke's chair. "I'm not going to get you in trouble. I mean, I don't want to."

Cole found his breath and felt his feet on the floor. An instruction his therapist gave him years ago that he resorted to when besieged by panic. Combined with Chris's patience, it seemed to be working. With newfound resilience, he remembered what he had said to Bella and what she had said back via speakerphone. Was anything here salvageable? Or maybe the conversation had not been heard. "I was just curious why Eliza was stressed. I thought maybe I could find a reason by looking through the files."

"Oh, you and the woman on the phone were curious about Eliza's mood?" The mocking tone was back, and with it, Cole rose. "No. Wait!" Cole sat. "Just tell me what you were looking for, Cole. I don't want to get your aunt or grandpa involved."

"I wasn't going to do anything with what I found!"

"Okay. And what were you snooping for?"

He could at least be honest here. "I swear I don't even know."

"But you were going to copy all the files and send it?"

"I—"

"I heard you say it. Why?"

Cole kept his mouth shut. He kept searching for an out. He couldn't find one. Another lie and he could be done for. "I feel like sometimes," he said at last, "that my family is up to something."

"Conspiracies?"

He shook his head. "It's not like I thought anything would show up."

"You should have searched *evil shit*, maybe then…" Chris stopped himself. "I don't know what you're looking for or what you planned to do with it, but I'll tell you this…there isn't anything on this computer. Before your grandpa left, we did a full security audit."

Cole perked up, sensing an ally. But he couldn't be too sure. "So you're saying there used to be stuff?"

"No. I didn't say that."

"Just please don't say anything. I'll stay out of your way. I'll go back to SF."

"I won't say anything."

It seemed too good to be true. He tried to put himself in Chris's shoes. The inquiry led nowhere, so he found the courage to ask. "Why?"

"You're the grandchild of my boss. What could ratting on you do for me?"

And yet Cole knew, and expected Chris knew, that it was a questionable argument. Duke would value truth, would reward the messenger no matter any inconvenience caused by the message. Duke, Cole reflected, was the king of *tell me the bad news first*. No, he would want to hear.

Cole didn't press the point further. "Thank you," he said. "I know I shouldn't have been…snooping."

As he was almost out the door, Chris called him back. "One more thing."

"Yes."

"If you're curious and want to know more about the work we do, you should go to your grandpa."

"Okay."

"No, really. Go to him. If you're scared to ask, you can read some of his emails."

"Emails?"

"Yeah," he said, so casually. "You know, I send him emails a lot. But there was a good one I sent at the end of August."

"A good one?"

"A board meeting follow-up." He smiled. "I actually have to run. It was good seeing you though, Cole. You're looking good."

Cole didn't know what to say in response, and it wasn't until Chris was in the hallway shutting the door that he managed, "You too."

19

Richard is dying (but so is everyone)

Richard had no time or use for introspection. In college, he shunned drugs because, he told himself, he had no interest in them. Deep inside, perhaps in his inaccessible gut, lived the realization that his aversion to drugs wasn't from a lack of interest but rather from an abundance of fear. He snuck closer to this truth when he tried, for the first and last time, a pot brownie. He was a sophomore at Stanford. The respectable frat boy who could party and did party, but only after finishing his work. Partying consisted of beer and the occasional three, six, or nine shots of vodka.

Alcohol had a unique power to imbue Richard with confidence. After enough drinks, self-doubt would dissolve and a singular narrative would materialize: he was Richard Peterson, successful and charismatic. Everyone wanted to be near him, or even be him. This clarity emerged in his head as his actions became increasingly sloppy. A small price to pay.

He went into his pot brownie experience expecting the same effects. "It's like getting drunk, come on…" his fraternity brother had said, holding the brownie in Richard's face.

Feeling especially adventurous, Richard had consented, eating the whole brownie.

What followed was horrible. "It's laced! It's laced!" He had yelled, stumbling around the frat house, his nails in his scalp and his mouth twisted open. "Bahhh!" And he stormed to his room and shut the door. *What am I? Who am I? Where am I? I'm dying. I must be dying.*

It took him a few days to bounce back, but he did at last, with a newfound resolution to never do drugs. That experience, which had felt like a near-death experience, had been reframed in his mind as merely uncomfortable. But deep down, he knew it had been more than that, and whenever the topic of drugs came up he recoiled. Drinking was different though. Life was especially easy when he drank, but even sober it wasn't so hard. Things remained that way until he was forty-five, in Hawaii, facing a wife who, inconceivably, was "fucking miserable."

Looking in the mirror, in a moment of heightened panic, he asked, *Who am I? Am I dying?* He knew the answer. I'm dying. Face-to-face with his wrinkled skin and saggy neck, it occurred to him that he was dying a little bit more every day. Soon he would be in the ground like his mom and her mom and all the moms and dads that ever were and will ever be.

He was dying, and he had never noticed.

Like he had lost a friend, he looked back to the past, as recent as yesterday, and wished that he had appreciated his ignorance.

He went to the kitchen, to his father's section of the pantry, and found an impressive selection of whiskey. He liked vodka and beer because Duke did not, but now he poured himself whiskey because this opinion, he realized, like so many others, was futile, irrelevant, one card atop a tumbling house of many.

He wasn't drunk, not yet, when Cole called him. He wasn't expecting the call and was sad to realize that his son's face on the vibrating phone made him nervous. Cole wasn't going through a phase any more than Lily was going through a phase. And in that way, mother and son weren't so different: united in a shared resentment toward him.

"Cole, how are you?" He wondered if Cole would hear what he heard: forced exuberance, lingering panic. But Cole seemed unfazed, and they had a surface-level conversation, equal parts disingenuous and easy. Richard realized that his relationship with Cole had always been superficial, and that's why even in the midst of suffering, he could so easily turn on autopilot, returning the ball in a conversational rally, devoid of anything real. If he overstepped, Cole would lash out. They'd argue about politics. Cole would call him evil. He'd call Cole spoiled. It was best to avoid the confrontation and pretend that there wasn't anything bubbling beneath.

"Dad," Cole said when they had seemingly exhausted every prosaic topic, "I want to come visit you in Hawaii."

If Richard had any courage, he would have asked why. But he didn't ask and preferred to assume that Cole missed him, even if he suspected otherwise. "Great," he said. "We'd love that."

RICHARD WAS A FEW DRINKS IN, between buzzed and drunk, when Duke came home. If Duke was surprised to find his son stooped on a kitchen stool with a bottle of Lagavulin, he didn't show it. Instead, he poured himself a glass and sat on an adjacent stool. "Rough day?"

"You know it." And like that, another superficial conversation was in motion. It rattled on until Richard couldn't stand it, perhaps the booze at last rendering the normally tolerable intolerable. "Lily's miserable."

"Is she?" Duke asked, like the statement was no different than the twenty banal ones Richard had made in the minutes prior.

"She's miserable! She told me. I don't know why. It's like…she seemed to say it was my fault. Have you noticed? That she's miserable?" He didn't tell Duke about the pills, that felt like too personal an admission.

Father and son met eyes. Richard squirmed first, attention moving back to his drink. He had looked for compassion in his dad's face, but all he saw was intensity and righteousness.

"Women are fickle things—"

The use of *thing* was unnecessary enough for Richard to tune out the incoming rant, sure from the get-go that it would be fruitless. The man was sexist, keen to bash women, and joke at their expense.

"Was Mom ever…depressed?" He wanted a better word, but wasn't that what Lily was?

"We had our hard times." Duke took a drink. Whatever stories he had would be tough to extract.

"Like?" It wasn't a good enough prompt.

"Women are always on the verge of losing it."

"Even Mom?"

"Everyone, men, women, pick your pronoun," again unnecessary, "everyone wants the same thing. To be noticed, to be respected, to feel like they matter. So tell her you're proud of her, tell her you would have achieved nothing without her. Maybe it's true or maybe it's not. It doesn't make a difference. With your mom, it was true," he added. "I really think it was. I needed her. I didn't say it enough, though. I wish I would have said it more."

Duke's words, which Richard knew were genuine and inspired, still landed badly. They evoked jealously. How could he be jealous of his own mom who wasn't even alive to hear the compliment? While alive, she only knew what Duke called tough love. She never complained, but Richard and

Eliza knew it to be true. Her pride could only disguise so much, even though the mask seemed effective for Duke, who assumed her to be happy even as he verbally berated her and made her feel small. Now he remembered his marriage as some perfect and precious thing, an artifact from a better time, from a better generation.

Perhaps if Duke outlived him—and it was possible, it had never felt more possible—he would tell Cole and Emmett that he had needed his kids, didn't say it enough, and wished he had said it more.

Driven by jealously, spurred by drink, Richard couldn't brush aside the advice. "You could tell us, you know, too." He felt small suggesting this, like he was back in middle school, holding his report card before his dad's unimpressed face.

"I guess I should."

Half-admission, half-dodge, now Richard was unimpressed. "But you won't, huh? You can't say it. Are you proud of me?"

"Of course." But he didn't look at his son when he said it, and there was no feeling in his words.

"I'm on a panel at ALOHA 2028, if you want to come watch? It's a big deal, you know. Even Lily is proud of me for that." That wasn't true but he hoped it would be effective.

"What's that?"

"It's a big tech conference here. One of the biggest tech conferences of the year"

"When is it?"

"Next week. It starts Tuesday. It's three days, but I forget when I speak."

"Maybe. Yeah, maybe. You're gonna talk about that VR stuff?"

"Yeah. And maybe some other investments."

"Oh yeah?"

He knew what his dad was getting at: he didn't have anything to speak about other than Trance. It was his only great deal, the only one people respected him for. Behind his back, he knew other investors called him a one-hit-wonder. Somehow, a few years ago, his dad heard the taunt.

"If you would approve the bitcoin company I could talk about that one…"

"The one in Russia?"

His dad was just stalling again. He had told him about the deal hundreds of times. Duke knew it was in fucking Russia. But maybe this was his chance. "The government is giving them special approval. It's such a unique opportunity."

"Isn't bitcoin terrible for the environment?"

For Duke of all people to ask that question…but he looked serious. Richard allowed himself a sliver of hope. "You know the mining equipment gets pretty hot and so a lot of the emissions come from cooling them down. But that's the beauty of doing this in Russia. It's fucking freezing there. There are fewer emissions and you're not paying as much for electricity."

"But still it's pretty bad, right? For the environment?"

"Dad since when do you fucking care about that! Who cares! It's a great deal. If you don't say yes soon, we're gonna lose it."

"Well, I'm still thinking about it."

Richard wanted to leave, but like a handcuff, his drink kept him tethered. He changed the subject back to Lily and spoke as if his dad wasn't there, more to his drink than to anyone else. "I see all the signs now, clear as day. Little things keep popping up. Each one hurts, each specific incident that I ignored then but now seem so fucking obvious. Even the good moments, and I think that's the worst part of all, are fucked now. Because I feel like while I thought something was good, she was just putting on a little show. Maybe she was deluding herself, I don't know. But I was blind. It's unbelievable. She used to say 'I love you honey' in that sing-song voice. I smiled like a fucking idiot each time. I said it back, you know, 'love you too.' Matching that fucking voice. And you know, it's because she couldn't say it in her real voice. She had to make it a little performance. It was the only way it was bearable."

"You're drunk."

"So? So are you."

Duke was, all of a sudden, suffused with disdain. "I am not." Then, with just as much venom, he said, "Get over it."

"What?"

"Lily says she's miserable, and this is how you react? Get over it."

Richard wanted to get up and leave, would leave the drink in an instant, but was now locked in place by primordial fear. He had been on the wrong side of his dad's tirades before but past experience didn't make things easier.

"Look. You need to hear this."

"Why?" The plea was disregarded, the question taken literally.

"Because you're too soft."

"Fuck you."

"What?" Duke hissed.

"You're an asshole."

Duke expanded, seemingly bursting at the seams with vitriol. "It's my fault. I made your life too easy. I made you soft. You grew up in luxury. I grew up suffering."

Richard had heard this insult before, many times. It was an unfair invective, and when blessed with a clear head, Richard knew why. Duke's upbringing wasn't the depression-era shit-show he made it out to be. Richard knew that Duke had been rich, spent the bulk of his childhood in post-war suburbia, playing baseball and even golf. But Duke, perhaps thanks to conditioning from his own father, really believed he was made from better stuff: hard-worn, tough like leather, a product of grit and grime. Later, Richard would remember this; post-fight he always did. But in the thick of battle, all he could say was, "You played golf too." As he got up from the stool, freed at last, he felt wretched but almost, just almost, victorious.

"What?" Duke called back after him.

And like a twelve-year-old, he prepared to slam his bedroom door, and shouted back, "YOU PLAYED GOLF TOO!"

Unfortunately, the door was unslammable and, slowed by some fancy mechanism before closing, it rendered Richard's outburst anticlimactic, albeit less overtly childish.

20

Emmett finds drugs but for once doesn't take them

Emmett made the unfortunate decision to search his parents' room. He resorted to such a desperate measure only after interrogating his mom and dad about why they were acting so strange and getting the same response from both: *we're fine, don't worry.* They weren't fine, and he was worried.

He wished his parents would be honest with him now, but he understood they wouldn't be. If he asked his mom why she was acting weird, he would get back some dishonest, pacifying response because she didn't think he could handle the truth without turning to drugs and alcohol to cope.

"You know I'm fine, Mom. I'm not an addict." He had tried to reason with her once, just to see if there was any chance he could change her mind.

"Oh, I know. Honey, I know." And she had hugged him as if to say that she knew he was suffering but just didn't want to say it should she make the suffering worse.

He had never understood why she felt this way or how it could be merited until he searched the Maluhia master bedroom. He entered with no expectations, at best hoping he would find his dad's iPad and learn something from intra-marital text messages. Instead, in the bathroom, he found a mess of bottles and scattered pills, too many to count. He learned enough on Google to know that Lily Peterson was being treated for bipolar disorder, depression, and anxiety. He didn't have to look up Ambien but wondered how often and how much she took of it. A few of the compounds were supplements available to anyone, though known to treat the same ailments or, in a few cases, were supposed to suppress appetite or burn fat.

He spent the rest of the day away from the house, wandering through a paradise that his mind was unable to notice, let alone appreciate. In a crude imitation of a TV detective armed with a corkboard, he linked blasé memories to calls for help, petty arguments to evidence of deep suffering. Like when she took handfuls of pills every day. "I have to take my supplements," she always said. He tried to reconcile the mom he thought he knew and the one she so obviously was: over-prescribed, numb to life.

He had never thought about his mom as anything but a mom—and the traits he ascribed to her in his day-to-day musings now seemed archetypal and false. She was chatty like other moms, equally protective, a gossip among friends. But she was concealing something dire, and when alone, he now knew she was none of the things she pretended to be. He imagined her tearful and broken—reaching for the handful of pills every day.

He used to think that his mom's worrying, while uncalled for, was reassuring: proof that she could take care of him should anything go wrong, that she had a maternal drive to protect him and keep him safe. After finding the pill bottles, he no longer believed that she could protect him, even if she wished to. He would have to save his parents. There was no one else.

It was a tremendous burden, and he was only seventeen. He would do anything to be older.

He didn't see or speak to anyone while he was out, and when he got home that night he went straight to bed. When he awoke, he wondered if he had dreamed of the pills and was almost ready to believe it, but each waking moment added another brick of reality, and by the time he was up and in front of his mirror, all hopes were abandoned.

Before escaping the house for the day, he passed Lily in the kitchen. A week prior, he would have seen nothing of significance. A smiling mom asking questions: "Why aren't you eating?" "Where are you going?" "Are you feeling okay?"

He responded as he normally did: "I'm not hungry." "I'm going out." "I'm fine."

Cursed with context though, the scene played out differently in his mind. She was unsure of herself and in her pleas, needy.

He wished he could call Kacey but couldn't do it. After he slept with Chloe, he had called her and told her he needed space to think.

"Is there another girl?" She had sobbed after finally figuring out that "space to think" meant breakup.

"Of course not! I would never," he had to answer. It was that kind of guilt-tripping that made Kacey impossible to be with. If he had wanted to keep sleeping with Chloe or anyone else, he would always hear Kacey in his head—crying and pleading, acting very distressed.

He had many friends, but as he scrolled through his contact list, he realized that he couldn't share the issues with his mom with anyone. They wouldn't understand and it would be embarrassing. Not just the admission, but the sharing itself.

He and his guy friends didn't discuss stuff like this. They talked about sports and girls and how they had each other's backs always. In this case, they might have his back, but what would they repeat to others and what would he become in their eyes? He imagined them walking on eggshells around him, perhaps not passing him drinks and drugs because they imagined some associated trigger, or even worse, walking back jokes in fear that he would be offended.

He had a few girl friends but figured that their allegiance lay with Kacey. And anyway, if he wanted to get with them later, he couldn't show them how weak he felt.

So he scanned his phone to no avail and wondered if he would bear this secret alone for the rest of his life until his mom was dead and even after. He heard her voice in his head lecturing him about the dangers of drugs. "It would kill me," she had said once, "if you ever took too much of anything."

"Mom, what do you think I'm doing?" He had countered. "I smoke weed sometimes, and I drink sometimes."

"I know," but her eyes said otherwise—like she somehow knew about the times he did coke or MDMA or mushrooms or, perhaps most likely, when he went through that NyQuil phase. Now it seemed reasonable that she had expected all these things and more, not because of anything she had seen or heard, but instead because she saw herself in him.

He hated himself for having no friends to talk to, and he hated his dad and Duke for being equally unapproachable. He couldn't give his dad the bad news, and if his dad already knew, then he would have to confront a sad father who did not want to be seen that way by his most doting son. It wasn't something they could talk about. It never would be. With Duke, the visualization was fuzzier but also unpromising. Would he tell Emmett to man up? Or would he take the news right to Lily, confronting her and making a horrible scene? Either outcome was undesirable.

On an impulse, he called Chloe's number. She was quick to pick up. "I'm with my mom."

"Can you get away for a few minutes?"

"Not really."

He thought of something to make her reconsider. "Oh. Well, I just wanted to talk about the working together thing. I think we'll be able to do it."

"Oh yeah, about that, I don't think we need investors anymore."

"You don't?"

"No."

"Well okay. Let's hang out soon?" He was desperate but determined not to sound like it.

"For sure." Then she hung up the phone.

He found himself outside the house as the sun was coming down but did not know if he would go in or keep walking. Both options sounded miserable.

He heard a car and moved to the side of the road and watched as it approached the home. When he heard a familiar voice and then saw a familiar set of shoulders, he walked quickly toward the car, thinking the whole time that he must be imagining it. Cole was in San Francisco, away from this. Lucky to be away from this.

It was Cole, though. Dressed as he always was, black hoodie and jeans and those black shoes with the hidden lifts that made him taller, and which made Emmett sad no one had told his brother the gimmick was obvious and that the shoes looked clownish on his small feet.

Neither brother smiled until they were an arm's length apart, and then they did, concurrently, because it was the polite thing to do.

"How are you?" Cole asked.

"You came to surprise us?"

"Mom and Dad didn't tell you I was coming? I told them."

"Um, well… I'm glad you came." Emmett was surprised to find his arms widening and then more surprised to find Cole's body between them, accepting the hug but keeping his arms inward. They swayed there for a second, and then Cole slid out, mumbling something about too much touching. Still, he seemed pleased by the hug, even sheepish, and Emmett grabbed his brother's bags in a gesture of continued appreciation.

"Why did you come?" He asked as they went into the house.

"I missed you guys," Cole said. "Even you!"

21

Everyone likes Tesla (Even Cole!)

"You seem nervous," Duke said from the passenger seat as Richard pulled his Tesla up to a valet line of Teslas. A man in a yellow vest came running.

"Valet?" asked the man.

Richard handed him his keys without saying anything, and then stepped out of the car. Duke, Emmett, and Cole followed.

Once out of earshot, Duke could complain. "You should have parked in the lot."

"This is their job."

"You trust that boy with your car?"

"It's his job to park cars; that's what he does. That's what he's good at. So yes, he can park my car."

Richard seemed exasperated, so Duke didn't press the issue. Instead, he fell in line behind his son, with his grandsons in step behind him. They made their way toward a massive banner—*AlohaTech 2028 Check-In*. A woman took their IDs and then handed them badges. Duke's read *Duke Peterson—Peterson Ventures*.

"That's not right," he said.

"Dad, come on."

"Has there been a misprint?" the woman asked.

She seemed nice enough to deter Duke from being an asshole. "I guess it's okay."

"You can write your own." She handed him a blank name tag and a Sharpie. He scratched *Duke Peterson—Peterson Lumber Company* and stuck it to his shirt. The result was far worse than the printed one, which, with Richard's logo, at least looked professional, but all the better to make his point.

"Happy?" Richard asked.

"Euphoric. You want to do the same, Emmett?"

Emmett had a Peterson Ventures tag, too, and seemed proud of it. "Well, I work for Peterson Ventures, so…"

"Suit yourself."

Cole asked for a blank tag and a Sharpie. He wrote his name, no title or workplace.

Richard grimaced. "Why do you have to do that Cole? They made you a nice badge."

"Oh…I just."

"He doesn't like VCs," Duke said.

"No. I'm just not a VC. I don't want to be a part of the bullshit."

Duke laughed. "There's a lot of bullshit here."

"There's a lot of bullshit everywhere. No one wants to be honest about anything anymore. Not even me, I guess. It makes me sick. At least I'll be honest about this," Cole said.

Ignoring this, Richard started toward the security checkpoint. The rest followed behind. It was a crowded lobby filled with attendees, mostly men. They all looked very busy. This was Duke's first year at the conference and Richard's fifth. Duke had expected Richard to say as much. Richard liked to tell anyone who would listen how he had attended "the very first Aloha Tech Conference" and how "ATC just isn't the same anymore."

It was a sad claim to fame as far as Duke was concerned. The other investors were bragging about their portfolios and there Richard was, bragging about his conference tenure.

But Richard didn't seem interested in bragging about anything now. He looked wretched. Father and son hadn't had a real conversation since their one about Richard's marriage a week ago. So when he said that he was going to the green room, it was a relief. Duke could roam around alone now, or perhaps with the boys in tow, and mock these insufferable people.

"Which stage will you be on?" Emmett asked, studying a map display of the sprawling complex. There were restaurants, bars, hundreds of exhibition booths, and four stages.

Richard looked down at his badge, which had the eminent caption *Renew Stage Speaker.* "Renew stage is," he traced his finger over the map, "right here. My panel is at twelve, in case you want to watch."

"Of course, we're gonna watch," Emmett said.

"Of course," Cole said, somewhat surprisingly—perhaps feeling bad about his name tag.

Duke said, "See you soon." And just like that, Richard was walking away, lumbering into the crowd until he was out of sight.

Duke, Emmett, and Cole cleared security and found an exhibition hall. Some recognizable companies, so significant that even Duke knew them, had demo booths. There was Microsoft and Alphabet and Richard's magnum opus: Trance. Whatever VR trapping on display was attracting attention—the line stretched into the next booth over. But no Peterson seemed interested in the Trance booth or any other, even as conference reps called them over or approached them directly.

In the food court, an eager man, hand extended outwards, made a beeline for them. "If you don't mind, I noticed your tag," he said, addressing Emmett. "I'm Paul. It's a pleasure to meet you." His hand wiggled, and Emmett shook it. "I'm a founder here to connect with investors. I hope you don't mind me saying hello. I see you work for," he squinted. "Yes, Peterson Ventures."

He looked at Duke's and Cole's tag, then pivoted away. "Well great. I started a company called Hop. So I guess I'll say, Hoppy Thursday. We're a vertical AI platform for quantum technology." The man had a horrific smile, like it was duct-taped to his face.

"We're not interested," Duke said, but Paul didn't go away.

"We're raising our A, but it might as well be a C. You know, those rounds don't mean much anymore. We have big-name contracts about to materialize. And so that's why we're raising money."

Paul, Duke noticed, had an uncanny ability to speak incredibly fast and then abruptly shut up. Now, with no more words, he looked frozen in time, no sign of life on his automaton face. Emmett gave him his number, and, when Paul left, turned to Duke. "My first pitch," he said.

"That guy is a sleazebag," Duke said. "He's pitching every VC here."

Emmett frowned. "I mean, he came on a bit strong—"

"Hoppy Thursday. Jesus. He should go fuck himself."

Cole laughed, Emmett didn't. They sat down at a restaurant. It was 10:45. Duke ordered a beer. "You know," Emmett said, "it was a stupid name, but the idea itself, I don't think it's so bad. A vertical AI platform."

"Maybe you'll love investing," Duke said. "I mean, if you liked that shit, wait until a good pitch. How about you, Cole, you're working for a consulting firm?" Cole looked embarrassed, perhaps afraid that Duke was about to pick on him. Duke clarified, "I think that's just fine. We work with consultants, you know. Maybe one day you could consult for me."

"I think I would like that," Cole said. "I don't think this," he gestured vaguely to the surrounding pandemonium, "is the right fit for me."

Duke perked up. "I think it's awful."

"It feels like Las Vegas or something."

"Yeah, ha. In the middle of this beautiful island. Tech has to ruin this too, you know? Maybe we'll find a forest management startup. I'd tear them a new one."

"When we get back, maybe I can help you with some of your work?"

"What's gotten into you?" Emmett asked.

"What?"

"Since when do you give a shit about Grandpa's work?"

Duke couldn't help but chime in. "Maybe after sitting at a desk all day, pretending to solve pretend problems."

Cole nodded along. "I think that's right." Duke looked at Cole with affection. For so long, he had thought of Cole as intelligent but misguided. At his most charitable, he dismissed Cole's leftist streak as a product of youth. It seemed like he was correct again, especially as Cole started peppering him with smart questions. He knew a lot about forests already. He asked about clear-cutting, harvesting techniques, the sawmills. Duke got the sense that he was being brown-nosed, but it only vaguely annoyed him. A few seconds into an answer, he would get so immersed, so excited, that he forgot his audience entirely.

—

EMMETT COULDN'T BELIEVE what he was hearing. His brother, who behind his grandpa's back had called the lumber company terrorism against the earth, was now groveling. The craziest part was Duke, who Emmett thought so highly of, was eating it up, saying he was "very impressed" by Cole's "great questions." Emmett chimed in, hoping he could get some of the same recognition. But his question about team dynamics (one his dad often asked) was pushed aside in favor of Cole's about elevation range.

Cole had been acting strange ever since he had arrived. It had been five days, and Emmett couldn't recall a single insult, condescending remark, or disagreement. Despite himself, he was becoming jealous of his brother and eager for his attention, like he was seven again and Cole could do no wrong. The brothers had even shared a moment of closeness when Emmett, after a few days of internal debate, decided to partially share what he had found in their parents' bedroom. He wouldn't tell the whole truth, he had decided, just in case Cole turned on them all again, but he dropped a hint. When the two of them were alone, he said, "I'm really glad you're here because Mom and Dad have been off."

Cole didn't look concerned. "How so?"

Emmett said that they weren't really speaking, Dad was moping, and he heard something about Mom being on prescription pills.

"I wouldn't be surprised," Cole said, but then added, in very un-Cole fashion, "Life can be tough on everyone, you know. Maybe it's a rough patch for them both."

The brief exchange was enough for Emmett to feel better. So much so that he arrived at the conference optimistic, once again, that his dad would come through and make everyone proud.

Cole and Duke seemed, if not less optimistic, less excited. When Emmett said, "We should go to Dad's stage," they did not move from the restaurant. Only when he said they would be late did Duke slap a twenty on the table and rise. When they arrived at the auditorium, it was somewhat crowded, and while there were plenty of open seats, the middle rows were taken. Duke pressed forward, approaching a VIP section.

"Sir—" warned an attendant.

"My son is speaking next." Duke pointed to the screen displaying the agenda and then to his tag. "Peterson," he clarified.

"It's just for the VIPs, you have to buy—"

"Come on," Duke said, gesturing them by.

"Sir—"

"Come on, guys, it's fine." They followed his lead. Emmett with curiosity, and Cole with what looked like horror.

The attendant had followed them. "If you're still here after your son speaks, I will have to escort you out."

"Unless I have a stroke, I won't be anywhere near this cesspit."

Emmett hadn't seen his father speak before in public. He would be the first to tell him that he did a wonderful job. He hoped he would do a wonderful job. He expected he would, knowing that this was his dad's fifth time at the conference, but still, Emmett was anxious, remembering his dad's nerves from this morning and his unmissable fatigue and sadness over the past week.

—

COLE HAD SEEN HIS DAD speak publicly once before. Richard had come to Stanford for a venture capital conference, and Cole, even though he had said he was busy, had shown up, wedged in the back of the room where he could not be seen. He remembered feeling a mix of pride and resentment as his dad spoke and then self-resentment as he acknowledged his pride. Money, he reminded himself, doesn't matter. The people who make money get the most respect but contribute the least amount of value. It was the activists, the artists, even the scientists that were fighting for a better world, but it was always the wealthy that got the respect.

Now, about to watch his dad speak for the second time, he had no idea what to expect.

No matter his feelings, he would match Duke's assessment, determined to earn his grandpa's trust as quickly as possible.

A man stepped up on center stage. He introduced himself as one of the conference organizers and a journalist at *TekFox*. He shouted into the mic, "ALOHA, ALOHA TECH!"

There were a few cheers, enough for the mic man to play it off. "Good stuff," he said, "Good stuff! So I'll be moderating this panel, and it's going to be great."

Richard, he explained, would be joined by another two investors to discuss "investing in a better tomorrow." The topic both interested Cole and incensed him. If the other panelists were anything like his dad, they would be full of shit. They and the other very rich benefitted more from the status quo than anyone else. This was their better tomorrow. A tech conference in Hawaii was VC nirvana.

Richard was introduced as the founding partner of Peterson Ventures. "An early-stage investor in Trance and Rosegate." Cole had never heard of Rosegate; he wondered if any techies had.

He was joined on stage by Casey and Dana, who Cole wasn't very surprised to see were men. The panelists were asked about planet-friendly investing, the threat of climate change, sustainable foods. Richard looked tired and nervous but was doing okay. The audience seemed to like his answer to "What do you look for in investments?"

"I'm always looking for the next Tesla," he said, with little passion and just enough enunciation to pass a sobriety test. "The green companies, the sustainable solutions, are among the best opportunities I'm seeing. Every year I meet with thousands of incredible sustainable companies. They're doing stuff with green hydrogen, quantum, AI, blockchain—sometimes all at once, you wouldn't believe it. It's inspiring. It's become my life's work."

"And," asked the moderator, who seemed to be getting increasingly schmaltzy, "why do you care so much? Why is this work important to you?"

"Because," Dana cut in. "This isn't just our planet; this is our kids' planet. They will be here longer than we will be here, and, and it hurts me to say this, it really does, but it's true, we're not doing good enough, we can do better. So every day, I commit myself to doing better. If not us, then who?"

The crowd clapped, and some sorry sucker let out a cheer.

"It's a good point," said Casey. "I don't have kids, but I feel like for us VCs—not to sound self-important, believe me, this is a humbling job—everyone in the world is our child. They're depending on us to keep them safe, entertained, you know, healthy. Without innovation, the world becomes a much worse place, and we are literally the fuel for innovation."

"Let's talk about fuel," said the moderator.

They went around again and again, each investor getting increasingly more applause. Toward the end, though, Richard began trailing off and rambling.

"What are the hardest parts of the job?" The moderator asked Casey.

"The stress, the burden of feeling like humanity is depending on you. I think I do a good job handling the stress. I practice a lot of meditation. I do ice baths, psychedelics. To handle this job, you have to get your ego in check first, or else the stress will get to you, it really will."

"And for you, Richard?"

He was staring, Cole noticed, right at Duke, and then right at Emmett, and finally right at him. Richard's head settled there, his eyes laser-beams, his body slouched but still. "I think it's about the children," he said, "the children are our future."

People still clapped. The moderator moved on, but Cole stayed glued to his dad, who seemed to be quickly losing steam, who still had not stopped staring at his family.

Then his dad's face changed, like he, at last, had the solution to an all-consuming problem. He sat up straight. He looked re-engaged, re-energized. Cole shot Emmett a look, both relieved their dad would make it through just fine.

"I want to keep this last question open-ended," said the moderator. "What's a kernel of wisdom you want to leave people with today? Perhaps something they can take with them and chew on. It can be about sustainable investing or anything else. Dana, why don't you lead us off?"

"Every day when I wake up, I ask myself, what can I do better? Sometimes, I decide that I'll work a little harder, or be more present with my kids, or go for an extra five minutes on the Peloton. I urge you all to ask the same question every day, multiple times a day, twenty times! As much as you can. Everyone else will tell you there's a ceiling, but that's not true. Ceilings only exist in your imagination."

Claps and a couple of cheers. They were sad, desperate people and Cole didn't care about them at all.

Then it was Richard's turn. "Don't believe everything you hear," he said, this time enunciating, this time with good posture. Everyone expected him to say more. He didn't.

"I'm not surprised that people are so depressed," Casey said at last when it became clear that Richard would not speak more. "When you turn on the news or scroll on X or TikTok, all you see is doom and gloom. More fire, more riots, impeachment here, impeachment there. White supremacy, rising seas, wealth disparity—" he put air quotes around wealth disparity, "I urge all of you to turn that shit off and have some faith in humanity. We are building incredible things. I know we are because I'm funding them! The news doesn't tell you about the robot that can perform heart surgery, or the drones that prevent terrorism, or the fact that your wearables will know you're about to have a heart attack before any doctor ever could! I'm not surprised that you're depressed, but after today, you don't have an excuse. Meditate, go in your ice bath, go in your sauna, take mushrooms, ride your Peloton…but most of all, stop whining. If you don't like something, go make it better. Get off the sidelines and join us."

Huge applause, more cheers. "I want to thank each of you—" started the moderator.

Richard interrupted. "I think that's bullshit."

He said it very quietly but enough for the moderator to pause.

Richard spoke louder now, and the crowd was quiet. He didn't look at Casey or Dana when he spoke. He looked right at Duke and Emmett and Cole, who was once again sure that Richard was looking just at him.

"You think my answer was bullshit?" Casey's face was inflated with malice. But Richard didn't notice.

"I think my answers were bullshit too. I think this whole conference is bullshit." Then he stood and, like some preacher, took his microphone to the center of the stage.

Cole wondered if he should do something. Would a more courageous son run up and restrain Richard? Emmett wasn't doing anything. He also looked stunned. Duke whispered, "Your dad's lost it—"

People pulled out their phones; the moderator seemed to be salivating.

Still looking at his family, Richard said more forcefully, "I'm sick of everyone pretending that we're superheroes."

"No one's pretending you're a superhero, Richard," spat Casey, who must have been withholding that venom the whole time.

Richard didn't seem to hear him. "We're not saving the world; we're just saving our world. We all know it." Richard, who hated making a scene, looked unperturbed, even at peace. "I'm in Hawaii because California is literally on fire. Think about that. And when we fuck up Hawaii, we'll go somewhere else."

"Panel's over," Dana said.

"I know that I'm full of shit. I don't know if me saying that matters."

"Get off the stage!" Someone shouted. But then, one or two people started to chant, "Richard. Richard. Richard…"

Cole started to chant too. So did Emmett. Duke looked riveted.

Richard waited for the noise to die down before he continued. Now with a somber face, he said, "Don't believe everything you hear. Everyone has an agenda. They'll lie to you. You'll see, they'll lie. The hypocrisy has to end."

—

RICHARD DIDN'T HEAR THE CLAPPING, the cheers, or the much louder jeers. He staggered through the outer hall in a daze. A man came up to him. "That was amazing," he said. "Really, really amazing. Heroic, even."

"Oh. Thank you."

He grabbed Richard's hand. "My name is Paul. You said you were looking for the next Tesla. Well, wait until I tell you about Hop!"

22

Lily, very fleetingly, feels bad for Patricia

Lily spent her days walking, often only stopping for water or a snack (she allowed herself almonds and the occasional cashew). She also stopped to write in her notebook. This was a new habit inspired by Patricia's love for journaling. Lily had written *Insights* on the front cover, and she was about halfway through its 200 pages.

She wrote with a bold black pen; she underlined and capitalized words; in some cases, she drew geometric patterns along her borders.

When she let herself fantasize, when she really let go, Lily imagined that in the future her journal would be an important book. Scholars would devote time studying its motifs, patterns, even contradictions. They would discuss it at schools and universities.

Would future readers deem the author a genius, a child, a lunatic? Sometimes what she wrote made sense. For example, there were five or six pages chockfull of specific memories from childhood. Good ones and bad ones and ones that she didn't know how to brand but knew they had to be significant since she hadn't remembered them until that moment.

She wrote, *I was on my mother's lap bouncing up and down and laughing, and then my dad came in. He had his shirt tucked in, and when he was in a good mood, I would put my hands on his protruding belly and say, "Squishy squishy." I remember assessing if this would be one of those times and deciding, upon hearing his voice and reading his face, that it was obviously not.*

Sometimes her insights didn't make sense. She wrote them down anyway. Partly because why the fuck not, but also because maybe, just maybe, they obscured genius, truths not yet accessible to their creator. Like *beneath the layers of soot and silk is the unknowable strength of serenity.* This just came to her, while she was walking, the words like flowers in a field ripe for picking and arranging and preserving in the notebook.

When Lily walked with Patricia, she didn't write in her notebook. Any spontaneous insights were filed away, although in most cases forgotten in a few seconds. When a thought seemed appropriate, she would say it out loud, and Patricia, in her no-nonsense way, would either nod along or add fuel to the fire. These disclosures were more presentable than those in the journal. Often Lily would reflect on a memory or relationship and draw a line to her present state or more recent past. "I think I was so stressed my whole childhood, constantly doing things. Piano and pageants and school and volunteering. It was pedal to the metal twenty-four seven, and then all of a sudden, I had nothing to do but be Richard's wife. Like he had no problem with me not working and not doing anything, and it was so tempting. But you know, I miss doing things. It feels so worthless just to sit around."

"You were feeling burned out when you met Richard." Patricia knew just what to say to make Lily keep talking.

"Exactly! Burned out, and more than that, Richard was like the life event that said it was okay to burn out. Because I had achieved what I had set out to achieve, or, well, what my mom said I had to achieve. It was always about a good marriage, you know? And anyway, I went from a hundred and twenty percent to like five percent. Even in college. I was taking hard courses, and then I was taking classes with the athletes, you know sociology and…not that I'm saying sociology was easy, it was just those certain—"

"I was a sociology major."

"Oh, I didn't mean—"

"I'm fucking with you."

Lily grinned. Patricia was the only person she knew who fucked with her. "When I was a kid, I was so sure I wouldn't grow up to be boring. If that kid could see me now, what would she think?"

"You still have time."

There was a section of the notebook, less stream-of-consciousness than the rest, called *goals*. Some were underlined, like *Travel BY MYSELF* and *Meditate MORE*. The underline was a way of saying this goal was a sure thing. The more speculative ones were followed by a question mark. *Try Psychedelics?* And *Have an affair?*

She decided to share this last one with Patricia. The fantasy had been weighing on her mind for the last few days. She had thought about sharing it on other walks but hadn't yet summoned the courage. Today though, in the middle of September, now very comfortable with her new friend, she decided that it was time. She had never considered herself the type of person who would have an affair, and for her to do so would be proof that she had changed—that she wasn't the *"perfect little wife,"* something Richard often would actually call her. "You're a perfect little wife…"

And she would giggle as if consenting to the role. Sick Lily, under Richard's thumb, pretended to like it; if she fucked someone else, she would still giggle perhaps, but more sinisterly. *If only you knew.* Which was getting to the darker side of the impulse. Richard didn't know what it was like to suffer. Well, this week, perhaps he was suffering, but it was long overdue. And even if she wouldn't tell him about the affair, which was still nebulous in her mind, knowing how he *would* feel if he *did* know, would be enough. She would sleep better knowing that she had that over him. He would be the *perfect little husband* plodding along in fantasy land.

"I'm gonna tell you something," Lily began.

"Okay."

"Don't judge me." It was a habitual but unnecessary disclaimer; Patricia seemed to love it when Lily was provocative.

Lily waited until they were clear of a passersby and near the koi pond. "I want to cheat on Richard."

Patricia's mouth contorted into a frown.

"I mean, I don't *really* know if I want to—" Lily managed, hoping to deflect some of the awkwardness. To make matters worse, they had stopped walking, and Lily had no choice but to look into her friend's motionless face, bewitched by its ferocity.

Then, as if she, too, had been under a spell, Patricia shook it off, shrugged, and started to walk. Lily followed suit, refusing to speak first. But her resolve only lasted a few seconds. "You think that's a bad idea?" she asked.

Patricia shrugged again. "I don't know."

"You just seem annoyed all of a sudden."

"I'm not annoyed," but her tone was very annoyed.

Then Lily understood. The realization wasn't shocking, not at all when she considered the circumstances, but still had unmissable power, changing the way she saw Patricia. Not for better or worse, but altering that picture of her that, until then, had been static. "Your husband cheated on you!"

Patricia looked surprised and then reverted to indifference. "It doesn't matter," she said.

For the first time since meeting Patricia, Lily felt bad for her. Not in a pitying way—she tried to demonstrate that by not acting *too* interested—but more in an empathetic way. Patricia, too, had problems. Of course, Lily understood this rationally. But day-to-day, she had lived with the belief that Patricia didn't. She was an uncanny example of realized potential. Now she was, if less venerable, more relatable.

"Do you want to talk about it?" Lily asked.

"I don't think so."

They were cutting back through the flower garden and soon would be going back toward the beach and their homes. It seemed like Patricia had picked up the pace. "I didn't mean to sound so surprised," Lily said.

"I know."

"It's just…" Patricia was walking very fast, at an almost uncomfortable pace for conversation. "It's just it made sense why you thought me doing that was so bad," Lily explained. "I wasn't actually going to do it, you know? I just wanted to be funny."

"Mhm-hm."

"You don't believe me?"

"No, I do. You wouldn't cheat. You don't have it in you."

"What? Can we slow down?"

Patricia looked annoyed but slowed down. They stopped by some *Birds of Kauai* infographics. "I didn't know the Nene Goose was the state bird," Patricia said.

"What do you mean I don't have it in me?"

"Look, I'll say this once, and then I don't want to talk about it again, okay?"

"Okay—"

"The truth is, and this is going to sound, I don't know, cold-blooded… look, the cheating was the best thing to ever happen to me. It sounds crazy, but it's true. I didn't like myself back then. Frankly, and I think I've said this, I was a lot like you. Do you know how much better it feels to not give a fuck? I can go to Hawaii whenever I want, at the drop of a pin. But not just Hawaii, I can go *anywhere*. I can go to India. I can go to Iran. If I want to

172

work, I work, and I do a better job. If I want to fuck somebody, I can do it, you know? And you can't. " She exhaled. "You look mad. I'm offending you."

"No." And then to prove that she was not offended, "I want to do those things too." There was an awkwardness between them now that Lily hadn't felt since their first few meetings. She had to change the subject to something Patricia would want to talk about.

"I can invest in your company, by the way," she said.

"Really!" Patricia's face lit up. "What are the next steps?"

"Um…"

"Text me your email address, and I'll send you docs. What do you think makes sense, fifteen million? I know it's a small investment. I just can't take on much more cash right now. This is great news! I'm so excited for you. I'm so excited for *us*."

The awkwardness was gone. They walked back to the pool. "Dream team!" Patricia said again, shaking Lily's shoulder.

23

Cole (for more than ten seconds) is a good brother and son

Emmett and Cole had always fought. When they were younger, they fought with their fists. Cole, five years older, always won, but that didn't stop Emmett from asking for it.

And yet, it was never a relationship defined by violence. Emmett idolized his older brother. When Cole stopped eating fish, so did Emmett. When Cole listened to rock music, so did Emmett.

Then Emmett got taller and more popular. People gravitated toward him in a way they never did with Cole. By the time he was in eighth grade and Cole was a senior, Emmett decided that he didn't want to be anything like Cole. Now that they were older, though they didn't fight with their hands, the fights were worse. Emmett knew just what to say to provoke Cole. Even better than a stealthy slap was the charge, "You have no friends," or "You've never kissed a girl." His brother would shrivel up, redden, and then scream back. "You are so stupid," "You're a retard," "How the fuck does anyone's brain move so fucking slowly?"

Emmett, who knew Cole was much smarter, would scream out in defensive agony, "At least I'm not a fucking freak! Everyone thinks you're such a freak!"

Like the fistfights, these blow-ups went away. When Cole got into Stanford, Emmett was actually proud of his brother, even though part of him had hoped Cole would be rejected. He still thought that Cole was brilliant.

Those conflicting parts remained as Cole left for Stanford and proceeded to return home as little as possible. They had three trips to Maluhia together, where they more or less stayed civil. Cole read while Emmett golfed, and when they met for dinner, they spoke like long-acquainted, albeit distant dinner guests, constrained by decorum and presumed maturity.

On the ride home from the conference, neither brother spoke, but they shared a comfortable silence in the back seats, sometimes glancing over at each other when the awkwardness between Duke and Richard became impossible to ignore.

Duke called Richard's performance "foolish but ballsy."

"What does that mean?" Richard looked sick, eyes glued to the road ahead.

"It means what it means."

Back at the house, Emmett snuck away and pulled down his blue duffel from the top of his closet. He was the only one in the family tall enough to reach it. He looked through the contents. Bags of cocaine, bags of weed, some mushrooms, LSD, and then in the side pocket, a vial of ketamine lozenges.

He took out the vial, zipped the duffel, and returned it to its hiding place. With the ketamine in front of him, he considered dosage. He was overwhelmed, perhaps slightly sad. Was it his dad's panel? To him, it had been more foolish than ballsy. Or was it Cole's return? His former tormentor, all of a sudden playing nice.

The only thing he knew for sure was that he was overwhelmed. He would take a lot, then run to the beach and zone out for an hour. Vanquish his thoughts entirely. He counted out the white chalky spheres. Ten would do.

The door swung open. He dropped the vial, and the remaining lozenges fell on the floor. He held his ten with a death grip.

His mom was looking at him and then looking at the floor. "Emmett—"

"Knock, Mom! Jesus!"

He moved in front of the spilled vial. She walked around him and bent down. "Emmett, honey." He sensed her budding worry before it was full-fledged. She picked up the vial. "What is this?"

"Um." So Lily knew every other type of drug, just not this one.

He cursed Google as she typed on her phone. "HORSE tranquilizer?"

"Mom, it sounds worse than it is."

"You couldn't just take a human dose? You needed a horse dose." Her eyes were welling up. "Richard!" She called out.

"No, Mom!"

His dad and Cole entered.

"He's taking horse tranquilizer!"

"What?" his dad said.

"Look!" She handed over her phone and the vial.

"You're one to talk," Richard mumbled.

"Really? Now? You're gonna pull that shit now?"

"I was just…"

"Just what? Our son is taking horse tranquilizer, and you take it out on me?" Cole took the vial.

"How much does a horse even weigh?" She typed, then exclaimed, "Nine hundred to two thousand pounds!"

"Mom, it's okay," Cole said. "It's a popular drug. They're studying it at Stanford and psychiatrists are prescribing it."

"To humans?"

"Yes."

She actually seemed to relax a little. Emmett picked up the lozenges on the floor. He put them back in the vial, then she snatched it away.

"We're going to talk about this." She said it just to Emmett, like there was no one else in the room. "We're gonna figure this out. It's okay."

"Let me talk to him," Cole said. She looked back and forth between them. "I can talk to him," he said again, this time more strongly.

She still seemed unsure.

"I'll talk to Cole," Emmett interjected. He didn't want to talk to anyone, but figured a compassionate Cole was better than his reeling mom. He followed his brother to the door and wondered if his dad was thinking what he was thinking: Mom had probably just found her new drug of choice. It was just a matter of time.

They walked to the main road, and when the house was far behind them, Cole laughed. "You brought ketamine?"

"Just to try."

"Sure."

"Well, thanks for helping. That could have been bad."

"Seems like you need all the help you can get."

"It was bad timing too. I found a bunch of pills in Mom and Dad's room."

"Yeah, you said Mom was on prescription pills."

"Yeah, but…I mean, I found them on the floor of the bathroom. And not like a few. Like a lot of them."

"Why can't you guys keep your pills off the floor."

Emmett shook his head.

"How many?"

"I don't know, like fifteen or twenty different bottles. Prescriptions and supplements."

"Fifteen or twenty bottles?" Now Cole sounded concerned too.

"Yeah. Well, like bottles and vials, you know?"

"Okay."

They sat on grass away from the trail, overlooking a pocket of trees and flowers, with the ocean further out. "I think this is a nice spot," said Emmett.

"Twenty?"

Emmett communicated as best he could. Naming some of the prescriptions he remembered, most significantly trying to convey the disarray. "She had dumped them out, or maybe Dad had. They were scattered all over, the pills, all different colors."

"Do they know you saw?"

"I don't think so. Someone picked them up later."

"Why didn't you call me?"

Emmett ignored the question and drew with his shoe in the dirt. "It's just, I never thought of her like that, you know?"

"I know."

"Do you think we should talk to her? After this ketamine shit, it probably won't go over well."

"I don't know." Then Cole stood and stepped away. Emmett kept drawing in the dirt as his brother looked off into the distance, and he didn't know what Cole would say when he turned around, but it felt like their relationship would never be the same, for better or worse. They had never spoken about something like this. Perhaps because nothing like this had occurred before. But here they were, having their first adult conversation, and he didn't feel anything like an adult. He hoped that his brother would reveal himself as one, perhaps as the Cole that he remembered: so fucking smart. If Cole came back with a recommendation or direction, he would accept it because the alternative, stewing in misconception and confusion, was much worse.

Cole turned around. "It'll be okay," he said. "We'll talk to her. We can figure it out. She's still our mom."

"We'll talk to her together?"

"Yeah. We can do it together. Maybe not right away. We should give it some time after this."

"Yeah."

"And," he added, now looking away, "I have to go back to SF first and wrap something up. But I'll come back after! And we'll talk to her, and Dad too. We'll be okay."

"I don't think I can be here alone."

"Just do your thing, and I'll be back as soon as I can, and we'll figure it out. Who knows how bad it is, anyway. Maybe we're missing something. The drugs were prescribed, right?"

"I guess. I mean, some of them you can buy right off Amazon. Like the Skinny Gal and Bliss Boost."

"Bliss Boost?"

"Bliss Boost."

"Well, at least it's on Amazon. She's not some black-market buyer…."

"Well, we don't know…do we?" Emmett asked.

"No," Cole conceded, "we don't know, but we will." Then Cole sat back down. "Let's be better to each other," he said after a while.

"Okay."

"We're not always so good to each other."

"Did you take my ketamine?"

"No, I'm being serious."

Emmett decided to be serious too. "I feel like you hate us."

"What?"

"Me and Mom and Dad and Grandpa. It feels like you hate us."

"I don't hate you."

"Dad and Grandpa agree with you more than you think, you know?"

"What do you mean?"

"Just about the earth burning and society collapsing and all that stuff. They think you could be right."

He sighed. "We'll see. I guess."

"That's why you're always angry? Because you don't think we believe you?"

"I don't know." Then thinking more about it, "Sometimes, but sometimes I just get angry. I'll try not to. I don't hate you guys."

They listened to the wind. Emmett thought about something to say, but nothing came to mind.

—

AFTER ENSURING THAT DUKE and his dad had indeed left to go fishing, Cole entered his grandpa's room and found his laptop on the bedside table. He dropped it in his backpack and, without saying a word to anyone, left the house and headed to one of the Maluhia cafes. It was one of the less popular spots on The Preserve, and he was practically the only one in the restaurant.

Even though he knew Duke was fishing, the prospect of his grandpa coming in and seeing him was stomach-turning. He tried to cover the front of the laptop with a menu and positioned himself so he was facing the door, just in case.

Luckily, the laptop had the same password as Duke's desktop in Redding: *Margie.* With Bella out of his sight, the whole mission felt that much more absurd. He was telling the truth when he said that he wanted to come to Hawaii. He felt a gut-wrenching pain when he thought about his mom, and then his dad having to deal with her, and then his brother having to deal with them both. Here he was, though, hiding away with his grandpa's laptop, digging for dirt.

All he had to do was send one text, and it would all go away.

Hey, he typed to Bella. *I can't find anything in his email. I've looked all over. Sorry.* After clicking send, he felt, all of a sudden, much better. The waiter approached. "I'd love a beer."

"Can I see your ID?"

On his phone, he saw three dots. Bella was typing. *What do you mean? You said there were emails.* The beer came.

I can't find them.

He took a sip. He waited for her to say it was okay. He might have to quit Aid for Earth. He might have to give up on his dream of being with Bella. That was okay. He knew she didn't like him. He had hoped that things would change, but they wouldn't, and that was okay. He could stay here with Emmett. He could find another job.

Not with the family. He wouldn't stoop that low. But he wouldn't ruin them. He wouldn't prove that he hated them.

She sent him a longer message.

I know this is hard, Cole, but I need you right now. He heard her voice as he read. *If there is any way that you can find something to help me, I would be so grateful. I was thinking a lot about you this week. I can't imagine what it feels like to betray your family. I don't think that's what you're doing, BUT I know it might feel like that. You're one of the bravest people I know, and I don't want you to give up! I'll make it up to you!*

He reread it. It felt like he was being pulled apart by two forces, equally strong and equally malignant. *I need you…I'll make it up to you!* He decided to look, just to see if something was there.

As he expected, his grandpa was still logged into his Gmail. Cole searched *Chris Hill.* He had to go back a few pages to find emails from the end of August. There were dozens. He thought about what Chris had said: it was something about a board meeting. About halfway down the page, there it was: a two-email thread. *Subject: Board Meeting Follow-up*

Duke—I didn't communicate my point effectively in today's meeting and I appreciate the opportunity to circle back. I'll keep this short and to the point. While I mentioned ethical concerns, the far more important consideration is business risk. If this were to get out, the repercussions for the company could be far more significant than what we have to gain by silence. You've always let me speak my mind, and I'm asking you to consider a more reasonable approach where we cooperate and help Chester. I suggest we take this off-line and discuss. Thank you, Chris

Duke responded two hours later: *How would it get out unless we say something??? I'm very disappointed.*

It wasn't a jackpot, and he didn't know what to make of it, but it was a lead, and maybe enough to make Bella happy.

I might have something, he wrote.

She responded with a heart emoji.

Whatever I send you, whatever you get, you have to PROMISE me that it won't come back to me.

It won't.

Okay, I'm sending you two emails between my grandpa and his coo.

He forwarded the thread to his email and then deleted it from Duke's sent folder. Then, from his phone he forwarded the message to Bella, just as she was sending him another text. *You're doing the right thing.*

He cleared Duke's browser history and charged his beer to the family account. He ran home and went right to his grandpa's room. Still empty. He put the computer where he found it.

There were three new messages from Bella. She wrote,

This is shady stuff. Thank you!

Great work Cole.

She sent some more heart emojis.

He felt sick and used and had to keep reminding himself that he was fighting for a better world. Really though, he knew that he was fighting for Bella.

Maybe it wasn't a big deal. Maybe it was something small. But what if it wasn't? And if it was a big deal, what if it came back to him? Then what would Emmett think? For the first time in a long time, they had a chance to be close. He would ruin that too.

Bella, it can't come back to me. You have to promise.

It won't.

She didn't promise. He needed her to fucking promise. He heard shuffling outside his room. He couldn't talk to anyone, not now. He waited for the shuffling to subside then snuck into the hall and went out the door.

24

Bella sends a mysterious email

Bella started knocking and then didn't stop. Even after Brandon screamed "COMING!" from the inside of his apartment, even when she heard him fidgeting with the lock. When he finally opened the door, she stormed past him. "Did you get my messages?" She dropped her backpack and didn't stop moving. Since getting Cole's email, she hadn't stopped moving.

"Is everything okay?" her Uber driver had asked on the ride over.

"Excuse me?"

"You're shaking!"

Bella had looked down to see that her right leg was dancing on the floor mat. She wasn't even embarrassed. At first, the email hadn't made sense, but after a few searches, it did. Chester had burned down in the Lasco fire— a fire *very* close to Peterson land. Maybe it was an accident, but they were somehow responsible. They had to be. She knew it.

"All those people who died in Chester," she told Brandon, "who lost their homes, it's because of Peterson Lumber! Don't you see?" She was pacing before Brandon.

"What?"

"Did you see my messages?"

"I saw them."

"And?" At last, she stalled, open-armed, starved for recognition.

"I think it's interesting."

"Interesting?" She went from expectant to apoplectic. "Are you fucking kidding me?"

"What? There's nothing conclusive." He wore that teasing smile that she usually found attractive. Now she wanted to slap it out of him. Instead, she opened up her computer. "I saw the email," he said again.

"Clearly not!" She pulled it up and for emphasis highlighted *I'm asking you to consider a more reasonable approach where we cooperate and help Chester.* "Don't tell me you're not going to do anything. I'll bring it somewhere else. I'll quit right now, in a heartbeat."

"Whoa. Slow down. I'm not saying we're not going to do anything. We just need to talk it through. This isn't enough."

She was about to push back but collected herself. He went to make her a drink. She sat down on the couch, and when her leg started to shake, she steadied it. He came back with a tequila on the rocks, her drink of choice. "No, thanks. I'm good."

She realized she was getting carried away, that all the energy and anxiety wouldn't make the next few hours better or her actions more effective. But it was easier to wrestle and wrap herself tighter than to relax and slip free.

Since joining Aid for Earth, she had waited for a moment like this one. She had spent her few months on the job pushing papers. Her Aid for Earth peers, Brandon included, weren't like the men and women she had revered. Instead of Malcolm Xs and Susan B. Anthonys, she was working with grandstanders and desk jockeys.

When she logged into TikTok and Instagram, she saw her Stanford and high school friends on beaches and in rainforests and at 5-star resorts. Meanwhile, a click away, she would field private messages from her uncle and cousins in New Orleans. They weren't vacationing in the Bahamas. Climate change would only make things worse for them. There could be other hurricanes like Katrina. Eventually, there would be. And she would see all of this and think about the future and hear that calling that she had been hearing for a long time to do something about it all.

Now, finally, she had ammo. But here was Brandon telling her to ease off, calm down. "So," she asked, "what will we do?"

"I already reached out to a reporter."

"Okay, good. Someone you know?"

"Yes. She covered Aid for Earth when we were still hot."

Bella knew what he meant. This was the first time he was admitting, albeit subtly, that the organization had lost its buzz. "We'll be back," she said. They sat down at his coffee table, and he brought up his phone contacts. "Sandra Perry," she read. "*Wall Street Journal*...you're kidding me?"

"She's always been fair."

Bella searched Aid for Earth in Perry's articles. There was a piece about the Martha Clancy protests. A quick skim showed that Perry was anything but fair. "Looters in the house," she read aloud. "That's bullshit. No one looted the house."

"You guys tore it apart. There was nothing left to loot."

"Clancy was a hypocrite and a hack."

"Do you want to call the *Stanford Bugle* instead?"

She didn't correct him with *Stanford Daily*. She let her glare say it instead.

He softened. "I already sent Sandra the emails. Let's just hear what she thinks?"

The phone rang four times, then Sandra answered. "Mm-hmm."

"Sandra, it's Brandon."

"I know." It wasn't rudeness as much as impatience, although Bella wasn't impressed. The next minute of small talk didn't help. Sandra said she was working on a big story. She may as well have said she didn't want this one.

"I'm here with an associate," Brandon explained. "She's the one that obtained the emails."

He gestured for her to speak. "Hi, Sandra." He kept gesturing. "I'm Bella. It's a pleasure to speak with you."

"Mm-hmm."

"Brandon says he sent you the emails?"

"Yeah, you know, I read them. It doesn't seem like there's anything there. And how did you even get these emails?"

She spoke franticly, "See at first I didn't know if there was anything there either, but then I realized that Chester burned down in the Lasco fire and Lasco was just an approximate location and the Peterson Lumber company owns…"

Sandra interrupted, "But you're saying that. The emails don't say that."

"But they basically do."

"Unless you can get me a source to say what you're saying, there just isn't enough here."

Sandra laughed. Brandon shrugged. Bella wanted to throw the phone. Instead, she pressed on, "I said I wouldn't share his name."

"Look, Brandon and, I'm sorry, I forgot your name?"

"Bella."

"Brandon and Bella. It's not a story until we get a source to come forward. At best, the email can be part of a bigger story."

"There are other places that we can send it."

"I'm sure there are, but we have standards here."

"Look," Brandon said, "we appreciate your time. We would prefer you to write the story. If we get you a source or some more evidence, you'll write it?"

"Yes, *if* they can make it a story."

After he hung up, Brandon asked about Cole.

"No chance."

It should have ended there. As much as she wanted the story out, and she couldn't imagine anything she wanted more, she had given her word. More so, she couldn't compel Cole to speak on the record. He didn't want his name attached to the leak, let alone his name printed. No matter what she said, though, Brandon was unconvinced.

"He's obsessed with you." There was jealousy there, perhaps spite. "He'll do anything for you."

"He won't do this."

"You should see the way he eyefucks you. It's pathetic."

"Stop it. We're in this position because of him. Because of him, we have our first shot in a long time at doing something big."

"So you like him now?"

She didn't. She found him needy. But she was used to needy men. What made her feel gross in his case was her actions, more than his. She pretended to enjoy his company and to appreciate his mind. She pretended like they were friends. She was her most disingenuous with him.

With Cole, she said the right things. She pulled him along, and as long as she kept him close enough, she knew he wouldn't stray.

Part of her, though, did appreciate him, despite everything else that she found so off-putting. He was like everyone she hated in almost every way, except he said he was willing to do something about it. Whether it was genuine or not was another question. "I'm not saying I like him, but I won't throw him under the bus."

"It doesn't matter anyway," he said. "Sandra barely thinks we have a story."

"Sandra is wrong. The right story would show the world that one of the richest families in America started a fire and destroyed a town. I could write that story in my sleep."

"How about the guy who sent the email…Chris?"

It was worth trying. According to Cole, Chris had even tipped him off about the emails. She started to draft a message as Brandon watched over her shoulder.

"There's no rush."

"Brandon, half that town is still living in hotels. They all know someone who had to go to the hospital. Some people died. And you want to sit on this?" She didn't wait for his response and sent the email.

Subject line: *Chester*.

Body: *I heard you want to make things right.*

"It's a very mysterious message," Brandon said.

She shrugged. "Now what?" he asked.

They didn't have to wait long. In minutes, a response came in. It had a phone number. Bella stood and was pacing, all the excitement from the evening again in full swing. "Okay, okay," she spoke more to herself, "so we need him to agree to go on record?"

"Or at least talk to Sandra."

"Let's do this."

"Bella, just hang on a moment…"

She put her phone on speaker and paced with it in hand. Brandon stayed seated.

"Hello," Chris sounded calm.

She tried to explain her reason for the call.

He cut her off. "Cole sent you some emails." Again, there was only calmness, but she still reeled at the charge. Especially because she hadn't mentioned Cole. Some quick thinking, though, and it all added up. He was expecting this very call, wanting it, perhaps. At minimum, he had googled her after reading her email. One quick search, and he would find that she and Cole were in the same Stanford class.

"So you have the emails," he continued, "what now?"

"Well, we can do a number of things. We can post them on the internet."

"Or…"

"Or…" she repeated.

186

"I can speak with a reporter."

"You would do that?"

"No."

Bella scoffed. "Okay then—"

"What's the reporter's email address?"

Bella looked to Brandon. He pulled up Sandra's email and she read it off. When she was done, he hung up.

"What the fuck was that?" She asked.

Brandon shrugged. "I don't know. I guess we have to wait."

"We have to wait…"

"Yeah, nothing to do but wait."

25

Emmett gets KO'd by an iPad

Emmett would have expected Cole to stay silent during the ketamine incident. Instead, his brother had come to his rescue. Whether the moment was an anomaly or evidence of real change, Emmett didn't know. But he was desperate to find out. If Cole was still being nice, he would show him the waterfall—a secret that he only shared with his very best friends or, as in the case of Chloe, more important conquests.

He walked to his brother's room and knocked. No answer. He knocked again. He could have sworn he had heard his brother moving about twenty minutes ago. He stepped into the bedroom just in case Cole was asleep or listening to music, but the room was empty. Cole's laptop and iPad glowed on the desk.

When the iPad buzzed, Emmett approached. He looked down, more curious than suspicious. Cole, as far as Emmett knew, had few friends. This seemed to be a work text. From the lock screen, he read a message from someone named Bella Jones.

Thank you again for sending those emails. I know it's hard to go against your family.

He tried to click into the message, but the iPad was locked. It was a numerical password. He entered Cole's birthday. He was in and could see the whole message thread. For someone so smart, Cole had set a very stupid password.

Emmett read a long message from Bella, "*I know this is hard, Cole, but I need you right now. If there is any way that you can find something to help me, I would be so grateful. I was thinking a lot about you this week. I can't imagine what it feels like to betray your family. I don't think that's what you're doing,*

BUT I know it might feel like that. You're one of the bravest people I know, and I don't want you to give up! I'll make it up to you!"

At first, he didn't understand, but then he reread the message. His confusion crumbled. He imagined Cole in front of him, his condescending ugly smirk. That smile always meant the same thing: *I hate this family.*

He sat down in the desk chair. Anger boiled, then simmered, boiled, then simmered again. Maybe he had it wrong. He always jumped to conclusions and was probably missing something. He hoped he was missing something.

He read more messages. Cole wrote, "*Okay I'm sending you two emails between my grandpa and his coo.*"

Cole was sending her company secrets.

Emmett slunk to his room. He considered leaving to find his brother and confront him. But he was frozen in place. The prospect of a confrontation was abhorrent. To face his brother would make the horror show real.

He went back to Cole's room to read from the iPad. Even as he moved toward it, he wished he were going anywhere else.

This is shady stuff. Thank you!

Great work Cole.

Emmett picked up the iPad, ready to smash it on the desk, but then he heard a door open. He quickly put it down and stepped out of the room. It was his dad and grandpa. "Emmett—" Duke started. Then squinting, "Are you okay?"

"I'm late for something. I have to—"

"Is this about the drugs?" his dad asked.

He shook his head.

"What's going on? Come sit down." Duke sat down at the table and gestured Emmett to do the same. Emmett had never disobeyed his grandpa, and by reflex, he obeyed. Richard took a seat as well. Richard didn't look too concerned about his son. He was so obviously not present, and his face changed as different thoughts arose then faded. Duke, conversely, wouldn't let Emmett out of his gaze.

"How was fishing?" Emmett managed.

"It was fine," said Duke. "Your dad is in a rut." Richard shrugged. Duke continued, "He caught a massive blue marlin." He pulled his hands apart in demonstration. "But he didn't even care. Anyone would have been excited, but he didn't even smile."

Richard shrugged again. "It was just a fish."

"Just a fish! I don't understand you at all." Then, turning to Emmett, "So what's wrong?" Beneath the directness, there was a flash of compassion, and Emmett was so surprised and in need of kindness that he broke down, sniffing tears back and looking down in shame.

Only now did Richard look, and his face turned from absent to concerned. "Emmett, what happened?"

"I don't know. I just…" Then it occurred to him that he would tell the truth, not just about Cole but about everything. "This trip has been shit."

Duke smiled. He must have been thinking that he would make everything better with a good pep talk, one that he had given both his grandsons many times. Except Emmett knew that this time was different. There would be no pep talk.

He looked at his dad. "I saw Mom's pile of pills."

Richard looked unsurprised. "She's unhappy," he said.

"What kind of pills?" Duke asked.

Emmett deferred to his dad, who didn't seem like he was interested in responding, but at last said, addressing Duke, "Yeah, I didn't tell you before, but she's on some meds. They're all supposed to make her happy. She dumped them all out the other day. Emmett, I guess, saw them."

"Well, that's good," Duke said. "She shouldn't be taking so many pills."

"No, she shouldn't be."

Emmett shook his head at his dad. "You knew about this?"

Richard nodded. "I just never really thought about it until she dumped them all out."

"Why did you never talk to her!"

"About the pills?"

"About why she was taking them."

"I don't know." He seemed to consider the question for another minute but then repeated himself. "I don't know. I guess I didn't want to know."

"It's good she's off them," Duke said. "People these days take way too many pills. It's terrible."

"How are both of you so calm about this?"

"Emmett," Richard explained, "Your mom and I are working through some things. Have you noticed? Is that what's bothering you?"

It was such a trite line, so devoid of any substance that he wanted to scream. He decided to go for the jugular, move his dad and grandpa from aloofness to action. "Cole's going to fuck you." He said it to Duke, but only Richard flinched.

"Fuck me?" Duke asked.

"I mean, screw you over. All of us over!"

"What?" Duke was still and emotionless, the flash of compassion gone. Emmett wished the confession back, aware that his grandpa's anger was a tremendous force, but it was too late. And there was no reason why he should temper the truth. Cole deserved it.

"I saw texts from someone on Cole's iPad. I think Cole sent some email where you say that you did something bad."

"Cole sent someone an email?" Duke still wasn't getting it.

"He sent someone one of your emails, or emails between you and your COO."

"Why would he send that?" Duke asked.

It was Richard who responded, afraid of his own words. "What did you say in the emails?"

"In my emails? I send thousands of emails."

"Something shady," Emmett tried.

Then Duke's face soured, and he got to his feet. Emmett, looking to his dad for guidance, saw Richard tilt his body away and gaze downward.

"Let's not jump to conclusions." But Richard might as well have said nothing at all, so ineffective were his words, and so defeated his tone.

"You're sure of this, Emmett? That he hacked into my email?"

"I don't know if he *hacked* it."

Duke, with a swing of his hand, slapped the table. "Dad—" Richard warned.

"Where is he?"

"I don't know."

"Dad—"

"Call him. Right now. CALL HIM." Duke was seething. His eyes bulged.

"Emmett, did you read the email?" Richard asked. Emmett shook his head. "See, Dad. He hasn't even read it. He read some texts."

"So you're just, what, full of shit?" Duke asked.

Emmett felt small and trampled over and desperate for relief. "The texts said enough," he said. "You think I would make this shit up?"

"Your dad—"

Richard rose for the first time since sitting. "I'm just saying let's talk about this calmly and figure out what is actually going on."

"All right, Emmett." In a histrionic flop, Duke was back in his seat. "Tell us what you know."

Holding back sniffles, Emmett tried to sound composed. "I think Cole sent some of your emails to a coworker. She said he was betraying the family; she said the emails were shady."

"Cole works for what? A consulting firm? What do they do?"

Richard shrugged. "I don't think he's been working for a consulting firm."

"So he's working for what, the government? A goddamn DA? What?"

"Maybe like a nonprofit," Emmett suggested.

"So he's going to fuck us."

Emmett nodded.

The front door opened. All heads turned to find Cole, wraithlike in the hallway, immobilized mid-step by three miserable gawking faces.

26

Lily discovers that she's very conservative and/or boring

Fifteen miles away from Maluhia was the rival fire-season preserve, Pōhaku. Maluhia residents thought of Pōhaku as a second-string community but still visited when bored by Maluhia. Lily had been over a few times. When Patricia asked her about it, she repeated what everyone at Maluhia said: "Pōhaku is fun, but I would never want to live there."

"Well, can we check it out?"

Lily had asked the shuttle driver to take them to The Boathouse, the best restaurant on Pōhaku. The food was good, but more importantly, it had a lively ambiance and a younger crowd. "Maluhia," she explained to Patricia as they waited to be seated, "is more, well, classy, I guess." She felt odd using the word, especially since The Boathouse was a classy restaurant. "I think the crowd here is much younger, more of an LA playboy scene." Patricia seemed to understand, or at least nodded along.

The women glanced around. It was still early, so there weren't many people. Those there, though, were well-dressed and attractive and wealthy. Lily wondered if the Pōhaku residents dismissed Maluhia the way she dismissed Pōhaku. "I don't know, maybe it's not so bad here."

"Hmmm?" Patricia didn't look surprised. One of the best things about Patricia was she rarely, if ever, looked surprised. Except for when Lily had floated the idea of cheating on Richard. That, in hindsight, had been a mistake. Since that moment, Patricia had become the chief advocate for the pro-affair stance. Even now, after sitting down, she elbowed Lily and nodded to some suave gentleman in the corner. He was thirtyish and handsomeish and wore sunglasses even though the sun had set.

"What do you think?"

"I think we should talk about something else." They sipped their first drinks. "It does just feel more…lively here?"

Patricia nodded. "Maluhia is stuffy."

"Did you not consider Pōhaku?"

"No. I rushed into it. I'm always a sucker for a good deal, and the Bells were selling…Not that I regret it! I met you."

Two drinks in, and they were talking about Richard. Lily had told herself before the evening that she would avoid the subject. But Patricia knew just what to say to egg her on. "He doesn't listen to you."

"You know he poured my pills out on the ground? Just poured them out, like an eight-year-old."

"He thinks the pills are why you're mad."

"The pills, and these drinks, are the only things keeping me sane."

People started to pile into The Boathouse. The lights on the terrace glowed red and festive. The music got louder.

Lily could count the number of nights spent at clubs on one hand. Even on the nights she had gone to The Boathouse with her family, they always left as soon as Richard said it was getting "too loud."

The years that she could have been partying and traveling and finding herself had been stolen from her. As a teen, she would have been okay making that sacrifice if it would have meant more time building a resumé, but she had missed those opportunities too. Instead, she had given her youth to her mom and then, with no break in-between, Richard. As the music blared and she looked around at a swarm of attractive people, she felt like she would do anything to get those years back. She downed what remained of her drink. Patricia called over a waiter and ordered her another.

Richard and their friends at Maluhia said all sorts of things about Pōhaku that just didn't seem to be true. She looked around with new eyes. It was, in fact, delightful. Outside The Boathouse, there was Hawaiian grass swaying and a gentle breeze, and the smell of bonfire in the air.

They went to the lounge area and sat down by a stone fire pit. The flames and the red string lights rendered the ocean unseeable, but out there in the blackness, they could hear it, and under their feet, they felt the cool, damp sand. Around them, people buzzed and congregated, and eventually, the bench opposite them was claimed by two men.

As Lily prattled on about Richard, she took mental note of them: successful, cool.

Patricia must have noticed them too. She cut Lily off mid-diatribe and raised her voice. "If he's so bad, you should take some accountability and do something about it."

"I don't know if—"

But Patricia shot back with another point. "I mean, I understand that some women need that. You know, security and safety and protection. Really, I get it. Me, though, I'm not interested. And I'm telling you, if you just had the courage to try it, you would see it's an incredibly liberating way to live."

"I just—"

"You two look intrigued," Patricia said.

Now Lily faced the duo. The man across from her was Asian, strong-jawed, tall, and slim. He had a golden watch on his left wrist and her same fitness tracker on the other, and he stared her down, her specifically.

The other man, white, bearded, and at first glance friendly, gazed over her and Patricia with amusement. "Intrigued?"

"Well, what do you think?" Patricia asked, matching his teasing tone.

The Asian man asked, "What are your names?"

"Um," Lily was rattled by his abruptness.

"Patricia. And this is my best friend, Lily."

Lily loved the sound of "best friend" and, never having been referred to as one, smiled.

Her admirer noticed. "Well, I would hate to come between best friends, unless you're into that kind of thing." His lips lifted into a smirk.

Patricia laughed. "Just get her back to me by morning."

"I'm Ben," said the bearded man. "This is Aaron. He's quite the comedian."

"Comedian?" Asked Aaron. He took a sip of his drink. "I'm deadly serious."

"It's a nice schtick," said Patricia. "Do you ever break character?"

He laughed. "Sometimes. For you two, maybe."

"So, Ben and Aaron, what do you do?"

They were movie producers. They had a whole resumé of movies that they pretended to be tight-lipped about until the slightest invitation came to share more. Then they were off to the races. And Lily, despite herself, was impressed. "You worked with Timothée Chalamet?"

"Tim's great," said Ben.

Patricia seemed less impressed. "I was just saying to Lily that I think marriage is terrible and unnatural."

It was a complete non sequitur, but Ben didn't miss a beat. "Are you married?" he asked.

"No. I was. It was suffocating. I think the idea that we should be with one person our whole lives is crazy."

"I think—" tried Lily.

"Lily is," Patricia interrupted, "you know, a very conservative person. Not politically. No, but conservative. And I love you, Lily, I do, but I just can't do what you do. And all the power to you! But I need freedom, adventure, and that's what we were talking about before you two decided to butt in. Why would someone choose to be tied down? To be restricted?"

"I don't think I'm conservative."

"Lily told me she wanted to have an affair, and I couldn't believe it! But of course, she took it back in an instant."

"Oh, you're married?" Asked Aaron.

"She's married all right, to a loser."

"Hey—"

"What? Can we speak freely here? He's a loser. He plays iPhone games all day. You said he's like a four-year-old."

"Eight-year-old," said Lily, unable to look up.

"I don't think every married person is conservative," said Aaron.

"Maybe conservative is the wrong word. But, I don't know, boring? Is boring better? For some people, boring is good. There's nothing wrong with boring. All the power to you, Lily. All I'm saying is that it's not right for me, that's all. That's all I'm saying." This was the first time Lily had seen Patricia drunk and by the way she was gulping down her latest margarita, it seemed she had no plans of slowing down.

"I think I'm ready to go," Lily said.

"Go? It's like eight thirty. See guys," Patricia grinned, "She's boring."

"I'm not boring."

"Then stay a little. Live a little."

"Okay." It was one thing to let Patricia call her boring, but another to help make her point.

"I think," Ben said, "that when women have sex, there has to be an emotional connection. I think it's different for men. But that's why most women can't do what you do, right? Isn't it natural to want that security?"

"You're conflating connection and security," Patricia said.

"Okay," Ben conceded. "Isn't it natural for women to want a deep connection with their partners?"

"You don't have to be exclusive with someone to have a deep connection."

"That's true," said Aaron. "But polyamory has its drawbacks. You have to admit that."

"I mean, it's not like being single and open and free is easy. It takes a lot of courage. I don't think people talk about that enough. You have to be okay with yourself fundamentally, you know. To be alone with yourself, you have to be okay with yourself. And I think that's the main reason why most women can't do it. They get married because they're fundamentally not okay with themselves."

Lily cut in. "Ben, tell us your best Hollywood story." The line had been on her tongue for the last minute. She had waited her turn.

As he answered, it took everything Lily had to nod along. Like she was programmed for it, she laughed when the others did and leaned in when the others did but absorbed nothing. The booze in her stomach swished and burned. Her thoughts, jumbled as they were, vacillated between self-loathing and defensiveness. Then she was no longer engaging, even superficially.

"Lily?" Patricia shook her. "Are you all right?"

"Yes. Um. What?"

"Aaron asked you a question. You must be sloshed." Patricia laughed so hard that she spilled her drink.

"No. I'm fine," Lily said, wiping down the table with a napkin.

"I asked what you do for fun."

"I, um…"

"You do a lot of yoga, right? You go for walks."

"I think Lily can answer for herself," Aaron said.

For a second Patricia looked irate, and then composed herself. She was nursing a smile. "I don't appreciate you giving me advice on my relationship with my best friend."

Lily couldn't stand the conversation's sudden awkward plunge. She watched Aaron's face for clues on how to proceed. He looked unperturbed.

"It's fine," Lily said, unable to endure another silent second. "I do like yoga. But I like it here too! I like going out. I like this place, it's beautiful. I'm just tired, that's all."

"Right!" Patricia exclaimed, ignoring the tired part. "We should be here, not Maluhia. I'm going to sell the house. I'm going to move here. Lily, you too, let's do it."

"I don't think Richard would—"

"See! Richard, again. That's her husband. He's all she talks about."

Lily excused herself.

In a bathroom stall, she rifled through her purse. She dry swallowed two Inner Peace pills. They were filled with ashwagandha, reishi mushroom powder, and she didn't know what else. She stared for a moment at Emmett's ketamine. Maybe she could take one or two. She read the instructions on the vial. *Hold under tongue for five minutes and then spit.*

The tablets were bitter and chalky. She watched the time on her phone. Around the three minute mark, a woman came out of a stall. Young and attractive like everyone else here. Lily turned away. The woman washed her hands.

"Is everything okay?"

"Mm-hmm." She couldn't look the woman in the eyes.

"You sure?"

She nodded vigorously, hoping it would do the trick. It didn't. Lily glanced up and saw that the woman looked very worried. Lily checked the timer. Almost four minutes. Close enough. She spat. "Sorry! Mouthwash!"

"Oh. Got it. You were scaring me."

When Lily returned to the lounge, she found Aaron alone. "They went to get drinks," he explained.

"Oh." Her mouth was numb.

"I don't think you're boring."

"She was just kidding."

"Yeah?"

But she didn't relent. "Yeah." He moved to sit next to her.

He was handsome, and despite his wryness, she sensed kindness in him. She liked how at ease he seemed. If Patricia couldn't faze him than nothing could. Her mind went to Richard, who couldn't sit still without something in his face, be it a phone, game console, or football game. "Do you have a home here?" she asked.

"No. We're just renting for fire season."

"You and…?"

"Just me and Ben," he smiled. "Bachelors on the prowl." The line should have made her uncomfortable, but instead, she laughed. "You have beautiful eyes," he said.

"That's nice of you to say."

"I'm sorry things are tough with your husband."

"Thanks. They're fine, though, really."

"Well, honestly, that's disappointing, for me at least."

That was crossing the line. Lily tried to think of what Patricia would say. Patricia would flirt back, perhaps even escalate. Then it occurred to her that Patricia's best qualities—courage, independence, nonconformity—now seemed less appealing. Lily felt trapped between what Patricia wanted for her (what she had thought she wanted for herself) and what it seemed like she wanted now.

Now she wanted to be home. She wanted to see Emmett and Cole and Richard, even if he was swiping up and down on his phone.

"I forgot," Aaron said, "you're very conservative." He put a hand on her leg.

"I should find Patricia."

"She's fine."

"I should really—" he kissed her before she could finish. He put his right hand on her thigh and squeezed.

She was shocked and, for a moment, didn't move as his lips and fingers clamped down in a simultaneous seize. In a burst of clarity, she threw her head back and pulled her body up from the couch. "No! I need to go."

"I'll hold your seat." Aaron was unruffled. He sipped his drink.

She found Patricia at the edge of the lounge speaking to Ben and some other strangers. Lily nudged her. "Can we talk?"

"Of course. New friends, this is my best friend, Lily. She—"

"Can we talk somewhere else?"

"Excuse me, guys."

They walked toward the open beach away from the lounge. Patricia held onto her new drink and almost lost her balance on the sand. Lily's sandals sunk with each step. She felt light and fuzzy, a little dizzy.

"So, what's up?" Patricia asked when they were away from the noise.

"Aaron tried to kiss me. Well, he did kiss me."

Patricia looked ambivalent. "Was he a bad kisser?"

"I didn't want to be kissed!"

"What. Why? It's a kiss. Come on."

"Well, he groped me too."

She didn't feel like she could meet Patricia's face and instead looked toward the ocean.

"You guys have been flirting all night," Patricia said.

"No! What? I was just being nice. I thought he was being nice."

Patricia laughed. "Don't be stupid."

"What?"

"He's very handsome."

"I don't care! I don't want anything to do with him! I want to go back."

"You said you wanted to have an affair."

Lily shook her head. "I just want to go back."

"It's like eight."

"I don't care." Lily felt a wave of fortitude, what she imagined was a ketamine-induced confidence. "I know your husband cheated on you. And I know you're trying to show yourself that it was okay and that everyone should do it, but well, I don't want to do it. I don't like picking up guys and flirting and all this shit about openness and freedom. I just want to go home."

Patricia squinted and lowered her voice. "What's up with you?"

"What's up with you?"

"I'm trying to have fun, and you just want to feel sorry for yourself."

Lily searched for a response. Ideally, something to pacify her "best friend." She couldn't find the words though, and instead sat down in the sand.

"What are you doing?"

"I'm sitting."

"Come on. Get up. They're waiting for us."

"I want to sit here."

"You're making a scene."

"I don't care."

Patricia walked away, and Lily sighed with relief. But Patricia turned around. "Okay. Get up. Let's go."

"You'll go too?"

"No. But I'll walk you to the front desk and wait with you until the shuttle comes."

"Thank you. Will you be okay?"

"Me?" She asked in disbelief. "*I'll* be just fine."

27

Cole has a thick Marxist skull

"Is everything okay?" Cole asked.

No one spoke, and Emmett didn't look at his grandpa's face, but he imagined that it was awful.

"Sit down," Duke said, pulling back a chair. He waited there behind it, like some butler, hands clenched around the chair's frame. Cole's body didn't move, but his face vacillated. "COLE, SIT DOWN!"

Cole, like a puppet, wobbled over. "What's going on?"

Emmett, who a minute ago would have assaulted Cole if he had the chance, who a minute ago had basically indirectly done so by spilling the beans, looked at his older brother's face, marked by terror, and felt a swell of pity.

Emmett had never been hit, slapped, or spanked growing up. Richard had. Duke had been beaten by his father, sometimes to the point where he was bloody and blue. He used to tell them about those times with equal parts pride and disdain. "It sucked," he would say, "and I don't wish it on anyone, but it made me strong."

Now Duke, old and frail, looked like at a moment's notice he could summon the horrific strength of his own dad—the fabled belt whipping, hard-driving tyrant. It wasn't so much Duke's body, but rather his posture, vulture-like over Cole's chair.

"Dad," Richard said, "let's talk this out."

Duke retreated to another chair. The four of them sat around the table, Cole next to Emmett and Duke straight across.

Emmett considered that he would have to speak to explain the situation. "Cole," he said, "I saw your texts."

Cole gulped. "What?"

"I went looking for you in your room and your iPad buzzed—"

He stood. "Those are private texts. I don't know what you think you saw but—"

"Stop it, Cole." Duke's words outmatched Cole's, and his grandson was rendered silent and skittish. "Only you give a flying fuck that Emmett read your texts. Before you mutter another word, get that through your thick Marxist skull."

Cole looked like he was about to cry. "I'm leaving."

"Sit down," Duke said.

"Cole, we need to discuss this." Then Richard turned to Duke. "Dad, you need to calm down."

Duke shook his head. "I don't think so. Is this really something to calm down over?" Then, to answer his own question, "You fucking sent out my emails!"

Cole's breathing was fast and jittery and seemingly wet. He looked like he was dying from fear and grief and poison all at the same time.

———

COLE WANTED TO LEAVE and was ready to do it. But he couldn't. He wanted to stop crying too, but he just couldn't. He was betrayed on all sides, inwardly and outwardly. The world was closing in and beating him down, and each unwanted sob and unwanted second in the horrible chair was proof that he was powerless to resist. He wasn't sure if what would emerge hours from now would still be him or, instead, some forever-cracked forgery. He sucked back another throbbing cry.

"We just have to figure out what you did and come up with a plan," Richard said.

Cole didn't look up at his dad but imagined that he was confused and, like him, unmatched by the moment. And sure enough, the reconciliatory gesture was ignored by Duke, who, still seething, said, "A fucking plan? You fucked us, didn't you?"

Cole buried his face in his clammy hands.

"Fine," Duke said, "sit there and have your tantrum, like a baby."

"Cole, it's okay," Emmett said.

"No, it's fucking not!" Duke contorted his face and leaned over the table.

Now inches away, Cole felt his grandpa's breath and permeating heat. He lowered his hands and was terrified by the closeness of the old man, who heaved a finger away.

"I never thought it was possible that someone could be such a pathetic, dense, deplorable piece of shit. And I've seen some pieces of shit. But you? Going against your own family? Who gave you everything? Your prep schools and your fancy degrees and your name. Everything that makes you anything. It's fucking pathetic. I can't even look at you." Duke slumped backward and shook his head. "I just can't believe it. I never thought I'd see it. My own grandchild." Then Duke turned to Richard. "You raised one fucked-up kid."

"Cole," Richard pleaded, "can you please explain what happened?"

"I don't, I, um…"

"Cole, goddamnit!" Duke banged his fist.

"I sent some emails to Aid for Earth."

"Aid for Earth?"

"What's that?" Richard asked.

"It's a nonprofit," Emmett said.

Cole nodded.

"You work there?" Duke asked.

Cole nodded again.

Duke shook his head. "Why?"

"It's a good organization…"

"No, you fucking nimrod. Why'd you send the emails?"

"They asked me to. They are looking for dirt."

"Looking for dirt? Jesus! What the fuck is wrong with you?"

"I…"

"It's because you hate this family. Emmett was right. You hate this family."

"I…" Cole's thoughts zoomed through him and seemed to rip pieces of his mind out as they came and went until he was an incarnation of fear itself: retracted, withering, wrecked.

"Cole, are you okay?" Emmett's voice seemed to be from some far-removed dimension.

"I think I'm having a panic attack," Cole said.

It could have been seconds or minutes. Cole didn't know. But then he was back enough to find his breath and feel his feet on the floor. He was back in the world just in time to see Duke stepping out of the room. "I'm leaving," he said. "I'm going back to Redding. We're going to fix this mess."

"I'm sorry," Cole called out. "I really am sorry."

PART 3
October

28

Duke feels betrayed by a newspaper

"Save it for my deathbed," was the last thing Duke said to Cole before packing and leaving. When he arrived in Redding, Eliza was waiting for him at his compound. It was the middle of the night, and it showed on her face. He knew, without having to look in a mirror, that his old face showed more. But there wasn't time for sleep. Chris had intel that Sandra Perry at the *Wall Street Journal* was covering the story, and Cole had sent her the transcript of the last board meeting.

By 8:00 a.m. the next day, there were ten people crowded around a conference table at the corporate office.

"The *Journal*!" Duke felt betrayed. It was the only paper he read.

"They'll be reaching out for comment before running it," Becky, their head of PR, added.

The team reviewed the transcript. Six quotes were flagged. Chris's insistence that they likely started the fire, Eliza's recommendation not to cooperate with investigators, and Duke's comments about the financial burden of a scandal were deemed gratuitous.

"This is bullshit," Duke said. "We didn't start the fire on purpose."

"Yes," Becky conceded, "but it's the coverup that will get us in hot water. And the, well, some of your comments make you seem…" she looked for the right word, "ambitious."

"What's wrong with ambition!"

"You said in response to Chris," she read aloud, "*Let me get this straight, you would defer hundreds of millions of dollars to get us wrapped up in a scandal, that could cost this company billions.*"

"So?"

Eliza rested her head on her arm. She sighed. "It doesn't sound good, Dad. You sound evil."

"Or," Becky said, "ambitious."

Becky was a seasoned PR lead. She had joined Duke two years prior when *New York Magazine* ran the hit piece on post-fire logging. Becky had done an admirable job blunting the worse effects of the smear campaign. "By salvaging the trees, we're preventing future fires," she responded on behalf of the company. "By leaving the trees, we'd be leaving fuel on the ground. If people think fire season is bad now, just wait until we stop salvaging."

"We'll just have to spin it the right way," Duke said. "Like you did with the magazine article."

Of course, Becky wasn't a magician. That article had pushed his board member Ronnie to make Duke choose a new CEO and step into a chairman role. If he wanted to remain with the company in any capacity, he would need her to overdeliver.

Their head counsel, Seth, cut in. Duke liked Seth. He, like Becky, had covered the company's ass a number of times. Now, he looked troubled. "It's not just the story we have to worry about. There will likely be an investigation."

"An investigation?" Duke slammed his fist against the table. "Fuck! We're fucked."

"Let's worry about the story first," Becky said. "We have a day, maybe a few, to limit the damage. There's not a lot we can do other than a strong response. But if it's possible to slash the credibility of the source, that could be effective."

"But there is a transcript," Chris said.

She shrugged. "I wish we could delete the transcript, but that ship has sailed. We have to find out where the leak came from and plug it. And then, if we want to be aggressive, we have to publicly discredit the person, or persons, responsible."

"Discredit?" Eliza asked.

"We won't release anything directly. We'll give other people the story. But we'll have to reveal that whoever did this isn't some virtuous whistleblower. We'll have to find whatever skeletons they have in their closet and shine a light inside."

Duke turned to face a wall, and Eliza sunk farther into her seat.

Becky continued, "It's usually a disgruntled employee. If it is, we might even get them to walk back what they said and not cooperate. We might even—"

"It's not an employee," Duke lamented, still facing the wall. "It was my grandson."

No one spoke, and Duke, made uncomfortable by the silence, sidestepped to face a window. Outside, the gray morning looked suffocating and unfriendly. "Does anyone have a cigarette?" he asked.

He looked back to see some shaking heads. He hadn't smoked in twenty years. He had given up the habit easily, compared to other smokers. "I wasn't going to die over something so stupid," he had explained. And with pride, would add, "I can't see what the big deal around stopping is. It just takes some willpower. I just stopped."

Few people in the room remembered him as a smoker, maybe just Chris and Eliza.

"You shouldn't smoke, Dad," Eliza said.

"Who cares." He wasn't angry as much as withdrawn and tired, and the room seemed more disturbed by this than any past display of wrath. He saw them shuffle about, at a loss for words, no one wanting to take the first swing.

Eliza stood and with crossed arms, looking at her dad and no one else, she said, "Okay, so we have to throw Cole under the bus to save the company?"

"I don't think it's as black and white as that," Becky said. "You should at least talk to him."

"I'm not talking to him," Duke shot back.

He and Eliza knew enough about Cole to mount a defamation campaign. Becky lined up a list of possible reporters and outlets. Seth and his legal team covered everyone's tracks. Duke, despite his shame and exhaustion, was impressed with the urgency and diligence of his team. He began to refer to the conference room as the war room and his eight-person squad as his security council. The terms caught on. People went home late and returned early. Eliza, he was impressed to see, slept in her office. "Even I'm going home," he told her in a show of support. He wondered if she would ever sleep at her house again.

A week passed before Sandra Perry reached out. "They have some emails and as anticipated, the transcript. And yesterday she spoke to someone on record, a credible source. She wouldn't say who," Becky relayed.

"Cole," he said.

"She wouldn't say."

"Cole," he said. "Did you tell her the things about Cole?"

"She didn't seem interested. I sent in our written comments." They had prepared a response where they emphasized that they had done nothing illegal, there was no coverup, and their actions were industry standard, and so on.

They couched the response with a lot of legal mumbo-jumbo, saying that the company had always planned to support the town of Chester's rebuild. Chris was put in charge of the project and left for the small town. He called in to report that there were lots of opportunities to make things right. "We can start by funding the school rebuild, then the post office, then some of the local businesses—"

"I want a budget," Duke said. "I want the most bang for our buck." By "bang" he meant good branding, praise, and forgiveness. He sensed that under each of Chris's comments was a tacit I-told-you-so. If they had cooperated in the first place, they would have paid less money overall. He didn't give Chris the satisfaction of acknowledging that fact.

To Eliza's apparent chagrin, though, he told her as much. "We should have listened to Chris."

"We didn't know that Cole—"

"I don't care. You made a mistake. You have to own up to it."

He watched her unravel and then try to recover, but it was obvious she was reeling, barely able to keep her voice down. "You agreed with me."

"I know. I won't do it again."

He expected her to cry, and for a moment it looked like she would, but she took a deep breath and stepped out of the room.

THE STORY RAN ON OCTOBER 10. It wasn't the top story, but it was still above the fold on the front page. "*Peterson Lumber Company Burned by Scandal—How a ten-billion-dollar family business started, and covered up, a deadly fire.*" Duke and his security council read in silence. Duke read it until he had practically memorized the piece. He broke the silence and pointed to Eliza. "They mention you a lot."

She looked down.

"They barely mention me," he said.

But the piece was as bad as they could have expected, perhaps worse. Sandra wrote that she had received confirmation from a reliable source that cover-ups at Peterson Lumber were common occurrences. While she didn't state everything directly, the implications in the article were clear: the Petersons were corrupt and immoral, and the Chester fire was spit in the ocean compared to their other offenses.

"There's nothing else, though," Eliza said. "Right?" Duke was too tired and distracted to feel bad for her.

They called Chris on the conference line. He sounded disgusted. "It's unfair! Most of all," he said into the phone, "it's so unfair."

"Chris," Duke said, "find out who on the team spoke to Sandra. Maybe it was someone Cole knew? Maybe they did it together."

"Yes, sir!"

Duke paced around the room. The more he thought about the story, the worse it seemed. He imagined all of his friends and acquaintances and enemies reading it. The worst part was, he had been in their shoes many times. When scandals broke, everyone disavowed. It was easier that way. There was too much blood out for the rich. They could band together only so much before it became a liability for them all. In the days, perhaps hours, to come, he would hear from his museum boards and his academic boards, and so on. *We're sorry, Duke, but—*

He had seen it happen to others. In some cases, he had even been on the other end of the phone calls, telling colleagues that while he appreciated their contributions, their services were no longer needed.

Now when friends called Duke, would he apologize, deny, or push back? Who did he have dirt on? Was there anything he could say to survive? Anyone he could blame instead so he would emerge scraped but intact? He thought back to his first impressions from the piece and his comment to Eliza, *They mention you a lot.*

He paced. "Let's cancel Cole. Let's ruin him." Then he turned to the room and looked at everyone except his daughter. He spoke like she wasn't there. "And, Eliza, you have to step away from the company."

"What?"

"We'll say you stepped away. It's the only way."

She ran her hands through her hair. Like some melting wax figurine, she oozed desperation. "Please. No."

"Stop making a scene."

She put her hands over her eyes and slurped back snot through her nose. "Please. Don't put this on me. It's not right. Dad, please."

"Control yourself!"

But she couldn't, and she retreated to a wall and leaned against it for support and just kept saying, "Please, please, please."

Duke was repulsed. He wanted to strike her. Instead, he turned away to address the others in the room. They were frozen and tortured. Seth looked the least afflicted. Lawyers, in Duke's experience, always did.

"I will step in as CEO again," he told him. "Draw up the paperwork and get the board signatures tonight. If anyone shows even a smidge of reluctance, you tell them to call me, but tell them I won't be happy to be getting their call. And Becky put out a press release."

—

Eliza didn't wear a mask in the parking lot and didn't get into her car. She kept walking, zombielike, to a field across the street. The air was bad, dry with white ash. It speckled her black blouse and irritated her eyes. She had looked at the field from her window every day but had never once gone over there. Now she looked back at the building she had known her whole life. In the smoke and heat, it looked drab, even antiquated. She couldn't imagine a more conventional office building. There were millions like it, all over the world. But only this one housed a multibillion-dollar corporation. "Why do we need a new one?" Duke would always ask. "I think it's just fine."

She had believed him. At times, she took things a step further, showing off the building to new employees, sharing that she was proud that it was unremarkable. "We're not showy. We're about results."

Now it looked dismal and evil, and she wondered if she would ever step inside again. She shouldn't want to, but she couldn't help herself. It was all she had.

It was gone now. Her whole life reduced to this moment. She hated her dad and hated herself for hating him, but most of all hated that she had wasted everything to be here. Outside in a smoke-blown field, choking on rotten air.

29

Lily won't think about the Africans

Lily, usually the first out of bed, awoke to her husband's voice in the kitchen. For the last week, since the Pōhaku night, she had been staying up late drinking and sleeping in. Mostly she drank alone, at first, just a few glasses of wine, but after Cole left, perhaps more than a few. She tapped her phone and saw that it was barely 7:00 a.m.—two hours before she wanted to wake up. But after a few seconds of listening to her husband, she knew something was wrong. She crawled out of bed, struggled into a robe, and then found Richard on a barstool, bent over with his headphones in, his hands clenching and unclenching, his right foot tap-dancing on the floor.

Lily turned up her wearables to their maximum stress relief settings.

"Max, buddy, come on." Richard pleaded. "Let's just talk about this."

Max Lewis was Richard's college roommate. Richard had been Max's first investor in VisionaryVR, later renamed Trance. In all the years that the two had worked together, she had never sensed even a rumbling of conflict. Other shareholders and journalists even complained that Richard was an "enabling" board member: loyal and spineless, unwilling to challenge Max or vote against him.

Lily also knew that other investors whispered that Richard was nothing without Max. They never said as much to her, of course, and because Richard was rarely invited to their exclusive parties, no one had a chance to tell her even if they wanted to. But word got around. She read insinuations in newsletters and blog posts. They said it was a small check and Richard took too much credit for Trance's success.

Now here he was, seemingly begging Max for much less than a reference. "Just let me explain to everyone. The money I invested in you wasn't my dad's money! It was my money. It has nothing to do with the lumber business." He listened for a moment, then shot back, "It was from *my* trust fund!"

Lily put a hand on his shoulder. He didn't seem to notice. "Come on! As a friend, I'm asking you, I'm begging you, don't do this." He closed his eyes and waited and then lashed out, "It *is* up to you!" The outburst made Lily flinch and Richard, at last, noticed her. He gestured to his laptop. There, open on the browser, was the *Wall Street Journal.* There was a bold headline: "Peterson Lumber Company Burned by Scandal—How a ten-billion-dollar family business started, and covered up, a deadly fire."

"Oh, the conference?" Richard moaned. "What does that have to do with anything? People liked it. They cheered for me."

She scanned the story. She looked for her kids' names and was grateful not to find them. She and Richard were also absent, but the Peterson name was everywhere on the page.

Richard continued, "You weren't even at the conference, so how would you know! Everyone who talked to me said I did a great job! Don't kick me off. Please. This company, this board, they're the most," he sighed, "important thing I do."

"I can't believe it," he said to her after hanging up the phone. "I just can't believe it."

She hugged him, but he didn't open his hands, and it was like she was hugging a tree. Swaying, inanimate, he rocked back and forth in her arms. "It'll be okay," she said.

"He wants me to resign from the board. Me! His first investor."

"I don't get it. What does the lumber company have to do with Trance?"

She let go, and it looked like he didn't know what to do with himself. She helped him to the table. "Max said that the rest of the board thinks it'll be a distraction."

"The story?"

"The scandal, they said. Well, he said it wasn't just the scandal. He says I *embarrassed* him at AlohaTech. He wasn't even there but he said everyone was talking about it. It's all such…." He searched for the right word but didn't seem to find it, and so, instead, let out a hand-clenched roar of exasperation.

"Do you have to resign?"

"I don't think I have a choice. He thinks he's doing me a favor by letting me resign. As opposed to kicking—"

He couldn't finish the thought.

Lily was about to lean in and kiss him on his forehead. She hadn't done something like that in a long time. But seeing him like this now made her want to kiss him there.

Before she could, though, her phone buzzed in the pocket of her robe. She felt a sickening feeling before reaching for it. Then she read the name Randolph, and her stomach dropped.

"Who is it?" Richard asked.

"It's Randolph, the chairman of InhaleAfrica."

Richard nodded. "It's making its rounds."

"Maybe it's about something else?" The prayer sounded stupid even as she said it and then more so as she let the call go to voicemail and he called right back.

"Are you gonna answer it?"

She didn't know until her finger tapped the phone. "Hi," she said.

"Lily!" Randolph was his usual phony self. "How are you? How is paradise? How is the family?"

Randolph was an overdramatized, habitually insincere person, impossible to imagine as a child. She hated him but to his face pretended like she revered him.

She expected him to move on, but he was waiting for an answer. "It's fine. Everyone's fine."

"Great. And the weather's been good?"

She indulged his spiral of small talk for a minute. If he intended to relax her, he failed. Finally, she asked, "Randolph, why are you calling?"

"Um. Yes, well. Well, you know. News travels fast these days. Twenty years ago, it wasn't like this."

"Randolph."

"Yes, well. You know the board saw the article today about your family. Personally, I thought it was very unfair. Are there any good journalists left? It's a shame, really. But this is the world we live in. And it's a shame for your family, really."

"What does this have to do with my family?"

"Well, your wider family, per se."

"It has nothing to do with me."

Richard nodded, looking encouraged by her bravery. She felt like making him proud and repeated herself. "It has nothing to do with me."

"Yes, well, I see that. And that's great, you know."

"Great?"

"I mean, it's great that it's not you, is all. I would never expect things like that from you. And it's not fun to be judged by the actions of one's family. If only you knew my aunt." He gave the fakest laugh. "Well, anyway, depending on what you think and what you want to do, it may not be the worst thing for InhaleAfrica to have you take a temporary leave of absence."

"You're asking what I want to do?"

"Well, I would implore you to think about the Africans. If you really think about them, it would be a shame if our work got swept up in something so perplexing. And I think you can just step away for a few months until things cool off."

"It would be a shame for the Africans?"

He mistook her shock for sincerity. "Yes! For the Africans! Exactly."

"Randolph, for God's sake, this has nothing to do with them!"

"Yes. Yes. I agree. I agree. But, you know, it's about optics."

"Optics?"

"Yes."

"I don't want to leave the board."

"Just temporarily."

She wouldn't beg like Richard. "You'll have to kick me off. I'm not leaving, temporarily or otherwise."

"Hmmm." It was like she could hear him coming up with something to say. At last, he murmured, "You see, the board voted already."

"ALREADY?"

"Yes and—"

"Fuck."

"Well, there might be another way. You know you committed to a very generous pledge when you joined us, and it certainly was well received by the board. And if you were to give another gift, perhaps of a greater amount, we could certainly find a way to ensure your future participation."

"We gave you ten million!"

"Well, you pledged ten million. I don't think it's all been sent yet and... just to remind you, you're obligated to give the gift in full."

"I'm obligated?"

"Well, you made a commitment to the board."

"Well, I didn't know you would be asking me to resign!"

"Lily, it's the optics that we need to overcome, is all. It's about the optics."

She wasn't nervous anymore. Instead, she was enraged, indignant. She turned to face Richard head-on before she spoke. She wanted him to see it. She wondered if Emmett was in the house and would be listening. She raised her voice. She didn't mind him hearing it.

"Fuck you, Randolph, you little shit. Fuck you." Richard reached to grab her phone, she swatted him away. "You fucking clown. You piece of shit. You pompous greedy motherfucker. You dried up waffle. You ugly fucking shoe. You're like a shoe with eyes. You just step in shit and drag it around and—"

Richard put his hands over his eyes. Lily grinned. "You fucking shoe man."

She wondered if he would hang up. He didn't. "I understand this is a tough moment for you and—"

"Shut the fuck up."

He did but didn't hang up the phone. She imagined him fidgeting in place, embarrassed and disturbed. "Lily, are you still there?"

"Yes. Fuck you."

Richard was smiling. It made her smile too. She put Randolph on speaker. She gestured for Richard to wait, and when the man's voice came skittering through, "Lily, I—" she interrupted, "Randolph, go fuck yourself."

Would he lose his temper? She didn't know. She was curious. Richard was too, still sporting that astonished grin. After his longest silence yet, Randolph spoke, "Lily, please let's try and be professional."

"Suck my dick."

Richard muted her phone. "How much of the ten million did we already wire?" he asked.

She beamed, thrilled that he understood. "It was tranched. We only sent half."

"Ha," Richard exclaimed. "Make him squirm!"

Lily unmuted. "I stay, and you'll get your gift. The first one. Nothing more. Or I'm out, and you'll get nothing else."

She heard a deep sigh. "Lily, let's try and be reasonable."

"It's your move, dude." She suspected that no one, ever, in his sixty-plus fussy years of life had ever called him dude.

"I'll have to discuss with the board."

"Fine. And Randolph?"

"Yes?" He sounded miserable.

"Send them my best."

"Okay."

"And tell them you're a little bitch."

"What?"

"Tell them you're a scaredy-cat chicken-shit bitch." She hung up. She felt electrified, equal parts nervous and thrilled.

"Where did that come from?" Richard asked.

She had so much energy that she had to pace around the room. "I don't know! It just felt right. I wasn't going to let him push me around, you know?" She realized that she sounded like Patricia.

Richard's phone rang. His momentary respite of excitement dissipated. "I don't want to pick up." He sunk.

"Who is it?"

"It's Jill. From Rosegate." Rosegate, a service that provided on-demand private security for high-net-worth individuals, was his second-best company. It was small compared to Trance but had just raised another fundraising round, and Richard's stake was worth five times as much since his initial investment. The company was often in the news for its own controversies (their security contractors had a habit of profiling, doxxing, and in a few cases, assaulting innocent people). Lily grabbed him. "Look at me!" He did. "Do what I did! Don't bow down. Stand your ground. You got this!"

"I don't know—"

"Stop it! You got this!"

He answered on what must have been the final ring. "Hi, Jill." He didn't sound strong. Lily flexed her bicep to help him along. He looked away, though. "I think that's—" he said, but was interrupted. "I don't think—" he said a minute later but then also was interrupted.

Lily reached over to put Jill on speaker. "Maybe if it was just your breakdown at AlohaTech or just the article, but, Richard, this is a pattern. We don't have a choice."

"But, Jill, you do. Just let me—"

"You'll be receiving documents this evening. All further correspondence should be between you and our lawyers. If you choose to reach out to me personally, I will not answer. This is a courtesy call."

"I think that—"

"Richard, this isn't a discussion. This is a courtesy call. My counsel will be in close touch."

"Um." But he muttered into a vacuum. She was gone. "Fuck!"

"Also off the board?"

"Yeah. And they want me to sell my position."

"They can't make you do that!"

"No. But the fact that they want me to is awful."

"I know someone who can make this right!"

Richard perked up. Lily explained, "My friend Patricia. She has a ton of money, a ton of influence, people listen to her. She'll do anything for me. In fact, she's the one we're investing in! In her company! She probably knows Jill! She's probably the largest LP in every other fund that backed Rosegate! I'm telling you, she can help. She will help. She knows everyone!"

"Patricia…" He was thinking it through and then entertaining the idea. "Okay. Okay! Maybe she could help! What's her last name?"

It occurred to Lily that she didn't know.

"She's your new best friend and you don't know her last name?"

"I guess I never asked, and she doesn't do social media and…" she trailed off. "She can help us though! She bought the Bell place. That was like fifty million!"

Richard groaned. He covered his eyes with his hands, pulled his hair back, and looked like he would collapse.

"What?"

"Patricia Otto," he muttered.

"You know her?"

He went to his computer, and Lily followed. He typed Patricia Otto into Google, and her best friend popped up. The first hit was a *NY Post* article. "Taste of her own medicine: Relationship 'guru' and billionaire-wife busted for serial cheating."

"What?"

"She was married to Arthur Otto," he explained. "The hedge-fund billionaire. She was in a huge cheating scandal. It got a lot of press because she was a relationship coach, and well…she was like seeing fifteen guys at once, I guess. And everyone thinks Arthur is the nicest guy. His kids love him. I can't believe you've been hanging out with her! She's been shunned by everyone else here. She barely got anything in the divorce. I hear she spent everything she did get on the Bell place. She's a laughingstock."

"Patricia? This must be someone else." But he gestured back to the article, and Lily leaned in. It was her Patricia. "Essential oils…" she said. "That's what we're investing in?"

He shook his head. "There is no way in hell we're investing in Patricia Otto."

"So, she can't help us?"

"Lily, honey," he wallowed to the couch and collapsed. "I can't imagine anyone worse to have in our corner."

30

Cole gets canceled

After leaving Maluhia, Cole went to his Pac Heights childhood home. He lived there like a ghost, hiding every sign of his presence so his family would find the house undisturbed when they returned. He didn't go outside. When he ordered food, he had the courier leave it by the front door. Only his hand would extend outwards and then retreat with its sustenance.

The home was like a former best friend now far-removed. Its expensive art, its ornate banisters, its bathroom clad in limestone were as familiar as ever, but unsettling. He imagined he was living in a simulated world, where the home was cloned and only he, acquainted with its every detail, could see through the charade.

Perhaps it was because he wasn't supposed to be staying here. When his dad had first forbidden him to stay at the house, he had taken the words in stride. But now he couldn't go back to hostels. He was too fragile for that life.

He saw the article when it made it to Reddit, a few hours after the *Wall Street Journal* had run the piece. Instead of escaping to a realm of mindless scrolling, he was now face-to-face with his treason. The emails played a minor role, but the reporter had also gotten a source to provide a transcript of a board meeting. These quotes were excruciating for Cole, who knew that his family might conclude that he was responsible. He wanted to explain to them that while he had regretfully sent the emails, perhaps had even been coerced to do so, he would never have spoken to a reporter or sent the transcript. That was someone else. Someone much worse and more deserving of scorn.

A day later, a blog post materialized on the internet. The author, Ed Gross, had around 100,000 followers on X and a couple thousand subscribers to their Substack. Previously, Ed Gross had argued against cancel culture, identity politics, UBI, and other examples of so-called "Marxist hysteria." Cole had seen his stuff pop up on his timeline and once had even heard him on a podcast. Never in a thousand years did Cole expect to see his grandpa's business in an Ed Gross piece.

The Left, swept up in another cancel campaign, has (surprise, surprise) missed its target. Every week, like toddlers on a soccer field, they kick without aiming and score on themselves. Their latest temper tantrum is over a WSJ *hit piece on Peterson Lumber Company. Supposedly, a forest fire, as forest fires are apt to do, broke out on Peterson land and then spread through a small portion of the state. Did Peterson Lumber purposefully start the fire? Of course not. Peterson Lumber is a family-owned business that has created thousands of well-paying jobs, has sequestered one-hundred-thousand metric tons of CO_2, and has singlehandedly saved species like the Dart Spotted Owl from extinction. Could Peterson Lumber have been more forthcoming following their bad break? Perhaps. But let's remind ourselves, and the subset of our leftist comrades who still have a shred of intellect, that fires happen every day in the forest. Forest fires are natural and necessary. Peterson Lumber manages two million acres of timberland. They can't possibly monitor every acre and respond to every fire.*

This should never have been a story. But it was, and in the Wall Street Journal *of all places, a historically hysteria-proof publication (unlike the* New York Times*). Curious how a story like this got its legs, I reached out to Peterson Lumber and the* Journal. *What I learned is interesting, albeit unsurprising. The spoiled, Stanford-indoctrinated, justice-warrior grandson of Duke Peterson, racked with rich guilt and resenting his family's success, decided to throw the people who gave him everything under the bus.*

Cole stood up from his chair. There was no escaping it now.

Cole Peterson is another example of elite university inanity bleeding out, graduate after graduate, into the real world. My sources tell me that by his sophomore year at Stanford, Cole was radicalized, calling out microaggressions, protesting free speech, shaming his loved ones, and so on. It's a familiar story, but for one stark differentiating detail: Cole remained, in all the worst ways, half-baked. While he had no problem villainizing his family, he also had no problem living extravagantly off their dole. He flew on private jets, withdrew from his trust funds, and most hypocritically used family money to buy bitcoin and bitcoin miners for himself. Imagine the type of person who spends his days ranting about climate change and his nights exacerbating it.

He had to get rid of the fucking bitcoin.

Perhaps we can forgive Cole for these offenses. After all, what snowflake social justice warrior isn't living off of daddy's money? But few have the audacity to be proudly anti-racist in some circles and a full-blown bigot in others. A scroll down Cole's X feed tells us all we have to know. More recent posts are par for the Gen Z course. He rails against cops, conservatives, and systemic racism. But if you keep scrolling, you discover someone who cares less about stopping Asian hate than spreading it.

Cole looked with horror at three time-stamped screenshots. He had no memory of the tweets or Facebook post. If he had been asked at gunpoint if he had ever been racist, he would have denied it. Here was the proof, though. It made him sick.

"Thanks Asians for ruining the curve #ApChem."

In another, he retweeted a local story about Chinese restaurants growing in popularity with the addition *"Hide your dogs."*

Then there was the Facebook post. Cole had commented on his semi-formal photo where he and his group of dateless losers, many of them Asian, posed in front of a fountain. Perhaps to lessen his embarrassment, he had commented, *"I've got Asian eyes in all of these!"*

Each post individually was excusable, perhaps. Together, they demonstrated a pattern.

He scrolled the rest of the article. There was a lot about Aid for Earth and the Martha Clancy incident. There was more about Peterson Lumber. And finally, there was the hook, line, and sinker.

Cole is a warning to all of us. No matter how much you give and teach your kids, the wrong environment can ruin them. Let's hope that Peterson Lumber emerges stronger than ever, and let's hope that their trust fund baby traitor of a son is kept far from the business.

It was unreal. It was unfathomable. He rubbed his face and wondered what he was supposed to do. He was paralyzed by what felt like an ocean of hatred. It wasn't a foreign feeling. In middle school and high school, he swam in that same ocean. Kids called him names, sneered behind his back, relegated him to the library for recess. He was the class weirdo. They hated him for it.

Here was the same hatred, no longer confined to the schoolyard, but now on the internet, on Substack, X, Facebook, TikTok. He imagined the story everywhere. He imagined his name and face everywhere.

Ed had included a photo from Cole's LinkedIn profile. People were just starting to comment. Someone said he looked like a pedophile on puberty blockers. Someone else said they didn't know that ball-hair grew on faces.

No one would defend him. Not even his family. Emmett had ratted him out. His parents had stood by. Duke and Eliza had skewered him. It had to be them behind the story. It had to be.

He heard his phone buzz. His mom and dad had been calling him all evening, and he had refused to pick up. He checked, and in addition to five missed calls from his mom, there was a text from Bella. *Hey, I saw the blog. Are you okay?*

The walls of the house began to push in on him so he could not breathe, and he had to get up or face what felt like death. There was that one voice, now on repeat in his head, repelling the despair. Bella asking, *Are you okay?*

He texted her to ask if she would see him. She seemed reluctant. She said she was working from home. But then she gave in and gave her address.

It was a smoke-cloaked dusk, and he walked through the city with a black mask, sunglasses, and hoodie. No one, not even his family, would have been able to recognize him. It was a long walk from Pac Heights to Lower Haight, and when he stopped to catch his breath after climbing a big hill, he would look around and see masked people scurrying, never enjoying themselves, always in a rush. He had never lived anywhere very cold, but he imagined that people moved the same way in the dead of winter, desperate to get inside and rid themselves of discomfort.

He knocked once, and Bella's door cracked open. She stepped into the hall and kept the door ajar. He had to back up to make room.

"We can go to Starbucks?" She suggested.

"Um." He wanted to know what she was hiding inside. "I just wanted to ask about a few things, is all. I don't think it'll take very long." After not seeing her for a few weeks, she looked especially beautiful, more so because she looked at him with compassion and warmth and he hadn't felt anything like it in a long time.

"I'd let you inside, but, well, I have someone here."

"Oh."

"I asked him to leave, but he was in the middle of something."

"Oh. It's fine. I—" He was embarrassed and jealous but did everything he could to suppress it. He failed.

"It's Brandon."

Now he was embarrassed, jealous, *and* angry. Brandon hadn't thanked him, not even once, for sending the emails, for making the story possible. Even now, the man was hiding inside, unwilling to greet Cole. And to add insult to injury, he was sleeping with Bella. *Of all people,* he wanted to ask, *why him?* He knew the answer of course. Brandon was everything he wasn't: handsome, successful, confident. It didn't make things any better.

"I mean, you can come in," she said. "It's my place. He doesn't control me."

"Well, I don't need to. I just wanted to hear what you thought about what happened and—" she put up a finger, told him to wait a second while she went inside. He could hear muffled speech inside the apartment. He heard Bella snap, "Deal with it!" When she came back and opened the door wider, he retreated. "No, it's fine. I'll go."

"Stop it! Come inside."

He didn't notice anything in the apartment except for Brandon. Tall and strong, leaning back on the couch, typing on his laptop. When Cole's presence became undeniable, he offered a head nod, and a few seconds later a, "Hey."

"Hey," Cole responded, feeling stranded in the middle of the studio. There was a small table by the fridge. Bella gestured him over. They were only a few feet away from Brandon, and it was going to be a different conversation than he had intended.

"You want something to drink?"

"Um, I'm fine." His throat was itchy from the smoke though, and he wished he had asked for water. "You read the article?" He asked her when she sat across from him, delicious-looking glass of water in hand. "The second one, about me."

She nodded.

"I just, um, I guess I want to thank you for supporting me and for giving me an opportunity, and I just wanted to reassure you that I'll keep working hard and doing my best for you and Aid for Earth." He hadn't planned on being ingratiating, but considering he hadn't planned anything at all, wasn't surprised by his meekness.

"We're grateful for what you did," she said and then called Brandon into the conversation. "We both are."

Brandon closed his laptop and came over, sat down on the last remaining seat. "Thank you," he said. It was a forced admission. They were cramped together, pressed against the fridge, and Cole felt small beside Brandon's big arms, his unaffected glare.

"I hope that I showed you guys that I care a lot about Aid for Earth and that I will keep helping."

Bella looked morose. Cole didn't dare look at Brandon, but when his words came, they were expected and chilling. "About that, Cole." If he was nervous or uncomfortable, he didn't sound like it. "We appreciate you sending us the emails and supporting that side of our advocacy work. But we're not convinced that there is a long-term role for you with us." When Cole looked up, he saw a poised, placid expression.

It didn't make sense. He had ruined every relationship he had, all four of them, five counting Eliza, and now everyone with a Substack or X account hated him. Brandon seemed to hate him the most.

Bella reached over to squeeze his hand. He shuddered but not as much as Brandon, who scooted his chair back and shot Bella a look. The man was quick to recover, but his tone shifted. "Frankly, Cole," he said, "We just need someone who doesn't harbor those kinds of prejudices. That story and those tweets mocking Asian people. That's not the kind of culture we're trying to build here."

"That was in high school. I didn't mean any of it. I'll apologize. Bella, please—"

"Cole..."

"Are you kidding me? *You too?*"

"Those tweets are vile, Cole."

"I know! I'm sorry. But look…I mean, think of what I did for you guys! I told my family that I was on their side and then…" It sounded awful as he said it, and he couldn't look at either of them, but he hoped it would get the message across. "You told me to find the emails, and I found them. I drove to Redding, then flew to Hawaii and stole my grandpa's laptop and—"

Brandon interrupted. "And we said thank you."

"We really are grateful," Bella said.

Brandon rolled his eyes. "Cole," he said, "we just don't have a place for you anymore at Aid for Earth. If that stuff in the blog is even remotely true—"

Cole hadn't even been sure he wanted to go back until he saw Bella again. Now he didn't even have the option.

"It's not because we don't appreciate your work," Bella added, confirming that she knew this had been coming. "We do, or we did." He began to doubt her. How much of this was an act? How much had he been used?

"All right," Brandon stood. "I have to get back to work. Thanks for coming by, Cole. We'll have official documentation forwarded tomorrow."

Cole sat dumbstruck for a second and then, aware he was unwanted, like so many other times in his life, moved to the door. Before stepping out, he felt a surge of energy, like all the day's suffering had been combined, militarized, and was now roaring to life. The impact was jarring.

He looked at Brandon. Brandon wasn't looking at him. He was typing away. "Hey," Cole said. Brandon put up a *give-me-a-second* finger. "Hey!" He screamed. Now Brandon looked up. "You think my family's evil? This shit is evil. You're fucking evil. And you're full of shit."

"What?"

"Cole," Bella tried.

"I do everything you tell me, go above and beyond what anyone else would do, get paid like shit, get treated like shit, and then you pull this fucking shit. Fuck you. That's some evil shit."

"Cole." Brandon looked back down and started to type again. "You need to leave."

"Fuck you. I'm gonna sue you."

That seemed to fire him up. He stood. "Oh yeah?"

"Yeah!"

But Brandon was walking Cole's way, looking extra big and strong.

"Stop it, guys," Bella said, grabbing them both.

Brandon stood a foot away and dipped his chin to look into Cole's eyes. "You want to know the real reason you're not wanted?"

It was easier to yell from far away. Now Cole felt trapped, backed against the door, and small before Brandon's hulking frame. "I'm leaving." He turned around and put his hand on the knob. Brandon's hand grabbed his. The grip was firm, and Cole was terrified.

"Let go of him!" Bella screamed.

Brandon looked down, seemingly noticed his closed hand, and released. He moved in front of the door, in front of a petrified Cole.

"You want to know the real reason you're not wanted?"

"I want to go," he begged. "I just want to go home."

"No one likes you. Not a single person on the team likes you. You suck the energy out. You suck the joy out. You're like a fun sponge. And," he smiled, "you're such a creep."

Cole felt tears in his eyes. His hands rattled, laced together in a futile attempt to hold it together.

"That's enough, Brandon," Bella whispered. "Stop it."

"Bella thinks you're a creep. Has she not told you? She says you stalk her Instagram. She gets notifications in the middle of the night. It's fucking creepy."

"Stop it, Brandon!" She screamed. She stepped between them and shoved Brandon away. He stepped back, and she opened the door, grabbing Cole's sleeve and pulling him through.

She walked with him to the staircase and through the *use in case of fire* door. They were alone on the fourth-floor landing, and there were spiders in the corners and the sound of construction work below, but it was the safest-feeling place Cole had been all day. He sat on the stairs.

"I'm fine," he wiped his face. "You can go."

"It's not true what he said," she sat beside him, but a few feet away, like she was leaving room for someone else. "I don't think you're a creep."

"I liked your photo by accident," he said. "I just thought you were pretty. It was the first time we met."

"I thought it was funny, that's all."

"I just really liked you. I really like you."

"Oh." He twitched as she hesitated. She must have noticed. "I like you too!" But it was forced.

He stood up with wobbly knees. "I'm gonna go."

He started down the stairs. She followed him. "I do appreciate what you did."

"Mm-hmm."

"I really do!"

Then he stopped and turned. "Then don't go back!"

"What?"

"If you really appreciate it, then don't go back! How can you work for him? How can you like him?"

"It's not just about him, Cole. Thanks to you, for the first time, we can do something here. Aid for Earth is relevant again. People are donating. We're putting together events and a march."

"A march?"

She considered her words. "A march. At your grandpa's office."

"Peterson Headquarters?"

"Yes. I know this is a lot for you—all of this. But now, we finally have a platform. Thanks to you!"

"Stop saying that!"

"What?"

"Stop saying that it's thanks to me." He felt like he had nothing to lose. "I can't believe you're fucking him."

"*What* did you say?"

He didn't know he had the capacity for more pain, but her look of disgust tore through him, the latest blade in a parade of predecessors. It made him double down. "It's odd, that's all. I thought you would have more respect for yourself."

"Wow."

"I thought you of all people had self-respect."

She laughed in a way he had never seen her laugh before—teeth bared, head shaking. Like she couldn't believe what she was hearing. Like he was absurd. Then she stopped and looked at him with a somber and insolent face. "You don't even know me."

"Yeah *clearly*. I didn't know you were a whore." He regretted it the second it was out, but it was too late.

She pointed. "Get out of here."

"I didn't mean that."

"Sure, Cole. Please leave."

He walked away. He didn't wear a mask, and on his long walk home, he breathed toxic air. He felt very alone and very sad, and he wished that someone would say that they didn't hate him.

31

Emmett breaks his bong (and heart)

Emmett sat on his bed, switching from app to app on his phone, overriding the voice in his head that oozed discomfort. The phone, in time, was overmatched. He needed to get high, he needed to fuck, he needed to be anywhere else but the Maluhia house.

He had a backpack that he used to pack his bong and weed, but he couldn't find it in the clutter of his room. So he put the bong in his left hand, stuffed his pockets with its accoutrements, and left through the back door. Under a pink fading sky, he must have looked like a junkie washed ashore, scampering to some refuge. Except he had nowhere specific in mind and was spurred by habit more than location.

Off the road, he crouched in the bushes and packed the bowl. The water percolated, and he sealed his lips to get everything out of the smoke. He waited for a second and then took another hit. Now he was high but still horny and considered his options.

Chloe was probably at Logan's. He had declined the invite to his friend's weekly party, citing exhaustion, but was now enticed. He didn't know if she would fuck him again. They hadn't spoken a lot since his first dismal performance, but she was his best prospect.

He would ask about her mom, so it didn't seem selfish when he told her about his family and all the shit that was so fucked compared to whatever angst she harbored. Hopefully this time she would talk to him. This, more than the fucking, would be therapeutic. As he made his way down the steep hill toward Logan's, he ran the scenario in his head. He would take her somewhere quiet, perhaps to the beach. Would they talk after or before? He didn't care.

Cole had been there for him for an hour—an hour filled with promise. Two Petersons united against forces only they could understand. Now Cole was part of the problem, and Emmett was alone again, a bong-clad silhouette under the falling sun. He had to find Chloe.

He passed an elderly couple he had seen once or twice around the pool, perhaps at dinner. He stopped in front of them and, presented with the opportunity to show them (and himself) that he didn't give a fuck about anything, took a massive pull.

They were terrified. They scurried off like mice. He was very high now, and he ran up the hill after them saying he was sorry. They tried to run too. He was younger and faster, and soon they were cornered. The man with his golf hat and wrinkled face stepped in front of his wife. "Get away from us!"

"I didn't mean to scare you. I was just—"

The woman chimed in. Less scared now, it seemed, her face ripe with judgment. "Doing your drugs!"

"I'm sorry. I didn't mean to scare you." The world swayed around him, but there was nowhere to sit. "I'll be on my way. I didn't mean to scare you. And it's legal here. It's legal!"

A few minutes later, he didn't know if the couple had been real or fake, and it was nice not knowing. He packed the bowl and took another pull. Now at the bottom of the hill, he could see Logan's house. When there were people over, they usually gathered on the bottom floor and on the patio. The lights were on, but he didn't hear any voices, and he wondered if everyone had left. He walked around the house to see if anyone was by the pool. He had to move off the road and walk up a dirt hill, but from the top, under a canopy of trees, he could see. Empty as well.

They were probably enjoying a family dinner. Maybe a family game night in the confines of the house, where even he, perched on high ground, could not see in. It was a nice family. They weren't in the newspaper this week.

He packed another bowl and inhaled even as his throat cried out for him not to.

Everything swirled and he was coughing, and even as his mind ascended to a level of highness that he hadn't known for a long time, he wanted more and imagined a summit so supreme that the world and all its problems would be out of sight and beyond comprehension.

He drifted in and out of consciousness. He heard voices below, and when he looked, he saw figures in the moonlight. He could barely make them out at first, then realized it was Logan and Chloe. He wanted to run down and see them.

When he stood, his legs were jelly, and he sagged back to the dirt. He couldn't hear what they were saying over their music, but when they turned on the lanterns, he could see they were in their bathing suits. They got into the jacuzzi. Logan put an arm around Chloe. Then she kissed him. They kissed for a long time, and Logan's hands found Chole's chest. He felt a wave of nausea. Of course she was with Logan. He remembered the first time he met her. Her saying, "Logan's pretty rich."

His left hand grasped the neck of the bong for support.

He poured out the water and started back to the street, but the hill was steep, and the ground was dark beneath him and his feet gave way. He tried to stabilize himself, but he kept slipping, and then he was on his ass, sliding down the hill, and the bong went flying. He hit the fence as the bong hit the concrete. It shattered.

Logan and Chloe were looking at him, squinty-eyed. He tried to sit still. He hoped they couldn't see him. "Emmett?" He heard Logan call out. "Emmett, is that you?"

Emmett scampered up and started to collect the pieces of his bong. There were many pieces, and they were sharp, and he had nowhere to put them. He grabbed what he could in his hands. He felt pieces cut him and he felt his hands start to bleed. He didn't look up as he shuffled away. His heart was pounding as he ran away from the house and up the steep hill, dropping pieces of glass. He heard footsteps pounding behind him. He heard, "What the FUCK, Emmett?" He heard, "Slow down!"

32

Lily and Patricia are losers

Lily sat on the bed as Richard packed. Her mood-boosting wearable buzzed on her wrist. She had taken four Inner Peace pills and one ketamine lozenge. She listened to a binaural beat soundtrack to "eviscerate stress at the source." It wasn't a pleasant tune, but she powered through. She was paying twenty dollars a month for the "world's most advanced neuroacoustic software," and, goddamnit, she would get her money's worth.

Richard asked her something. She didn't want to remove the headphones, but when he stood in front of her, she had no choice. "Are you feeling okay?"

His laser beam stare made her feel like a schizoid behind museum glass. "Yes," she said. He wasn't convinced. She had to redirect his attention. "Should we try him again?"

"Cole's okay."

"How do you know?"

He got into bed beside her and wrapped his arms around her waist. "He's okay," but he didn't sound convinced and his hands were unwanted and stranger-like. "We're going home."

"I wish we never left."

It was a foolish wish and pinning her mess of a life on Maluhia was a foolish trick. Pain had been in the cards for a long time, and she would have known it had she allowed herself to look. Because it was about more than the fire or the articles. It was about more than revoked boards and public shame. Her family was divided, her sons were suffering, and her husband, even as he consoled her, was as lost as she was. She should have seen it coming. She should have done something to stop it.

When her phone buzzed, she sprung up. Richard also jumped, betraying his projected composure. It wasn't Cole.

"That vile woman," Richard said, reading the text.

"You don't know her."

"I know enough."

Why was she defending her? Patricia had lied to her, led her astray, and now she wanted to meet up.

"Don't go," Richard told her, "it's not worth it."

It would be easy to take his advice. Instead of facing Patricia, she could forget her, move on with life and pretend like everything was okay. She had gotten good at that over the years. She had, in the suitcase before her, everything she needed to ensure success. Supplements, prescription pills, and now ketamine. Wearables, biohacks, and self-help books. In a couple of weeks, Patricia would be a passing thought, and in a couple of months, ancient history.

But when her phone buzzed a second time, she had already decided to go.

She found Patricia at the beach bar, sipping a luminescent drink, watching the waves. Before approaching, Lily looked for signs of irritation, for proof of guise. There was nothing to be found. If Patricia was playing a character, it seemed she was invested in the role, no matter the audience.

When she saw Lily, she stood and opened her arms. "I can only imagine what you're going through. Come here." Lily suffered through a hug. "Let me get you a drink," Patricia said.

"No, I'm good, thank you."

"What? Come on. You need it."

"No, I'm really okay. Thank you. We're packing up. I just wanted to—"

"You're leaving?"

Lily had two paths before her. The first, and the easier of the two, would involve chitchat and culminate in a goodbye hug, perhaps with a resolution to stay in touch until next fire season. Then there was the second path.

"You're leaving?" Patricia asked again.

"Why did you lie to me?"

There was, at most, a quiver. "I didn't lie to you."

"I googled you."

"Well, good for you. I hope it was informative." She drank her cocktail. Then rolled her eyes.

"Your company is an essential oils company?"

"No. We're revolutionizing the health and wellness field through personalized, patient-centric, and evidence-backed interventions. But yes, our *first* product is essential oils."

"Essential oils? That's what I was going to invest in?"

Patricia raised her eyebrows. "Going to?"

"You were using me. *And* you cheated on your husband? You told me it was the other way around!"

"For fucksake, I never said that. And so what? You cyberstalked me and decided you're too good for me?"

"What? No. No! I have to pack. I'm tired. Can't you just let me be?"

Patricia squeezed Lily's shoulder. "Ohh...I like this side of you. It's fierce."

Lily brushed off her hand. "I need to go."

"Could you be any less fun?"

Lily hopped off the barstool and started across the beach. Patricia was calling out behind her. "Oh, come on. Really? REALLY?" Lily didn't slow down until she hit the trail heading back to the homes.

Patricia was close behind. Lily didn't move toward her, but waited, made her come. "You're really mad, aren't you?" Patricia had her hands on her hips.

"I'm not mad. I just don't like being lied to and I don't like being used."

"I never lied to you, and I wasn't using you. You're acting crazy."

"I'm not crazy."

"I didn't say you were. I said you're *acting* crazy."

Lily started again on the torch-lit trail. Patricia followed her, but this time kept her distance. It took thirty seconds before she was interrupted by someone else. "Lily?" The voice was squeaky, injected with elation. She looked up to find Cathy smiling back. In past years, Cathy had been her constant fire-season companion. Now the bubbly chatterbox was the last person she wanted to see. "Lily! My God! I haven't seen you all season."

"Oh, hi, Cathy."

"Why have you been hiding?"

"Oh, I haven't. It's just—"

"You must come over! You know what? What are your plans tonight? I'm heading to dinner to meet some of the ladies. Come with me, please! They'd love to see you."

"Oh. Thank you. I don't have time right now. I promised Richard—"

"You know, a little birdie told me that you've been hanging out with the woman who bought the Bell place."

Patricia was standing off to the side, away from the trail and obscured in shadow, but in earshot. Lily saw her smirk.

Cathy leaned in, "You're so open-minded! I like that about you."

"Cathy, I would love to catch up, but I need to go."

"Oh, of course. Did you know that we brought a Nigerian exchange student with us?"

"Yes, I think you mentioned it." Lily started to walk, but Cathy swiveled and joined her.

"You need to come another night for dinner and meet him. I insist. He is something else. You work with Africans, right?"

"Um, Cathy, I would love to. But I need to—"

"Don't you do something African?"

"Um. There's a nonprofit." She sensed Patricia behind them. When Lily turned, there she was with an outstretched hand. "Hi. I'm Patricia. I bought the Bell place." Cathy's smile, against all odds, remained. It seemed extra-taut, as if pinned to her cheekbones.

"Hello," Cathy said, too loudly. She shook Patricia's hand.

"You were talking about me."

Lily couldn't help but laugh.

"What?" was all Cathy could say.

"Yes," Patricia said, "And I was right here listening! What a coincidence."

This time Cathy composed herself. "I was saying that it's so great that Lily and you are friends."

"Oh, jeez, it really is!"

If Cathy knew she was being mocked, she didn't show it. Instead, she turned back to Lily. "I'm going to dinner. Great to see you." Then looking back at Patricia, "And great to meet you. What's your name again?"

Patricia dropped her histrionic, mirroring smile. "You know my name."

For the first time ever, at least by Lily's estimation, Cathy returned a glare. "Excuse me?"

"You know my name. Don't bullshit me."

"I don't know what you're talking about." And then, as if it had never left, the smile was back, "Lily, let's catch up soon."

After Cathy rounded the corner, Patricia sneered, "These are the people you hung out with before me?"

"At least she doesn't lie to me."

"Are you kidding me?" Patricia stepped forward. "All that woman does is lie. She's a living, breathing lie. I haven't seen someone so full of shit since you."

"Since me?" Lily knew what she was going to say but asked anyway. She wanted to hear Patricia take credit for saving her.

Sure enough, she explained, "Since the old you. Do you really want to go back to being like that?"

"You always think you know best, huh? Like everyone in the world would be so happy if only they were you. Well, guess what, we're not all you."

Patricia shook her head. "You feel smart saying that? Proud of yourself?"

"Oh, stop it!" Lily sighed. Her hands were hot. Her breath overwhelmed. She planted herself, though. She found courage through her anger.

"I was happy to help you."

"Oh, cut it out with the patronizing shit. I can't believe I looked up to you. I can't believe you just wanted me for my money."

That was a dagger for Patricia. Her expression changed from annoyed to irate. "I do not need your money!"

"That's not what I heard."

"Heard where? From your manchild of a husband?"

"So it's all bullshit?"

"Most of it!" She raised her voice. "And you don't know the first thing about any of it! If you want to ask, then fucking ask—"

Lily spotted a couple heading their way. She put a finger up to quiet Patricia, and the two of them stood at attention as the intruders approached.

"Hello," Lily said.

"Hello," Patricia mimicked.

The husband and wife nodded with sewn-on smiles and then hurried by.

"You have to make a scene like that?" Lily whispered.

"Do you have to be so goddamn insecure? So we're having a fight? God forbid anyone hears sweet Lily having a fight. What would the good people of Maluhia think?"

"You're being mean."

She cupped her hands around her mouth, dipped her head back, and shouted, "Lily Peterson is having a fight!"

"You're being a child!"

"I'm the child? You read a gossip column and think you know everything about me."

"I don't. In fact, I don't know anything about you! I had this idea in my head that you were some super successful person who didn't give a shit what anyone thought and who was cheated on and blah blah blah and I felt bad and—"

Patricia laughed. "You felt bad?"

Lily nodded. "I felt bad. But it turns out you cheated, and you aren't that successful, and you're more of a nutcase than anyone."

"A nutcase?"

Lily felt like being mean. "You sell essential oils! I thought you were a CEO!"

"I am a CEO!"

"Fucking oils!"

"They're doing super well."

"For fuck's sake. I'm going."

She turned, but Patricia grabbed her shoulder. "Wait!"

"Don't touch me." She saw that Patricia had tears in her eyes. It was a sight that Lily had never expected to see.

"Fuck you. You think you got me wrong? I got you wrong."

"What?"

"I got you wrong. You're just like everyone else. You're a loser." Patricia wiped her face. "You think you're better than me because you went to Stanford? Because you sit on some fancy bullshit board? Well, guess what? Do you think anyone would give a shit about you if you didn't have your husband's money? And it's not even his money!" She grinned through her torment, seemingly impressed with her own realization. "It's his daddy's money. You're the worst type of person. Freeloading. Scared."

Now Lily felt tears coming, "Please stop."

"No fuck you. Look at me," she mimed. "I'm Lily, the victim. My life is so hard that I have to take a bunch of pills so I don't kill myself."

"Stop...please."

"I raised psycho-fucking kids."

Lily turned red and stood up on curled, stress-stuffed toes. "FUCKING STOP!"

One more comment from Patricia, and she would have lashed out in a whirlwind of fists and nails.

The apoplexy must have been obvious. Patricia stopped speaking. The malice disappeared from her face, and only the tears and torment were left. But Lily didn't have any appetite for forgiveness. She composed herself as best she could and, before turning around, managed, "Well, now I know what you think."

She was, once again, walking away. "Oh, come on," Patricia called out. "We both said mean shit." This time, she didn't turn around. Even as she heard Patricia following behind her, shouting, "Let's just talk about this. Come on. Okay. I'm sorry! I didn't mean to talk about your kids."

Lily picked up her pace and was about to round the corner and hit the main road to the house when she saw a figure approaching her. Even in silhouette form, there was a glimmer of recognition. Then she saw that it was Emmett. He was wild-eyed and scampering, out of breath and clutching something in his hands. When he saw her, he froze. In the dim torchlight, she noticed that his hands were cut up and bleeding. "Emmett! Baby, are you okay?"

He was lost for words, disoriented, and looked high as hell.

Then two other figures emerged and came toward them. They slowed down but peering out, she could see it was Logan. He was with a girl.

She looked at her son's bloody hands and then into his dazed eyes. Had he hurt someone? Killed someone? It was all the drugs. He didn't know what he was doing. Her baby. She brought him close. He sagged in her embrace. "What did you do?"

"What?" He asked. Then he looked around. "What are you…"

"Hi, Mrs. Peterson," Logan said. He and the girl moped over. They were both in swimsuits.

"What's going on?" She asked.

Logan spoke to Emmett. "We didn't know you would come by."

"It's fine."

"Why are your hands bleeding?" Lily asked.

He looked down and only then seemed to notice the blood. He was clutching pieces of glass. "I dropped, um…"

"Let's go, Logan," the girl said.

"No, wait," Logan said. "Emmett, I didn't know that it was like that."

"It's fine."

"Well, I can tell it's not!"

Patricia finally caught up to them. "Lily, can we please talk about this?" Then, as she moved closer and noticed the others, she froze.

"Chloe?" Patricia asked.

"Mom?"

"What are you doing here?"

"What are you doing here? Why is your face all fucked up?" Patricia's face was makeup smeared from her tears. She wiped it again, but it didn't improve anything.

"This is your daughter?" Lily asked.

Patricia nodded. "Chloe, this is my friend Lily."

Emmett stumbled over to the bushes and puked. Lily went over. "You okay?"

"I hate that girl," he whispered. And then he puked again. "I hate her."

"Well, I don't care much for her mom."

They walked off toward their Maluhia home. This time, no one ran after them.

When they were back at the house, Lily washed Emmett's hands in the sink.

"What was up with you and Chloe's mom?"

"She was trying to use me." She dried his hands with a paper tower. "Use us." She studied his cuts. "Okay I think you'll be all right."

"Use us?"

"To invest in her company."

"Oh." He walked over to a chair and slumped down. He was out of it, droopy and rattled. But then, all of a sudden, perked up. "I guess Chloe was using me too."

She sat next to him. "Let's forget about them. We're going back to San Francisco."

He looked confused then content, like one side of him had won a battle over another. "Good."

33

Cole and Chris, unlike the air, come clean

Compared to San Francisco, Redding was about 160 points higher on the AQI scale. On the digital air quality map, it was an eerie shade of red. But the forecast couldn't prepare Cole for the smoke-laden stench from the adjacent burning forest. In San Francisco, the air was gray. In Redding, it was darker, opaque, as if made by a machine to color a haunted house or seedy club.

As he walked from his dad's car to his grandpa's front door, he felt like his head was suspended over a campfire, mouth pried open to better vacuum up the smoke.

Duke's chef, Santiago, ushered Cole in. He said something to Cole as they walked to the living room, but Cole couldn't make out the words over the whirring purifiers. Santiago left Cole in the living room, probably to get Duke, but then five minutes passed, and then ten, and Cole wished he had asked Santiago to repeat himself.

Cole moved along the edges of the room. There were gold-framed maritime paintings, a globe, an African mask above a bookshelf. The books were leather-bound and worn, and he was reminded that his grandpa was a reader like him.

Duke entered at last, stone-faced.

Cole lowered his gaze and wished he could blend into the room; he felt small and insignificant beside the literature and art.

"What are you doing here?" Duke asked, still staring.

Cole lifted his chin and found that his grandpa didn't look mad so much as tired. He wondered if the last few weeks had been as hard on Duke as they had been on him.

"I wanted to clear the air."

Duke coughed. "Follow me."

Cole accompanied his grandpa through the winding halls of the house, past the kitchen, past the dining room, past the TV room, to Duke's office. He remembered it differently, clean and organized. There were papers scattered across it now, and photos strewn across the desk.

In one, he and Emmett, Mom and Dad, and Duke and Grandma stood together in the forest, smiling in front of towering trees and foliage. Emmett had a big smile on his face. Cole had puckered lips and angry eyes. He wasn't surprised to see his preteen angst in the frame. He hadn't always been so self-conscious, older photos on the desk suggested as much. As a baby and toddler, at least, he smiled.

"Do you want something to drink?" Duke asked.

Cole shook his head.

"It's no problem. Santiago can get you something."

"No, I'm okay."

"Okay."

Duke couldn't seem to get comfortable in his chair, and he couldn't find a place to rest his arms. Cole hadn't seen him like this before. It was a far cry from their last interaction, where Duke had been apoplectic, consumed with a young man's rage. Now, whatever anger was left was overmatched by fatigue.

"I, um…" Cole looked at one of the photos of a younger Duke, it was easier than looking at the real thing. "I don't know where to start."

"You can start by sitting."

He took a seat opposite the desk. "Last time, I, um, didn't get a chance to explain myself."

"I think you had your chances."

"I guess so. I guess I didn't know what I was doing."

"Look at me, Cole." Cole looked up and met his grandpa's gaze. "If you're going to apologize, just do it."

He took a deep breath. It was hard to keep eye contact. Every part of him wanted to shift away. But he held on. "I have more to say than sorry. But I'll say that too."

"You will?" A sly, hurt smile.

"I will. I'm sorry."

"Good."

"You know…Can I get up?"

"What?"

"Can I get up and pace around? It'll help me think." Duke looked confused. "I mean, I can sit here too. It's just…" he exhaled.

"Fine, pace around."

It was always easier for him to speak while moving. "I was driving over, you know? And I knew what I had to say to you. I knew it was sorry, first off. And I am sorry. But I also wanted to explain myself. But I don't want it to be an excuse, okay?"

"Okay."

"It's not an excuse. It's just an explanation. You think I did it, maybe, because I'm a radical and don't like your business or your politics and, you know, all of that." He hadn't planned what he was going to say next, but something about his grandpa's frailty, the morbid idea that the man was close to death, imbued him with courage. Not just the courage to say it to Duke, but more remarkably, the courage to say it to himself, to say it aloud. He would say things now, he discovered, that he wouldn't have said in front of a mirror weeks ago. "I don't believe in anything."

"Hmmm?"

He looked at his grandpa. "I don't believe in anything, you know? All the stuff I think I believe, I'm just regurgitating. I'm full of shit. And that's not why I did it. I wish that was why I did it. That would have been defensible, you know. But I'm going to tell you the truth. I am telling you the truth. I did it for a girl."

"For a girl?"

He nodded. "I did it for a girl because I wanted her to like me. And in general, everything I do and say and believe, it's all so people will like me." He felt a lump in his throat. "I hate myself. I hate myself so much. I hate everything about myself. I hate what I did, and I hate the people I did it for, and, well, most of all, I just hate myself. But it's okay."

"It's not okay."

He clasped his hands together and stood in front of the desk. "No! I know. I'm not saying what I did is okay—"

"I know," Duke said.

"Oh. Good. I'm just saying it's okay that I hate myself. I don't want your pity. I just want you to know that. Not that it'll fix anything. I know it won't fix anything. But I have a plan to fix things. I'm going to make it up to you. You'll see."

Duke looked unconvinced.

"I will. I can't explain it, not yet anyway. Or maybe ever, I don't know. But I'm going to make it up to you."

Duke waved a hand, like Cole was crazy. "It's fine."

"Okay. Fine. But there's something else, and it's not an excuse, and I'm not saying it doesn't make what I did any better, okay? I sent the emails to the girl. I own that. I did that. But I didn't send the transcript. And you should know that the other stuff in the article, there was some other stuff," he was pacing again, "you know about the company culture and Eliza and all that stuff, that was Chris. And I bet he sent the transcript too."

"What?" Duke's eyes narrowed. It was like the accusation had pumped him full of life. "What are you talking about?"

"It was Chris. I know it was Chris because he told me you had emails in the first place."

"He did?"

Cole nodded. "But it's not an excuse."

"I have to make a call."

—

DUKE CONSIDERED LEAVING THE ROOM, but his legs were weak, his head hurt, and he hadn't slept well for days. Last night he had stared at photos with a whiskey in hand and felt rotten. Last night and the night before that and so on.

So he stayed put and, with Cole pacing, dialed Chris's number.

Chris picked up on the first ring. "Duke. How are you?"

"All right. I'm all right." Even Duke could tell that his voice suggested otherwise. He was no stranger to uncomfortable conversations, but over the last few weeks, he had had so many of them. He didn't feel bad about anything he had done, not even scapegoating Eliza, but he was sick of having to solve problems. Work used to be a mix of problems and victories. Now it seemed there were only problems.

This was perhaps the worst problem yet. Cole's betrayal hurt because he respected Cole and loved him. Considering the causes Cole championed though, the unfaithfulness wasn't shocking. But he never would have expected this from Chris. Even now, he couldn't quite believe it, but Cole, while he had many other flaws, wasn't a good liar.

"You want an update on the Chester efforts?"

"No." He sighed. "I have a question."

"Shoot." Seemingly no fear in his voice.

"Did you speak to the *Journal*?"

"Me? What? Come on."

"Did you? And did you send the transcript?"

"No. Absolutely not."

Cole paced but didn't look fazed by the denial.

"If Eliza or Cole said so, I hate to say it, but they're full of it." Chris took a deep audible breath. "Well, look. I made a mistake when Cole showed up in the office and said he was helping Eliza. I pointed him toward some emails and the board transcript. I didn't know that he would send them! I didn't even know what he wanted with them. I thought it was for you. How was I supposed to know? He's your grandson, Duke. What was I supposed to say?"

Duke found the response convincing but rehearsed. "Cole's next to me, Chris."

"Fine." Chris laughed. "Maybe you can get him to be honest."

Duke addressed Cole. "What do you have to say to Chris?"

"I, um…" A few seconds of silence crawled by.

"See, he has nothing to say. Of course, he has nothing to say. Duke, this is insulting. Of course Cole is going to make up lies. Of course he's going to try to pin this shit on me. I'm the outsider. I'm the easy target. It's such an obvious move that I'm shocked you're even considering it!"

"No, wait." Cole leaned over the desk, so his head was suspended over the cell phone. "I never even knew about a transcript."

"What?" Chris said.

"You said you told me about a board transcript. You didn't. I just saw two emails—"

"Really? You're a Stanford grad, and you're telling us you don't know about boards. This is fucked. Duke—"

"I mean, I didn't think to look for a transcript. You told me—"

"I gave you what you were asking for. I didn't know what you would do with them."

Duke listened to them go back and forth. He closed his eyes. Chris was persuasive, strong-willed. Cole was keeping up but less confident, body-shakingly nervous. And yet, with his eyes closed, with one hand on his chest, he felt his gut say that Cole was right. He interrupted Chris, "I think you spoke to *The Journal*, Chris. This will be easier if you just say so."

"I won't say so. It's his word against mine. This is insulting."

"No, Chris. It's our word against yours. I think you did it. I think you wanted to be a whistleblower."

"That's bullshit!" For the first time, Chris raised his voice. Duke knew he was getting warmer.

He pressed on. "It killed you that I made Eliza and you co-CEOs."

"No."

"It killed you that—"

"No. Listen. I didn't do it, and I shouldn't have to sit here and take this. I'm in fucking Chester, bumfuck nowhere, cleaning up the mess that I tried to prevent! Why? Because I'm loyal. You know that. For twenty years, you've known it. Should you have realized that when you made Eliza my co-CEO? Maybe. But I took it in stride. I went on with my work."

"It doesn't seem like that, Chris."

"If I was mad at Eliza, it wasn't because she was my co-CEO. It was because she wanted to cover up a fire! And you listened to her."

"Shhh!" After all that had happened, he didn't want it said so blatantly, not over a phone line.

But Chris didn't stop. "A fire that killed people. That was our fault. It was fucked, Duke."

"And you said that to *The Journal*?"

"No!"

Duke looked at Cole. With the phone muted, he asked, "What do you think?"

"I...I know he did it. I don't care as long as you know it wasn't me. I mean, I sent the emails. I told you that. But I didn't send the transcript and I didn't talk to a reporter. I wouldn't have."

It was a slight difference, and while the distinction seemed to matter to Cole, Duke wasn't sure if it mattered to him. More importantly, if Chris had spoken and was denying it now, he had no future with the company.

He had one move left. He would push even harder. If Chris stood his ground, then he had every reason to assume he was innocent. If he folded, the bluff would be warranted.

He unmuted. "Chris. I spoke to my contacts at *The Journal*. I just wanted to give you a chance to come clean."

There was silence on the other side. Duke could imagine Chris weighing his options, perhaps running probabilities in his head. Duke was doing the same thing, unsure what Chris would say next, but ready to react accordingly depending on the result.

With a deep sigh that made it through the speakerphone and then a single word, "Okay," Duke knew that Cole was right. Then Chris asked, "Who did you speak to?"

"People who told me what I needed to know."

"Okay," Chris said again, more firmly. "So I spoke to them."

"So you did." Duke looked to Cole for signs of relief, even pride. But the boy was his same nervous self.

"And you sent the transcript."

"And I sent the transcript."

"You can't work with this company anymore, Chris. You know that, right?"

"Listen to me, Duke. Please. Just let me explain." He had never, for as long as he knew Chris, thought of him as desperate. The man had weaknesses that Duke was aware of, that he had seen. Like overconfidence and the occasional bout of bitterness. Never though had Chris shown even a smidge of desperation. But here he was, as desperate as they come. "Everything I did," he continued, "I did for you and the company."

"It doesn't matter." Chris had gone behind Duke's back and lied to him. No justification mattered.

"I tried to do it the right way. You read the transcript. I stood up to Eliza. I explained my rationale to you. If you had only listened, then none of this would have happened."

"Don't you dare pin this on me."

"Duke, listen to me. Please. Eliza was going to run this company into the ground. I know it, and if she weren't your daughter, you would have known it too."

Duke had his complaints about her but most of those she had assuaged. She had shown him that she had the work ethic and drive to succeed.

She had shown him that she could be confident and competent. What Chris took issue with, her ethics, wasn't even on his radar. Perhaps because small blunders like the Chester fire were bound to happen. Chris didn't know it but Duke had done far worse over the course of his career. In the old days, little infractions could be taken care of by bribe or blackmail. When Chris joined, Peterson Lumber was well beyond its scrappy, not always above-board, adolescence. If he hadn't been willing to skirt some rules, he never would have succeeded. Who was he to chastise his daughter for doing the same?

"You stood up for what you believe in. I don't begrudge you that. But you betrayed us."

"Duke, did you notice that you weren't implicated in the article? Not at all."

"Chris—"

"It's because I made sure to protect you. And protect the company. It was about Eliza. It was always about Eliza. She had to go. You couldn't see it."

"That's enough, Chris."

"If you let me go, the company has no future. Zero. Do you understand?"

"I can see that you think so."

Duke expected that to be the end of it, but for the second time in the conversation, Chris fucked up.

"If you fire me, I'll ruin you." He didn't sound like himself when he said it. There was grief in those words. Grief and everything else that desperation excreted.

"Ruin me?" Duke wasn't nervous. He was too old to be ruined and stronger men than Chris had tried before.

Cole, who had stopped pacing and had for the last few minutes seemed content with merely fidgeting, began pacing again.

"There are things I could share that you don't want me to."

If Chris was willing to go this far, there was no place for him by Duke's side.

"If you think that blackmail will change my mind, you're sorely mistaken."

He heard Chris sigh. "Whatever, Duke."

"All right then."

When he hung up, the two Petersons were quiet. Cole approached the desk and sat down.

Duke glared, "If you plan to say I told you so, I advise you not to."

"I don't want to say it."

"Well?"

"Well, there's something else."

"Hmmm?"

Cole looked around like there were ghosts in the room. "They're coming to Redding."

"What?"

"Aid for Earth. They're going to protest outside the headquarters and they might come here."

Duke laughed, but quickly stopped after seeing the look on Cole's face. "How do you know?"

"The girl I like, or *liked*, told me about the headquarters…but I think they'll come here after. It's what they used to do, anyway, go after private residences. They ransacked a senator's house… They'll probably just break your windows."

Duke looked out the only window in the office. "I hope not," he said. "I don't like smoke in the house."

34

Eliza branches off

Sheila Nesbit was small-statured, wizened, and frail. Eliza made the mistake of dismissing her, believing that a nod would be a sufficient hello. It wasn't. "I don't like your dad," Sheila said.

Eliza hoped that Gary would interject and curb the awkwardness of his wife's comment, but he just sat down and sipped his coffee. No one told Eliza to sit. She did so anyway.

She hadn't expected Gary to host her. When she had reached out, she had suggested the same diner as before, but Gary had insisted on his house. It was a large house but poorly maintained. The flowers outside were dead or dying. There were fruit flies in the kitchen. It smelled like smoke and Febreze.

"He's very intense," Eliza responded to Sheila, hoping to end things there.

"That has nothing to do with it," Sheila said. "I'm intense. He's rude."

"Oh."

"I think he doesn't like women in his meetings. I think he's a misogynist."

Eliza didn't dispute the point. Despite a whole life's worth of trying to prove herself, she knew that Duke doubted her abilities. For him to punish her after the Chester scandal, even though it had been as much his doing as hers, was just the latest injustice. This one, of course, was notable. Never before had she been actually fired, although the man had threatened to do it many times.

After he had dismissed her, she had sat outside in the smoke, waiting for her anger and sadness to fade. It went nowhere. Even after a night of sleep, she awoke to the same feeling of vindictive betrayal. She started to fantasize about a world where Duke Peterson couldn't control her, where the man would have no capacity to ruin her day, or her life, with a rash decision.

She withdrew money from her trust fund and spoke to a bank about bolstering her cash position with a loan. They wanted to see more clarity around the specifics of the deal she described but gave her enough of a thumbs-up to feel comfortable proceeding. Now she just had to convince Gary, and apparently Sheila, to sell her a piece of their land.

"So I was hoping we could discuss the plot that I emailed you about?"

"You've bought almost everything already, including everything that burned in August," Gary said. "What's another two hundred acres?"

"I'm not buying this one for my dad. It's for me."

Sheila's eyes contracted. Gary looked confused. "What?" he asked. "For you?"

"I'm branching off."

Sheila laughed. "Daddy issues?"

Eliza shrugged away the slight. It didn't matter what Sheila or Gary thought of her. It didn't even matter what her dad thought of her. If she could keep that from mattering for as long as possible, she would be okay. "I'm starting my own shop," she said. "The Eliza Peterson Lumber Company."

"That's cute," Sheila said, "but if you think you're gonna get some rookie discount, you're mistaken."

"I'll pay a fair price. I have the cash."

Gary left and returned with what seemed like a rolled-up poster. He cleared the table and spread the paper out. It was a map of the Nesbit holdings. The Petersons had transitioned to digital renderings almost two decades ago. Her dad had maps like this, but primarily for memory's sake. She felt bad for Gary, managing his business the same way he had in the seventies. She assumed they had no satellite mapping, fire detection, smart sensor capabilities. No wonder they were selling everything off.

"You think I'm old school?" Gary asked, perhaps sensing her condescension. "Well, it gets the job done. It always has."

The map was marked up in a thousand places. She saw the most recent sell-offs circumscribed by red pen. "PLC," Gary had written in brackets. She noticed other sell-offs too. Gary had little left. "We're moving to Costa Rica," he said.

"That doesn't mean we're desperate," Sheila said. "In fact, I bet your dad would pay extra for the piece you want. Maybe we'd get a daddy issues premium?"

Eliza couldn't shrug that one off. As much as she hated to admit it and wouldn't dare say it aloud, she suspected that Sheila was right. When Duke found out that Eliza was breaking off, he might become incensed. That was a problem for another time, though. Right now, she had to lock in a price.

She spotted the plot she had her mind on. She had sent Gary an email with the coordinates, and he zoned in on the allotment with his index finger. It was a good plot; they both knew it. There was easy road access and no recent burns. It was mostly White Fir and Ponderosa Pine, timber that would sell.

"You could work with my dad," Eliza said. "He'd probably pay you more for it. But do you really want to sell him another good plot?" She was nervous but did her best not to show it. The setting, the context, the future, all of it reeked of uncertainty. As she watched Gary and Sheila before her, old and proud and determined to beat her, she wondered if she was up to the challenge. She willed herself on. "He'll keep winning. He'll buy up the whole state. You know that."

Unless I'm there to stop him. She didn't say this next part. It wouldn't be vengeful. At least eventually, it couldn't be. Vengeance, she knew, could only spur her for so long. She would persist because it was what she was good at. She was good at her job, no matter what Gary, Sheila, Chris, her dad, or anyone else thought. *I'm good at my job,* she said over and over again in her head.

"I don't care about who buys what," Gary said.

"You're telling me you don't care where it goes? Your life's work?"

He wasn't bluffing. Unlike her dad, who cared about legacy and reputation, Gary seemed practical and unattached. There was grace in his position. He knew he was beaten. He wouldn't let it get to him. "Costa Rica will be nice," she said, shifting gears, buying time. "I would love a glass of water if that's okay?" She looked at Gary when she said it. She wouldn't ask Sheila. He didn't either. He left the room to get it himself. And just like that, she knew what to do. "Sheila, how do you feel about leaving?"

Sheila studied her, perhaps unsure of what to make of the question or perhaps wondering if it was worth answering. She waited for her husband to return and then said, "I've wanted to leave for years."

Eliza sipped the water. It was lukewarm. "You hate it that much?"

"It's on fire."

"And yet I'm staying."

Sheila laughed. Eliza was growing on her, she could tell. She wasn't used to growing on anyone. It was an exhilarating feeling. She pushed it further. "You think that's crazy. That I could go anywhere, Costa Rica even, but I'm staying. This is my home."

"We used to think that way too." Sheila glanced over at Gary. "Or one of us did."

"I'm not asking for a favor, and I'm not asking for a deal. I'm just asking for you to choose me over my dad and let someone else win for once."

Gary rubbed his eyes. "She thinks she's some kind of upstart."

"I didn't say that."

"But you think it, yeah? Your dad is a billionaire."

"I'm not saying I'm an upstart, but you weren't either."

"I took what my dad built and tripled it."

Eliza didn't know the full history but didn't think that was true. Perhaps there was a time when he had overexposed himself, but land holdings didn't always correlate with business performance. If she wanted to make something happen though, pushing back would serve no purpose. "I'm just asking for the same chance."

"You think you can build what your dad built?" Sheila asked.

Eliza knew she could do a better job than the Nesbits. She was born into lumber and raised by it. She knew the business and any knowledge gaps could be filled by the right people. Of course, it was hard to be starting small. If lumber prices dipped or she couldn't build up salvage capabilities fast enough after a fire, she might not survive long enough to bounce back. It was a worst-case scenario, but not improbable. If things turned sour enough, she'd have to turn to Richard to pay back the bank loan. But she wouldn't let doubts derail her. "I'm going to build something different than my dad," she said, "but I know it'll be good."

"You know it?" Sheila smiled.

"I know it."

"It's only two hundred acres," Sheila said. "And I have to pack." Then she turned to her husband, "It'll be fun to see what she'll do with it."

Gary grimaced. "We'll be long gone. I hope to God I'll have no idea what she'll do with it."

Sheila's gaze turned from amused to serious. "What did your dad do to you?"

"He fired me," she said. And it seemed to be a good enough answer for Sheila, but Eliza knew it was a distortion. It wasn't Duke's fault that he was like this. It was who he was, and he couldn't change that any more than she or anyone else could. But he had made her feel small for her whole life. By dismissing her, by judging her, by doubting her. She wore his views like they were her own and, for years, was ruined for it. Firing her was the best thing he had ever done.

They went back and forth for a little bit longer. After Sheila had flipped, Eliza knew that Gary would follow. He dragged his heels, but by the afternoon, they had a deal.

35

Bella makes a speech

For the first time since Bella had joined Aid for Earth, the Dogpatch warehouse was being put to good use. Maybe one hundred activists clustered around tables and desks. They were making posters and banners. Some of the slogans were catchy. She liked *Trees before Fees* and *Planet over Profit*. One sign had a crude drawing of Duke Peterson with the caption *Chester Molester*. The artist was proud and showed everyone.

Bella found Brandon lingering outside his office. He looked disinterested. "Have you alerted the press?" she asked.

"Yeah." She waited for more. He humored her. "The local news will be there. I'm sure their three viewers will be riveted."

"Hey," she walked inside his office, and he ambled after her. She shut the door. "Why are you sulking?"

"I'm not sulking." He took a seat and kicked his legs up on his desk. Since firing Cole, he had been distant and passive-aggressive. She hadn't had time to worry about it. The protest was shaping up to be an event. She wasn't going to let Brandon ruin it.

Of course, she needed his media connections and, should things turn ugly, his help. When they had defaced Martha Clancy's house, Brandon had placated the mob, but only after throwing a stone himself.

"You are sulking. Why don't you care about this? This is big."

"It's childish."

"No. This is marketing. This is brand awareness. This is—"

"No one will care. There are bigger things happening than a corporate scandal." He must have noticed her grim face. "The story was good, don't get me wrong. I'm glad we were a part of it."

"A part of it? We made it happen."

"But it's run its course."

She looked through the window at the cluster of activists. Most of them weren't the typical protesting crowd, although those people were there too. Chester molester man, she wasn't surprised to see, was one of them. Ponytailed, bearded, and most telling of all, sandaled. But she had also met a plumber, a school teacher, a gardener, a barista. They each had a different reason for showing up.

Some of them were outraged by the article. Some of them hadn't read it at all. They had heard about the protest on X, Instagram, or TikTok. They were social justice warriors who jumped from cause to cause. She didn't care and wasn't in a place to be picky. For every ten fair-weather protestors, there was one who cared, who joined today because they didn't have a choice—because Peterson Lumber's behavior was too insulting and offensive to ignore. For the ones that didn't feel that way now, there was always the chance that they would feel differently by day's end. She had seen it happen before. She'd seen crowds radicalize even the most passive of people.

She had done her best to meet everyone. She had a conversation with a group of self-dubbed long-timers. They brought their *Stop clearcutting California* signs and *Save our Trees* shirts. For them, the fire coverup was news. "We've been protesting Peterson Lumber for decades," a wizardly man told her. "We didn't know there was more to the story."

She also tried to speak to those who stood on the outskirts of the gathering, like a man dressed in all black.

He was young, her age perhaps, and short, and his eyes traced the room in an eerie synchronous loop. "That's a big bag," Bella had commented, pointing to it. It was practically his height. She couldn't imagine it on his back.

He didn't smile. "It's a big day." He had a deep voice, and even as he spoke, his eyes continued to survey the room, not once straying from their fixed course.

"I'm Bella," she tried.

"I'm Tom."

"How'd you hear about this?"

"The internet," he said.

She expected him to say more, but he slunk away. He was creepy but at least he was here, and with him and others in mind, she told Brandon that people cared. "And if they don't care right now, they will."

"Well, I wish you guys the best of luck."

"What? You're not coming?" She was more annoyed than surprised.

"I have stuff to do."

"What stuff?"

"Running this fucking outfit, since no one else will."

She clenched her fists but didn't speak. He wasn't worth a fight. "All right then."

"Just do your thing and be back to work on Monday."

She couldn't believe that he considered paper-pushing work and the protest frivolous. But again, he wasn't worth it. They had to leave soon if they wanted to get to Redding by late afternoon. It was a four-hour drive. Some people were bussing it but most were carpooling. She was riding with two others from the Aid for Earth team and the school teacher. They would have to stop twice to charge. Her cheap-ass car had two hundred miles of electric range, and that was with no AC or filtration running.

She left Brandon and saw him draw his blinds. She imagined him alone in his office, stewing. He had revealed himself in the last two weeks to be selfish and petty. Had it been his idea or his campaign, she knew he would be leading the charge, perhaps holding the megaphone as he used to at old Aid for Earth events. He resented her and this new generation of activists. He hated that the team followed her instead of him.

Perhaps he was stewing because he knew he was losing her, both as a lover (any attraction she had toward him was waning) but also as an adherent. If she stayed at Aid for Earth, it would be on her terms. And truth be told, after the protest, she didn't know if she would stay. This would be as good a swan song as any; it could be the foundation she needed to start something of her own.

Before addressing the group, Bella took in the scene. Even if Brandon was right and no one outside of this group cared about the protest, the fact that this group showed up was a victory. Big movements always start small. She didn't know it for sure but hoped that this was the start of something big. A few of the protesters were social media influencers who Bella had befriended at Stanford or in the city. They would stream the event and post about it for days, potentially spreading the news to millions. Like Marco, a Berkeley student who streamed protests on the Citizen App, and Jenny, an Instagram influencer who baited her audience with bikini photos before serving up social critiques.

If the influencers were successful and the Peterson protests trended on social media, the message would be heard worldwide. *Peterson Lumber is evil.* There wouldn't be nuance in the message. The best messages were never nuanced. Nuance was the enemy of progress.

"Okay, everyone," Bella stood up on a chair. It took a moment for the group to settle down. When they did, she told them to bring megaphones, horns, speakers, and anything else to make a racket. "We'll meet in the field right outside the corporate HQ. If you don't have the address, it's in the Signal group. If you're not in the group, just ask someone from Aid for Earth to add you. And bring your masks. Thanks to these fuckers, it'll be smoky." The last jab was effective, but the crowd wanted more. She saw that Marco and Jenny were recording her. She raised her voice and looked at their iPhone cameras.

"We're all here because we believe in justice. Justice for the earth, for our forests, for the men, women, and children of Chester."

There were a few claps. "The Peterson family makes billions of dollars from cutting down our forests, from burning our forests, from selling burnt forest, from making us breathe this shitty fucking air. They're corrupt. They're criminals. But because they're rich, they can do whatever they want. Duke Peterson has been featured in magazines. He dines with presidents and prime ministers. He makes more money every day than all of us together will make in our lifetime. I don't want to make this about too many things, but you see, and I truly believe this, all of these things intersect. They all form one giant..." she looked for the right word, "mush pile of injustice. The environmental degradation, the wealth inequality, the criminality, the blatant nepotism..." Those in the crowd that knew Cole booed. "It's all one giant horror show signifying everything that is wrong with the world. The Petersons epitomize that. Everything that is wrong with the world is thanks to them and people like them.

"The things that we will fight for today aren't frivolous, they're not overreactions. We're not lazy or victims or brainwashed, no matter what conservative hack jobs will say. We are brave and determined, and we know in our hearts that we are doing the right thing by standing up and standing together.

"Today, you made a choice to join us in showing the world that we're not okay with corruption, criminality, and motherfucking arson. Peterson Lumber doesn't think they have to play by the rules. And why should they? For decades no one has said a thing. When our forests burn, they profit. When people die, they walk free. Who holds them accountable? Not the state. Not the police. These are goddamn billionaires raping the earth and laughing at us for letting it happen!" Bella raised a finger.

"But not anymore. Not today. Today we will show the world that we won't stand down while Duke and his family burn everything but their vacation homes. If you're out there today, wondering if this is worth it, if any of it is worth it, just remember who you're doing it for. Maybe it's for Chester. Maybe it's for your children or your children's children. Maybe it's because, like me, you're sick and tired of being told that everything is fine the way it is. Things are not fine. Look outside. Look at this city and this state and this country. The people at the top are destroying this planet for their gain, and everyone else, the voiceless, the oppressed, the animals, the trees…we've all just been taking it. For fucks sake, I'm sick of it." She felt a burst of anger. She pulled from it and belted, "And you're here because you're sick of it too."

36

Richard, submerged in darkness, finds his true self

Richard didn't bother to turn the lights on. It had been light in the game room when he had started playing, but now it was dark outside. He didn't care or notice as he stared into the shining screen like a man possessed. His thumbs danced on the controller. He was thirsty and hungry, but he didn't stop. The load times between matches made him reach for his phone and open Instagram. He liked the way the screen bounced and spun like a slot machine when he refreshed it. The posts themselves were of little interest compared to the bouncing screen, and by the time he read one or two, he was usually in another match.

He was playing a violent game on his Playstation. He had been playing constantly since arriving back to San Francisco a few days ago. He was good but didn't compare to the fifteen-year-olds who had grown up on the games. What he lacked in natural talent though, he made up for in grit. When Lily would nag him for playing too many games, he would tell her that it was the only thing that took his mind off work. She usually let it go after that. But now, it didn't seem to be taking his mind off work or anything else. The worries, and there were plenty, loomed.

Then the power went out.

It had been a hot fire-soaked day and now a windy, smoky night. Richard was sure this was another public safety power shutoff. Such power outages were frequent outside San Francisco but were becoming more common in the city too. The Peterson's generator had broken prior to their trip. They weren't supposed to be around this time of year, and he had put off getting it fixed. He didn't let go of the controller. He heard Emmett and Lily upstairs.

He knew he should get up and light candles, pull out the battery-powered purifiers, help Lily put ice in the fridge. The best he could do, though, was put down his controller. That alone was a big job. Afterward, he scrolled X as a reward. Many people were mad at PG&E, California's electricity provider. And to his dismay, many people were mad at him. He was an X lurker, never a poster, and he was surprised that people had found his account and bombarded his page with vitriol about Cole and Peterson Lumber. He could only read a few posts before putting his phone down.

He lay back on the couch in the dark room. Perhaps smelling smoke or maybe just imagining it. With the purifiers stopped, it would just be a matter of time. He began to ponder the choices of his past, wondering what he could have done to ensure a better present.

His first big mistake was joining up with his dad instead of starting his own firm. He had been insistent his whole life that he wouldn't go into the lumber business. It was one of the things he had been proudest of then and that he was proudest of now—that he had forged his own path. Yet, perhaps the true story wasn't so cut-and-dry. After his first investment success with Trance, he could have raised a fund and managed other people's money. That was what most VCs did. Instead, he took an easy way out and, on the back of the success, convinced his dad to spin out a venture arm of the family office. He told himself and others that it was what he wanted to do. That way, he said, he could focus on making investments and not worry about raising money to invest in the first place. But maybe he really did it because managing other people's money scared him. He was used to disappointing his dad, but disappointing others was terrifying.

He felt sorry for himself and wondered if he had always felt sorry for himself and had just ignored it. He had felt good on a few occasions. Like when Trance went public, and he got to go on CNBC to talk about it. And then when he spoke his mind at the AlohaTech conference. The two were very different kinds of feeling good. On CNBC he had felt confident, proud, and aware that his dad was watching. At the conference he had felt honest, genuine, even courageous, also aware his dad was watching. That, of course, had backfired. Maybe if he had just stuck to the script he'd still have his board seats. Still, in the moment it had felt incredible. He wanted so badly to feel courageous again, but it seemed impossible. He couldn't even get up and help Lily with the house.

He waited for her to come to him. Eventually, she came and sat on the corner of the couch. He sat up and scooted toward her, not so close that they were touching but close enough for him to see her even in the dark. He saw that she was tired and worried and wasn't surprised to see it.

"Can you be here with me?" she asked. It was an odd question, but he understood it. He wanted to tell her that he wanted to be. All he could really do was shrug. "One of our sons," she explained, "is upstairs with a bong, and the other is holed up in Redding."

"You spoke to Cole?" He wasn't expecting the sudden burst of energy, but there it was. They had arrived to an empty house that, at first glance, hadn't been used. But there was trash in the bins and one of his Teslas was gone. Richard was about to call the police when he got a text from Cole. *I'm fine and will see you soon. And I borrowed the black Tesla.*

"He called me," Lily said. "He went to Redding to warn Duke."

"Warn him of what?"

"He says Aid for Earth is going to protest outside the HQ."

Richard relaxed. While unfortunate, he couldn't imagine a leftist protest making things worse than they already were. He didn't even know if it would get a lot of coverage or if more than five zealots would show up. He said as much to Lily, but she dismissed his unconcern. "Cole thinks it could be worse than that. He says it'll be the biggest thing Aid for Earth has done in years."

"So?"

"So he thinks they might end up at Duke's house. And remember, Cole's there." Even as she spoke matter-of-factly, he sensed her fear. She didn't want to say it directly, that Cole was in danger. Not just for the article, which revealed him to be everything Aid for Earth disliked: a racist, rich-boy hypocrite. But also because he had decided to stay with Duke. If they saw him there, behind enemy lines…

As Richard ran the scenario in his head, he felt his lethargy and self-pity lift. Lily saw it too. She took his hand and squeezed. "What should we do?"

He didn't have to think twice. He stood up. "Let's go over there."

"Tonight?"

"Tonight."

"Emmett doesn't think we should go."

"Pack your things. I'll talk to Emmett."

"I haven't unpacked."

Before stepping upstairs, he turned to find his wife still sitting. He wouldn't disappoint her. "We got this," he said.

"Hmm?"

Now she looked at him. He saw she had been thinking of something else. He repeated himself, and this time stood up extra tall. He imagined himself looking young and strong in the darkness—this capable guardian here to save the day. "We got this. Those protesters won't know what hit them."

Whether she believed him or not, he didn't know. And what that actually meant, he didn't know either. But it sounded good. It sounded very manly.

—

EMMETT DIDN'T EVEN BOTHER hiding his bong when his dad knocked. Past versions of Emmett would have stashed everything under the bed. The smell was one thing, but seeing it all out in the open—bong, weed, grinders—was another. When his dad knocked, he sat there. He didn't even say come in.

Richard looked at Emmett and then right at Emmett's desk, where the evidence was spread out, spotlit under a battery-powered lamp. "Isn't there enough smoke in this house?"

Emmett shrugged. His dad sat next to him on the bed. He didn't know if he was about to be lectured or coddled, but neither sounded good. Instead, his dad said that they were leaving in an hour for Redding.

"I'm staying here." Being home with his parents was one thing, but adding Duke and Cole to the equation was a nauseating prospect. He didn't think he had enough weed to get through it, and he had a lot of weed.

"They need us," Richard said. He looked injected with purpose.

"I'm staying here. You can go without me." This time the words came out mumbled. He rested his head against his bedside wall and closed his eyes. The darkness spun.

"Sober up. We're going."

He wasn't used to this version of his dad. It made him push back harder. "No!" He knew the refusal sounded juvenile. He didn't care. If he had to have a tantrum to get his dad to leave him alone, he would. Tantrums used to be Cole's thing, but he should be allowed one. Especially now.

Standing up, Richard asked, "Why don't you want to go?"

"Don't you know?"

His dad should know. He was there, after all, in the Maluhia dining room when Cole and Duke had combusted. Richard had stood there as the minutes had ticked by, unwilling or unable to quell either family member's pain. And Emmett had sat there as if he were pressed between two closing walls, young, powerless, and scared. He hated Duke at that moment for hurting Cole. But afterward, he hated Cole just as much. For letting himself get hurt and for putting them all in a position where so much hurt was possible. Duke, despite his rage, was acting accordingly with Emmett's view of him. The man was hard-nosed; his dad had once called him a train, and his anger was nothing new. Cole was supposed to be becoming someone else, an older brother he could talk to. Emmett didn't need protection from him. He didn't even need love. He had just wanted closeness. Instead, Cole had made things worse than they ever had been before.

Now watching his clueless dad trying and failing to save the day, Emmett resolved that once he went to college, he would be done with his family. It would be easiest to leave Cole, but still not so hard to leave his mom and dad, who couldn't see that the world they inhabited was marred by awkwardness, depression, apathy. They fed off each other. Emmett got the spillover. He always had.

He couldn't care less if his dad and mom left for Redding, and he couldn't care less if they didn't speak to each other the whole car ride. He wouldn't be there to infuse the vehicle with small talk, to help everyone else pretend that things were fine. If his dad lost confidence, he wouldn't be there to build him back up. If his mom worried about him, he would let her worry. No more reassurances. She hadn't accepted those anyway. To her, he was always as broken as she was. It was all she could see in him. He would let the prophecy come true.

He stood up, and his dad maybe thought he was going to pack, but the only thing he packed was the bowl. "Emmett."

He flicked the lighter and inhaled. He would do anything to go back to August. There were problems then, but not like this.

"You're just gonna do that in front of me?"

He took another puff and blew the smoke in his dad's face. He wanted the man to get mad because he wanted to get mad back. He wanted to fight like they had never fought before. He wanted to see if his dad had it in him.

He was so proud coming in. The big man here to save the day. Was he just going to stand there and take it?

He couldn't even do that. Sapped of any fortitude he had entered with, and without saying a word, Richard bowed his head and left the room.

Emmett sat in his desk chair for a minute, still angry, still determined to let them leave without him. But his dad's sad face wouldn't leave him. His whole life, he had reacted to that sad face with a strong show of support. He knew that he was the only one who could help his dad feel better. Not doing it now, despite all the hurt in Emmett's heart, seemed unconscionable.

He stumbled outside the room and, in the dark house, made his way to the media room. He heard his mom and dad talking.

"So he won't come?" his mom asked.

"He won't come."

In both their voices, Emmett heard disappointment.

He didn't want to make things better. He really didn't. But he felt bad for blowing smoke in his dad's face and undermining him, and he felt bad for his mom too—for letting her think that things were as hopeless as she believed them to be.

He sighed. They must have heard him. "Emmett?" his mom called out.

He stepped into the room and told them he would come. He saw his dad perk up. "Okay then."

"Are you sure?" his mom asked.

"He's sure. He said so. Let's do this. Let's go help Cole."

"All right, Dad. I'll go pack a bag."

Emmett lingered just long enough to watch his dad clasp his hands together. He looked strong again. But Emmett didn't feel much better. He wondered why he always had to help everyone, and he wondered why nobody ever helped him.

37

Bella is underwhelmed then overwhelmed

Bella arrived outside the Peterson Lumber office at 4:30. About half of the group was already assembled. With their masks, sunglasses, signs, and horns, they looked like performers in some post-apocalyptic circus. Her mask, serviceable in San Francisco, stood no chance against fumes from Redding's burning forests. The smoke was so heavy that Bella couldn't recognize anyone unless she stood a few feet away.

Marco was recording with a handheld camcorder. "The phone isn't picking up anything through the smoke," he explained to her. Then added, "Are we safe here? How close are these fires?"

Bella couldn't see the fires burning but knew that they must be close. There was ash in the air. It fell and swirled like snow.

"There are fuel breaks around the town," she said, refusing to add that she didn't know how effective the breaks would be when it came to halting a spread.

As more protesters arrived, the group started to chant. Within minutes though, Bella sensed that the energy was waning. The office building looked empty, there were no TV cameras, and one lone cop stood by, chewing gum. Whatever enthusiasm the group had on the drive up would be gone in a matter of minutes.

Bella considered that the location was as much the problem as anything else. For a billion-dollar-plus corporation, the Peterson office was tiny and unassuming. She knew that most of their employees worked in the forest, cutting and hauling lumber, but she wasn't expecting so little fanfare. She had read about protests in virgin forests, where men and women clung to trees, delaying clear-cuts through sheer force of will. Prior to arriving, she had imagined something similar. Now it was obvious that such a projection

267

had been nonsensical. They were in a lumber town outside a concrete office. There was no majesty here, nothing remarkable or beautiful. It was too indirect a jab, too futile a war cry.

Despite herself, she realized that Brandon had been right. He had realized it would be like this long before they came. Perhaps she should have yielded to his hints, but they had been so passive-aggressive and angsty that she had dismissed them instead. If he had wanted to be helpful, he could have been. Instead, he had set her up for failure. She imagined him watching them now, perhaps tuning into Marco's stream, laughing.

A news truck drove up. Two people walked out. A cameraman and a female reporter. Bella went to speak to them but stopped short after hearing their conversation.

"This is a joke."

"Let's just get some footage and bail."

The cameraman started to roll. Bella got in front of the crowd and, with a megaphone, led a "Peterson is Poison" chant. She pumped her fist and raised her voice. She marched back and forth like she was leading troops into battle. The news truck left a few minutes later. She moved to the back of the crowd to regroup.

"Aid for Earth staff," she said, "come with me."

Five of them huddled a few feet away. They, like her, looked depleted. In the back of her head, she had been nursing a Plan B. Perhaps she had always known that it would come to this and just hadn't wanted to admit it. Now it seemed like the fate of the protest depended on it. "We're going to march to Duke Peterson's house."

"His house?" asked Toby, always the first to doubt her.

"His house," she confirmed. "We have to show everyone that we're not fucking around."

The message spread, and the group was on the move. They walked down Market Street. A few people came out of their stores and homes to sneer. "Go back to San Francisco!" an old woman yelled. Bella wanted more of that. It would get everyone riled up. But most people just watched, unimpressed and unmoved by the display. They had vacant eyes and droopy heads. The ones without masks looked like they were perpetually yawning.

In the hot and smoky air, each step was draining. "Save your energy," she called out, stifling the few vacant chants. "We'll explode when we get there."

Tom, the backpack-wielding stranger, marched by her side. He didn't talk to her but occasionally repeated her phrases. Like, "Explode."

She didn't worry about Tom or anyone else. It was all about getting in front of Duke. Perhaps Cole would be there, too. If the group saw Cole, they would go crazy. The guy had given his summer to her, and all he got in return was vitriol. Well, that and the nerve to call her a whore. The Aid for Earth team detested him and thanks to the trending Substack article and some trending tweets, so did most of the protesters.

To the Left, Cole was a hypocrite and a racist. To the Right, he was a reactionary tree hugger.

They arrived at the gate and were met by two security guards. They couldn't even see a house, just a long winding driveway. The security guards looked unimpressed by the protest. Like everyone else in the town, they seemed to have other things on their mind. "Stay back," one guard said. He was maskless, double-chinned, and mustached. "As long as you stay back, there won't be any trouble."

She should have anticipated the guards, let alone the gate. Martha Clancy was rich but nothing like Duke Peterson. Of course, he would have security. Of course, his house would be nestled away from prying eyes.

The group, worn out in the smoke, tired and hot, craned their necks, awaiting her instructions. She wanted to take solace in the fact that there was a real crowd but, framed by backwoods and pummeled by smoke, the numbers lost their effect. She felt small, and the task before them impossible. If they stood here and protested, no one would care, no one would hear them.

"We're going in," she told Toby, Marco, and Jenny. "Start recording. We're going in!"

"It's private property," Toby said.

"That's right," said the other guard.

Bella stood in front of Marco's camera. "There are two of you and hundreds of us. We're going in." The guards crossed their arms and tried to look menacing. It didn't work. Bella led the group to a shorter fence. She climbed over. It only took a few steps up and then was an easy jump down. Even the old-timers navigated the move with ease. She knew the guards would call the police and felt compelled to remind everyone that they could get arrested. "Anyone who isn't comfortable with that, feel free to turn back. Your contribution is just as important."

As she moved forward and found her way back to the driveway, it seemed that no one took her up on her offer. After a long day of driving and walking and yelling into a vacuum, the people wanted some action, wanted a story. Most of all, they didn't want to be the ones too scared not to stand with the others.

For the first time that day, there was real energy and enthusiasm. Beneath the house now, they started to chant. "Look what he bought with blood money!" she shouted into her megaphone.

Marco pointed off in the distance, and she saw an even larger house, just barely visible in the smoke. She understood at once. "This isn't even his main house," she shouted. "This is his guest house!"

The people booed. She started the procession toward the mansion. Close-up, it was even more extravagant. They had to cross a footbridge over a river. "He built a fucking moat," she heard someone say.

There were yellow flowers, blue flowers, rows of cacti. There were statues and fruit trees. It was a paradise in the most desolate of places. A fuck-you to the pedestrian town a few miles away. She saw a few younger protestors stomp on the flowers. An older man stopped that, fast. "Don't hurt those," he hissed. "It's not their fault."

Everyone was filled with rage. And Bella was there with her megaphone, spurring them on. "They make money off of forest fires," she screamed. "They started a goddamn fire! They pay jack shit in taxes. They live like this. They burn trees and live like this."

Now beneath the main house, Bella was encouraged by signs of life inside. It was so big and so sprawling, but she could still make out faces in the windows. She could have sworn she saw Cole, ghost-like, appear and swirl away. On the second floor was a balcony. A woman stepped out: blonde, pretty, rich, white housewife. Before Bella could address her, she too was gone. At last, they had an audience, and not just bored townsfolk and perfunctory newscasters, but the very people who needed to hear what they had to say.

"You pillage the earth," Bella shouted. "You profit on pain. You murdered a town!"

"Murderers," the protestors called out in unison. "Murderers."

She felt the crowd condense and swarm around her. All of a sudden, she wasn't leading the mob but instead was immersed in it. People paid her no mind as they passed. They crept closer to the house. She had to hop up to see over the taller heads. In the smoke, in the noise, in the chaos, she lost sense of where she was and what was happening. Then she heard soft splatters. At first, just a few sparse hits, then the sounds came more frequently. She moved to the side and finally, in a pocket of space, saw the source of the noise. Eggs and tomatoes and paintballs and all kinds of things were being hurled. A window broke. People whistled and howled. She couldn't find Marco or Jenny. She imagined they were recording at the front of the crowd. She didn't know if that was good or bad. Another window broke. That was probably bad.

With her heart racing, she sprinted into an open pocket in the crowd. She screamed into the megaphone. "Let's regroup at the gate. Regroup at the gate." But everyone was screaming and blowing their horns or blaring their speakers. Her voice was hardly audible over the clamor.

Then the crowd started to chant together. At first, she couldn't hear what they were saying. The noise was coming from the front of the group near the front door. It sounded chaotic. There were boos and hisses. Someone must have come out. And that someone took on a name in her head when she heard the chant. "Bitcoin bitch. Bitcoin bitch."

She moved forward to look. It was too smoky, and there were too many people, and she was too small. By the time she had a view of the front door, it was closed. People were still screaming out. She saw one of the protestors being tended to on the ground.

She had to get everyone out. Within moments, she heard sirens. Then on the other side of the house, she saw a figure moving quickly, pouring something. He was very far away and obscured by smoke, but she knew by his huge backpack that it was Tom. She knew it too by the way he moved and by the way his head seemed to tilt in every direction at once. "Hey!" she screamed. But he wouldn't hear her. The sirens were getting louder.

She pushed through the crowd. She didn't care who she swiped or stepped on. But by the time she caught sight of Tom again, he was farther away again, hitting another side of the house. "Stop it!" she screamed. She thought he saw her briefly, although his head never stilled. Was he pouring lighter fluid? She hoped that she was wrong. She didn't think she was wrong.

"Stop it," she screamed into the megaphone. "Stop it!"

Her cries weren't audible over the chaos. She knew that even if he did hear her, he would not stop.

38

The Petersons (for the most part) stay inside

Cole paced around the house, not sure what to do, unable to ignore the rabble outside. "The police are coming?" he asked again and again.

Duke nodded. He was posted by the window on the second floor. "These people need to get a fucking life," he said, staring out the window, shotgun in hand. He, unlike the rest of the family, seemed unfazed.

Richard and Lily were doting over Cole. "Don't worry about it," they told him. "We don't blame you. It'll be okay."

"I know," he tried.

"We don't blame you," Richard said again. "We came to help you."

It was a nice gesture, but there was little they or anyone else could do. Outside, people were chanting and throwing things. He saw Bella in the crowd and felt sick. Even if his parents said they didn't blame him, he knew they did. And to be fair, it did all seem like his fault. He had never intended for these two parts of his life, activist and heir, to clash so violently. But here he was, stowed away in his grandpa's mansion, waiting for the police.

"I'm just gonna shoot some of these motherfuckers," Duke said.

Richard grabbed the gun. "No, you're not."

Lily put her hand on Cole's shoulder. "It'll be fine, honey. We'll move away to a place where no one will know you."

He brushed her off and looked down to find his face on signs. It was an unflattering picture, his Aid for Earth website photo. He looked like a camera-caught convict, plastered over poster board in black-and-white. The posters read *Bitcoin Bitch*. He couldn't recognize the people holding the signs. They wore masks and hoodies. Most of them also had sunglasses. They hated him, like so many people before them.

"I'm not going anywhere," he assured her. "Not until we deal with these assholes." It felt like a brave thing to say. He didn't feel brave. He was grateful to be in the house but knew they would have to escape soon.

Emmett scowled from across the room.

Cole walked over. "It'll be fine."

"Fuck off." Emmett pushed him away.

"What the hell?"

Emmett stepped back like Cole was diseased and contagious. Below them, they heard louder chanting. Eggs splattered against the walls and windows. "I'm here because Mom and Dad wanted to be here. I'm here for them, not for you."

"I know," Cole said. "I know."

"You think this shit is okay?" Emmett asked. "Look what you fucking did, dude. What the hell? It's fucked."

"I know it's fucked."

"Stop it!" Lilly hissed. "Stop it, both of you." She came running over and put her arms out to separate them. "You are brothers. Start acting like it."

"Tell Cole to do something, for once!"

"Do something?" Cole asked.

"Make them stop! They're your friends!"

"Will you forgive me if I make them stop?"

Emmett shrugged. "I don't care, dude."

"Cole, stay inside," Lily said.

Richard echoed her from farther away, still looming over Duke. "Stay inside!"

But Cole felt like he had nothing to lose. He walked down the stairs and, with his family chasing after him, opened the front door and stepped outside.

He was hit by a swell of smoke and then a fast-closing, electrified crowd. It was a wash of chaos. They were chanting. His knees wobbled.

—

EMMETT DIDN'T THINK THAT Cole would actually go. That hadn't been his intention. Never in a thousand years would the Cole that he knew go outside and face the mob.

Emmett ran after him, a dash ahead of his parents but still too far behind to stop Cole's exit. Emmett waited by the door, not sure himself if he could do it. He heard them outside, but from here, they were louder, angrier. It took a deep breath to know he had to go and then another to open the door.

He saw Cole a few steps in front of him, inches away from leering faces. They were chanting "Bitcoin Bitch." They were yelling into his face, and he seemed paralyzed. "Get away from him!" Emmett screamed. It was so loud, though, that he didn't know if they could hear him.

"BITCOIN BITCH! BITCOIN BITCH!" they chanted.

Emmett turned around, pushed back a couple of hands, and typed in the code on the keypad. He put his body in front of it to make sure no one saw. When he slammed the door behind him, he heard knocking and banging.

"What's going on!" Lily yelled.

"Cole's in the crowd. I need something."

"Something?" Richard asked. His parents stood side by side, static and petrified. It was up to him again, the youngest son, the practical teenager, to take control.

He ran upstairs to the second floor. "Grandpa, I need a bat!"

"A bat?" Duke stood. He had gotten his gun back. "Take this," he said.

"No! No!" Emmett ran up and down the hallway, looking into each room. He found golf clubs in the gym. He grabbed a wedge.

"No," Duke said over his shoulder. "Take the four-iron. You'll hit 'em farther."

He grabbed it and was back out the front door. This time he had to force it open against prying hands. He started to swing the club. He hit someone's arm, someone else's leg. "Get the fuck away!" He screamed. This time they listened. All but one taller man, bearded, masked, strong. Emmett swung at the man's legs, but the man caught the club.

He tried to rip it out of Emmett's hands, but Emmett kicked him in the stomach. The grip loosened, and he could swing freely. He hit the man in the balls. And then the head. Emmett screamed at the top of his lungs, louder than all the chanting and horns and speakers. "GET THE FUCK OFF ME!"

He was someone else entirely, barely a person. Just a vehicle for adrenaline, for violence. If the man had stayed, he would have beaten him to death. The worthless-justice-warrior-freeloading-hypocritical piece of shit.

He would have kept swinging until there was nothing left of the man but blood and bone.

He directed that adrenaline forward now. Even as the crowd stepped up to challenge him, he took no notice. He halted their charges with rabid swings of the club, and they steered clear like he was behind a razor-sharp propeller.

He found Cole in the middle of the chaos, on the ground. Twelve or so masked protestors surrounded him. They were screaming "Bitcoin Bitch" and "Chester molester." He started to swing his club. Again, his careless urgency caused the group to step back.

That bought Emmett just enough time to get his brother to his feet. "Let's go."

"What?"

"LET'S GO!"

Cole took Emmett's arm, and they pushed back toward the front door. People booed and hissed, but no one touched them. Emmett held the club up, though, just in case.

"We need to get out of here!" Cole said.

"Inside first!"

The scene slowed down. Emmett saw the mass of masked people waving their signs, chanting. He felt their energy and anger. If the police didn't come soon, they would get hurt. He imagined them breaking windows and climbing into the house. He knew they'd be outmatched, even with Duke's gun and his golf club. Sure, he had done the bulk of the hitting so far, but that could change. If they didn't get help soon it would change.

"MOVE," he yelled at the congregated group by the door. But they didn't move, so he had to brush Cole off him and swing the club. He hit a stomach and a leg. Cole punched in the code, and Emmett slammed the door.

—

As EMMETT AND COLE retreated inside, Lily watched from the second floor. She didn't want people to see her face. She sat up just enough, so her eyes rested above the bottom of the window. She let the curtains cover the top of her head.

They were throwing eggs and chanting. They would break a few windows, perhaps. But the police were on their way. She thought she heard sirens; surely they would come soon. And then they could leave this awful place and forget about it.

Emmett and Cole were back inside and okay. Richard and Duke were together by the opposite window. They were a real family once again. Together they would figure this out.

Then, through the window, she saw someone at the corner of the house pouring something. She watched, at first, with interest, unsure what they were doing. But when they moved closer to her side of the house, she saw their twisted face and knew it was something sinister.

"This guy's pouring gas," she screamed. She pulled the curtain apart. "He's pouring gas."

Her family crowded around her in the window. The protestors saw them and eggs came flying. But they were too focused on the grimacing man pouring liquid down the side of the house.

"Fucking hell," Richard said.

"Where the hell are the police?" Duke screamed. He cocked his gun.

Then, on cue, the sirens became much louder. They saw four police cars zooming in. "Oh, thank God," Lily said. The police got out. They shouted into their megaphones, telling the protestors to leave. Two cops started to cuff people. But most of the crowd did not react. They kept throwing eggs and tomatoes and what looked like red paint. The man kept pouring the gasoline.

"Why is no one moving?" Lily asked.

"They don't care," Cole said. "They don't care."

"They don't care?"

"Getting arrested is a badge of honor. They want to be cuffed."

Lily imagined the house burning, her two sons burning. She wasn't going to let it happen. She wasn't going to wait for the police to save them.

She walked to a guest bedroom with a balcony and stepped outside over the crowd. "He's burning the house," she screamed, pointing at the man, who still paid her no attention. "He's trying to burn the house."

If the police heard her, they didn't show it. And then she was pelted with eggs and tomatoes. She started to cry and scream even louder. "He's burning the house! He's burning the house!"

A policewoman shouted into her megaphone. "Ma'am, return inside. For your own safety, return inside."

"HE'S BURNING US!"

"Return inside," the cop repeated. "Return inside."

"You're fucking psychos!" She screamed. "You're fucking psychos. We're gonna die. Is this what you want! You want to kill us!"

The crowd cheered. Some of them turned up their music and blared into their horns.

Lily took another tomato to the nose. She was drenched in stickiness. "Look! Look at him!" She said, pointing to the man. "He's going to kill us! HELP! HELP!"

Only then did the man look up. He stared, for a split-second, and then returned to his work, without another glance. Lily felt a tug on her arm, as Emmett and Richard grabbed her and pulled her inside. When the doors were closed, she saw that they had been hit too. Only Duke was clean now. He was ready to start shooting.

"We need to leave," Cole said.

"You're right," Richard said. "I'm gonna get us the fuck out of here."

—

RICHARD WAS OVERCOME WITH CONFIDENCE. In the face of peril, in the face of death, he wasn't going to let his family down. "In the car," he said. "NOW!"

Everyone started toward the garage but Duke. He didn't move at all.

"Dad," Richard explained, "we don't have a lot of time. We need to leave."

"I'm not leaving." Duke didn't look at Richard. He just looked out the window. It was splattered, and the view was opaque. But he didn't take his eyes off the sight. His fingers crawled up and down his gun.

"You're coming with us!" Richard said, raising his voice now, feeling the urgency of the moment. "Come on!"

"No, I'm fucking not. If they want to burn me, they can burn me. This is my house."

"So you're going down with the ship, huh?"

"Grandpa," Cole tried, "Dad's right. We have to go. Now!"

"You'll have to drag me."

Richard reached out to grab his dad, and the muzzle came flying downwards. It was pointed right at Richard's chest. "Fuck no," he had never had a gun pointed at him before. He stumbled backward.

"Leave me," Duke said.

277

"WHAT THE FUCK!" Richard screamed. "YOU SELFISH FUCK. YOU'RE GONNA SHOOT ME? YOU'RE GONNA KILL US."

"Just leave me."

"You're coming with us," he seethed.

"Son…" Duke's voice was calm, even mocking. "I've made it forty-five years without listening to you, if you think I'm going to start now, you're dumber than I thought."

Richard flew at his dad, grabbed the gun away, and then pulled Duke's collar, so he was in his grasp. "Come on," he screamed at everyone else. And like Duke was his suitcase, he lumbered toward the stairs. Duke was heavy but Richard was strong. He still had it.

"Let go of me!" Duke hissed.

"No. I'm not going to let you die."

"I can look after myself!"

"Obviously not." They walked down two flights of stairs to the garage. Cole opened the back door of the Tesla, and Richard sat his dad down into the middle seat. Cole and Emmett climbed in on either side, so Duke was sandwiched.

Everyone buckled. Richard opened the garage and accelerated. Protesters banged against the windows as he drove by. They were just passing through the gate when flames shot up behind them. He kept driving, and only when the house was far in the distance did he stop.

More police flew by them. The fire was terrific. He always thought the house would burn and had told his dad so many times. "I have a moat," Duke would say. "Wildfires won't hop the moat."

This wasn't a wildfire, though. The house stood no chance.

"We're safe," Richard said finally, glad to be the voice of comfort in the aching silence.

"Let's go," Lily whispered. "Let's go to the police station."

Richard nodded. He put a hand on his wife's leg. "We're safe now," he said. "I wasn't going to let anyone hurt us."

39

Bella has big plans (that hopefully don't include jail)

Bella was relieved but not thrilled to hear that it was Brandon outside her apartment door, knocking and repeating her name. She knew that the police would come eventually. She was in too many videos and tagged in too many posts. Still, she wasn't ready for the inevitable interrogation.

She cracked open the door, and Brandon squeezed by her. It was a cramped shithole of a studio apartment, but she did what she could to keep it neat. He kissed her on the cheek and told her he was glad that she was okay.

She tolerated these advances because she was too tired to oppose them. He seemed to sense her discomfort though, and backed off toward the bed, kicking off his shoes and sitting up with his back against the headboard. "You don't think I'm glad?"

"I think you came here to rub it in." He spent a long time looking at her. He stared at a bruise on her left arm (someone had knocked her over in the chaos). He seemed more interested than worried.

She brought a chair over from the kitchen, only a few steps away. The bed looked more comfortable. After arriving home, she had sat where Brandon was now, unable to sleep, unwilling to even try. Now she would settle for the chair. "Why'd you come here?"

"To see if you were okay."

"You weren't worried about waking me up?"

"I had a feeling you'd be awake." It was 5:00 a.m. and even the Tenderloin was quiet. "I'm not here to rub anything in."

"Okay."

"Everyone's talking about us, so I don't know what I'd rub in. That's what you wanted, right?" He smiled a cocky smile. For him to be cocky now, when she had to spend the next twenty-four hours looking for a lawyer, was unforgivable.

But she wasn't in the mood to fight. There had been too much fighting already, and the truth was, even though things had gone too far, Aid for Earth was all over the internet. Duke Peterson was trending, so was the Chester fire and the name Bella Jones.

In a day, the potential for her to be conventionally successful had been stripped away. There would be no prospect of law school, a banking job, or a career in venture capital. The mainstream would shun Bella Jones, the activist, the radical. Her mom and dad would be crestfallen.

But as one door closed, another one was opening, perhaps the one she had been gunning for all along. Those mainstream options were insurance policies, they always had been. Now all that remained for her was the life she had really wanted.

"Have you spoken to the police?" Brandon asked.

"No." After the fire had started, she had rushed to help whoever she could. Then before the police could grab her, she had run with the crowd back to the cars, one of many militants sprinting down Market Street in the smoke. "I have friends in law school. They're helping me find someone for when..."

"For when they come?"

"Yeah. For when they come."

"Do you know who started the fire?"

"I didn't know the guy. He was a rando, but I saw him pouring the fuel."

"And you didn't stop him?"

He had a horrible opinion of her. He didn't respect her, not as a person. To him, she had been something useful—at work and in the bedroom. She had always known it, but had put up with it, had tried not to think about it. He had been useful for her, too, after all.

"The fact that you would even ask."

"What?" The cocky smile came back.

"The fact that you think I wouldn't stop it, or worse, that...I would be a part of that. Fuck off, dude. Get out of here."

He didn't move from the bed. "You don't have to be so defensive."

"You don't have to be such a dick."

"So you're going to sit there and tell me that this isn't what you wanted? All that talk about how we weren't doing anything big, that was just talk? Now that it happened, you regret it?"

"I didn't want a fire. I didn't start it. But if you're wondering if I feel bad for them, I don't."

"It's not going to help anything, you know that, right? Everyone now thinks of us as arsonists, even eco-terrorists. The Right is going to have a field day. Anyone protesting, even peacefully, will be lumped in now. The Petersons, for fucks sake, will be victims. You guys made them victims."

At least people were talking about Aid for Earth. At least people would learn more about Peterson Lumber and the Chester fire. People like Brandon have been marching in the streets for decades but have accomplished nothing. "Peaceful protests don't work," she told him. "We've been trying them forever. They don't work."

"They've worked before. Like for the Civil Rights Movement, like in India."

She scoffed. "The Civil Rights Movement was a goddamn war! What whitewashed history have you been reading?"

"The one that doesn't end with me in jail."

"You've been to jail."

"And it fucking sucked and has made my life ten times harder since."

"Your life is a cakewalk! You traded in everything you used to care about for stars on Charity Navigator." She sprung up and swung the front door open. "I'm not gonna sit here and get lectured by you. Telling me your life is hard! I can't believe it! We're supposed to be helping the people whose lives are really hard. You just want to help yourself."

"Close the door."

"I'm telling you to get out."

"Really?"

She tapped her foot and held the door. Seconds passed, and she didn't look at him. Then he moved toward her. He put his body in front of her, then he slid by into the hallway.

"I didn't start the fire. I didn't want the fire. But I want you to know that this is the first time since joining Aid for Earth that I don't regret being here."

"Well, we're not gonna do that kind of stuff anymore."

"Well, *we're…*" she pointed at him and then back at herself, "not doing anything anymore."

"Really. Not anything?" He raised his eyebrows. Even as he was being thrown out, he had the gall to tease her.

"Nothing. I resign."

She expected him to push back. Instead, he shrugged, and said, "Well, I wish you all the best."

"I thought you were a fighter. When I joined you, I thought you were a fighter. But you're scared. I'm not scared anymore. The Earth is already an ashtray. We can't be scared."

"We can't be stupid."

"Stupid is twiddling our thumbs as everything around us burns."

He walked off. She shut the door and lay back in bed. She wondered if he'd see her again. She imagined him coming to visit her in prison. He'd say I told you so. She'd make him eat his words.

She was scared of prison, even if she hadn't said as much. It was a peaceful protest until it wasn't. And that wasn't her fault. She hoped that she wouldn't have to go.

She picked up her phone. It was 5:15.

On X, there was a ton about the protest and fire. People were even linking to a *Wall Street Journal* article. Not the old one. A new one. She skimmed it. It wasn't very complimentary.

Many people on X were though. People kept linking to the Chester fire, citing the number of causalities, displaced families. #Karma was trending.

40

The Petersons, except for Duke and Eliza, go to Europe

The family arrived at Eliza's house at 10:00 p.m. Duke took a seat on the couch as the others went to the kitchen to get water. Lily brought him a glass. He took a sip. Eliza sat down next to him.

"Dad, I have to talk to you," she said.

"Do you have anything else to drink?"

"I have wine. I have beer. I have—"

"Beer's good. Gimme a beer."

She came back with a beer. He took a slow sip, and then she sat again. "Dad, I have to talk to you."

"Now?"

"Yes, I'm sorry but it has to be now. I want to tell you before you hear it from anyone else." She took a deep breath. "I started my own company."

Duke rested his head back and rubbed his eyes. It was like he had lived five lives in the course of a day. "Your own company?"

"Are you…" Eliza bent down, her eyes searching him for signs of sickness.

"I'm fine!" Duke looked around to see if anyone else was following. Cole and Emmett sagged against a wall. They looked uninterested. Richard and Lily were seated nearby on chairs, listening politely. "Your own company," he repeated.

"I bought a plot of land," Eliza said.

"Lumber?"

"What else."

First, Duke felt defensive. He could think of a hundred reasons why she would fail. Before sharing them, though, he caught himself. His competitiveness was being overrun by something stronger, perhaps spurred by fatigue, perhaps spurred by age. He didn't dissect it.

"Anyway," Eliza said, "You should rest. I just wanted you to hear it from me. You must be very tired."

He saw a nervousness in Eliza and, he was surprised to see, a nervousness in Richard. They feared what he would say next. Even as he was frail and hunched over on the couch. They had always feared him. It was that way because it was the only way, or so he had always assumed. It occurred to him for the first time that it was a nasty feeling. They were, all of a sudden, very young again, and he was about to crush their adolescent dreams like he had so many times before.

It'll never work, he would say, to Richard's sophomoric video game ideas, Eliza's plans to start a fashion line. *What the hell do you know about fashion?*

He could say the same thing now about lumber. It would really fuck her up. She was waiting for him to say it. Richard, too.

He wouldn't say it, though. Why did he always have to say it?

"Your own plot," he said again, breaking the silence.

"It's a small plot," Eliza hedged, "nothing like your holdings."

"I started small too," he said, surprising them. So he said it louder and sat up straighter. "I started small too. It's the best way to start."

He could feel their relief. It felt better than their fear. Take note, he told himself. And it was the truth too. When he shot down their dreams, he always justified it by saying it was the truth. But this was the truth too. Those days, when he was starting small, were some of his best days. There wasn't time for headaches. There was only time for work. He said so. "I'm jealous. I wish I could start small too, again."

"You can," Richard said. "You can do whatever you want."

What he really wanted was to keep going, glory days be damned. But he knew he couldn't do it for much longer and with Eliza and Chris out of the picture he had no one to take over. He needed Eliza, even if it pained him to admit it. It was that, or bring in some third-party that he had no control over. The board had granted him temporary CEO status, but they wouldn't let him keep it for long.

"I'll acquire you."

"Dad, I already said—"

"No. Listen. I'll acquire you for double what you paid, and I'll make you CEO. Not co-CEO, not acting-CEO, but CEO." He would remain chairman and keep a firm grip on the company.

Eliza looked torn. "Can I think about it?"

"No," Duke said. "Take it or leave it. I'm too tired to draw this out. I don't want to compete with you, but I will. We both know what the better option is."

"I'll be CEO?" she asked.

Duke nodded. "Starting tonight. CEO." He reached out his hand. She looked around at everyone.

"And you'll acquire me for double?"

"Double."

"And I want a raise."

"I'll pay you whatever you want," Duke said. She stared at him for what must have been a short time but felt to him like a long time. He knew she would take it, but her gears had to spin all the same. As he watched her it was almost like he could hear her thoughts. She was justifying it, pretending that it wasn't a weak move but a strong one, pretending that things would be different now. They wouldn't be different. He knew it, and he expected that somewhere deep down, she knew it too.

Finally, she shook his hand. "Welcome back, CEO." He smiled at her.

"Thanks, Dad." She shyly smiled back and then looked away.

Duke stood with shaky knees. "This is a fine family." Richard stood up to help him, but Duke brushed him off. He headed for the guest bedroom. "And I'm proud of you. All of you. You guys." He looked at his kids and Lily, and then he looked at his grandkids still pinned against the wall. "And you guys too. I want you to know that. Today they tried to take us down, but they failed. No one can take us down."

They looked sheepish. Richard broke the silence. "Dad, I know this isn't a good time but it's our last chance to invest in the mining company. If you could—"

He was feeling generous, even in the face of Richard's blatant opportunism. "Fine."

"Really?"

"Yes, fine. I believe in you. I'm proud of you. I'm proud of all of you." He looked at Eliza and Richard. He could see they were uncomfortable, albeit very proud of themselves. Seeing their pride made him want to take back the compliment. He was just being nice; after all, they didn't deserve it. But he was tired and it was late and where was the harm in letting them feel good for a moment?

—

"Look at this," Lily said, holding her phone in front of Richard's face. There were forty text notifications and even more emails. Randolph from InhaleAfrica had called her three times. She only had to read a couple of the messages to understand how quickly things had changed. "They don't hate us anymore," she said. She broke out in a grin. "Look," she went to show Emmett and Cole too. And then, for fairness sake, Eliza. "They're all so worried. They all say they want to help."

"Well, you guys did almost just die," Eliza said.

She wasn't understanding. "They weren't texting before, though. They were ghosting me, all of them. We were pariahs. They were ghosting Richard too. Richard, open your phone."

He did as instructed. He showed her messages and emails. One, in particular, made him beam. It was from Max Lewis, the founder and CEO of Trance.

Richard grabbed a beer. He offered one to Lily. "What the hell," she said. It was late, and she should be exhausted, but she was revitalized. And it occurred to her that in the tumult of the day, she hadn't had the time or impulse to take a pill, mix a juice, or even turn on one of her wearables. It was her first supplement-free day in the last year, perhaps for years, perhaps since college. She didn't even want the beer, she realized.

"Are you gonna call Randolph back?" Richard asked, taking her beer and putting it back into the fridge.

She considered the question and imagined the conversation. He would ask how she was. He would feign sympathy. Then he would welcome her back to the board, encourage a gift, perhaps apologize with a sycophantic plastic appeal. There would be more conversations like that one. In a few hours, they had gone from lepers to champions, surviving and standing up to a changing tide that their elite brethren would do anything to stop. "We're like a warning to them," she said aloud, dodging her husband's question. "They see themselves in us. It scares the shit out of them."

Richard nodded. "It's gross when you think about it. That we have to almost die to get them on our side…"

"We didn't almost die," Cole cut in, surprising Lily, who assumed he wasn't listening. She saw her two sons hunched together in the corner. They were the most tired in the group. But she wasn't worried. They would get rest. They would be okay. The whole family was going to be okay.

"What's important," she said, "is that we have each other." They nodded like it was some banal point pulled from a Disney movie. That wasn't her intention. "No, really, though. We can move on now. I feel good now."

"Why?" Emmett asked.

Part of it was the adrenaline. Most of it was the belief that whatever lay ahead would be different, that they wouldn't go back to living as they were, living scared, but instead could do what they wanted to, what she always wanted to do. Her laundry list of dreams no longer seemed so impossible. She could go to law school if she wanted to. She could start her own business, just like Eliza almost did. It was her life. She didn't owe anyone anything.

She had been sleepwalking through life. She had dragged Richard, and perhaps her kids, with her too. She had blamed everyone else, Richard most of all, but it wasn't anyone else's fault. It wasn't really her fault either. It was just the way things were, and now things were going to be different. All thanks to a rowdy band of tree huggers. Who would have thought that some of her least favorite people—those entitled, rebellious wokesters who had corrupted Cole, corrupted so much of the country—would set her free? They would be going to prison, and she would be free.

"Can you feel that?" she asked Richard. Sensing his bewilderment, she asked everyone else, "Can you feel that?"

"Hun, are you all right?" He put a hand on her shoulder. She clasped his hand and held it there.

"I'm all right! I think everything's all right."

"Feel what, Mom?" Emmett asked, concerned. He was always concerned. She loved him for that, felt bad for him too, that she made him feel that way.

"I just mean, things are looking up. I can tell." She looked at Eliza, "You're gonna be CEO!" She looked at her husband, "You'll be back on boards." Then finally, she turned to her boys. "And you'll be whatever you want to be. Me too! Let's make sure of that, okay?"

She thought about what her mom or Patricia would think and realized that Patricia and her mom weren't so different. They were very much the same in that they thought they knew what was best for her and everyone else. People, she thought, shouldn't tell other people what to do.

"We're going to Europe," she announced.

———

RICHARD LOOKED AT HIS WIFE, tried to make sense of her excitement. It wasn't just the emails and texts, it couldn't be. Perhaps she had been impressed with him, wrenching the gun from his dad's hands, piloting them to safety. Perhaps she had seen what he had felt: power, authority, competence, and everything else a man should be rolled up into a breathtaking display of courage.

His dad must have seen that. *I'm proud of you.* He replayed the scene. He was proud of himself. Best of all, Lily was proud of him. She didn't have to say so directly. He could feel it.

"I don't know if I want to go back on the boards," he tried, testing if that was why she was inspired.

"Then fuck it, don't!" she said, beautiful words that relieved his doubt.

"Mom's gone crazy," Richard heard Emmett whisper under his breath.

She heard it too. "I have not! I'm for the first time, not crazy." She laughed and pulled Richard in. She had wide eyes. But they weren't crazy; she was right about that. They were determined. "Europe," she said. "Let's do it. We have to."

Her confidence was convincing, and he liked Europe. Plus, he would be closer to the Russian bitcoin company—that was his next big break, he could feel it. Maybe the last investment he would ever have to make. He imagined a new vision of Europe, where he could be whoever he wanted to be—after the Russian company went public, he wouldn't have to invest anymore, by that time everyone would consider him an amazing investor and he could step away at the top of his game. No more connections to lumber or familial baggage. That was all too time-consuming anyway. The work was too hard, too thankless. All the wasted minutes in front of his computer, the hours on the golf course, the pointless and forced golf course banter. He didn't even know if he liked golf or if he just played it because everyone else did. Maybe he was supposed to be an artist or a poet.

In Europe, he would sleep in until the afternoon and walk down cobbled streets to a corner cafe, where accordions played. He would drink wine and read a book or write a poem. He hadn't read a poem in his life, not one he could remember anyway, but he would write them in Europe with a glass of wine and some fresh bread, and he would be living for once. That would take real bravery, to try new things in a new place and not worry about what anyone thought, what all his "friends" in Maluhia thought. He would call them and say he was abroad and, for the first time, really living. They'd be jealous. They'd never say so, but he would know.

He had been all over Europe for work, but he didn't think of any of those places, not now. He imagined some breeze blowing, old-world movie set. There wouldn't be any fires. There wouldn't be any protests. Not in his Europe, anyway. He wondered if he could ship his Teslas across the Atlantic.

"Let's do it," he said. "Let's go to Europe."

—

EMMETT FOUND COLE OUTSIDE, sitting in a lawn chair, typing on a phone. It wasn't his iPhone, he realized, as Cole quickly tucked it away. Emmett didn't say anything. What was there left to say?

Other than comment on the air, of course. The air was shit. "You'd rather breathe this," he asked, "than listen to them?"

Cole smiled, recovering, "They've gone crazy, huh?"

"I mean, I guess it was a crazy day."

Emmett took the seat next to him. He took a deep breath and closed his eyes for the first time that day. If he wasn't careful, he would fall asleep and suck in a night's worth of smoke.

"I'm sorry. I can't say it enough," Cole said, on the other side of Emmett's closed eyes. "But I'll keep saying it."

"It's fine," Emmett mumbled. "Let's just sit here."

His mind drifted to all kinds of places, and he wouldn't remember any of them once fully awake. He wondered if he was sober. He didn't remember drinking or smoking or pill-popping, but he felt glued to the chair and miles above it at the same time.

"We'll be good now," Cole said from somewhere far away. "Are you listening?"

"Mm-hmm."

What Emmett wanted most of all was to skip the next year of his life and wake up in college. His family would be far away, and with them, his responsibilities. But he would be dragged to Europe and privately tutored or enrolled in some foreign school, or worse, homeschooled. It didn't seem very fair, but he could tell he wouldn't convince them, or maybe it wasn't worth convincing them. They were happy thinking about it. He didn't have the heart to take that from them.

"Will you go to Europe with us?" he asked Cole.

"If we go. And," Cole added, "if you want me to."

Emmett realized that he did. At least right now, he did. Cole wasn't so bad when he was trying to be a good brother. But he couldn't trust him. He wouldn't let himself trust him. He could forgive him, though. Those weren't the same thing.

He thought about the next year and the rest of his life, and he wasn't excited for it but wasn't dreading it either. It would come as the last few months had come, in waves, without warning, without sense. And it would be up to him to keep everyone else afloat. It didn't seem like a burden anymore, but instead a fact. The drinking and the drugs and the girls were vacations from his real life, his real job.

When his mom was worried, he would pacify her. When his dad became insecure, he would pump him up. And when Cole broke their trust, he would forgive him. Not because *that's what families are for* or some other bullshit, but because it was all he knew how to do. And when they called him a stoner or a slacker or anything else, he would smile because they didn't know how hard he was working for them. He would forgive them for that too.

"Let's go inside," he told Cole. "This air is rough."

"I'll stay out here one more minute."

"Suit yourself." He didn't look at Cole suspiciously, he just smiled and walked away. He would find out what Cole was doing with that other phone soon enough, and then accept Cole's apology for whatever he was planning.

Inside, his parents were seated on the couch. "You ready to go to the hotel?" his mom asked.

"Yeah. Are you guys all right?"

She smiled at him like it was a silly question.

—

COLE HAD TO START from the beginning, from before Emmett's interruption, to ensure he wasn't forgetting a step. He started his VPN, confirmed that his burner phone's internet had been routed to Japan, and then sent Thomas an encrypted message on Signal.

Sending second half of ur bitcoin now.

Thomas had done what he had been asked to, and even though nothing was stopping Cole from shirking, he would stick to his word.

His wallet and his conscience would be clean.

He read through the chat to confirm that he had the right address and then sent the Bitcoin with a crypto tumbler to obfuscate the transaction trail.

After all these years, it had been hard work tracking down Thomas, Cole's first and maybe only high school friend. The two of them had lost contact after Thomas had been expelled for his 4chan posts, but Cole remembered some of Thomas' Reddit posts and eventually found his old account. He found the same username in other places, most recently on YouTube, where sirfrogfucker would comment on conspiracy theory videos. The posts were angry, desperate, and, in a throwback to high school, violent. Cole reached out under a pseudonym, laid out the job, and paid five bitcoin in advance.

Half now, half later, he said. And don't light the fire until the car is past the gate!

There was a slim chance that Thomas would go through with it. There was nothing stopping him from taking five bitcoin and ghosting Cole forever. But then again, ten bitcoin was a lot more than five, and Thomas was very angry. Cole was careful not to reveal anything about himself, but he couldn't help but wonder if Thomas knew. As long as he didn't know for sure, Cole would be safe. He had taken all the right precautions and would now ditch the burner phone.

He waited a few minutes to see if Thomas would respond. Nothing came in. Cole assumed he was locked up and phoneless.

He took a big rock and smashed the cheap pre-paid piece-of-shit phone. He scattered the pieces in the bushes.

If he could go back in time, he would have never stolen Duke's laptop. He probably wouldn't have worked for Aid for Earth. He probably wouldn't have talked to Bella at all. But he couldn't go back in time, and burning down Duke's house was the next best thing. He wondered if Bella would go to jail and then realized that he didn't care. What mattered was that he made things right. The Petersons were no longer the scandal but the victims of one. It was a slight shift, but it made all the difference.

When he went back inside, he found his parents and Emmett on the couch, waiting for him. "Let's go to the hotel," his dad said.

"And then Europe?" Cole asked.

"I think we should," his mom said.

The idea sounded nice, he had to admit. If he could stand his family for a few months, the idea was nice. They would be easier to stand now that he had saved them. He wondered if he could get a finance job in Europe. If not, there would be protests to join. He really didn't have a strong preference between the two.

THE END

Acknowledgments

I am deeply grateful to my agent, Emma Dries, at Triangle House, for believing in this book from the beginning and championing it every step of the way. To Hailie Johnson at Rare Bird, thank you for your keen editorial eye and tireless dedication to shaping this story into its best version. To my parents, siblings, and wife, your encouragement has meant everything to me. This book exists because of all of you.